MIDNIGHT STRIKES

MIDNIGHT STRIKES

ZEBA SHAHNAZ

DELACORTE PRESS

Text copyright © 2023 by Zeba Shahnaz
Jacket art copyright © 2023 by Luke Lucas
Map art copyright © 2023 by Priscilla Spencer
Interior chapter opener art used under license from Shutterstock.com

Visit us on the Web! GetUnderlined.com

Educators and librarians, for a variety of teaching tools, visit us at RHTeachersLibrarians.com

Library of Congress Cataloging-in-Publication Data is available upon request.
ISBN 978-0-593-56755-5 (hardcover) — ISBN 978-0-593-56756-2 (lib. bdg.) — ISBN 978-0-593-56757-9 (ebook)

The text of this book is set in 11-point Sabon MT Pro.
Interior design by Cathy Bobak

Printed in the United States of America
1st Printing
First Edition

For Mom and Dad, for everything. Thank you.

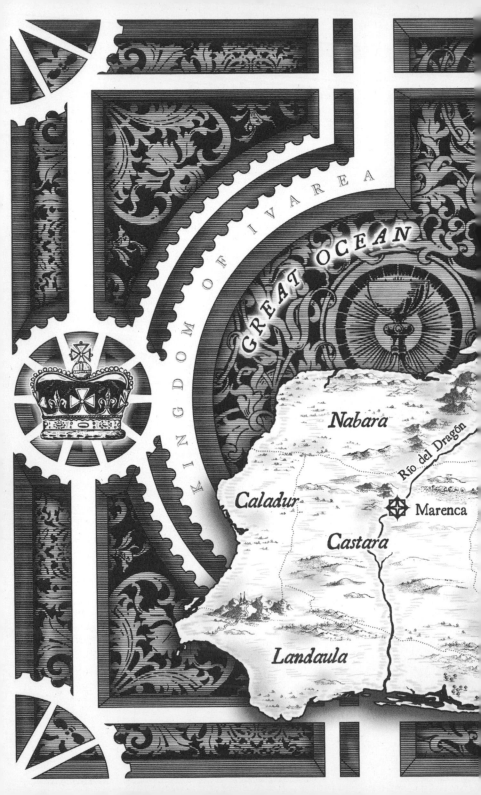

I

CHAPTER ONE

ONE NIGHT. YOU JUST HAVE TO SURVIVE HERE ONE MORE night.

Unfortunately, for a Proensan nobody in the royal court of Ivarea, that's easier said than done.

Tonight is the crown jewel of the social season, the most important party the provinces of Ivarea have ever seen: the celebration of four centuries of the Cardona dynasty's reign. The Anniversary Ball is the opportunity my family has been waiting for ever since our people were first conquered by the Ivareans—the reason my parents dragged me seven hundred miles across the sea and over land to the capital. If they can defy the odds and arrange my marriage into a prominent courtly house, our family will be launched to the highest tier of Ivarean elite society. To a position of respect and power that our people, the Proensans, have not had since the Cardona conquest. This is a prize more than worth the cost of my future.

Or so I'm told.

Eight weeks ago, when I was first shoved through the grand double doors of the palace for my debut, I thought that the rigors of this historically grueling season would get easier to endure with time. I used to hope that each dazzling ball, each refined tea party, each perfunctory dance, would feel a little less like a living nightmare, because each one meant that the season was coming that much closer to an end. I hoped that each moment was bringing me that much closer to home.

But it never got easier. It never *will* get easier in a royal court that looks down on Proensans just because we're Proensans, regardless of our titles or lands or wealth. And now that I've finally made it to the Anniversary Ball, I'm not at all sure I'll make it out intact.

Tonight, I throw myself into the centers of gravity within the grand ballroom of the Alcázar Real de Marenca as earnestly as any of the hundreds of grandes from every corner of the kingdom also in attendance. Beneath shimmering chandeliers that float across the elaborately painted ceiling, ladies in voluminous gowns clash with lovers and enemies alike from behind fluttering fans, and gentlemen bearing ceremonial swords that have been passed down through storied bloodlines for centuries shout gaily to their fellows in privilege and glory. Each and every one of them is desperate to emerge at dawn with something—or someone—they didn't have before, but then again, so am I. So I smile at them like I'm deranged and flirt with them until I feel sick. When the dancing begins in earnest, I even manage to snag a minuet with young Don

Fernando Peláez, who is everything I'm supposed to want in a future husband: well-connected, wealthy, a *real* Ivarean. He smiles at me as we take our places on the dance floor, which my foolish heart takes as a good sign.

Maybe this one will be different. Maybe this one will finally put me out of my misery. Maybe this one will look at me and not find me wanting.

"You look absolutely enchanting tonight, Doña Anaïs."

Fernando twirls me by the arm, and the satin skirts of my gown flare out with me. My mother designed it to match the depths of my red opal locket, with gold and garnet beading down the bodice and a blood-red brocade underskirt. Contrary to what some of the grandes who dominate the capital might assume, I'm no stranger to overwrought ensembles, but I have never hated one more than this—less because of what it looks like, and more because of what it means for my family's future. What that future will demand of me.

"And by the saints," Fernando adds with a quicksilver grin that matches his celestially spangled waistcoat, "you're a surprisingly great dancer."

My lacquered lashes flutter as we trade steps like feints in a duel. "Why is that so surprising, Don Fernando?"

"Oh, I don't know. I suppose I didn't think you Proensans paid attention to dance crazes here in the capital."

I bite down a grimace. To people like Fernando, who hail from the central heartland of the Ivarean peninsula in the province of Castara, us Proensans are not *real* Ivareans, not even two hundred years after we were absorbed into this kingdom.

People on the peninsula see us as barely domesticated country bumpkins whose inclusion in elite Ivarean society makes for an amusing trifle at best and a bewildering insult to *their* culture and people at worst.

"What is it you think we do, then?" I challenge my partner lightly. "Lie around our farms all day and do nothing?"

Fernando leans down toward me, silvering the very air around us. "Well, I was going to say that you are too busy lying with your livestock, but I must admit, I like your version better."

If he wasn't forcing me around the dance floor, I would stumble and fall. The whole of the royal court could run me over without a second glance at the girl lost in the spill of satin below their feet. But we're still dancing, face to incredulous face, and he seems wholly unmoved.

"Let me assure you, Don Fernando. My people do not lie with animals." I offer him a rigor mortis smile. "Like pigs."

Fernando waits for me to break character, to invite him to laugh with me, but I stare him down and do not yield. His grin disappears. Without its warmth for cover, his expression turns imperiously, pointedly blank.

I know that look. I know it better than the freckles on my face.

"Barbarians, the lot of you."

From each cardinal direction, the Alcázar's four clock towers begin to strike eleven. Even they cannot drown out my pulse as it thunders in my head. Fernando takes the opportunity to let

4

me go and melts back into the crowd as easily as if the minuet didn't happen at all. As if none of it mattered.

Because for him, it didn't.

Ever since I was old enough to understand my family's position, I haven't asked for true love or even a grand romance— the stuff of poems and ballads, the relationships that nights like these are supposed to inspire. In my more optimistic moments, I imagined finding someone who could understand the pressures I bear and possibly share their burden. Someone who wouldn't make me long too much for Massilie, my backwater hometown on the northern coast of Proensa, once I left it behind for a life on the peninsula.

But after the season began, what kept me going was the small, wild, stupid hope that I might manage to find someone here who sees me as worthy of respect. And every night, the grandes and courtiers who my parents nudge me toward wring that hope out of my heart. I thought that after eight weeks of failure, one more wouldn't hurt.

I was wrong. It always hurts.

Around the ballroom, the royal court rejoices in the sound of the bells. After all, the night is just beginning, and it is yet full of possibilities untold, of destinies unmet.

At least, that's what my mother believes.

She swans over moments after Fernando abandons me, positively beaming in her dove-gray taffeta gown. "The future duke of Varillo! How wonderful, Anaïs. Your father and I are thrilled!" From farther along down the ballroom, where he stands on the fringes of a group of rather grave-looking Galvaise grandes, my father inclines his head vaguely in our direction. "You must make sure to dance with the Peláez boy again before the night is out."

She's feeding off this chaos, and here I am, getting quietly devoured by it. "I wouldn't start planning the wedding just yet."

Briefly taken aback, Maman drops her smile, revealing the contours of her cheekbones. The gesture lends her a strange, almost ghostly air. "Ah." She recovers herself with a brief shake of her head. "Well, not to worry. There's still an entire palace of eligible young men clamoring to have you on their arms."

If that were true, I wouldn't still be running around like a headless chicken two months into the season in search of someone, anyone, who would have me for a wife and my family for allies at court. And even if it *were* true, I cannot imagine willingly giving myself to any of these puffed-up peacocks.

"Don't look at me like that, darling. You're positively *destined* for greatness."

That can't be good, coming from her. "What do you mean, *greatness?*"

"I *mean,* you're going to be the triumph of the most important social season in Ivarean history! You're going to strike a match that will leave the entire court in awe. I'd swear it on the fairies—that's how sure I am."

Invoking the fairies—mythological beings that legend holds once dwelled in Proensa—to help me find a fiancé feels like a new, desperate low. "Maman, *don't*. You know what they'll all think if they hear you." *Silly Proensans. Crazy Proensans.*

Ever impervious to my bleating, my mother chastises me with a look. "Let them think what they will. The fairies *were* real—"

"*Were they?*"

"—and even if they weren't," she continues with a note of insistent triumph, "you shouldn't be ashamed of who you are or where you come from, Anaïs. The right man is out there, and he will cherish everything about you, even the magic running in your veins, for the *blessing* it is."

The humid air trapped in the ballroom seems to press against my hollowed chest. "That's not funny."

"I didn't mean it to be funny."

She could have fooled me. "The blessing" is what we call the magic that runs in a small number of Proensan families. When I was a girl, my father taught me to draw power from my blood to cast spells: repairing accidentally beheaded dolls, warming my bedroom without lighting a fire, even speeding the growth of a new lavender garden. Blood magic depends on both the continuation of blessed bloodlines *and* the potency of a given bloodline's magic, and between those two factors, it has withered away a little more with every passing generation.

The blessing is one marker of my heritage that can't be taken away from me, so despite its weakness, I suppose I am grateful to have it. But all it's really ever done is further separate me and my people from the rest of Ivarea, who see blood magic as a blasphemous practice.

Unlike us blessed Proensans, Ivarean magicians manipulate the world around them. Here on the peninsula, magic suffuses the very earth, and people born and bred here have the potential to use that power without sacrificing even a drop of blood. So really, it's no wonder Fernando looked at me the way he did. The way they all do, in the end, whether they know about my blessing or not: with absolutely impenetrable derision.

"Maman, those men you've had your eye on all season, all of those powerful peninsular families—they're never going to look twice at us. We're just fairy-worshipping, blood-magic-wielding *barbarians* to them."

For the first time since before we were admitted into the ballroom, my mother looks me in the eye. The need for discretion dawning, she herds me behind a nearby pillar. Spiny marble branches of a pomegranate shrub drip garnet fruit all the way down from the painted ceiling, offering us a bloody veil of concealment. "I know the past two months haven't been easy on you, child. None of us were under any illusions otherwise. But we traveled here to the capital for you. For *tonight*. Now all you have to do is be your sweet, charming self, and your father and I will manage the rest." Her dark brown eyes glaze over as she envisions the wonderful future, the grand destiny, I'm to build here in Marenca, the capital city. "It will all be worth it in the end, you'll see. You'll belong here. Just like any other Ivarean."

Maman's been giving me this speech in some form or other

since I was a child. Hide behind topiary plinths to avoid my Castaran lessons? *You can't be an Ivarean if you can't speak the language of the court.* Complain about my dancing instructor tying an oak branch to my back to improve my posture? *But don't you want to be able to waltz like an Ivarean?*

All that training, all that work, all my life to belong to a court and a kingdom that turned my people into second-class citizens in our own land.

The thing is, I don't *want* greatness as Maman sees it. I don't want a destiny I don't already have in my hand, waiting for me seven hundred miles away. I don't think I could bear it.

But how I live my life has never been up to me. That's not about to change tonight.

My gloved hand wraps around my locket out of habit. Maman first entrusted the family heirloom to me when I was young. I should have hidden dried flowers or a perfumed scrap of silk inside before coming to the capital—something that would remind me of where I come from. Now the necklace is just a hollow touchstone in a world not mine.

"I just want to go back home." To our countryside château in Massilie, surrounded by precious little other than grass, cheese, and livestock. I want to go home and let the capital and its glittering palace fade away into nothing in my memory.

My mother merely hums over the confession. "This is your time, Anaïs. We have to make the most of it." She adds with a note of pointed cheerfulness, "Don't we?"

My life has always been forfeit. A sacrifice to forces greater than I really understand. But if my future is a sacrifice that could change my family for the better, that could ensure our safety, our *survival,* what choice do I have but to give it?

"Of course, Maman."

After Tristán de la Cueva, another Castaran grande's son, suggests that I'd be more *comfortable* in the royal stables, I decide to give up. I don't care that sitting out from the Anniversary Ball would really just be a pause in the inexorable trajectory of my life. My parents might force me here all over again next year, or they might let me settle for another, slightly less ambitious season in Lutesse, the capital of Galvain Province, but . . . what's the point of worrying now?

Well and truly hopeless, I plant myself at the feet of a column in the northeastern corner and close my eyes against the chaos before me. In my mind's eye, I trade the free-floating banners featuring the Cardona dynasty's crowned dragon sigil for ivy draping the stately, whitewashed walls of my home. I set the hummingbirds that haunt Papa's hyacinths loose among the enchanted limestone animals that flank the arches at either end of the palace ballroom. I shake loose the antique-gold and bone-white stones of the mosaics adorning the walls overhead to let in the temperate Proensan sunlight. I imagine miles and miles of open space instead of the gilded inland capital, where there's not a soul to dismiss me because of my home, my beliefs, my magic, my name.

When I finally open my eyes, someone is staring right at me.

His eyes are dark and radiant in the bright ballroom. I don't realize who he is until he begins to advance like a burnished shadow in my direction. A wave of panic causes me to choke.

The prince.

Infante Leopoldo Cardona—known as Leo the Lush for his signature vice—has a servant trail him across the room with a bottle of wine at the ready. As the youngest and most irresponsible of the king's three children, he usually pops into a given event only long enough to ensure that no one can deny he was, at one point, *there*. Then he slips away to carouse in Marenca proper, or gamble with sailors in the river district, or whatever activities are more to his taste. I have no idea what those are. More importantly, I have no idea what someone like him would want with me.

When he finally draws up before me, his eyes like embers taunting an innocent onlooker with the possibility of their igniting, my legs twitch, begging me to run. But his presence fixes me in place, and like a proper Ivarean lady, I begin to curtsy.

The prince waves me up before I can complete the gesture. "No need for such formality," he remarks, magnanimously drunk, his hand loose on the hilt of a ceremonial sword he's carrying for the occasion. "I am simply your Infante Leo."

"As—as you say, Vuestra Alteza Real." *Damn it.*

"And you're that girl from the Duque de Tarrazas's ball, aren't you?"

I can't believe he remembers that. The prince scrawled his name on my dance card a few weeks ago to avoid dancing with some poor Castaran girl who had never gotten in the habit of carrying breath mints. The second the girl's back was turned, he stole a bottle of Vornolmian red and abandoned me with little more than an insouciant wink.

I still have that dance card in my room. If my mother ever found it and realized I failed to use that chance encounter to my advantage, her screaming fit would break all the windows in our rented Marenca townhouse. She could not accept the truth: the story of an insignificant bumpkin and a prince who is second in line for the Ivarean throne will never end well. And I *know* I don't want to be just another Proensan for a Cardona to conquer, like his ancestors did mine two hundred years ago.

If I'm nothing but a nameless girl to him now, I must have been right.

"My name is *Anaïs*, señor."

Despite his intoxicated state, the prince curves his lips in an indolent grin. "Now, what makes you think I do not remember who you are, Doña Anaïs? Daughter of Don Eduard Aubanel, Conde de Massilie?"

Oh. Well, whether he's drunk or bored or trying to stir up a bit of scandal, I am not in the mood to indulge him. Not after everything I've already had to endure at the hands of people like him. "Maybe the fact that it's taken you all this time to remember me."

Only the last remnants of my dignity stop me from clapping my hands over my mouth. Leo is almost as taken aback by my insolence as I am, tucking his chin into the gilt-embroidered collar of his black tailcoat and letting go of the hilt of his sheathed sword. Briefly distracted by the way his gray-gold brocade waistcoat sets off his bronzed complexion, I almost miss the fact that he's slowly grinning back at me.

"Luckily, my lady, I'm no oath breaker. If I promised you a dance, a dance you shall have."

Somewhere, my mother is surely swooning. I manage to stay upright for now, but giddy disbelief still rushes through my veins as I take his hand and let him lead me to the center of the dance floor. Couples bow and part as he passes, my scarlet skirts casting nearly as wide a berth as those of the ladies already glaring daggers at me behind their fans.

"If I may be so bold," he says once the music has begun, "what has been the highlight of your time in the capital this season, Doña Anaïs?"

"Oh, the . . . the picnics at the riverside, I suppose." I add with a wry undertone, "At least I didn't spend them praying the sun would evaporate me."

"Ah, nothing quite so alluring as sweat in the capital. I'll bet you're missing Proensan weather terribly by now, aren't you?"

"Well, not just the weather, señor. Proensa is my home."

Is it me, or does he set his jaw slightly? "Then this place," he says quietly, "must feel like your own personal hell."

For a moment, I think he understands the costs of merely *existing* as a Proensan in the heart of the Ivarean court.

But that can't be. He's the *prince* of these vipers.

Isn't he?

"Certainly not. Hell is not nearly as hot."

He laughs now, a true laugh. "Come outside with me, Doña Anaïs. I think you'll enjoy it."

This dance—this proposition—it's simply too overwhelming to be real. An intoxicating fantasy. I feel as drunk on the thrill of his attentions as he is on wine. But his hand feels like my only tether to the world as I spin and twirl like a storm about its eye. And underneath it all, he looks at me as if he doesn't want to stop.

To my great confusion, I find myself feeling the same.

So, as the last bars of music reverberate off the mosaic tiles of the wall, I let Leo lead me away from the dance floor and out of the ballroom entirely. Over the last four hundred years, the Cardona kings have turned the Alcázar Real, a medieval fortress crowned with arched gateways and sun-kissed bell towers, into a seat of power carved in their own image, modern and glorious. That extends to the Mirror Garden, where Leo leads me. Torches flicker on either side of the soaring arches that surround the garden's four quadrants, divided by narrow rectangular reflecting ponds. Each quadrant houses mazes of fragrant rosebushes that close and open again, independent of the breeze, and shrubs enchanted into animal shapes, which seem to be dozing this late at night. This garden might as well be a gateway to another world.

An involuntary gasp slips out between my lips. "*Oh.*"

We stop in the middle of the bisecting paths, the bombast of the ball distant at our backs. "Hell this may be," says Leo graciously with a sidelong glance at me, "but it can do a reasonably good job of disguising itself from time to time."

I have to shut my mouth before he notices my gaping. "Yes, well . . . it must be very impressive in daylight," I lie smoothly.

A curl plays on the corner of his lips. "I think you're the first girl who's ever been unimpressed by Jardín de Espejos."

"Maybe they didn't admit it for fear of offending you."

"But you are not afraid of causing royalty offense. Are you, Anaïs?"

All of a sudden, he grabs my hand and pulls me closer, as if we're about to dance again. But this is like no dance I've ever been taught.

No, this is so much worse.

I'm already in a full-fledged panic when Leo closes his dark eyes and begins to lower his lips. By the time I figure out what to do with my arms—namely, flap them about like wings—his lips have already brushed mine. A strange heat spreads through my tingling body like a spell.

A moment later, he registers the batting of my arms and releases me at once. We stare at each other, each more alarmed than we'd probably like to admit. When he speaks, his voice is soft, unsteady. "Did I do something wrong?"

No. You did, Anaïs.

I *let* Infante Leopoldo Cardona sweep me off my feet. I flirted with him. I danced with him. I went off with him. I forgot myself. It was stupid, and *far* too easy to do, with those shimmering eyes inviting me to indulge myself just a little more. But that kiss brought the brief, reckless fantasy to a grinding halt. After all, a prince of Ivarea will never want anything more from a Proensan count's daughter. And I've been through too much with too many people like him at this goddamned court to let Leo the Lush just *seduce* me.

He didn't cast a spell on me with that kiss. He broke it.

Without a word, I back away slowly and turn for the palace. Just as I cross the threshold of the western arch into the ballroom, the first chime of midnight clangs across the entirety of the capital. The royal court erupts in cheers and cries in its wake. *"Four hundred years and four hundred more!"*

I keep going, drowning myself in the cacophony. On the royal dais, Rey Rodrigo and Reina Isabel stand from their jewel-encrusted, dragon-winged thrones to bask in their triumph. Their elder son, Príncipe Felipe, and his wife, Princesa Helena, cheer at the left end of the dais, their daughter, Infanta Clara, at the right. Behind me, Leo has taken up a position beneath the western archway, calling loudly for more wine.

My parents must have seen us disappear together. By now, they are probably itching to commence talks for our swift betrothal, gloriously heedless of what the king and queen would have to say about such a thing. But somehow the thought of my parents accosting our monarchs no longer brings me any anxiety. Tomorrow, we'll sit with my failure, but at least it's over.

At least we can finally go home.

A high, shrill voice nearby exclaims, "Out there! Fireworks!"

For a moment I think I hear them, a popping sound as they ascend into the silken night sky. The sounds are too loud to be coming from the hills, though. A courtyard? The garden I just abandoned?

No . . . no, not out there . . .

The windows are blown out. The air is suddenly thick with eviscerated tile and smoke. I'm knocked onto a bed of glass and rubble. My heart pounds so hard that I can't feel my lungs fighting for breath.

The wall mosaics burst like grenades in showers of glass. Proud columns and arches shudder and begin to crumble. Floating chandeliers plummet to the ground. Servants and grandes alike flail for leverage to pull themselves clear, choking on plumes of dust and smoke. The whole of the ballroom is suddenly molten with flame.

Explosions.

Explosions in the Alcázar.

Minutes, days, hours later, the palace stops shaking. I don't know how long I lie there, atop the rubble of the windows. It feels like the whole world has been counting time as the Alcázar was decimated, and me inside it. Shards of glass seem embedded in my scalp. The broken boning in my corset nearly pierces me through with new, alien ribs. Spent gunpowder and sizzling flesh invade my nostrils, force their way down my throat. My vision hitches on the stubbornly gleaming thrones, overturned like beached whales.

The king and queen. Their elder children. *Gone.*

I hear people begin to call for their friends and family

members. Rifles and shotguns blast through the smoke. I flinch into my jagged shroud and don't move. Don't understand. The detritus of the ball falls on me like heavy silt—fans, rings, hats, feathers, shoes, brooches, an appendage or four—but if I look at it, I'll look for my mother in those orphaned objects, or my father, and I can't do that.

"SURVIVORS!"

Staggered by the word, the absurdity of it, I try to raise my head. Blood trickles down the back of my neck, too fresh and deep to clot. But there—there, across the way. *Leo*. Climbing atop an upturned table. His stupid sword raised like a beacon. He spits blood onto the ruptured floors of his home.

What the hell just happened?

"TO ME, SURVIVORS!"

What did we just survive?

He shouts again, and his voice, clear and singular and terrible in the chaos, stuns me into motion. I force myself to roll over. Glass and gravel press into my arms and chest as I start to crawl. There are bodies everywhere. Heads misshapen with shrapnel. Limbs gone black with soot, still warm beneath my palms. Screams frozen in death.

I don't look longer than I can help it. I don't stop for anything. Not even when I notice a familiar celestial jacket melting into ashen skin, its owner's mercurial grin replaced with a mask of horror. I can't even look up when Leo heaves me to my feet. Without a word, he drags me toward the Arco de Léon on the eastern side of the ballroom. A girl I might have recognized before midnight shoots with an orphan rifle into the room to cover our retreat.

From whom?

Leo shoves me under the shadow of the arch. Enchanted limestone lions mewl piteously at the base of its pillars, missing haunches and tails. Each person Leo's stowed here seems more stunned than the one before, but they're alive.

"Stay here," he snarls pointedly at me. Then he dives back into the melee in search of more survivors.

I'm too numb to disobey. Instead, I tug my singed gloves off, press my fingers against the wound on my neck, and close my eyes. I don't know exactly what my blood magic can do to protect against *this,* but I try to focus my thoughts into a coherent intention: *Keep me from harm. Don't let me die here.* Eventually I feel the spell settle in my skin with a faint blush of power, but it doesn't feel much like armor. Not when everything is falling apart around me.

But I guess it's more than others can do. I shuffle vaguely toward the person closest to me, bloody hands raised as if in surrender, but stop short when I hear a new, insistent sound. The stomp of boots. Coming from the tiled walks beyond the ballroom. And beneath the marching, the cold snick of steel being unsheathed. The click of revolvers at the ready.

I peer into the corridor.

You really, really shouldn't have done that.

A many-headed wave of people crashes inexorably down the hall toward the ballroom. Their faces are indistinct in the lithe shadows that sprang up around the fallen chandeliers, but their weapons are nothing like the aristocratic ornaments that now litter the ballroom floor. These are efficient, ruthless, practical. And the people bearing them do not seem afraid of using them.

All thoughts of gentle protection spells dissipate in my head. Nothing I do will be able to stand against so many people, so many weapons. So I throw myself back into the chaos. The chain of my locket thuds against the hollow of my throat as I run.

"Alteza! Leo! *Come back!*" I scream. "Intruders—from the arch—"

Behind me, a bloodcurdling shout. Someone crashes to the ground, followed by the clatter of a rifle rolling through limp hands. The girl, the one who was shooting. I whirl around as Leo diverts his bloody path to look for the assailant. But it's impossible to find that one person in the stream of the armed intruders. They fall on the little band of survivors I just abandoned with gleeful efficiency until the stalwart Lion Arch above crumbles at last, turning all of them, innocents and perpetrators alike, into a pile of twitching limbs.

If I had stayed—if I had offered them what meager protection I could—

But more and more intruders keep streaming in over the ruin of the arch. Over the bodies caught in the rubble. Armed and just as eager to kill as the earlier arrivals.

The ones who blew up the Alcázar.

Who are they? Where did they come from? Why are they here?

I don't know, but ahead of me, the prince isn't stopping to ask those questions. He roars, sword raised, to charge. And while I watch him, my mind comes to a sudden, precarious stop.

The *prince* . . .

But Leo's still alive and his family is not . . . so . . . so that means . . .

A thunderous crack of bullets. The new king collapses backward as the shots pierce him. Amid a growing chorus of guffaws from the attackers and strangled screams from the remaining guests, I dive to his side.

Leo raises a shaking arm to cup my face. He looks like a broken doll. The one I was taught to magically repair as a child. Helpless, I press my hand to his. His blood mixes with mine, with all of Ivarea, on my cheeks, down my throat and locket, before dripping onto his bleeding side. "You," he chokes out.

I don't know who I am. I don't think he knows, either.

"My king."

My skin prickles with residual magic—the protection spell. Then I hear another boom. Lightning tears through my body. A strange amber light blows out my vision. When I try to look down, I see a dark flower with jagged edges blooming from my chest.

The world turns black.

II

CHAPTER ONE

WITH THE PHANTOM TOUCH OF THE LATE REY LEOPOLDO Cardona still heavy on my cheeks, I open my eyes. And shoot up from bed.

My bed.

This is my bed.

My body. In my bed. In the townhouse we're renting in the capital for the season.

Alive.

But . . . but the ball . . . the prince . . . the explosions . . . all those bodies . . .

I saw them. I know I did. I crawled over them. I fled across the ashen ballroom toward a king in a battle for his life. I died with him in my bloody arms.

Didn't I?

Only just thinking it, I glance down at my body. My ribs are demonstrably not broken. No cuts or bruises crisscross my arms or legs. My hands fly to my throat and find the skin smooth, if pale, and my empty locket quite whole and unbothered. I seem to be wearing a plain linen chemise, but the more I run my fingers over the hem, the less sure I am that I've ever touched it before. I stare at the wall across from me as if it will break open and reveal the Alcázar ballroom, burning just as I remember it.

Then, I hear footsteps.

Before my eyes, Lion Arch crumbles over the intruders once again. Everyone I know dies again.

A voice cuts through the memory.

"*One hour,* Anaïs, that's all I promised. Come on, come on, we haven't much time!"

I let out a shuddering breath. *Maman.* It's just Maman. See, there she is at the threshold: wide umber eyes, straight dark brown hair, cheeks so round even now that you can't really tell where her cheekbones are. Just as she should be. But I can't for the life of me understand what she's talking about.

"Time until what?"

Instead of herding me out from the flimsy butter-yellow hangings around my bed, Maman hovers where she is with a strange glint in her dark eyes. As if she, too, can tell that something's wrong. With all of this. With me.

What's wrong with me?

"Till the ball, dearest. Don't think for a second that you're going to sleep through the whole day."

The ball. The Anniversary Ball.

Memories—*real* ones, not visions from a nightmare—come

back to me now. The scent of wildflowers as my lady's maid washes my hair. My father evaluating kerchief options with his valet over breakfast. Onion-and-olive tart turning to sawdust in my mouth. My mother's brow creasing at the expression on my face. The snap of buttons as I shrug off my morning dress and dive into an old shift.

That was just this morning. Then I fell asleep. Before the ball.

Right. Yes. The smell of gunpowder in my nostrils is just the remnant of a stubborn dream. The amber light that flooded my sight was just the afternoon sun entreating me to wake up already. The voice that rings like thunder in my head doesn't belong to Leo the Lush. He's not a king, for goodness' sake. And I didn't die with him.

I didn't . . . It didn't . . .

It didn't happen. None of it happened. This was just a nightmare. A fantasy. My anxious brain conjured up an attack on the ballroom to distract myself from the *real* battle that awaits me tonight—the battle for my family's social standing and my future.

I draw a deep breath.

After tonight, it will all be over.

At last.

Hours later, my lady's maid, Béatrice, gathers my crimson skirts behind me so I can teeter down the staircase. The gown was built for a ballroom, not the narrow but well-heeled town-house, and it feels just as heavy and cumbersome as it did before, in the dream. With some difficulty, we shuffle into a drawing room and nearly mow down my father. Already dressed in a starched shirt, navy waistcoat, and matching breeches, he stands up from his carved oak armchair and, without relinquishing his pipe, comes closer to inspect me.

Upstairs, I was motionless when Béatrice swept my dark blond hair into a pile of curls at the crown of my head. I bit my tongue while she did her best to smooth away my stubborn freckles with powder and dabbed carmine on my lips. I had to dig my nails into my palms while she painted my lashes. When I saw myself in the mirror, I thought I would pass out.

The reality staring back at me was just like the dream.

Too much like the dream.

But . . . but my mother has been planning my ensemble for the Anniversary Ball for months. I went through innumerable fittings for the gown and sat through endless trials for my hair. Of course I would have committed her plans for me to heart before today.

Of course.

For now, I recognize the grimace on Papa's face as he takes in the sight of his battle-ready daughter. The gleam in his eyes, which are as round as mine but a lighter brown in shade, goes out whenever he sees me in Ivarean courtly dress. He prefers our wild, tranquil Proensa to the suffocating royal court, just as I do. And he doesn't want to lose me to this place, either.

But I'm not thinking of that right now. I can only see

Fernando Peláez's body crumpled under my feet. The dragon-wing thrones smoking in the rubble. Gunfire and screaming and corpses.

"Papa? What would you say to just . . . leaving Marenca?" I don't let his obvious surprise stop me. "We could go right now and be miles from the Alcázar by nightfall, and everything would be fine. For us. At home. Wouldn't it?"

Papa lowers his smoking pipe with a frown and glances at a newspaper folded on the armrest of his chair. I can imagine the sorts of measures he must have been reading about: Rey Rodrigo calling for higher taxes on common commodities, for new censorship laws, for the arrests of the king's critics.

"Your mother and I only want what's best for you, Anaïs. Difficult as it must be to accept, there is no better place you could call home than the court at the Alcázar Real. No safer place from which to stake a new position in this kingdom for yourself as well as for us. You know that."

Yes. Yes, that is a thing I know. The palace is safe, in more ways than one. *I* am safe. Whatever happens tonight, I'll be safe. We all will.

When Béatrice takes her leave a few minutes later and my father and I are briefly, mercifully alone, I drop my voice to a tremulous whisper. "Have you ever heard of the blessing granting visions?"

He blinks those round eyes, much as I would if asked a similarly stupid question. "Visions?"

Since my mother's family lost their blood magic decades ago, I owe my meager powers and even more meager understanding of them to my father. "Premonitions, Papa. Of the future. Those kinds of visions."

I know what he's thinking. When I was a child, he explained the blessing to me as best suited for hearth magic. Spells of protection and healing, of transformation and enchantment—in the present, *not* the future.

They say that the blessing was stronger during the age of the fairies. What exactly the fairies were, no one knows now. But the stories agree that almost at the moment of the Cardona invasion, the fairies disappeared, leaving Proensa to be swallowed up into Ivarea. There are still those among our people who believe that the fairies were real, and even some who worship them as minor gods. Others cling to the myth as a symbol of our pre-Ivarean past, to a time before the Cardonas forced their taxes and belief systems on our people; considering the efforts Ivareans have spent proselytizing their beliefs in the awesome power of their saints in hopes of making us *civilized,* that's an instinct that even more skeptical Proensans can indulge. I generally err on the side of practicality on the belief-in-fairies spectrum, much to my fanciful mother's chagrin, but after that . . . *dream* . . . this afternoon, I don't know what to think. What else could be possible.

In contrast to Maman's excitability, Papa sounds rather sanguine. "There's not enough blood in the world to buy premonitions. Of any kind." His voice is determinedly light, as if I'm a baby he's trying to distract from a growing tantrum. "Are you sure you're feeling all right?"

Absolutely not. But I don't know how to admit what exactly

is *not right* to him. He wouldn't understand if I told him about the dream, about my unease. He would try to talk sense into me, or call for Maman's help, both of which would only make me feel more pathetic.

At my silence, he takes out a miniature dagger from an inner pocket of his waistcoat and flicks off its tooled leather sheath. "If it's the ball you're worried about, this might help."

He pricks the pad of his smallest finger on the blade. Before I can flinch away, he presses the wound against my arm. His eyes are screwed shut, and his breathing slows for a moment. I can feel the intention of his spell flowing onto my skin, a flush that could have come from a blazing hearth if it were not the height of summer in the Ivarean capital. It dissipates quickly, but what he did is clear.

A protection spell. The same one that he would insist on casting for me when I was a child before he sent me off to explore the wilds of the forest bordering the château.

The same one I cast on myself in the dream.

He lowers his dagger back into its sheath and pulls out his chosen kerchief, a square of ivory silk embroidered with his beloved hyacinths, to blot the cut. "Just to make sure things go well."

As my father's blood dries on my arm, my hand wraps around my locket. "It's not too late. We could still leave. We don't *have* to go to the ball."

Papa has always been the grounded balance to my mother's determined flightiness. But right now, he doesn't seem grounded at all. It's as if he's floating so far above me that I can barely see him against the setting sun. "The world forces our hand sometimes, Anaïs. Wouldn't you rather choose where you're standing if that happens?"

How terribly easy he makes it sound.

Unfortunately, we both know it's not.

Once an ancient fortress, the Alcázar Real de Marenca has been made and remade with the faces of all the great cultures that have ruled the Ivarean peninsula for the last thousand years. The ornate pale stone facade of the palace emanates such haughty grandeur that guests from the highest of the high to the lowest of the low feel as though they ought to crawl through the doors in supplication. The gold veining of the marble columns that line the central plaza shift to depict a crowned dragon taking flight across the kingdom.

My stomach churns at the sight of it all—the Alcázar is a feast too rich to digest. We join the stream of perfumed and be-feathered grandes gliding through the double doors and up through the glimmering corridors toward Arco de León. The enchanted lions of my dream were crushed when the arch fell, but here they all are, amber eyes alert as they roar silently at the hall. My parents are too focused on their entry into the ballroom to notice how pale I've gone.

The royal herald calls out our titles before we enter.

"Conde Eduard Aubanel de Massilie. His wife, Condesa Aliénor Laborde Aubanel de Massilie." A professional pause as he clears his throat. "Their daughter, Doña Anaïs."

As I plunge through the archway, I wonder whether the dream wasn't a bad thing after all. It showed me the worst that this night could offer and then gave me a second chance. To do my best. To get it right. That's why I didn't tell my parents what I saw, isn't it? Because I *wanted* to do this. For them. For us. I was grateful for this chance.

I should be grateful.

But this Anniversary Ball is startlingly similar to the one I dreamed. The glances from other partygoers like stab wounds. The pleasantries exchanged like gifts no one wanted. Even the gowns look the same, and I *know* I could never come up with something as ridiculous as Sidonie de Courcelles wearing a tiny fishbowl with a sapphire tropical fish atop her head.

Bewildered to the point of dizziness, I press myself against the wall and tell myself I'll return to the crowd soon. I just need to work up my courage.

Which makes me easy prey for guests making the rounds of the ballroom's outskirts, otherwise free of flirting and dancing and alliance-making, in search of a social inferior to bully.

Guests like Jacinthe Vieillard and Paloma Nelleda.

Damn it.

Jacinthe draws herself up before me, her dark skin resplendent in a magenta satin gown trimmed with pink sapphire rosettes. Her father, a baron from the northernmost province of Galvain, is perhaps the wealthiest man in the kingdom, and she's never let anyone forget it, least of all me. Over the years of our acquaintanceship, born out of run-ins at Galvaise ateliers when Maman would drag me north for shopping excursions, Jacinthe has made it abundantly clear that she would never look at me as competition once we finally debuted. In moments like this, I can't bring myself to disagree with that assessment.

"Saints, Anaïs, don't you look lonely," she remarks with a dispassionate smirk, though I can only imagine how delighted she is to have found time to lord her successes over me. "What have you been up to all night?"

Just then, the bells chime and briefly drown out the unfeeling orchestra. Half an hour to midnight.

Which should not matter.

Does not matter.

"Oh. Nothing very exciting, I suppose."

Paloma, the granddaughter of a highly ranked Castaran duke, gives me her most saccharine smile. "How unfortunate." If it were up to her, I highly doubt she would have stopped to look at me, let alone exchange even those two words. But Paloma seems quite intent on tricking potential suitors into thinking of her as Jacinthe's equal in desirability, so here she is, stuck with Jacinthe and now, apparently, with me. "I can imagine what great dreams you must have had coming into tonight, Doña Anaïs. We can only hope that they come true."

Jacinthe wrinkles her pert nose, not quite in sympathy. "Perhaps it's not just Anaïs. This whole season *has* been rather quiet. I rather expected more fireworks by now."

31

Paloma raises a single elegant brow. "You want fireworks? Don't tell me you haven't heard . . . you know."

Fireworks. Why do I feel like I've heard talk of fireworks already tonight?

"You'll have to enlighten us," Jacinthe says, pointedly cheerful.

Paloma is so eager to press her gossip advantage that she no longer seems put off by my presence. "Infanta Clara is getting betrothed tonight."

Briefly shocked out of my melancholy, I squeak, *"Betrothed?"* Infanta Clara's engagement would be the news of the night, if it were true. The second-eldest royal offspring is doted on by her parents and beloved by the court both for her quick wit and for being the first magician of any talent to grace the royal family in decades.

Jacinthe blinks, cool and inscrutable. "To whom?"

"She's supposedly carrying a gift from him tonight," continues Paloma in a giddy undertone, skating over the gaping hole in her story. "If either of you is feeling brave, perhaps you could go and inquire whose it is."

"Oh, I'm rather inclined to allow the princess her little mystery. We shall simply have to find something else to solve instead." Before I can even imagine being drunk enough to ask the princess directly about her secret fiancé, Jacinthe seems to glimpse something behind me. A shadow crosses her face. "Well, look at that. Here comes a puzzle of our own."

Paloma and I turn to follow her gaze.

"And I think it's coming for you, Anaïs."

It can't be. Not now. Not for real.

But there he is. Infante Leopoldo, crossing the ballroom toward me. Like the last time we met.

Which was at the Tarrazas ball. Not here.

This can't be real.

But he's wearing the same clothes I saw in the dream—blood-red cloak, sword, and all—and that insouciant grimace is as magnetic from afar as it was then. Again, I feel my gaze catch on the brilliance of his. As if he set out a lure only I can see, and I am stupid enough to take.

Suddenly Jacinthe seems more interested in me than ever before. "What are you waiting for? This could be your last chance for a royal dalliance before you're back in that backwater town of yours."

"Don't you *dare*," Paloma interjects a beat too late, her voice full of panic. "You couldn't possibly think the *prince* would actually be interested in someone like *you*. If you were smart, you'd bow out now before you completely humiliate yourself in front of the whole court."

She's not wrong. I *don't* think the prince is truly interested in me. I *know* I'd just humiliate myself.

But for now, I don't have a choice.

He's coming this way.

And he's still looking at me.

Again.

The three of us girls curtsy before him. Even as I rise on shaking legs, I stare at his boots instead of his face.

"Vuestra Alteza Real. How wonderful to see you actually

taking part in the celebration. I was worried the nature of the evening would escape you." There's a genuine quality in Jacinthe's voice that she has never bestowed upon me. I suppose growing up as a dear playmate and friend of the royal children—a privilege bought for her by her father's staggering wealth and clever court politicking—would grant her that familiarity.

"Don't worry about me, Jacinthe," says the prince, returning her smile. "I know *exactly* what tonight is all about."

Paloma shifts so the width of her creamy satin gown dwarfs my figure. "And what is that, señor?"

His grin rusts at the question. Instead of answering, he casts his gaze around the ballroom to make it seem like a coincidence when it snags on me again.

It is not a coincidence.

"Have we met before, my lady?"

Well, now I know my dream-self gave him too much credit. "You promised me a dance weeks ago, Vuestra Alteza Real. At the Tarrazas ball."

Jacinthe's eyes gleam as she leans forward. She has never retained or passed on information that did not interest her, and nothing about me has ever been interesting. Until now. "Why, Anaïs, you didn't tell us you had danced with the prince."

"Because we didn't."

"Didn't we?" Leo furrows his dark brows. He really doesn't remember.

"No, señor. I'm certain." I wish I'd forgotten about the

dance card incident, too. But I am, apparently, getting very good at not forgetting the things I should. "I believe that means you're in my debt."

Paloma gasps. Jacinthe stands back, considering me more carefully than she ever has.

For his part, Leo smiles again, and it looks just like the one in my dreams, quick as lightning and just as dazzling. "We can't have that, can we."

For a second I think, *We really, really can't.* Because if this is happening again, even in this form, then . . . then what if the rest of the dream wasn't a dream? What if it really was a vision? What if—

This can't be right. This isn't happening.

But I don't have time to panic. I don't even have time to think. My hand is deliciously pliable in Leo's as he guides me to the dance floor. The whispers around the ballroom that I dreamed up earlier this afternoon echo now: *Who is that? Who told her red is her color? Doesn't she look Proensan?*

Partway through the sedate number, Leo makes a noncommittal noise in his throat. "You don't seem to be enjoying this as much as you should."

I suppose I don't know how to. I have never been so naive and stupid and reckless before.

He continues. "Perhaps you now wish you'd called in your debt for something more than a dance."

I almost freeze in his grip.

"What are you thinking about, Doña Anaïs?" His voice

is low and almost sinuously silky in my ear. "A ballroom as bright as this is no place for dark secrets. Tell me what's on your mind."

Obnoxious as he is, something about the sound of his voice triggers an avalanche of visions again. Fire and smoke and ash. The screams of the dying. The uncanny, gaping silences of the dead. And in the center of it all, Leo immovable before me. Somehow the only solid thing in the world.

I don't understand how I can hold both versions of the ballroom in my head at once. The real and the fake. The now and the nightmare. This is not a balancing act that people are meant to survive with their sanity intact. And it is definitely not something I should be confessing to the prince. But the same overwhelming instinct that sent me running to his side from unknown intruders is building in me now. As if something terrible will happen if I don't do something. If I don't try to reach him, right here, right now.

"I had a vision. Of the Alcázar getting attacked. At midnight tonight. The ballroom collapsing. People dying."

For the first time I've ever seen, Leo holds himself like an actual courtier. He schools himself into a determinedly diplomatic expression. "Have you had . . . visions . . . like this before?"

"Oh God, no. No, but it was so . . . it was so *real*." My voice cracks open, as if the memories have been written on my skin, my tongue, and I can't hold them in any longer. "And then I woke up, and it was this afternoon somehow—"

"You woke up," he repeats.

"*Yes*, technically, b-but I don't think it was just a dream. I saw you wearing this exact coat. You remembered me. From the dance card incident. We danced here. You took me to Mirror Garden and . . . and then the ballroom went up in flames and people with rifles stormed in and killed the survivors. And I—I'm sorry, I just . . . have a horrible feeling about all of this. *Whatever* this even is."

Leo's burning eyes slide to me again. Only now, they seem terribly and piercingly blank.

I don't know why I'm surprised.

"So what are you going to do about it?"

My mouth parts in an O of shock.

"I—I don't know. I just . . . you asked what I was thinking about." *You beneath the burning arch. Your screams as the people you risked your life to save were murdered. Your choking gasps in my arms.* "You said you wanted to know."

"And you couldn't bear to confess your delusions to people who *actually* know you."

"Perhaps I hoped you could do something about it."

He cocks his head to the side. "You would have to be pretty desperate," he observes, "to think I could save you."

The dance ends on a glorious chord. We break apart with the music, but do not applaud the orchestra with the other dancers. He's staring at me as intently as I'm staring at him. I am suddenly very aware that we are in the middle of the dance floor and half of the Ivarean court is watching us still. Waiting to see how this ends.

It has to end.

"It's almost midnight," says the prince.

What? Already?

The only thing I can do is try to salvage this second chance with the prince. The way Maman would push me to. The way Papa would expect me to. "Alteza, I must beg your forgiveness. I swear I didn't mean to disturb your night with my delusions of doom."

Even when banked, the embers of his gaze are deceptively warm on my skin. "Do you know, sometimes I think we've been doomed for a long time."

Dread prickles in the pit of my stomach.

"Till next time, then, Doña Anaïs."

I don't know if he means the next function of the season, or something else. But he turns on his heel and abandons me as easily as he first swept me up.

The orchestra picks up speed and intensity for the next dance, and the whole of the Ivarean court forgets the unsettling episode they just witnessed. Gladly they throw themselves into the frenzy of the moment, breathless and sweat-slicked with exhilaration.

It's not yet midnight, it's nowhere near morning, but I feel like no matter what happens in the next few seconds, everything is ending. For me. For my life. For the dreams I didn't know I had but sense that I'll never hold in my hands.

Soon, all too soon, come the bells.

The grandes burst into cheers directed at the raised dais. Just as they did in the vision, the Cardonas rise to meet the crushing vehemence of Ivarea's celebrations. This time, Leo is with them.

I send up a prayer to any deity or saint or fairy that could be listening.

Please let me have lost my mind tonight. Please let me just have ruined my life, not ended it. Please let me be wrong.

Goose bumps erupt on my arms. They tingle so urgently that I feel my skin trying to rip off my bones.

Papa's spell. The blessing. It's trying to protect me from bodily harm, but—

Then come the explosions.

With them, the screaming.

Again.

For a long, horrific moment, it's all I register. Screaming and sobbing and shooting and burning, everything burning. Like music weaving in with the chiming of the clock towers. The terrible sounds are trapped in my aching head, bells that never stop ringing. Massive chunks from the painted ceiling fall and carve chasms into the floor. A boulder with the ruined face of some Ivarean saint crashes down and pins me at the bottom of one of those craters. I am trapped between the roiling center of the earth and the burning of the ballroom.

It's happening again. It's all really happening again.

I was right. The explosions at the palace *weren't* just a dream. Not a dream at all. They were real. I died then. And then I woke up . . . and came back here . . . just to die again?

How? *Why?*

Why isn't it the same now as it was before? Why doesn't anyone else remember?

What's wrong with me?

My gown starts to smoke like a pyre.

I'm going to die here now. Truly. At least then the mystery of this situation won't matter. Not to me.

Something teeters on the lip of the crater above me, draped in a crimson cloak like a shroud. Coughing through the smoke, I crane my aching neck up to peer more closely.

A body.

"Saints, it's you." Blood drips from Infante Leo's mouth onto my throat. Detritus flies and fire burns behind his yet-gilded silhouette. "What the fuck is this? What do we . . . what do we *do*?"

My tongue is inert in my mouth. "I don't . . . Leo, I'm so . . ."

It doesn't matter what I am, in the end.

There is only the crashing of the painted ceiling, and in the rush before it splinters through the both of us, a whisper like the kiss of death:

"Till midnight."

III

CHAPTER ONE

THE AFTERLIFE FEELS ODDLY LIKE THE CAPITAL. SIZZLING heat. Oppressive humidity. Everything bathed in a slick molten bronze glow. It pierces through to my eyes even though they're shut.

Wait.

The afterlife?

The capital?

My eyes flutter open, smooth as a dream.

This is not a dream.

That, in the ballroom, was not a dream. I *died* there. I was crushed by the ceiling. The last thing I saw was Leopoldo Cardona flattened by a splintered piece of sky. It was real. And I was only there because I let myself believe it was a dream. I let myself be carried back to the ballroom even after what I'd seen because it was only a dream and could not hurt me.

But here I am now. In my room. In Marenca. After dying. *Again*.

I'm freely sobbing with anguish and shock and a twinge of guilty relief by the time I notice that my mother has perched herself gingerly on the edge of my bed. Her presence just makes me cry harder.

"Anaïs?" Fear fills Maman's eyes as she stares at me, bewildered concern etched in the elegant lines of her forehead. "Darling, what happened? Did you have a nightmare?"

A nightmare? *A nightmare?* Twice I've lived through that *nightmare* and twice now I've been killed by it. As have my parents and everyone else I know. But . . . but in this moment, as shock and horror continues to flood my senses, all I can do is gape.

"Ah. Let's just get you cleaned up, shall we? Petronilla," she calls to one of the maids on the landing, "bring Mademoiselle some water."

Petronilla bustles inside and hands me a glass of water. Béatrice follows behind her, discreetly heading to fill the porcelain ewer in the corner. I take a hesitant sip but cannot shake the unmoored feeling in my bones the longer I sit here.

"It's all right, Anaïs," Maman continues with a sigh, reaching out a hand. "We still have plenty of time before the ball."

The glass topples onto my lap. Water soaks my shift. "The . . . Anniversary Ball?"

"Of course the Anniversary Ball."

Maman clearly doesn't remember being killed there. If what

42

happened last time still holds now, then no one else remembers it, either.

And since it wasn't a dream . . . and the ball is happening again . . . then at midnight tonight, it will end the same way, all over again.

I roll to the other side of the bed, heedless of the spilled water, and round the tall bedposts. "We can't go back there. We *won't*. I refuse."

My mother is not the least bit fazed. She pats my cheek twice and then drops her hand, confident that she was exactly as reassuring as the situation called for. "Is this about my nagging? I'm sorry, dear, but there's really—"

"If we go there, we'll all die. I saw it happen."

Béatrice and Petronilla pause in their work. Maman sighs again, more sharply than before.

"*Don't* say I just had a nightmare. Something terrible is going to happen at the Alcázar at midnight. Don't make us go." I lunge forward and grab her arms. "Maman, you have to believe—"

"I do not have patience for such madness, Anaïs."

"*Please!*"

She wrenches free of my grasp. "How dare you try to manipulate me with this morbid fantasy."

If I had a gold real for every time my mother manipulated me, I would be richer than Jacinthe Vieillard. "It's not a fantasy, this is *real*! I don't know how or why, but I swear on the fairies that it is!" I slide to my knees, dizzy. "*Twice* now, I've seen what happens at the ball. I've been given a chance to escape, and we have to take it. Please, just . . . just *believe* me."

My tongue tastes of sandpaper. I don't have enough shards of dignity left to care how desperate I sound.

Maman doesn't break her stare for a long time. The maids don't have that kind of freedom, but I can feel their wariness. I wonder where Papa is. He has no idea that he's been delivered from the cold realm of death twice now. Or has he been brought back after crossing over? I don't know. I don't understand. My head is pounding. I never got more than a sip of water, after all.

"I am your mother, Anaïs. It's my duty to protect you." Her voice is gentle, tender. "And I will do so the only way I know how."

No, no, no, no, no—

"Girls," she says to the maids, "get my daughter cleaned up. We have a big night ahead of us."

My mouth gapes as she sweeps back out of the room, but as the maids help me up, I'm quiet as a tomb.

I've often thought my mother was going to be the death of me.

I didn't think it would prove so literal.

"Don Eduard Aubanel, Conde de Massilie. His wife, Doña Aliénor Laborde Aubanel, Condesa de Massilie. Their daughter, Doña Anaïs."

It's the same herald as last time. *Everything* is the same as last time, and the time before that. But none of it feels real. I should be able to dispel everything I see with a touch. Every proud painting, every enchanted statue, every absurd headpiece. I should be able to dismiss them all like so many gilded cobwebs and reveal the twice-decimated ballroom for what it is. It wasn't a dream. It's definitely not a vision. It was real. It happened. To *me*.

Which, of course, is impossible. Even I know that. Before we left the townhouse tonight, Papa quipped, "Any opportunity Rey Rodrigo gets to yammer on about his forefathers' benevolent rule *is* a calamity beyond compare," which effectively doused any hope I might have had that he'd believe my story. So when my parents force me to approach the royal dais to be presented to the king and queen, I have no leverage to resist.

I was six the first time we came to the peninsula. That winter, Rey Rodrigo convened the court in Bayirid, the grand capital of Tarracuña Province on the eastern coast of the peninsula and the city of origin of the Cardona dynasty itself. My mother, being my mother, persuaded Papa to make the trek across the sea—as an investment in our family's future, of course. The king does not generally make it a point to meet the tiny, screaming children of random provincial nobles, but one day, his own tiny, screaming children—Príncipe Felipe, Infanta Clara, and Infante Leopoldo—demanded new playmates, and Maman eagerly offered my service.

I don't remember much about that afternoon, but I do remember Rey Rodrigo and Reina Isabel peeking into the royal nursery on their way to some function or other. Infanta Clara poked me into curtsying. The queen laughed. The king asked who I was.

I don't know how I answered him then. I doubt he or his children remember that day in Bayirid. Now I can only stand rigid and blink at the great wall of paintings mounted behind the dais, at the glittering wings of the monarchs' thrones.

But when I look closer, ghostly visions of the kings and queens of the past two Anniversary Balls crowd the dais beside their current impassive counterparts.

Great. Now I'm seeing things.

Before I know it, my parents are making their genuflections to Rey Rodrigo and Reina Isabel. I smash my own foot under the cover of my skirts. The pain cleaves through my dizzy spell even as it raises an undignified grimace on my lips.

"Conde. Condesa," Rey Rodrigo rumbles. He looks more like a bear than the dragon of the Cardona sigil, with a fine, dark beard framing a prominent nose and beady, intelligent eyes. "I hope the Marenca heat has not treated you too badly."

"On the contrary, Vuestra Majestad Real," Papa responds in his accented Castaran, "it has made for an . . . exotic change for us."

"A *much-needed* change, I assure you, Vuestras Majestades." Maman's chirping strikes my eardrum like an arrow. "If I may now present our daughter, Anaïs."

Dazed and breathless, I stumble toward the dais and just barely manage to hurl myself into a curtsy.

"A pretty thing you have on your hands, Don Eduard," the

king says jovially as I force myself back upright. "That means trouble."

Maman answers for my recalcitrant father. "Oh no, señor. Our Anaïs is *incredibly* well-behaved, *exceedingly* ladylike. She's been quite the hit in the capital this season—"

I can tolerate a lot when I know I'm about to be murdered, but I won't tolerate my mother trying to talk up my marriage prospects to a king who will be dead in three hours. "My mother flatters me, Vuestras Majestades, but right now, I must tell you, I had a vision of an attack on the palace at—"

The king narrows his eyes. "I do not recall ever hearing Proensans claim visions of the future among their . . . gifts."

Neither do I, but regardless: "You are in grave danger, Majestad. We all are. You must have the palace evacuated and searched before mid—"

"Do you know what you're saying, child?" he sneers, so sharp that he could cut off my nose and possibly my very air supply. "Such talk would not reflect well on our grand celebration. Are you trying to cause a scene?"

Before I can respond, Papa steps around to block me from view. "Forgive my daughter, señores. She carries the blessing, you see, and is prone to flights of fancy. She means no offense."

Reina Isabel purses her full lips. "Of course, my lord."

Rey Rodrigo stares down my father for a moment longer, but the pull of a once-in-a-dynasty party is too great to ignore for long. "Don Eduard, you know my ancestors have shown your people great respect over the last two hundred years. I should not like to see that respect taken advantage of."

While plenty of peninsular grandes at court have been more openly hostile to me and my family since we arrived here, the king himself would not sink to that level with his highborn subjects. Certainly not in public. So he speaks of respecting Proensans' unique culture and traditions, and not-so-obliquely threatens me in the same breath.

The obvious insults hurt, but the threats couched in civil terms—that's what has always made the Cardonas' court so dangerous. Even before the explosions began.

For now, my parents recognize defeat when they see it. Papa bows again, even lower than before, to hide the shadow in his eyes. "Nor I, señor. We are at your service, always."

He and Maman make several more exaggerated gestures of deference, assuring Rey Rodrigo that he has nothing to fear from me or Proensans in general, tonight or ever in the future. It is with great relief and greater fear that they herd me away from the dais and pin me against the far side of a column topped with a crown of swaying marble olive branches.

"Ungrateful child! Telling tales! Antagonizing your king! Have you lost your *mind*?" Maman hugs the bodice of her gown, overcome with distress. "Do you even *realize* what he could do to us?"

"Give the countship of Massilie to one of his sycophants. Make practicing the blessing punishable by death." Papa bends down toward me so his grave face is directly at my eye level. "You've seen the papers, Anaïs. This is not a game. That man could throw you in the Torres as some political agitator, and you'd never see the light of another day again."

"*None* of us will see the light of another day if we don't get out of here *now*."

My mother wails high enough to rattle a gemstone olive off the branch. "Forget *prison*. If word of this gets out, no one will ever look at you as a suitable match again!"

"*Good!*"

She recoils, horrified. My father's eyes are hard, almost flinty in their depths. I can't imagine what he sees when he looks into mine now.

"I don't know what you've done with my daughter," Maman whispers, "but we haven't time to waste now. We shall discuss this in the morning."

I would give anything for that to be true.

But we're going to die first.

CHAPTER TWO

I GO THROUGH THE MOTIONS LIKE A CLOCKWORK CREATURE. Smile and avert my eyes when Maman attaches herself to a succession of noblewomen to scout out their sons. Parrot mechanical answers to questions meant kindly enough until all of a sudden they're not. I'm not a threat to many people in this room, but they believe in the power of a royal ball to change one's destiny as deeply as my mother does. Who knows what could happen tonight?

You do. You know.

After the feast, while the rest of the court stomps up and down the dance floor, I'm overcome by a wave of nausea, even though I barely ate anything—not rabbit in garlic sauce, not mussels perfumed with lemon and herbs, not even the rockfish stewed with fennel and orange peel from Massilie. I huddle in a corner, try to hitch my breathing to the beat of the music, but nothing I do calms the unsettled feeling in the pit of my stomach.

I am going to die at midnight. Somehow, somewhere. And my death will throw me back to this afternoon, and it will happen all over again. I don't know how, I don't know why, but it's clearly happening, and I have no indication that death will *stop* sending me back in time anytime soon.

So the only question I can possibly ask now is, *why* am I being killed? What's causing this chaos at midnight?

If I can find that out, if I can figure out how to stop it from happening, then at least for tonight, I won't die and wake up again. *That* is the one thing I could possibly accomplish. The one thing I could possibly change.

And besides, I can't just . . . hide here, while the rest of the world hurtles down an unwavering path to destruction. What else am I supposed to do with all this time?

Very well then, Anaïs. What do you know?

I know that we're facing a coordinated attack, not some freak unorganized accident. I saw the proof of it that first time at the ball, when those armed intruders swarmed in after the explosions. I didn't live long enough to see it happen last time, but there's no reason to think those same people weren't lying in wait then, too.

So. There is an armed group behind the attack at midnight. A group that attacks the royal court. The Cardona family's royal court.

They must want to kill the Cardonas. Take Rey Rodrigo's

crown. Rule Ivarea. After all, the explosions begin at midnight each time—when the royal family is gathered at the dais, give or take a youngest prince.

So are the bombs below the dais?

I have no idea. But even if they're not, even if I'm wrong about what the attackers are after in the first place . . . I have to do something. I *should* do something.

Now, how can I get close enough to the dais to investigate? There's nothing I could say to the guards keeping watch at each corner that would persuade them to let me anywhere near close enough. Not after the scene I made with the king and queen.

So . . . I need to get the guards to investigate *for* me.

Swallowing down the acidic taste in my mouth, I begin to cross the length of the ballroom to get to the dais, until a velvety silhouette stumbles into my path.

"Well, if it isn't the headstrong young lady who told the king to choke on his own almond cake."

I can feel trepidation building like vomit in my throat until I manage to glance up and realize that I've been interrupted by a silently guffawing Gaspard Plamondon. My instinctual panic abates. "That is *not* what you heard. You can't possibly believe I'd ever say something like that."

"It was either that or believing you told the king to shove a candelabra into his own eye socket," he answers in rolling Proensan, his hold on our mother tongue loosened by drink. "You never struck me as one for gore, so I went with death by baked goods."

Now it's my turn to bring my hands to my face. At least I can afford to look like a fool in front of the closest thing I have to a friend here. Gaspard and I are two of the few young Proensans in attendance at the ball, and we've known each other since we were children. I've seen him more often this season than I have ever since his father sent him off to study in the city of Lutesse, all the way up in Galvain Province, where he now attends university. Though the Plamondon family holds a major marquisate, and a marriage alliance with them would technically be advantageous for my own family, my mother would be less than pleased to see me waste my time in the company of a fellow Proensan.

Unfortunately for her, I can't bring myself to care.

"Gaspard, I think I'm going mad."

"That explains the death threats you're issuing to our beloved sovereign, then." He rolls his twinkling, dark brown eyes. "What is it really, Anaïs? Is your mother getting to you?"

"Among other things." I try to glance around to chart my way to the dais. And the bombs potentially planted near there. "You're, um, not going to dance?"

Instead of answering, Gaspard runs his hands through his shoulder-length black hair, which has gotten loose both with the anxious tic and the ballroom's humidity. "Should we be honest for a moment?"

"Do we have to?"

"Nothing we do tonight matters."

Hearing someone else say what I've been thinking for most of this cursed night makes me want to throw up. "What . . .

exactly . . . do you mean by that?" *And by any chance do you mean, "Nothing we do tonight matters because we're being forced to relive this night and this attack at midnight over and over again?"*

"I *mean,* our lives are already decided for us, aren't they? Don't you try to sugarcoat it either, Anaïs," he barrels on. "I could go dance with any number of girls tonight, I could steal a kiss or two from their brothers, but that won't change my future. Boys don't want more from me than I can give them in a night, and girls are certainly not looking for a *husband* like me."

I can hardly blame him for the sentiment.

As difficult as it is for me to be seen as a suitable match by Castaran power brokers, it's that much harder for Gaspard. His mother is Landaulan, an ethnically and culturally distinct people who settled on the peninsula from the far side of the Palancan Sea. The Landaulans have been here longer than there's been a united Ivarea; they even ruled the southern half of the peninsula for several centuries, until the last of their sultans was ousted by the Cardonas themselves. The Cardonas allowed the surviving Landaulans a province of their own in the newly united peninsula, carved of what had once been their kingdom; they and their nobility remain equal members of Ivarean society and the royal court. But Gaspard's mixed heritage and his attraction to both women and men may not make him the most sought-after of prospects as far as the richest and most ambitious Ivarean mamás and papás are concerned. Or their small-minded children.

"The point is," Gaspard continues, the silver braiding of

his jet-black velvet jacket bouncing with him in agitation, "*our* preferences really don't matter. They don't even have to be firm preferences. They could be idle fantasies about going back to Lutesse and becoming a distinguished, confirmed-bachelor professor of politics or history or something, but it wouldn't matter. It *can't* matter, not in this place. For my family. In this kingdom. So our fates are sealed, whether we know it now or not."

The sentiment is not unusual for Gaspard, who even as a child tended toward pessimism, but the emphatic quality of his little speech now seems different. Something he picked up at university, perhaps, if that fantasy life of his is less idle than he'd like to admit. Or something that's calcified after spending the last eight weeks here at court.

I could have related to much of his frustration if this weren't also the absolute worst possible pep talk for my current predicament.

"Fine, if nothing we do matters, not that I agree with you entirely"—*just in this one very specific and personal circumstance*—"would you dance with me?"

He shrugs again, and together we take our places among the other dancers, grateful to let the music and movement drown out all our more fatalistic thoughts.

Gaspard doesn't notice that I'm trying to tug him in a specific direction, but he does throw a few glares up at the clawed feet of the thrones. "Hypocrites," he mutters under his breath.

"What good is that fancy university of yours if they don't teach you how to hold your drink?"

The applause of the court and Rey Rodrigo's booming laugh drown out my voice. I don't know what's so funny, but it coincides with the end of the dance, so we all hang where we are, suspended in the moment. I glance over my shoulder to determine how far I have left to go to the possibly bomb-rigged dais. Close enough—just a few yards.

When I turn back around, I accidentally catch Infante Leo's eye.

I can almost trace the lazy intent in his eyes as he looks me up and down, focus sharpening. Whether he's remembered his unfulfilled promise, or he's simply decided that the freckled girl in the red gown is acceptable prey, I desperately don't want to find out.

Hiding behind Gaspard's tall, lean frame, I step out of the prince's line of sight. With my face and décolletage blocked from view, I reach behind my neck and undo the clasp of my locket. The chain falls like a snake in my closed fist. Then I, too, applaud the orchestra, and in my completely obvious and genuine zeal, send the chain soaring behind me. Toward the dais.

As the orchestra members adjust their sheet music, preparing for their next number, Gaspard turns back toward me with a self-deprecating bow that takes advantage of the lace of his cuffs. "Always a pleasure, Doña Anaïs."

"Five minutes ago you were spilling your angst-ridden self-pitying guts to me, and now dancing with me is merely a pleasure?" I click my tongue at him, trying not to smile. "This is just not done, Monsieur."

He sticks his tongue out at me—in extremely dignified fashion, of course. "I'm sure you'll find a way to make me pay for that another time."

Why not now?

I pretend to wave him away, but just as he turns his back, I bring my hands to rest at my neck.

My now-very-empty neck.

"My locket! It's GONE!"

Gaspard whips around.

"Maman is going to *murder* me!"

He knows my mother, so he knows I'm not really exaggerating. He guides me toward the wall to the right of the dais, muttering half-hearted apologies to the other dancers while I continue to blubber. From back here, I have a clear view of the king's profile—and a better view of the guards.

Gaspard clears his throat in a feeble attempt to distract from my hysterics. "Why don't you use the blessing to find the locket yourself?"

Oh. Oh, that is a thought. A good thought. That I didn't consider two minutes ago when I threw together this half-baked plan.

"Although," he adds, "that assumes the guards wouldn't throw you in the dungeon for attempting blood magic so close to the king."

I sag against the wall in relief. "Yes! That! Would be a problem." Blood magic may not be technically outlawed in Ivarea, but that wouldn't stop an overzealous guard from making what remains of my life more difficult than it needs to be. Thank goodness for Gaspard's highly honed cynicism. "Okay, I'll just have to ask the guards to look for it *for* me."

"You're not serious."

I can't believe myself, either, but I've come too far down this road to stop now. I pretend to steel myself to action, and the pretending actually does make me feel a little more determined. I bustle over to the closest crop of guards. In my head, I rehearse what to tell them. *Excuse me, señores, but would you terribly mind tearing this goddamned ballroom apart in search of my necklace and/or a series of bombs sitting right under your broken Castaran noses—*

A tap at my shoulder breaks my train of thought. I address Gaspard behind me without breaking my stride. "The longer we wait, the higher the chances that it could get kicked into a corner or under the dais or—"

"What could be under the dais?"

That's . . . that's not . . .

I stop at last. And turn.

"In-Infante Leopoldo," I stammer, belatedly curtsying.

"No need, my lady. I took you by surprise. Very unsporting of me." Leo's speech sounds steady, and his expression is open when I meet it.

Gaspard catches up just as I rise from my deep curtsy. He clearly saw who was trying to get my attention before I did and by the time he comes to my rescue, he has managed to school his features into a pleasant, noncommittal expression. "Vuestra Alteza Real." Under the politeness of his tone, I almost detect a bit of disdain.

The prince crosses his arms behind his back. "Is there some problem here?"

Considering what happened last time I asked Leo for help, I'm loath to tell him anything. But he already heard me mention the dais a moment ago. Might as well get this over with and send him on his way. "Nothing at all, Alteza. I seem to have lost my necklace. A family heirloom."

Leo glances between Gaspard and me as if he is a headmaster and we are students he caught committing some minor misdemeanor. "You are . . . relatives?"

"No, Alteza." Deference eats at him as much as it does Papa, but Gaspard is not quite as good at hiding it. "We are old friends, Doña Anaïs and I, and her locket disappeared while she was dancing with me."

"Then this is your fault," says the prince to Gaspard.

"If anyone is at fault, it's me for getting carried away. *Not* Don Gaspard," I add crossly. "I was just on my way to ask the guards if they might help me—"

"The Guardia Real?" Leo interjects. "With all due respect, they will not budge for anything less than a threat to my father's life. Trust me, I know."

Oh . . . right. That's the guards' whole job: knowing who exactly might be trying to kill their sovereign.

I knew I was desperate to do something, but forgetting that I could have at least *tried* to get a guard to investigate a very real threat to the king's life . . . How could I have been so *stupid*?

Leo cocks his head. "You know, *I* could summon your missing heirloom for you."

I must have been too busy beating myself up to have heard that correctly. But Gaspard seems to be as shocked as I am. "You . . . you're a . . ."

Leo grimaces in answer.

That can't be. There's no way the royal court wouldn't know there was a *male* magician in the Cardona dynasty again. Especially if it were someone as ridiculous as Leo the Lush.

While magical talent on the peninsula depends on the individual, not on inherited bloodlines, the Cardona family managed to produce and train the greatest magicians in Ivarea; their ability to keep up their command of magic over the centuries is what won them their mighty kingdom. First they united Tarracuña, their home province, under the dragon banner. Once they had swallowed enough of the smaller duchies and kingdoms dotting the northern end of the peninsula, they swept into this very Alcázar to overthrow the last Landaulan sultan. However, uniting the peninsula for the first time did not hold the Cardonas' hunger for long, and soon, their eyes began to wander across the sea—to Proensa and to the lands beyond.

But over the last two hundred years, since the peak period of Ivarean expansion, the Cardona family's ability to produce reputable magicians has weakened significantly. There hasn't been a magician-prince in the royal family worth the title for nearly a century. There was still talent enough for building the enchantments that animate the palace, but not enough to bring countries to their knees before Ivarean armies. Infanta Clara, Leo's older sister, was the first magician of note in the family in decades, but as a princess, her personal magical talents will not have significant implications for the future of Cardona magicians ruling Ivarea.

Unlike Leo.

Clearly, the fact of his power is a secret. But he just . . . *admitted* it. Out loud. To two nobodies from the fringes of the kingdom.

He doesn't seem that drunk tonight. So what on earth has gotten into him?

Whatever it is, this little mystery is not important now. Leo could have unfathomable power, but he'll never believe me if I tell him about the attack or ask him to help stop it. He said it himself: *You would have to be pretty desperate to think I could save you.*

So that's it: I have to stick to my plan—force the guards to find the bomb. I have a purpose. For tonight, at least.

"Thank you, Alteza. For your . . . help. But I'm quite capable of finding the locket myself."

"I don't doubt that in the least. However, you are our guest, and you are in need of assistance. I fear that I'm now honor bound to help you."

Out of the corner of my eye, I see Gaspard cock his head ever so slightly, considering. Then Leo extends a hand. His voice is low, pitched to carry to no one but me. "Let me help you, Doña Anaïs. Please."

The more I see of him, the more I realize there is absolutely no telling who Infante Leopoldo truly is. A drunk, a flirt, a king, a corpse.

And a magician, apparently. Who wants to help me.

Where was this Leo when I actually *wanted* his help?

"If you insist." Belatedly I add, "Thank you, señor."

Whatever self-control Gaspard marshaled for this conversation with the prince melts away as he snorts into his shoulder.

Leo seems to pay his little antics no heed. "Don't thank me yet. I'm going to need your earring."

Silently, I unscrew the post of my garnet earring and drop it into Leo's hand. He closes his fingers around its heavy gold backing like a storm would swallow starlight. Then he shuts his eyes. "Describe your lost object for me."

"Just a red opal locket. Nothing inside. Set in gold, with a gold chain."

That seems to be enough. Leo spins once where he stands, his fist taut. A moment later, I feel a current of wind flowing around me. Or I think I feel it, but my gown isn't fluttering, and my hair is decidedly in place. My cheeks chafe under its pressure, and it hooks into the bare skin of my upper arms as bitterly as a winter wind off the mountains. It's all I can do to not let it buckle my knees where I stand.

Abruptly, the current dissipates around me. Leo opens his eyes to stride into the shadows beside the dais. Startled, I gather up my skirts and hurry to follow.

Leo drops into a panther-like crouch and starts to root around on the floor, with one hand still closed around my earring. Then—"Aha!"

He stands and practically saunters over. The locket swings like a bloody pendulum in his fingers. My eyes follow its swinging, mesmerized by the flickering of the torches reflected in its scarlet depths. The opal looks like it's about to catch flame.

"I told you."

His voice seems fainter at the edges, as if exhausted from calling on magic. Peninsular magic doesn't require you to slice a thumb or limb open, clearly, but it must take a different kind of focus to work magic when it's not part of you. When it must be actively taken from the wider world.

"I didn't doubt you, señor. Thank you."

He quirks a very slight grin and jangles the necklace in front of my swimming eyes. "May I?"

Somewhere behind me, I'm aware of Gaspard watching this exchange. Behind him is the rest of the court. It would take only a moment for someone to tell her neighbor or his friend about the prince and the Proensan. In minutes, I might be the talk of the ball all over again.

In minutes, we'll all be dead.

And I still don't know exactly how it will happen.

The prince's proximity makes me feel far more uneasy than Gaspard's did: like I'm balancing at the edge of a cliff, and one wrong move will send me hurtling to my death. Leo loops the chain over my head, accidentally jerking me backward into him. His hands are warm on my skin, but he fumbles as he tries to work the clasp. Then, all too soon, the heat of his touch, the pressure behind it, is replaced by the cold gleam of metal on my skin.

When I turn back around, he's already holding out his hand to me.

I stumble backward and Leo lets out a low chuckle. "Your earring."

"Oh. Oh, of course." I pluck it from his palm like a chicken would grain. Great: livestock similes. The mark of a true Pro-ensan. "I saw you hold out your hand and I assumed—well, it was bold of me to assume—"

"Oh, I would certainly ask you for a dance. You were not mistaken there."

My breath trips over itself in my windpipes.

"But," he goes on in a low voice, "you've already indulged me more than you wanted to. For that, you have my sincerest thanks." Leo glances at Gaspard, who is now standing by me once more. "I shall take your and Don Guillaume's leave now."

"Gaspard," I say.

"The name is Leo."

My hands fall back to my sides. The earring and the neck-lace are back in place. I am in balance again. "*His* name is Gaspard."

Leo grins again, and again, I curse his stupidity, his eyes, his magic, his death. "Good night, Doña Anaïs."

A great cry goes up from the crowd when he melts back into it. Gaspard and I are both quiet for a moment, neither looking at the other, but I can feel him shift on his feet, can feel the frown on his lips.

"So Leopoldo the Lush starts flirting with you out of no-where, does a magic trick, saves the day—"

"Finding a lost locket hardly qualifies as saving the day."
It's not even sort of enough.

"What did he say to you after?"

"Nothing."

"It looked like he asked you to dance."

"I would have said no."

Gaspard raises both eyebrows, as he's unable to raise just one; I have no doubt this is a shortcoming that fills him with untold anguish. "You are absolutely full of surprises tonight, Mademoiselle."

They're not surprises when they don't work out the way you mean them to. That makes them mistakes. And I obviously made a mistake thinking I could *do* anything to stop this chaos. "Entertaining ones, I hope."

"Oh, immensely." Out of nowhere, I feel him seize up. He clears his throat and steps around me, his back to the rest of the ballroom. "But—uh, see you around, Anaïs."

I almost shout *How dare you abandon me* at his back, but, dimly thinking about the clock towers in each corner of the Alcázar grounds, I shoulder my way through the crowd—and suddenly see a creature in gray taffeta flying toward me.

I suppose I can't blame Gaspard for running away now.

With a huff, I head off Maman and drag her far from the dais before she can truly cause a scene.

"It's not what you think—I just lost my locket and he helped me find it. *That's it.* It doesn't matter. Gaspard was there, too!"

"Infante Leopoldo was on his *knees* for you, he put his *hands* on your *bare skin,* and you're talking about *Gaspard*?"

Maman is absolutely beside herself with hysteria, red-faced, panting. "Do you understand how close you just were to making all our dreams come true?"

"It takes more than five minutes of small talk for people to decide they ought to be together for the rest of their lives!" My back is to the rest of the ballroom. I can't bear to see the courtiers' glee at the coarse Proensan countess scheming above her station and the pathetic girl who wouldn't know how to land a man if her family's future depended on it. Which, hilariously, it *does*.

I wish desperately, ardently, that they would forget all about us. That we could just disappear.

Then the bells begin to chime.

"No, no, no, no, *no*—"

Maman isn't paying attention. "It's only midnight," she yelps in my ear over the joyous screaming of the crowd. "You still have time! Go find him, get him back now, before—"

And just like that, my wish is granted. With a vengeance.

IV

CHAPTER ONE

THE NEXT TIME I WAKE UP, I DON'T BOTHER WONDERING where or when I am. I scream, and scream, and scream into a pillow until I can no longer hear anything else. Until I can no longer feel anything.

The sound of muffled violence brings Maman running headlong into the room, skirts bunched in her hands, hair coming askew. She sinks to my bedside and wrenches the pillow from my white-knuckled hands.

"WHY ME?"

"What on earth—"

I throw the strangling covers off and pitch myself off the edge of the bed, banging my knee horribly in the fall.

Pathetic. Useless.

"WHY! IS THIS! HAPPENING! TO *ME!*"

My mother lets go of the pillow as I wail. Through my sobs, I can feel her staring, no longer sympathetic. Growing colder.

"The only thing happening is your destiny calling out for you, Anaïs."

"What DESTINY?" I erupt. "WHY AM I BEING PUNISHED LIKE THIS?"

She sends a sharp look to the side, where Petronilla and Béatrice are probably watching in consternation, before turning back to me. "If you think your parents sacrificing every waking moment, every ounce of energy, every gold real they have, to ensure that your life is better than theirs ever was, is some kind of *punishment,* then I am *sorry,* Anaïs, but you have no choice but to go to the Anniversary Ball and bear it with grace and elegance."

I can hardly breathe through the horror of it all, through the vision of explosions and burning and laughter that crowds the edges of my sight, that drowns the world anew in blood. "But why does it have to be *me*?"

"Who else do we have?"

Smelling salts to jolt me into coherence. Ice baths to calm my complexion. A tray of tea cakes to bribe me into settling down.

They are all so good at forgetting.

But I am not.

Here is the truth: between the first and last bells of midnight, the world will fall apart.

Wait—no, that's not right. When the world breaks down of its own accord, it does so slowly, unevenly. Like the eroding of a mountain. Sometimes acts of fate arise violently out of nowhere—earthquakes, volcanic eruptions, cataclysmic storms—but what's going to happen tonight is not a divine act. Not a freak accident that no one could have known was coming. *I* know it's coming.

And that must be for a *reason*.

I might not know what that reason is now, or more specifically, who's behind it, but I have a feeling I can find out. I *have* to find out.

How is a lone young lady supposed to investigate the reasons behind a future attack when stuck at court? By socializing, of course. For there is no one as savvy as a teenage girl.

They may not trust us enough to teach us more than the posh accents of Ivarea's major languages; piano and voice; watercolors and oils; classical poetry and theater if we're lucky; but high-born girls learn more about politics than most people suspect, even others here at court. Castles and fortunes and dynasties rest on the friends and enemies we make, the lovers and husbands we bring to our beds or to our parents. If we couldn't navigate the churning waters of this damned kingdom, we'd be sunk long before this, the ball of the season.

True, I didn't care too much about the particulars of Ivarean politics before I started getting killed. But even then, I was never able to just *ignore* who I am, or where I came from, or what it means to be where I am now. Everything girls like me do, or are forced to do, is political. Whether we like it or not.

And I *absolutely* do not like it.

As I make my way through the crowd, the elder nobles and grandes of the court bat me around like I'm the ball in a very sparkly, highly impractical game of croquet, and I emerge almost directly in front of Jacinthe Vieillard. She and I exchange air-kisses, and I do the same with the odious Paloma Nelleda and another of Jacinthe's close companions, a redhead from Galvain named Marguerite Lorieux. None of them seem particularly enthused to see me—not even Marguerite, whom I've begrudgingly gotten to know over the years since her family started wintering in Massilie—but it's early in the night, and they think they have time to waste. After all, as Paloma is quick to assure me, "Once you've been to enough of these things, they all start to bleed together."

"This must be especially overwhelming for *you*, Anaïs. How very different the capital is from Massilie!" Marguerite does try to be gracious, bless her heart, but it usually just comes off as horribly condescending. No surprise that we never managed to become close, despite Maman's best efforts to find me non-Proensan friends who could help me find a non-Proensan husband. Rumor has it that she herself has rejected at least a couple of suitors this season, though who else is in her sights, I'm not entirely sure.

Paloma's ensuing smile has the wide arc of a scythe slicing through stalks of wheat. "There would be no shame if you were feeling overwhelmed. Not everyone has what it takes to survive in Marenca."

Together, the three of them make for a blindingly bright creature, hungry to feast on the bones of lesser girls and inadequate boys. I grit my teeth and make my stare as unflinching as theirs. "I have every intention of surviving here." *Even though I know I won't.*

Jacinthe cocks her head. Her black hair is braided tight to her skull and pulled into a bun studded with pink sapphires. The granddaughter of a former merchant, she knows how to appeal to a demanding audience. "How interesting. I always thought you were dead set on staying in your *charming* countryside home. With that Plamondon fellow."

Paloma grins in uncharacteristic cheer. "Oh, that Don Gaspard *is* rather handsome. Half-Landaulan, unfortunately."

This is what being at the center of power has done to people like Paloma. As if Gaspard being part Landaulan makes him any less a *human being.* I shudder to think how she'd react if she found out that he's attracted to men as well. This kind of shit is why I could never willingly settle in the capital, surrounded by such cruel, small-minded people.

Still, I swallow the bile that threatens to rise in my throat. "Gaspard and I are not *together* and have no intention to be. So, here I am. Hoping to settle in Marenca. In . . . in the future."

Jacinthe, clearly losing interest in me, shrugs and glances toward Marguerite, who at least is not as smug. "Then you're much braver than me, Anaïs. I couldn't live here year-round. My nerves simply could not handle the unrest."

Unrest right under Rey Rodrigo Cardona's nose? That could well be the backdrop for tonight's mass murder. "What do you mean?"

"Well . . ." Marguerite seems to shrink into her goldenrod gown, its puffed sleeves half blocking the ducking of her chin as well as the upper half of Jacinthe's arm. "Haven't you heard all those vicious debates going around? About the taxation rates and all? Those . . . city philosophes and horrible students who keep getting arrested?"

"What philosophes and students? Where are they from? What did they do to get arrest—"

"Good-for-nothing rabble-rousers," Paloma cuts in at once, with the air of a governess trying to discipline unruly charges. "Don't pay them any mind. The lot of them should be thrown into the tower with their pathetic *leaders*."

Marguerite shudders. "They think we need to do away with the king."

With a cryptic smirk, Jacinthe adds, "*All* kings, dear Marguerite."

Oh. Well then.

Dig deep enough and you can find a vein of bitterness among Proensans toward our Cardona conquerors—my father and Gaspard are proof enough—but even that has dulled over the decades to a simmering grudge. From what Gaspard implies about his Landaulan relatives, I can only imagine they share similar grievances. But I had no idea that those grumbles were signs of anything other than the usual provincial frustrations. That they were echoing here in the capital, too. That they could threaten the very backbone of this kingdom.

I thought the attack tonight must be the work of someone who wants to steal the Cardonas' crown. It didn't occur to me that their goal might be destroying it.

Is this what I've been looking for? Are these radicals going to attack the palace at midnight?

"And what would they plan to do instead?" Paloma sneers in turn. "Put *peasants* in the palace?"

"My brother says a band of radicals at the University of Lutesse got expelled as soon as they were discovered. Their ringleaders were thrown in prison." Marguerite shudders again. "They had *pamphlets*. It was all *right there*."

Ah. That explains the arrests that Marguerite first mentioned. I wonder if Gaspard heard about this, too, since it happened at his school.

Paloma and Jacinthe don't seem as surprised. The former grumbles "Ridiculous" under her breath, clearly still discomfited by this topic; the latter responds with "Treasonous," as if we needed a reminder that advocating for the destruction of the crown is bad.

If these ladies are so scandalized by students printing pamphlets, I can't imagine their reaction if they knew they'd be assassinated by them. "Does the king know about these radicals?"

"He must know, surely," says Marguerite. "Why else would he have put in place all of these restrictions on public gatherings and the press and all?"

"I don't know, Marguerite. Has Rey Rodrigo's decision-making ever struck you as particularly foresighted?" Jacinthe asks dryly.

Much to my surprise, the redhead steps up to the challenge. "Are you saying he doesn't know, or that he didn't—"

Jacinthe clucks her tongue, seemingly disappointed, but her eyes twinkle with mischief. "Have you really learned *nothing* from me after all this time? You offend me, my dear."

Her brow arches. "Then you must let me make it up to you."

"I'd certainly like to see you try."

While I glance between the girls in consternation, Paloma rocks back on her heels, her incandescent cream gown bobbing like a boat on unsteady waters. "Oh, Saints above. None of this actually *matters.*"

I redirect my focus from the two Galvaise to the Castaran. "Why not, Doña Paloma?" I fix her with an innocuous smile, as wide and clear as the summer sky, but my hands are trembling. "What if something were to happen? Wouldn't you want to know if—shouldn't we be prepared for—"

"*Prepared?* What for? These stupid, ungrateful *radicals—* they're already graduates of the greatest universities in the kingdom. They have careers and lives that most Ivareans can only *dream* of. So forgive me if I think it's absurd that spoiled middle-class intellectuals want to tear down the whole world and build a new one just to give *themselves* power they haven't earned."

What would happen if Paloma were given a chance to pursue an education like those students? If any of us had that chance? Where might all our politicking energies go if they weren't hyperfocused on marriage alliances at the royal court?

Those are other thoughts for other lives.

God knows how many I have left to live.

I realize I've pushed this group as far as I can tonight, and frankly, I don't think I can stand their company any longer. "So that settles things."

"Does it, though?" asks Jacinthe.

"For now." I smile at each of the ladies and back away. "See you next time."

Marguerite calls out "What next time?" but I let the cacophony in the ballroom swallow up her voice and do not answer.

At dinner, I try to get my tablemates to talk more about these supposedly notorious pamphlet-wielding philosophe-radicals, but none of them have any knowledge about or interest in the subject. They don't have any theories about who *else* might be causing havoc in Marenca, either; if there *were* a problem, they imply, surely Rey Rodrigo would have snuffed it out by now.

However, the fact that some courtiers don't understand or take seriously the threats that face their own kingdom doesn't mean that there is absolutely *no one* in the Alcázar who does.

It's as Leo said last time: the only thing the Guardia Real cares about is a threat to the king's life. So if anyone might have an idea of what dangers lurk here, it would surely be those charged with the king's protection. They might even be able to stop them. If I can make the guards listen to me.

I'm still mulling over how exactly to go about it when the orchestra strikes up the first of the dances. I don't join in. Instead, I drift toward the nearest pair of guards, stationed at the northern doors of the ballroom, using a circuitous route to throw off anyone who might be watching me. Mostly my mother, but also—

"Doña Anaïs."

That honeyed voice makes me want to sink into the floor, but the prince's dark gaze pins me against the nearest column, this one crowned with ever-blooming wreaths of ruby and diamond carnations. He cocks his head as he approaches. Chandelier light hugs the hollows beneath his cheekbones as dearly as if they, too, were carved centuries ago by kings and princes long gone—an arresting beauty built for precisely this dripping-gold world.

I glance despairingly at the guards by the doors. How am I supposed to shake off the prince now?

He takes my stony silence for tongue-tied coquettishness. "I took advantage of you once, didn't I?"

Just once? "Not at all, Vuestra Alteza Real." I clear my throat and gather my skirts, making ready to leave. "You'll have to forgive me, I promised Don Emilio the next—"

"I'm the infante." The words begin to slide together, his tongue loose with drink. "Don Emilio'll understand."

My throat goes abruptly dry. "Alteza, I—"

"Don't you want to dance with your prince?"

A lucky thing that my blushing makes me look like the shy, decorous young stranger he apparently sees in me. "The waltz, then, señor." As long as it's not in the next five minutes, I have a chance to lose him.

Leo folds his arms across his chest. "No time like the present, hmm?" He glides forward, trying and failing to disguise a stumble with a flourish of his arms. It takes him a second to absorb my failure to fall over him; then his expression goes stiller than it should. "No?" His breath tickles my flushed cheeks. "Don't tell me this is about Emilio. You don't give a shit about that puffed-up sycophant. I can see it in your face."

Oh *no,* not this again. I cannot believe that the most consistently insurmountable force I've ever come across in all these nights, all these deaths, is Leo the Lush's *ego.* What did I do to bring this on myself?

"Tell me the truth, Anaïs." He whispers my name, unfettered by my title, as if he remembered it long before he set foot in the ballroom tonight. As if he knows, even in this state—especially in this state—how to say girls' names with such dangerous intimacy that they might go up in flames before the palace does. As if he's never said anyone's name like this before.

Leo the Lush indeed.

He adds, even quieter, deadlier, "What are you so afraid of?"

A riot would break out here and now if the rest of the court realized that he can use that voice on anyone he wants to, and that he chose a random provincial girl to be his toy. His delicately trembling prey.

I sigh. "Oh, nothing, just our impending deaths."

"Aren't we all."

"I'm *serious*. Someone is going to attack the Alcázar at midnight tonight. The ballroom will explode, almost everyone in here will die, and everyone else will be shot with the blood of their families still splattered on their faces."

If I were holding out any hope that explicit, gory detail would jolt the prince into sobriety, this moment would have quashed it.

"And here I thought Proensans were just our unorthodox fairy-worshipping neighbors. But I s'pose it's true what they say." He smirks down at me. "You *are* mad."

What I would give to be mad right now. How grateful I would be to simply have lost myself imagining all this blood, all this death.

"Also," Leo continues, blithe as his birthright allows him to be, "who's this *someone* out to kill us?"

"You tell me," I fire back. "Maybe those anti-monarchical radicals?"

"Those pathetic village attorneys and magistrates? They couldn't attack a wounded pigeon."

So he knows who they are *and* has an opinion on them. Which is more than I can say of most everyone else here, except for Marguerite, of all people. "If they're so pathetic, why has your father been having their leaders arrested?"

"Haven't the faintest."

I shouldn't have gotten my hopes up about him *intentionally* helping me. If there's anyone who seems remarkably out of tune with what's going on around him, let alone in his own country, it's the prince.

"We're really about to die?" he asks suddenly.

"I'm *not* mad. And I'm not a liar, either."

"Right. Then we don't have much time, do we?" He steps closer, letting his scent, citrus and sweat and alcohol, caress my bare skin. "We should dance while we still can."

My fists bunch in my skirts just as the clocks chime the half hour. "Forget those radicals, *I'll* kill you."

He cranes his neck back and peers at me down his straight nose. "Is that a threat?"

The only real threat in this room is the bombs about to explode.

But if I'm to be taken seriously, I have to be undeniable.

"No." I disentangle my fingers from my gown and raise a hand as if to take his in mine. "But this is."

I punch him in the face.

The crack of my gloved fist against his royal visage bounces up through my bones. Leo staggers back at the moment of impact as if he really were caught in an explosion. Blood seeps out from his nostrils and cuts dull tracks down his chin. I stare at my handiwork with horror even as I try to cradle my hand against my chest. But Leo's eyes don't seem quite as dark now as they did seconds ago.

"You . . ."

I don't apologize. I don't know how.

A cry breaks out in the ballroom. Leo and I are still staring at each other, each shocked by what I just did, when three guards begin to rush toward us. Courtiers swarm the men, half of them screaming and shouting and pointing at me.

"She did it! The Proensan! She attacked Infante Leopoldo!"

The guards draw up beside us, a human shield from the seething ballroom. Slung on one's back is a great black rifle. His fellows have broadswords strapped to their belts.

"Vuestra Alteza Real, if she—"

"Take her away." The blow to his nose has rendered Leo's voice tinny instead of honey-soaked. I almost like him more like this. Then, more coldly than I've ever heard, he adds, "I'm *fine,* by the way."

As the prince's sharp tone reverberates against the walls, the guard with the rifle jumps to attention. He barks orders in rapid Castaran to the other two, who grab my arms, sending jolts of pain down my aching hand, and drag me away. I don't thrash or fight. Still as a cat, I stare at the ballroom I left in bloody shambles.

Until the guards heave me through a side door, Leo stares back.

Tell me the truth, he said.

If only that were enough.

I have no idea where the guards are taking me or what the punishment for bodily harm of a Cardona is, but I truly couldn't give a shit. As awful as it feels now, with the pain in my arms and hand and the guilt in my stomach creating a delightful cocktail of disgust, I *improvised*. I did what I set out to do. I got two royal guards all to myself.

Now I have to make them talk.

"Come now, señores. I can't *possibly* be the worst thing you've seen here tonight."

The shorter guard with square ears grimaces, whether because of my Proensan accent or because he has no taste for stupid girls ruining his night. "You've got the worst arm, maybe. Not that *Vuestra Alteza Real* doesn't deserve it," he sneers under his breath.

His partner, a taller man with a red beard, smacks him over my head. "Saints, Oleastro." He tugs me harder so I'm half skipping behind them.

Paintings from centuries of Ivarea's past gaze impassively down at me from the walls of the wide palace corridors. The tapestries we pass, of mystical forests inhabited by mythical creatures, are embroidered richly enough that I could almost seek shelter under their enchanted boughs. But if the saints in their gilded frames or the creatures silhouetted in silver thread have seen any suspicious activity tonight, they aren't going to tell me so. The guards are my last hope.

"There's going to be an attack at midnight. The royal family is in danger."

Oleastro misses a step, thrown either by my words or the sweeping hem of my gown. "What are you talking about? What attack?"

I ignore the redhead tugging my other side like he's a wolfhound and I the little bedraggled fox he's bringing to his master, and try to steady my voice. "Bombs in the palace. Armed militias trooping in. Mass murder. *That* kind of attack. If we act now, we might still have time to stop it."

Oleastro's grip slackens. "Mendoza?" he asks his partner.

Taking advantage of their distraction, I plant my feet. "Think about it. Aren't there people who'd kill the king if they could? What if—*gah*—what if those enemies wanted to do it *tonight*?"

The redhead, Mendoza, jerks me closer. "If a king has no enemies, he's not doing his job."

"This isn't some—you have to understand, I know this is going to happen. I saw it, in a vision. I swear, I'm just trying to save our lives here."

"*Our* lives?" Mendoza echoes nastily. "Sounds to me like you're just trying to save your own skin from the dungeons."

"If I cared about my own skin, I wouldn't have—*agh*—punched the prince! You have to believe me! You have to find the bombs and stop the attackers *now*, while there's still time!"

Mendoza stares at me a moment before sighing, breath whistling through his teeth. "She's just some drunk girl, Oleastro. Doesn't know what she's talking about." He shakes me again, less violently than before. "Little Proensan lightweight."

They don't believe me. Of course not. Don't know why I bothered. It's not like there's enough time before midnight, anyway. There's never enough time.

But if there's anything I can salvage from what's left of this supremely botched night, at least let it be a suspect. "Fine! Fine, forget the attack," I squeak urgently at the guards. "Just tell me who the real threat is. Those radicals that want to get rid of the king—could they pull off an attack on the palace? Is it foreign assassins? Unhappy grandes? Pirates? Ghosts? *Please, I beg you, just tell . . ."*

The words die out on my tongue.

I know the look on Mendoza's face. It's the same expression that Leo had up in the ballroom.

It's true, what they say. You are mad.

I finally wrench my arms out of their grips before they can drag me away again. With one last chance to make my desperate appeal, I turn to the shoulders of the guard who seemed most shaken by my pronouncements. "Oleastro. Oleastro, you can take me wherever you need to. Do whatever you need, but please . . . *please,* just tell me who—"

There is no corner of this entire palace that the clock tower bells can't reach.

As I'm left paralyzed by the chimes, the guards snap me up again. I can't hear what they're saying, but I think I see a question forming in Oleastro's eyes as he darts them around the corridor.

Even this far from the ballroom, the explosion rocks the ground. Dirt and gravel and particles of dust fall around us. The guards let go of me to cover their mouths. The walls of the palace groan like old men on their deathbeds.

I open my eyes to find more royal guards running down the corridor. All have shields at their shoulders and weapons at the ready. They stream past us, coughing and shouting garbled orders to their fellows. Disoriented, I whip around in the dust storm. Mendoza joins the stream of people going up the corridor, dodging torches and bricks clattering to the floor. Oleastro appears ready to follow him into the crowd.

Before he can, I grab him by the shoulder. His eyes are wild but glassy. "You—" he stammers. "You knew—"

I shush him and drag his unresisting body to the wall, out of the way of guards and soldiers. I already hurt one young man today and consigned a thousand more to their deaths. If I can save someone who believes me, maybe this death will be worth it.

"Don't go back there. It's no use. Just help me, *please*. Who could've done this? Is there a radical—someone here in the capital—"

A great creaking from behind me interrupts my rapid questions. I twist my neck just in time to see a giant gilded frame three times my height tear free from the wall. I turn around so I don't have to watch it fall.

Oleastro, a true servant of Ivarea, is not so lucky. His screams will haunt me if I wake.

When I wake.

V

CHAPTER ONE

AS HAS BECOME UNDENIABLY CLEAR OVER THE COURSE OF my previous deaths, if Leo and I are in the same room all night, he *will* see me, and he will *probably* follow me. It's as if he can sense that I'm not one to be swept away by his attentions, and feels compelled to dig into that feeling, like it were a scab or an insect bite. It certainly cannot have anything to do with any memories he has of me.

But the pattern is clear: If he does find me, he will derail whatever I'm doing. My life will be over, again, and I'll be no closer to figuring out anything about the attack than I was when I woke up in my bedroom this afternoon. Which means that the only way I can accomplish anything tonight is by getting the hell out of the ballroom.

For that, I only have one easy, reasonably painless option.

Gaspard is still polishing off his lemon-and-strawberry meringue cake when I sidle up to him, the corners of his mouth covered with crumbs. He doesn't bother rising from the table, partly because he outranks me but mostly because he's lazy.

I gesture at the plate before him. "Enjoying yourself?"

"Immensely. Aren't you?"

"I do *not* look forward to being bandied about on the dance floor, I can tell you that much."

He wipes his mouth on his sleeve, just a boy now, not the heir to a beautiful Proensan estate on the shores of the Palancan Sea. "But Mademoiselle," he says, voice twisted with irony, "that's exactly what we're here for."

What I wouldn't give to make that true again. "I just don't want to waste my last night in the palace letting the Châtillon brothers trample my feet." I sink onto the arm of the empty chair beside him. "Come exploring with me."

"But the dancing's starting."

"And?"

He opens his mouth and closes it as quickly. The Gaspard who believed nothing we do tonight matters still dwells somewhere in this one; it's his influence that gets him to his feet. "You know what they'll say about us disappearing together."

Unfortunately, yes. But it's as I told Jacinthe and the others the last time I ran into them: Gaspard and I are friends, and that's it. If I hadn't been killed the first time we came to the Anniversary Ball, if all had gone as it was supposed to and we each still came out of the night with nothing to show for it, perhaps things would be different. Perhaps Gaspard would find himself willing to marry me after all, to spare himself the compounded humiliation of people rejecting him for where he comes from and who he is. And perhaps I would have accepted, if only to get myself out of Maman's crosshairs. After all, it's not as if I've longed for anything so impractical as *true love* since I was a little girl sneaking out of bed on feast days to listen to visiting troubadours and their romantic, lustful, tragic ballads. My parents trained me well.

But I *was* killed at that first Anniversary Ball, and now I'm stuck here for who knows how long. There's no use thinking about a future beyond this. For either of us. For anyone.

And if I am going to investigate the attack that traps me here night after night, there's no use in caring what anyone else might say.

"Are you coming, or not?"

Without another word of protest or warning, Gaspard follows me through Arco de Oso, and deep into the halls of the Alcázar.

We've passed the Mirror Garden, two more gardens I've never seen, and more arched entryways than even a palace of this size should be able to structurally support before Gaspard asks me what I'm looking for.

My fingers drag along the wall, rubbing against the dragons embossed on the wallpaper. Wings gilded, eyes burning. "Who says I'm looking for anything?"

"You have not been interested in a single magical or architectural wonder we've passed so far. You didn't even pause when I caught that enchanted topaz leopard staring at us from the jungle courtyard."

"I'm sorry, but once you've seen one garden here, you've seen them all."

His polished boots give him a heavy tread on the carpet runners. His eyes seem to bore into the back of my head, through the mass of pins in my hair, and into my skull. "This is the Alcázar Real. It's *all* gardens and arches and hallways."

And, somewhere, the people trying to kill us all.

We don't speak again until we stumble into a relatively humble antechamber somewhere in the western wing of the palace. Arrow-slit windows have been sliced into the walls. Winding stone stairs stretch above us into solid shadows. A dead end.

Gaspard turns a keen eye on the bare chamber, his gaze much brighter than the pinpricks of moonlight fighting to reach us. "Oh, I see now. What a treasure you've stumbled onto, Anaïs. *Such* an architectural marvel. *How* could the king have failed to parade the court here so we may all behold the full glory of his palace?"

"Oh, spare me. Shall we turn back?" I have half a mind to wander the other half of the Alcázar until midnight and see what happens in other wings of the palace, but Gaspard walks up to the stairs and cranes his neck back.

"Must have been the base of a tower." He runs a hand hesitantly along the railing and sneezes at the dust he disturbed. "From the pre-Cardona era, maybe."

And now it's an abandoned, caved-in symbol of a history we are not supposed to remember.

This ball is designed to make sure its guests do not think about Ivarea as it was before the Cardonas. We are not supposed to see the Landaulan sultanate, which rose to rule half the peninsula for longer than modern Ivarea has existed, in the soaring bell towers and elegant arches that make up the Alcázar complex. We are not supposed to remember the former dynasty, even as we stand in what was once their northernmost fortress.

No, all we're supposed to remember is four hundred years of glory, of triumph, of prosperity, the food and drink and gems and culture that have arisen with the Cardona kings' good fortune. Ivarea is one of the richest and most powerful kingdoms in the world. You don't have to wander the length of the Alcázar to see that.

But it makes you wonder what it took to get there.

"You don't like the Cardonas, do you?"

If Gaspard feels at all discomfited about walking the halls of the palace that saw the last gasp of the Landaulan sultanate against Carlos Cardona, the greatest of the dynasty's conquerors, he makes no sign of it now. He only says, "They're not there to be liked. They're there to rule."

"I'm not trying to pry. I just want to know."

"What's there to know?" he echoes. "For four hundred years, they've been telling us who they are and how we should see them. And tonight we're to renew our fealty based on the past four hundred years, not the present. Because without being able to rely on magic to prop up his rule, the only thing Rey Rodrigo has actually managed to do is create a police state. The taxes, the public gathering restrictions, all of that—you tell me what else this could be about."

Taken aback by his vehemence, I try to measure my words. "You mean if he were a magician . . . he wouldn't be doing all these things?"

"I didn't say that. All I mean is, what use is magic when you have power?" Gaspard's eyes flick to mine and stay there for what feels like a long while before he snaps back to himself. "People aren't happy about these laws, Anaïs. Up in Lutesse, anyone speaking ill about the crown in public is practically guaranteed a cozy jail cell. Rodrigo is cracking down on *any* room the people had left to engage with the government *or* with each other. It's goddamn disturbing."

So this is the experience that transformed the promising young discontented into radicals. Spending the last five years in the second-largest and second-most-important city in the kingdom seems to have exposed Gaspard to more than the gentlemanly academic pursuits his parents had in mind. He's seen a whole world beyond the wide-open pastures of Proensa. I can't even imagine what that must be like.

His righteousness evokes another wisp of a thought in the back of my head. "You're not opposed to there being a throne in the first place . . . are you?"

For the third time tonight, I've surprised him. From his slack-jawed expression, this might be the one that takes the cake. "Are you okay, Anaïs? You've been acting strange all night. And not in the ever-amusing, make-forts-out-of-potting-soil-in-my-mother's-morning-room sort of strange, which, admittedly, I wouldn't mind doing here. What's going on?"

It's one thing to be dismissed by your overbearing parents, and another to be ignored by strangers. I don't want the experience to be replicated by the only friend I have in a seven-hundred-mile radius. How I wish I could explain it to him and get him to help me. But for some reason, all I can think to say that can even begin to justify my behavior is, "Leo's a magician."

Gaspard's mouth falls open. For a moment I think it's because I called him *Leo,* as if I had a right to use his nickname. Then: "*Infante* Leopoldo? A magician?"

"It's true. I lost my locket and he helped me find it. With magic. I saw him do it. You weren't there." The falsehood leaves an ashen taste on my tongue.

"Huh." He forces his mouth shut. "Then maybe Rodrigo does have some cards up his sleeve after all."

I'm not sure *why* they're up his sleeve, though, and not in his hand. The king should be trumpeting the fact that not one but two of his children are carrying on their family's legacy. Not that I know very much about the *other* magical Cardona. Infanta Clara has pursued magic as her signature talent where other highborn girls might pursue watercolors or opera—as an advantage to be pressed among courtly rivals or as a talking point to be batted about in discussions of one's marriageable qualities. Certainly her powers were not meant for politicking or war, the way her illustrious ancestors' magical talents were infamously applied.

My mother has occasionally tried to use Clara as an example of how I might turn my otherwise unseemly magics into an asset in the hunt for a husband; if Paloma was right when she said that the princess was already betrothed, apparently it worked for her.

But *I'm* not the daughter of a king, and carrying the blessing does not mean having powers like an Ivarean. It means being burdened with a weak magic and dubious bloodline that has afforded my people little more than scars where we must split our skin to accomplish the smallest of tasks. It might as well not exist.

"I'm sorry about all this," I finally tell Gaspard. "I think this place is driving me mad."

He grimaces, as though all the feelings he's tried to keep to himself, with varying degrees of success, will break free if his lips quirk even a hair upward. "You're not the only one."

But that's the tragedy of my incredibly specific, particularly horrible situation. I *am* the only one.

Absentmindedly, I drift forward and hitch up my skirts to climb the narrow, winding stairs. The stone seems to shudder, as if shocked to be used. The dirt of centuries stripes my gown and smears my gloves when I drag my hand along the railing. I take a few steps and stop in front of the first of the windows. The view is less than breathtaking, the walls of the Alcázar complex dappled in palm-tree shadows, but it is *a* view. Of something other than a ballroom destined to cave in. Of gardens about to go up in flames.

"Maybe we should go back," Gaspard calls from the ground.

I can't go back.

"There's something you should know. Something I've been trying to say." I start back down the stairs, so I don't have to meet his gaze quite yet. "Promise you won't laugh."

He frowns. "If you promise to tell the truth."

It's easier to swear oaths than to follow through with them.

Luckily, my lady, I'm no oath breaker.

No. Stop it, Anaïs, you foolish, useless thing.

"The truth is, I've been stuck in this . . ." I pause on the second-to-last step. "I don't know what to call it, but it's as though time is loo—"

Footsteps.

Those are definitely footsteps. Coming from above—higher up in the ruined tower.

I freeze mid-step.

I hear pacing from above. Whoever's there, they're not descending.

Not yet.

I've spent all night trying to get close enough to the attackers to see who they are and how they pull off their plan. But my gut tells me that I don't want to be *this* close.

If I die before midnight, will I still wake up in Marenca this afternoon?

We stare at each other, each startled by the new arrivals. *Ball crashers?* he mouths.

I suppose that's right, in its way. Any other explanation would be too little, too late, at this point. *Let's go. Quickly.*

He nods and puts a cautious foot on the bottommost step to pick me up. He spins slowly around and sets me down in silence, as easily as if my gown weighs nothing at all. With one last curious look at me, he leads us outside.

We don't speak for several long minutes. By the time Gaspard tugs me down a tributary hallway, still half a palace away from the ballroom, a cold sweat has broken out down my back.

"What the hell? Who was that?" He glances back at the glowing maw of the corridor perpendicular to us. I can't hear anything but the pounding of my heartbeat at first. But then, just like that, a door squeaks, warped wood against cold stone.

We shouldn't have stopped.

Gaspard shrinks farther into the hall until his hands find another door. He turns the boar doorknob's bronze snout just as the footsteps make it into the central corridor of the west wing. I follow him inside. There are no windows in this little room, and what little carved wooden furniture is here has been covered with sheets. If the people stomping down the hall are heading to the ballroom, we could hide here until they pass.

Gaspard breathes shallowly, staring at the door he just locked. "Anaïs?"

A muffled sound from outside is growing louder. Out of some latent instinct for chivalry, Gaspard barricades me in a corner with his body. I can't bring myself to yelp.

"What were you going to tell me?"

Helpless, I gesture toward the door. "An attack. The ballroom. Midnight."

"What? How could you know that?" He's never held me like this, with barely contained frenzy. "Anaïs, what the *fuck* is going on?"

Laughter as bitter as tears boils up my throat.

"Anaïs!" Even his whispers are suddenly thunderous with fear, but I can't stop laughing. "Anaïs, *what's going on?*"

"What's going on? We're dying!" I double over, clutching my stomach. "We're going to die in this goddamned place, and there's no stopping it! We wait, and we die, and we live again!" Sobs twine with the laughter and burst from my aching chest. "Well. *I* do. No idea what happens to you."

The sounds from the hallway are louder now. Closer. I bite my tongue so hard that it bleeds. No time for follow-up questions.

"Right." Gaspard's terse whisper seems as loud to me as the horrible footsteps approaching the door. "Right. Forget midnight. First you have to make it through this."

I swallow blood.

"I'm sorry," I tell him.

With a hard, strange look in his eyes—the expression of someone staring down death—he lowers his head and kisses me.

I've never kissed Gaspard before, but even in my wildest dreams, I didn't think it would be like this. Awkward and panicked and desperate, my face plastered with tears, my mouth tasting like iron. One of his hands dips below my waist, clutching me close to his body; the other threads through my hair, catching on a cavalcade of pins. A stupid, suddenly lustful part of me says that if I'm going to die, it might as well be dragging my hands down Gaspard's chest, but the door opens, and I know I'll be robbed of that mercy before I duck my head.

"Oye!"

Gaspard doesn't break off the kiss for several beats yet, as if reluctant to let go. Finally, he slides in front of me and turns around, blocking me from the scrutiny of strangers.

A shield against death.

My lips are swollen. I still taste iron.

Three men crowd the threshold. Their faces are indistinct enough that they could be from any province. All three are clad in reasonably well-cut jackets and worn leather boots—not Anniversary Ball fare by any means, but nothing that would seem out of place or draw particular attention in the capital. None look like hardened killers, if you set aside the shotguns at their backs.

"What're you doing here?" one of them asks in coarse Castaran.

Gaspard flinches as he takes in the sight of the intruders. I can see his jaw clenching as though he's trying to swallow his own tongue to keep himself from saying the wrong thing. Though at this point, anything could be the wrong thing. I just don't know what he's thinking. What he actually wants to say.

It's only been a few seconds, but it feels like an age before Gaspard finally dips his head in a wooden impression of a gentleman. "Good evening, señores, forgive the trespass." As if we're the ones who *broke into the palace.* "My lady and I were in search of somewhere more . . . private. I'm sure you can understand."

Another of the men, with sandy hair and wide-set black eyes, steps forward. "We cannot blame young people for taking liberties while they can. Especially young lovers like you." He smiles blankly at me over Gaspard's shoulder. "Good evening, my lady."

I dig my hand into Gaspard's side, silently willing him to stall. Midnight can't be that far away. If I'm not in the ballroom, if I die before it happens—

He seems to take the hint and addresses the sandy-haired one directly. "Is there something we can do for you?"

"Well, that depends, my friend." He steps farther into the room, the others on his flanks. The closer he gets to us, the clearer it becomes that his eyes aren't black at all. They're a sickly, hypnotic green, glowing even in the semidarkness of the abandoned room. Tears and blood forgotten, I slip a little farther out from behind Gaspard to meet his gaze. "You are subjects of the Ivarean king? Celebrating this *glorious* regime?"

Gaspard shifts uneasily where he stands, choosing his words more carefully than ever before. "It is a celebration . . . señor. Few people ask for more than that."

"I see," says the green-eyed one, noncommittally enough, before he turns to me. "And you, my dear? Have you found what you were looking for tonight?"

I have to swallow several times to force something, anything, out of my mouth. "I . . . I'm beginning to think so."

The intruder's blank smile widens. "I'm glad to hear that. It's important in this world to go after what you want. Wouldn't you agree?"

The other two men chuckle. They've probably been told to make a sweep of the rooms, not to tarry and toy with young prey. Yet here they are.

Because *he* wants to be. Because he's their leader.

I step fully out from behind Gaspard. Now we're standing side by side, the two of us before the three of them. Even if we weren't outgunned and outnumbered, I would have some notion as to how this has to end.

I draw myself up to my full height. "And *you*, señor?" Gaspard stares sidelong at me, as if trying to warn me off baiting these people, and tries to herd me behind him again. But I find, in the face of certain death, that it's astonishingly easy to dismiss his concern. "Who are you? What exactly do you want from us?"

"From you?" The green-eyed one draws out those two syllables with dripping amusement. He opens his mouth, as if to actually answer my questions, but before he can, Gaspard steps forward.

"Please—please! Take no offense. My lady won't bother you, I promise. Just let her go, and whatever else . . ." His hands are out, already offering a surrender. "Whatever it is you want, I believe we can come to some sort of understanding. Just let her go."

An understanding? With these men? What does he think he's doing? In what world could that possibly happen?

You fool, Plamondon.

The green-eyed leader sighs with a heavy dose of irony. "Ah. A chivalrous instinct. Perhaps you are not the type of man I thought you were." He raises his voice but does not loosen the grip of his gaze on me. "But your lady asked me a question, and she deserves an answer before she takes her leave. What say you, friends?"

My hand snakes around Gaspard's in the silence.

The leader swings his weapon around and aims it squarely at me. "What is it we owe our fellow citizens, if not the truth?"

All he needs is one bullet.

But as I leap forward, he does not leave it to chance.

VI

CHAPTER ONE

IN THE PRECIOUS, USELESS SECONDS AFTER, AS I STRUGGLE upright in my bed half a city away, all I can think of is the desperate press of Gaspard's lips against mine. All I taste is his blood welling in my mouth. Violent, angry tears wear the skin of my cheeks to nothing. When my mother asks me what is wrong, again, I can't find the words.

I cannot fathom why the forces that shape human lives decided to steal mine that first night and replace it with this purgatory. An in-between space and time that isn't mine and that I can't hope to understand. If the only way to keep this curse from claiming me over and over again is to stop the midnight attack, surely there were hundreds of people in that ballroom who could have done so by now. Clever people, gifted people, people who know things, who care about something more than their lives and their loved ones' safety. People like Gaspard.

I'm not clever. I'm not gifted. I don't know anything, least of all what the hell I'm supposed to do next.

But as long as I'm stuck like this, and as long as that requires trying to stop the attack, I don't want to unnecessarily drag others to their deaths. Especially if they think they're *saving me*. No one can do that: not my parents, not Gaspard, and certainly not a Cardona.

As long as I'm stuck like this, I don't want to be killed without a fight.

At least not *every* night.

Before Béatrice can fasten me into my gown, I tear downstairs toward Papa's study. My robe flutters at the hem, hastily fastened over my corset and petticoat, as I slam the door shut behind me. He is in the middle of writing a letter to his brother, who is overseeing our estates while we're here in Marenca, probably promising him a speedy update as soon as my betrothal is set.

Unfortunately for him, there's no chance of that now.

"I need one of the Aubanel daggers."

He replaces his pen in the inkwell and peers at me carefully. "Those are blessed objects, Anaïs, not accessories."

"Exactly."

Proensan legend holds that blessed objects were transformed into magical wonders by the fairies themselves—books whose contents changed with every page, brooches that bled poison, pitchers of water that never went dry. But after the disappearance of the fairies, the Proensan houses that bowed to the Cardonas were forced to either send the blessed objects in their possession to Marenca as tribute to their new king, or destroy them. My father's ancestor, Conte Pèire Aubanel, protected a set of three daggers with gemstone-encrusted hilts from the Ivareans by hiding them in a cave normally home to aging cheeses. Of course, even if Ivareans *could* use blessed objects, their powers can only be maintained with blood magic, and all of the magical objects the Cardonas took as the spoils of victory have long since become punishingly ordinary.

That makes the Aubanel daggers, and any other stray blessed objects that escaped Cardona greed, the last of their kind; mythical origin story aside, the blessing is so weak these days that it cannot imbue new objects with powers anymore. As such, Papa is *extremely* circumspect about using them. If he didn't have to keep the daggers whetted with his blood, he never would have brought them with us to the capital.

"If I'm really going to get betrothed to some Castaran or whoever, then I'm about to lose everything I care about. My home. My family. My *name*." This last part I spit with more venom than the lie probably needs. "I'm going *mad* thinking about the future. You have no idea how much. So, please, let me have this. Let me be a true Aubanel. Just for tonight."

Papa absorbs all this with more grace than I probably deserve. There's even a melancholy twinkle in his nut-brown eyes. "I do not think the Guardia Real would be especially understanding if they found you smuggling a magical weapon into the ballroom."

"The other grandes always wear their family swords at these things. Why should this be any different?"

A rhetorical question if ever there was one: We're Proensan. We carry barbarous blood magic and believe in fairy-creature-god *beings*. We are not the same as the other grandes, and we never will be.

"Fool of a girl." Papa straightens his back and glances at the door behind me. "Can you keep a secret?"

I nod, not trusting my voice. He keeps staring until he hears my mother stomping up and down the stairs and shouting for me. Seeming to realize, as I do, that our time is limited, he withdraws one of his ordinary miniature daggers. With the tip of the blade, he draws a shallow line across his fingertip and dots a bead of his blood on his desk. He screws his eyes shut to focus his intention. I watch him set the spell closely, so I can replicate it next time. A few long, heavy moments later, a secret compartment rises from the desk.

Though I've only seen it a few times in my life, I recognize the wide velvet box inside the compartment. It's embossed with the Aubanel coat of arms, a silver stag leaping across an azure field, and it holds three of the last physical symbols we have of our pre-Ivarean heritage. The blessed daggers wink knowingly in the evening sunlight. Gorged with the blood of hundreds of years of Aubanels, the blades seem as sharp as the day they were magically forged. The sapphire dagger can transform ash into bread, and the ruby one can turn a sheaf of parchment into a roof overhead. Papa hands me the smallest one, its blade thin and needle-like, the emerald in its pommel the size of my pinkie nail, and replaces the box in the secret compartment.

"The cloth-magic dagger?"

"Quite appropriate for a young lady," he says.

I crack a grin. "Does Maman remember there's a blessed object in the vicinity that could create a magical gown?"

"If you wanted to wear something *more* elaborate for to-night, I'm happy to remind her."

"No!" My voice wavers as I close my fingers over the hilt. "No, please, Papa. Thank you."

He draws me closer and presses a wordless kiss to the top of my head. "Bear it in good faith, then, Anaïs. And be careful."

My mouth goes dry. "I'll try."

Béatrice does not ask where I got a brand-new matching sash for my gown, and Maman assumes that it was a stroke of her own past genius. In reality, of course, it's all the emerald dag-ger's doing—even though it was a minor spell, it was the first taste of its power in my life. Now it hums against my waist almost as though it's excited for its first real outing in centu-ries. Papa does a double take when I come downstairs, but of-fers absolutely no comment on my appearance, suddenly more focused on an impending social gathering than he's ever been in his life.

Perhaps I should take after his example.

By the time we arrive at the Alcázar, the main question on my mind is this: *How* do all those people, including the ones who just murdered Gaspard and me, sneak into the Alcázar without alerting the Guardia Real?

The quickest way to find out for certain would be to go back to that tower and watch it all happen again. Let them murder me all over again. But . . . no. Not now.

Not again.

I try to shake off the fear before it can settle in my bones, but when that doesn't work, I decide to redirect that anxious energy elsewhere. Like into investigating the tower when I know the intruders won't be there.

After some histrionics involving a truly unsavory combination of pungent blue cheese and spiced blood sausage, I bow out of the feast early, wipe my mouth clean, and hasten toward the west wing. I didn't make it to the top of the stairs last time, but I see now that the next landing of the tower has been sealed. The wall in front of me is solid stone—medieval stone, as Gaspard theorized, and therefore older than Ivarea itself, but unyielding stone nonetheless. I push against it from the topmost step, even kick at it a few times, but not so much as a pebble breaks from the shadows.

Gaspard and I definitely heard the intruders from above us. So either there's some sort of secret way through the wall, or the intruders use magic to destroy it.

If they can do it, maybe I can, too.

I stuff my gloves into the sash I conjured and pry out the

sheathed Aubanel dagger. I don't need its cloth magic right now: I simply need to spill my blood.

For only the second time in my life, I draw the dagger out of its little sheath and balance the naked blade on my palm. It feels strange to carry an artifact like this—a *weapon* like this—in the heart of the peninsula. I find my eyes drifting shut and my mind filling with flashes of home, as if reminding me that I am connected by a bloody chain to a place of legend and magic every bit as wondrous and legitimate as Ivarea, whether anyone cares about it or not. A place that's with me no matter where I go. Even here, in the stone heart of the kingdom.

I draw a light cut on my index finger. It stings more than I'd like, but the blood welling in the cut is still mine, and still, to whatever degree, magical. I press my bleeding finger to the stone wall at the top of the stairs and ask it for the truth: *Show me what's on the other side of this wall. Tell me how to get through. Tell me what this is.*

The Alcázar Real de Marenca should refuse me. It's not my home. It doesn't know me. And even if it did know me, Ivarean magic has been stronger than the Proensan blessing for generations, and the palace itself is clearly imbued with magic, from its medieval fortress foundations all the way to its Cardona-enchanted magical marvels. What right do I have to demand anything from this place?

I draw another cut on my middle finger and add that to the wall, screwing my eyes shut and turning my intention into an incantation: *Show me show me show me.* When that doesn't work, I add the blood of another finger. But I can feel the palace wearing away at my intention, as though its enchantment was designed to thwart the blessing specifically. Continuing to push against it makes the back of my head ache.

There's no way whatever's up there will be worth this.

Maybe not. But I have to keep trying. Otherwise I'll just end up here at half past eleven waiting to be chased down by murderers all over again.

I don't know how long I stand there like a fool, trying to focus both on my spell and on keeping my head from splitting open from the pressure of these opposing magics, when, finally, the wall begins to melt away.

Hope blinks awake inside me like a newborn grappling with daylight for the first time. *Look at that. Maybe you're not a* complete *fool after all.*

I have no idea what happened to the wall, but I'm not about to question the first stroke of luck I've had in ages. At last, I hurry through to the second landing.

Which looks exactly like the sealed-off second floor of a remote tower should look. Stone and more stone everywhere, no furniture or weaponry, no sign that anything here has been disturbed by more than the breeze from the narrow window in centuries. Certainly not plotting rebels or intruders or murderers. But I suppose that all comes later.

The stairs continue their spiral upward, leading to a third sealed landing. I draw another line of blood on my finger and try the same spell on that stone wall—and the palace yields, faster than the first time. Up here is another wholly unremarkable landing, though it is the last: The blessing shows me nothing else of note above the tower. Just the palm trees along the outer walls of the Alcázar complex and the wide night sky.

I lean back against the wall hugging the staircase and gaze back out into the murky darkness of the last landing. Once the initial resistance fell away, the rest of this has been, dare I say, *horrifically* easy. I haven't used the blessing much in Marenca, and certainly not in the palace itself, but . . . this feels . . . *wrong*, somehow. Blood magic should not be this easy in the heart of the Alcázar. Why else would Papa have warned me against it? Besides, no power that could erase walls that presumably stood here for hundreds of years should be so easy for anyone to magically dispel. Let alone me.

So why did the resistance I faced at the first landing disappear all of a sudden? Does this forgotten tower not have the same magical protections as the rest of the Alcázar? If so, how is it that the intruders know to enter here and nowhere else?

Wait. Who said they enter from nowhere else?

What if there are other areas like this across the Alcázar? There must be, considering all the intruders I remember streaming across the rubble of the Arco de León on that first midnight. A whole revolutionary band pouring in from weak spots across the palace.

This can't be a coincidence.

Someone must have removed the wards from the palace at the very moment that I was trying to break into the tower landings. So our murderous friends can enter without detection.

There's a traitor in the Alcázar.

Slightly winded after reinstating the seals on each of the landings in the tower, I return to the ballroom determined to stay the hell away from other people. When I recover a bit of energy, I surreptitiously test the blessing with a discarded crystal glass, but turning it into a croquet mallet offers me much more resistance than the upper landings of the tower. Which I can only assume means either that the palace's wards were broken at that moment, or that they were lowered deliberately.

As I circle the dance floor considering my next move, Marguerite Lorieux, of all people, waves me to her corner. She's probably too drunk to realize what she's done, but I head in her direction, thinking vaguely about interrogating her about her student radicals again. I don't even swerve when I notice she's with Jacinthe again, along with a third girl. I can't place her until I've already moved to greet Marguerite, who gestures to her side.

"Mi infanta, you know Doña Anaïs of Massilie?"

My eyes whip around to meet the third girl's, half hoping that it's not her after all. But it *is* Infanta Clara, the king's second child and Leo's older sister. Her hair is darker than Leo's, and her eyes a clear hazel to his rich brown, but the resemblance between the younger Cardona siblings is unmistakable. "Why, of course," she answers in her low trill of a voice. "Our dear Proensan friend."

I drop into a curtsy to forestall my panic. My vision narrows on the hammered gold blossoms flecked with diamonds that form an enchanted autumn garden on her emerald-green gown. If there were anyone in attendance who could bear a time-loop curse better than I can, surely it's the elegant, intelligent magician-princess of Ivarea. "You are too kind, Vuestra Alteza Real."

"I most certainly am *not* too kind."

I rise and nearly knock my head through the vellum of her folding fan, which is painted with scenes from an idyllic Castaran garden. Before I manage to run my own eyes through with its whalebone ribs, the princess shuts the fan and lets it dangle idly from a ribbon on her wrist.

"You are an honored guest at this ball," she continues, gracious as an eagle eyeing a rabbit who ventured beyond its underground warren. "Whatever kindness I might show you or anyone else here is exactly what you deserve."

Before I can cobble together a response, Jacinthe swoops in. "And what of those who could not be here tonight?" she prods her former playmate. "Do they not deserve your kindness, Alteza?"

Clara narrows her eyes, but otherwise seems unruffled. "Plenty of grandes were unable to make the journey to Marenca. That does not make them less dear to the king."

"And those who were not invited?"

Marguerite frowns earnestly. "Why would commoners be at the Anniversary Ball?"

Just like she did last time I saw her, Jacinthe appears to needle at Marguerite—but this time, she's looking straight at the princess. "Perhaps they would like to be."

Ah. Maybe this is why Jacinthe was so cold to Marguerite before, when we were with Paloma: Clara chose Marguerite to be her new favorite at court. That must sting for someone who is as close to the royal family as Jacinthe. But at least in her bitterness, Jacinthe actually paved the way for me. I send up a brief, bewildered prayer of thanks to Proensan fairies and dead Ivarean saints alike. "What would happen if someone *were* discovered to be crashing the ball? Someone who isn't supposed to be here?"

"That's quite impossible. The Alcázar is extremely secure, and the Guardia Real is out in full force tonight, as you can see." The princess gestures vaguely at the rest of the ballroom and adds with a wink, "Not to mention that which you cannot see."

Marguerite yelps, her sky-high hairstyle quivering with concern. "Spells? In the *ballroom?*"

"Of course, Alteza," I hasten to interrupt, "but no spell is ever quite foolproof. Especially not in a palace this large. Surely there may be weaknesses or blind spots that unsavory characters would exploit to . . . join the festivities?"

Clara fixes me with a purposefully opaque look. "I've snuck out of the Alcázar plenty of times myself. In my younger, wilder days, you understand. Parties my mother wouldn't want me attending. Performances by bawdy thespians. Demonstrations of foreign magics. You name it, I wanted to see it for myself."

Just behind us, Marguerite titters at the idea of a wild Infanta Clara. Perks of being the favorite, I suppose. Jacinthe glowers at their side, radiating mostly-concealed frustration.

"But if my father found out what I'd done, he'd have the guards seal off my own chambers. Once when he'd discovered I'd snuck out, he blocked me from the entire palace. I dawdled back up the hills at daybreak and was forced to rot on the drive all morning. In full view of the court."

Marguerite sucks in a horrified breath. "*My* father would have opened the doors just to kill me within his own walls."

"My point," Clara continues, still managing to bestow a dazzling grin on Marguerite as she addresses me, "is that even *I* couldn't get past the Alcázar wards, and I live here. I can quite assure you that no one gets in here unless they're wanted."

"How . . . reassuring," I offer meekly.

I'm tempted to press my luck with the princess, but the look on her face suggests she's growing annoyed by my questions. While I cast around for something less controversial to say, I remember what I heard before from Paloma Nelleda—that bit of gossip about Clara being secretly engaged. If it's true, her intended must be a foreign royal or other; princesses are never destined to stay in their homeland, after all. But if the announcement of a betrothal was ever in the cards for this evening's festivities, we will not get that far tonight. Clara will die an Ivarean, like everyone else.

In the silence, Clara dons another bright smile. This one somehow sets my teeth on edge. "Magic on the peninsula is very different from what you have out in Proensa, isn't it, Doña Anaïs? That blood magic—what do you call it again?"

"The blessing," I supply with a bit of trepidation.

"Ah yes, of course, how could I have forgotten? I find it

quite fascinating, though your countrymen are rather secretive about their power."

"Secretive? Señora, I can assure you, the blessing is not very interesting, or even useful, per se—nothing worth keeping to oneself, at least not in my experience—"

"You're kidding. You're one of them? Oh, how exciting." She grabs my hand and walks me down the ballroom, gilded fan aflutter. At first Jacinthe and Marguerite seem shocked by their sudden unprecedented loss. But when I try to shoot a desperate glance for help over my shoulder, I see them bend their heads conspiratorially toward each other, Marguerite's hand wrapping around Jacinthe's as if in the prelude to an embrace. They seem very glad indeed to have been left to themselves. Not exactly the behavior I would expect of warring favorites.

Clara, for her part, turns to me as easily as if I've been by her side all night. "Is it true that blood magicians don't need to use charms to cast spells?"

Taken aback, I can only squeak, "Y-yes?"

Unlike the limited blessed objects in Proensans' secret possession, charms are everywhere on the peninsula. They serve as conduits to the earth magic of Ivarea and bear no specific powers of their own. People here believe that charms with saintly origins are more powerful than other conduits because the saints' miracle-working was so much more powerful than the physical magic of ordinary Ivareans; all this season, I've seen Castaran girls wear combs made of saints' reliquaries to the theater and carry lockets filled with the dirt of holy places instead of reticules. Regardless of whether they're related to saintly miracles or to ordinary magic, neither the authenticity nor the effectiveness of charms seem particularly consistent to me. And despite the pushy pitches of peddlers I've run into since we crossed the sea, I can't use charms. With or without a conduit of whatever origin, this land's magic does not respond to a Proensan, especially not one who has the blessing. It doesn't belong to me, just as I don't really belong to Ivarea.

But the princess seems *delighted* with my answer. Which is not an emotion I thought I'd ever elicit from a royal. "How remarkable! A magic that depends on nothing but one's own self. And you think inherited blood magic is *uninteresting*! You mustn't sell yourself short, Doña Anaïs," Clara scolds me. "Self-deprecation is not an attractive quality in a woman. Particularly not here."

Suddenly, Clara snaps the fan shut. The violent clacking of its ribs puts me in mind of the other gossip Paloma revealed—about Clara bearing a gift from her husband-to-be. This fan must be the secret favor.

I don't have time to enjoy knowing something Paloma Nelleda does not before Clara directs another question my way.

"Are you already spoken for?"

Does she mean for the next dance? Or is she trying to ask if I'm betrothed?

The fact that she could be asking me either of those questions might be the most impossible thing that's happened to me since I started dying and reliving the same night. All I can tell her is the truth. "God, no."

"*Perfect.*"

The realization hits as we plow breathlessly through the crowd: *Infanta Clara is going to set you up with someone.*

It only takes a few minutes for her to find her quarry in the crowds. I forget to wonder who she could possibly be leading me toward until it's too late and he's standing before me, more disinterested than he's ever been to see me in his lives.

"Doña Anaïs of Massilie, meet my little brother, Infante Leopoldo."

CHAPTER TWO

THE LAST TIME WE WERE THIS CLOSE, I PUNCHED HIM RIGHT in his inscrutable face. If I didn't know better, I'd think he almost remembers that moment, hears the jagged cracking of my hand against his cheekbones. It would explain the way he's looking at me. A phantom from a half-remembered past, a future realized and undone.

Several beats too late, I curtsy to the prince, and something approximating charm smooths his voice into dull pleasantness. "Delighted to make your acquaintance."

"Oh, you should be more than delighted, Leo. Doña Anaïs is one of that mythical Proensan breed of magicians." Clara beams at the space between us and shifts to stand next to him. "He's also interested in regional magic, you see."

"Don't let the princess mislead you, my lady—I'm no scholar." He shoots her a barbed glance. "What is it you call me?"

"A dilettante." Clara winks. "Interested in indulging his curiosities."

Am I supposed to feel *grateful* that she's dangling me like a prize for her brother to snatch up?

"Now, I *am* sorry, but I do have a few other things to attend to tonight. Anaïs, my dear, I rather think you have as much to learn from Leo as he does from you." Clara leans forward and presses kisses to the air above my flushed cheeks, then does the same with her brother. "See you later, my loves!"

Even as the court swallows her up on her path toward the royal dais, new admirers materialize in her wake, desperate for her attention.

A soft chuckle breaks through the music and voices. "Of all the girls I expected my sister to foist on me tonight, I must admit my surprise that she picked a Proensan. First blood to Clara." He rubs his hands together instead of clarifying that last comment. "Right. We're here now—why don't we make the most of it. Do you really need to spill your own blood to perform magic?"

"Yes, Vuestra Alteza Real."

"Fascinating."

Since it wasn't his idea to talk to me, it doesn't appear as though he'll admit that he's a magician himself. But if Clara was hinting about his powers just now, why would she be so eager for her brother to tell me what he is? What on earth could I offer him that he doesn't already have?

He is right, however. We should make the most of this. And after Clara's not-so-subtle hints, I can't help but want to dig into the puzzle of Leo's magical talents.

"You know, Alteza," I murmur in a low, inviting voice, "*your* magic has always been fascinating to me."

"You mean the magic my ancestors cultivated in their time," he corrects me, unfazed. "The great magician-kings of Ivarea. That kind of talent has not graced my family in ages. Very unfortunate."

I feign shock. "What of Príncipe Felipe? He has no inclination for magic?"

Leo scoffs, a clear enough indication of his opinion of his own brother. I've seen Príncipe Felipe, the eldest of the Cardona children, floating around the ballroom—not that he's ever struck me as someone who would believe or help me. He's usually busy ingratiating himself with the most powerful elder grandes and ministers, or flirting with their daughters when his wife, Princesa Helena, isn't looking. "Even my dear sister's talents pale in comparison to those of the Cardonas who united the peninsula," says Leo. "Let alone those who conquered the provinces beyond the mountains."

Like Proensa.

I blink through the stabbing feeling in my gut so I can seem just as detached as Leo himself. "If I may say so, señor, you don't seem especially happy about that."

The shadow of a chandelier throws unnatural lines over his face. "For centuries, no other noble house in the peninsula could hold a candle to the Cardonas in the manipulation of magic. And now we can't even begin to recapture whatever it was that made them so great. Perhaps we were always going to lose hold of our legacy." He adds, with bitter irony, "It's not like magic runs in our veins."

Complaining. About power. In Ivarea. To a blessed Proensan. I suppose princely self-pity will never not be grating. "The blessing is dying out. We *are* losing our legacy." I can count on my hands and feet the number of people I know that carry the blessing. Nearly half of them are in this room, excluding Papa and myself. "We're going to lose everything."

He studies me more closely. I suppose no self-respecting prince can resist a magically gifted maiden wrapped in an air of melancholy. "If it were in your power, then, would you not try to preserve it?"

A tingling sensation slides down my back, like cold rain on a windowpane. "It's *not* in my power."

I can see the wheels of his gently addled brain turning in his eyes. He looks like he's about to say something, to offer me some hint of—

"Well, it's about goddamn time." Leo gestures toward a serving boy who dances through the crowd with a tray of wine-filled glasses. I bite my lip as Leo plucks one from the tray. Now if I'm going to get anything out of him about his and his family's magical and political attitudes, I have to be more entertaining than alcohol.

"Perhaps you'd like to escort me on a walk around the gardens, señor? Get some air?"

A grin I haven't seen since before I punched him spreads slowly across his face. He nods and offers his arm. I don't take it, and keep walking. Intrigued, or so I hope, he follows. Not once does he lose track of me, not even when I twist out from under Bear Arch and rush across the courtyard into another garden, this one called Night's Pavilion. Semiprecious stones that represent the stars are embedded in the white marble of the central pavilion, enchanted to reflect the rhythm of the Marenca sky above. As the gemstone stars shift and reshape themselves into the constellations, they tell the stories Ivarea has ascribed to nights just like this. It's beautiful, but as with so much of Ivarean culture, it holds no great meaning for me.

As I come to a stop beneath the pavilion, Leo leans against one of its outer columns. An arrow of stars embeds itself in his shoulder. "I must say, you know your way around the Alcázar far better than most provincial visitors."

And how lucky he must count himself for it. The country-bumpkin blood-magician girl has done half his work for him.

Let him think what he wants. I have a blessed dagger and a death wish. I'm not leaving here until I have something more to work with.

"I only thought we could talk more freely here."

"Yes, we can talk. If that is what you wish." He swirls the wine in his cup like he could catalyze a storm just as easily. And maybe he can. I have no idea how powerful he is; finding my necklace could hardly have been the fullest extent of his talents, though doing something similar may well mark the fullest extent of mine.

Leo was hungry to use magic then, no matter the less-than-pressing situation. He just needed an excuse to display his talents in public.

Under his father's nose.

I clear my throat to return to the topic we were discussing in the ballroom. "I suppose you think the kingdom would be in better shape if Príncipe Felipe were a magician."

"Are you implying the kingdom is *not* in good shape?" he retorts. I don't think he's well and truly drunk, but now he must wish he were. "It's hardly Felipe's fault that he's not a magician."

Tension builds like the music drifting in snatches from the ballroom.

"Ivarea wasn't always this way, you know. It wasn't always *this* horribly unfair. Back in the Dark Ages, Cardona grandes selected their heirs based on their *worthiness*. Their *abilities*. They would know in their *bones* what the answer was. They didn't rely on anything as arbitrary as *birth order*."

My gut instinct calcifies into horror. "And you believe *you're* worthy? Because you're the magician and your older brother isn't?"

He lowers his glass a fraction but is careful not to stare at me too openly. "What makes you think I'm a magician?"

"You told me so." I meet his gaze with cold certainty and lie through my teeth. "You were drunk at the time. You do not remember."

Leo steps out from the shadow of the column, frowning. "That seems highly unlikely."

"There's no use in lying to me."

"Do you think you're the first provincial girl to try to get strategically swept up by royalty? You've spent all night trying to get closer to my sister and, incidentally, to me. *You* are the liar here, Doña Anaïs. Do not mistake my indulgence as true foolishness."

My voice balances on the edge of a butcher's knife, curt and sharp. "You just told a near stranger that you don't believe your brother should inherit the throne when you already suspected she was using you. Now imagine what other secrets you might let slip with more alcohol clouding your already skewed judgment. Señor."

The knowing light in his eyes extinguishes as readily as a candle. It would be very easy indeed to forget that he has ever looked my way with anything except this utterly royal disdain.

"You devious bitch."

Then he exhales, and all at once the feeling rushes back into his expression.

"Fine. Fine!" He stumbles backward and bows, keeping his right arm level so the wine doesn't totally spill over his shoes. "*Yes*, I am a magician, and yes, I *do* think Ivarea could use someone like me on the throne. Our neighbors' ambitions are on the rise, and our own people tire of taxes and restrictions and hunger and everything else on which we Cardonas have ever emblazoned our name. Forget another hundred years—if Ivarea is to survive the next *decade,* we need a magician on the throne. That's the only way we keep our rivals in place and build a better future for our people. It's the only way we survive."

These grievances, self-serving as they surely are, remind me of the men who killed Gaspard and me. They had asked if we were loyal subjects of Rey Rodrigo. But they didn't say anything explicit about revolution against the monarchy, did they? Their leader only referred sardonically to the *glory* of the current regime. If he and his cronies are so concerned about the state of Ivarea under Rey Rodrigo's rule specifically, perhaps their intended solution is restoring Ivarea's storied magical leadership and installing another magician-king on the throne. And if the rebels care about restoring the Cardonas' own magical legacy, their options are limited: Felipe is as famously unmagically gifted as his father, and Clara may be a magician, but she's still a girl.

Which just leaves . . .

"If things are that dire," I say carefully, "couldn't you convince your father to alter the line of succession?"

Leo scoffs and turns away toward the gardens. His profile is unforgiving, carving at the flickering shadows as sweetly as one might caress a lover. "My father wouldn't listen to me."

"What would it take to make him listen to you?"

Sweat gleams on his temples. I think he's beginning to forget how we got into this mess. "More than a conversation. *Much* more." He blinks when he realizes I'm not standing where I was twenty seconds ago. "Wha—"

I whirl in front of him, and his glass crashes to the ground. Wine soaks into the soles of my shoes.

"What are you *doing*?" he yelps.

I can only stare, almost dumbfounded, at the point of my

dagger against his shadow-dappled skin. The blessed dagger thrums in my shaking grip, moving like static down my gloved hand and into the hilt, up through the gleaming silver of the blade—against Leo's throat.

Infante Leopoldo.

The magician-prince of Ivarea.

Midnight cannot be more than a few frenzied heartbeats away. But if I die at the prince's hand tonight—well, what's the difference?

I step closer to keep the blade steady. There are no guards out here, and if they do patrols of the gardens, they will only see two figures locked in a passionate embrace and lost in their own dueling gazes.

"Or maybe it's not worth the trouble to talk to the king. Maybe you thought killing your father and brother would be more politically expedient."

"My dear lady," he murmurs with a brittle, becoming smile, "what the fuck are you talking about?"

"I don't blame you, exactly. Assassinating everyone that might object to you becoming king is a tidy way to go about it. Except," I add, my voice shaking more than my hand, "you vastly underestimated the capacity of *bombs* to *kill people!*"

"Doña Anaïs—"

I remember his first death in my arms, his blood soaking my front, his gaze unseeing as he caressed my face. He didn't seem like a royal patricide then, or all the other times I saw him killed, too—by mistake, because of some betrayal by the rebels, I don't know, and I can't imagine it. But all those people—all those stories—all that mystery surrounding his powers—the raging discontent, the men marching through the halls—

"Doña Anaïs, what's going on?" Crystal shards crunch underfoot as he leans forward, heedless of how close he is to breaking his own skin. His breath seems to skip over the surface of the dagger. "Did you say *bombs*?"

"I saw them! All of it, with my own eyes. People dying. All of us dying. Over and over and over again."

"You're having visions?"

"Not a vision," I whisper. "A life repeating. A . . . break in time."

I expect him to swear at me again. Which would be fair, all things considered. Or maybe he'll roll his eyes and say it again: *You* are *mad*.

"Tell me."

It doesn't have the shape of a command. Yet the words tug at me like a rope cast out to a drowning figure. And . . . my God, no one has believed me all this time. Not until it was too late.

What do I have left to lose?

"I took a nap the afternoon before the ball. I woke up, got ready, came here. Ate, drank, made merry. And at midnight, the explosions started. I was killed." I can't bring myself to confess how he died that first time, a king for barely ten minutes, delirious in my arms. "Then I . . . woke up, or something. It was afternoon again. My mother wanted me to get ready for the Anniversary Ball. I thought it was a dream. So I went. And it happened again."

Tears stream freely down my freckled cheeks. Leo is several

inches taller than me, and he watches my silent sobbing with crumbling composure—jaw set, nostrils flared. He curls his hand around mine and lowers it to my side. His palm brushes the emerald embedded in the hilt of the dagger. I don't move to raise it again, and he doesn't go for his own sword.

"How is this possible? How are you reliving this same night?"

Another sob claws its way out of my throat.

He takes me by the shoulders and shakes me once, twice, three times. "*Anaïs.* Anaïs, how many times has this happened?"

I should leap at the chance to tell someone about what I've been experiencing. And somewhere inside, I *am* eager—to have an ally for the night, whatever is left of it, or at least someone who won't dismiss me as pitiably irrational. But the hysteria is too tall a mountain to climb. The dagger at my side feels like an executioner's sword. Would it be more merciful for me to kill Leo now, before midnight? Or kill myself and spare everyone in this goddamned place from one more painful death when they're destined for innumerable more?

He releases me, stumbles back, and swallows. "I'm not behind this. For the record." His laugh over my head sounds almost as forlorn as I do. "The dramatic flair of an attack on the stroke of midnight doesn't escape me, but . . . no, this isn't me."

"Then who?"

He seems too overwhelmed to think through the possibilities. "No one will believe you about the bombs without proof. And no one . . . We don't . . ."

"You don't remember." I crack an involuntary, slightly

crazed smile. "None of you ever do. You live out the day like it's the first time."

He nods again, his chin in his hand. "So we're about half an hour from dying again."

"Yes."

"And . . . and we'll wake up tomorrow—or today—and all of this will happen again."

"Not the exact same way, but . . . yes. We're doomed."

"But . . . *why? Why* is this happening?"

This is a question I cannot begin to approach. Every time it crosses my mind, I sense the depths to which I would have to descend to answer it and know I cannot make it there. Not without my mind splintering into madness. At how unfair it all is. At how horrific and cruel this situation is. The *why* is not more important to me than *what now*, and I would rather focus what little hysterical energy I have on the latter.

To Leo, I only say, "I have no idea."

The prince runs an exasperated hand over his face, but he relents. "Okay, then . . . then next time, come find me. I can't promise anything, but I'll try to help you. However I can."

Echoes of all my past failures make me ground my heels into the tile of the path. "Just telling someone what's happening doesn't work. Especially not with you."

"Right. Proof. Something you couldn't possibly know. About me." He begins pacing, treading the broken glass until pulverized crystal marks his footsteps in a glittering circle, before stopping suddenly. "Next time, tell me you know about my oath, and I'll help you."

"Your what?"

His eyes go wide as saucers, made brighter in the reflected light of the gemstone constellations—and somehow more panicked. It's like his brain is only now catching up to what came out of his mouth. "Saints, this sounds so much more embarrassing out loud, but—oh, fuck it. Just tell me you know about the time I tried to . . . I tried to swear a blood oath to the saints' service."

It's all I can do to stifle my disbelieving burst of laughter. I don't know what's more amusing: the idea of young Leo as a pious little acolyte of the saints, like any other religious boy in Ivarea, or the idea of young Leo as a little baby heretic. Because if even *I* know that Ivareans are not supposed to mix blood into their worship, a Cardona prince absolutely should have known better than to make up a heretical ritual.

A secret that combines both embarrassment and, in the right hands, no small danger. . . . Oh, it's perfect. I could not have asked for anything better. It's ridiculous. Flies against everything I have ever known or seen of Leo the Lush in all this time. Which, again, is what makes it perfect. I dissolve into smothered giggles again at the thought.

"Oh, stop it. Hard as it may be to believe, I did have my share of higher ideals when I was a boy. I didn't *intend* to commit heresy." He straightens his back, as if to defend his painfully earnest younger self. "I was always drawn to San Pedro in particular. You know the story? No, of course not. Your people believe in magical woodland creatures, not saints."

"Magical woodland creatures?" This is not the most important part of what he's saying, but I can't help myself.

Leo shrugs at my indignation and pitches his voice to near reverence. "Nine hundred or so years ago, in the northeastern foothills beside the Palancan Sea, there lived a blacksmith named Pedro Balmes. One day, the youngest son of a minor Tarracán lord turned up and asked for a sword. Balmes asked why. The lord said that his father's holdings were under siege by invading Castarans, and his people were depending on him to return with hope. Balmes was moved by the young lord's story and promised him a sword that could beat back the siege in thirty days."

Or he just hated Castarans that much. "So he promised the lord a charmed sword."

"Without asking for payment in return."

So Balmes really hated Castarans that much.

"The young lord returned to the foothills thirty days later and found Balmes with the great sword run through his abdomen. The Castarans had found out what the escaped lord was up to, and had come to cut off the last hope for the Tarracán. But Balmes was still alive when the lord found him, if only just. He told the lord to take the sword and leave him. The charm had not yet been wrought, but if they were doomed to die, it was better to die with a weapon in hand.

"The lord was shaken but in no position to object; there would be no saving Balmes anyway. He pulled the sword from the smith's body—and watched, amazed, as the blade transformed from steel to bone."

My earlier grin of amusement wilts into a grimace. For two hundred years, Ivarea has tried to supplant Proensans'

belief in the fairies; whether they were magical woodland creatures or little gods who once walked the earth, for most of us
these days, they are little better than distant mythical figures.
Instead, we are supposed to recognize the saints, who were
human in origin but more powerful than any magicians the
Ivarean peninsula ever produced; we are supposed to worship
them as if their example can offer us any guidance, as if the
miracles they worked were for our sakes, too. I learned enough
about the saints and their worship to survive on the peninsula,
but even my mother could not stomach those lessons for long.

But what I believe doesn't matter. This is about Leo. And I
still find it hard to believe that the boy who would grow to be
known as Leo the Lush would have been a devotee of anything
but his own amusement. Let alone a medieval saint with such
a macabre story.

"When the young lord returned to his father's holdings, he
used the sword to fight through the Castaran siege and kill their
duke. In gratitude for the lord's bravery and the new saint's
miracle, the people made the young lord Duc de Bayirid." Leo
quiets. "His name was Alejandro Cardona."

Ah. Now I see why Leo was taken with this particular
story. I knew that the Cardonas had started out as the lords
of Bayirid who united Tarracuña under the dragon banner. I
knew that they took over the whole of the peninsula and beyond. But I didn't realize that the dynasty's very origin was
so . . . gory. Or that there was power greater than politicking
at the center of it.

Magic and miracles.

Whatever it really was, I suppose no one beats a Cardona for mythmaking.

Leo sighs, though I can't tell if it's wistful or mournful— for his saint, or for the sweet believer of a boy he'd been. The one whose confidence he's now betraying.

"One summer when I was a child, my father took us to Alejandro Cardona's castle in Bayirid. On our last night there, I snuck out of bed to see the espasa òssia, San Pedro's relic. I got there and . . . honestly, I don't know what possessed me to playact a whole ritual, like I was some acolyte or knight or . . . or hero. But I did. I was . . . lonely, and stupid, and filled with all these stories of saintly glory and my ancestor's legacy, and I wanted a story like that of my own. So I made one up. I pricked my finger and smeared a drop of my blood on the sword like it would matter and swore to do as San Pedro had. To always serve Ivarea, with my life, my magic, anything, even after my death, if I was called to do so." He pauses, almost contemplative. "Pathetic, isn't it?"

"A nine-year-old making a fake bargain of his death just to feel like he was part of his own family?" I exhale, suddenly and strangely unsteady on my feet. "Maybe a little."

"Then we're in agreement."

I don't feel like laughing anymore.

Once upon a time, Leo insisted to me that he was not an oath breaker. He only meant it for a dance then, but I shrink at the idea of a child holding himself to that kind of promise. Even if it was just pretend.

I have never felt anything like destiny pulling at the flattened corners of my mind, the placid beating of my heart. Despite my parents' ambitions, I was content enough with what I knew. What I already had.

I don't know if my destiny now is to save Ivarea or to get myself out of this endless cycle. I don't know what I'm supposed to do. But I think I should do something. Anything.

"So next time we meet . . ." He breaks off, trying and failing not to picture his other self. "Next time, tell me you know what I did. Though there's stiff competition, as I'm sure you can imagine, that stupid night of make-believe and heresy. . . . I mean, it'd ruin my image, at the *very* least."

I swallow a reluctant grin. "And we certainly can't have that, can we?"

He doesn't answer. "All you have to say is you know that I tried to swear an oath like San Pedro, and I'd know you could only have heard as much from me. Then I'd *have* to believe your story. I'd have to do anything you say."

His deepest secret. A fake blood oath. The surprisingly sentimental truth of his character.

He offered all of that to me. He barely even hesitated.

"I always swore I'd take that to my grave," he mutters.

I swallow a lump in my throat. "You already have."

When the explosions begin, he is with his family, and I with mine. Our deaths are as they should be.

As they will be again.

VII

CHAPTER ONE

I DIE FOUR TIMES BEFORE I GET LEO TO DO SOMETHING.

Once, he lets me talk until I'm hoarse from hysteria, only to furrow his brows and ask me to explain it again. We die before I can finish.

The next time, he doesn't even show up to the ball until the last half hour, and his furious mother holds him hostage near the dais. I can't catch his gaze before I burn with him, half a ballroom away.

The third time, I faint in his arms during a dance, and he carries me off to a separate room. When I tell him that I know about his fake blood oath, he panics at my spilling of a secret he doesn't remember revealing and flees, leaving me to deal with his concerned servants and my indignant mother. She can't believe I ruined this chance. As the walls of the Alcázar collapse all around us, I can't either.

The fourth time, I don't even make it to the palace.

But—that was then. It doesn't matter. And now I'm back in the Alcázar, exactly where I'm supposed to be. Which makes me feel unmoored. I don't know why. I should be used to this by now, right? To the feeling that everything depends on what I say next and how I say it. To the knowledge that nothing I say or do really matters.

Yet every time I come back, I keep making the choice to *try* to change the future.

That should mean something.

Shouldn't it?

About an hour before midnight, I take a swig of summer wine and demand a dance in restitution from Leo for forgetting his promise to me at the Tarrazas ball. This elicits little but an arched brow and a muttered "Restitution indeed."

The dance begins as it always does, with sweeping strings and resonant brass and percussion that worms its way through your bones. As I have several times before by now, I explain to Leo what awaits us at midnight and appeal to him to help, as he promised he would if I invoked his pretend childhood oath.

In response, he calls me a witch.

"I assure you, I'm no witch, señor."

"Then?"

"I'm cursed."

The music stops with a flourish and we break apart. But—the way he's looking at me. It's like we're still touching. Holding each other. Dancing as we await the end.

I should have guessed that mysterious flirting would be the quickest way to capture his attention, but it's definitely not the *safest* way. Still, I spring the trap. "I know you're a magician, too."

Without a care for the young ladies preening in hopes that he will take notice of them, Leo steps in my direction and pulls me until I'm nearly flush against his chest. Our faces are mere inches apart, but I don't mistake it for anything like interest. "Watch what you say next. There *are* limits to my magnanimity."

I should try not to blame him for not knowing, not remembering. After so many attempts to see if his past word means anything, however, my patience is wearing thin. "*You* told me that you're a magician. *You* told me about that dramatic fake oath you swore. You said that you'd help me."

"And why on earth would I do that?"

"Because, saintly oaths be damned, you *really* don't want to die tonight."

Despite all the frustration he's put me through, all the unfeeling cruelties, the self-pitying jibes, I am sure—in fact, I *know*—there is a small part of Leo that believes in something. Maybe not in repeated breaks in time. Maybe not in the blessing. Absolutely not in me.

But I suspect that something is honor.

"There will be an attack on the Alcázar. Bombs go off at midnight. I don't know where they are or who planned this. Everyone here is going to die. You too, Alteza. But don't despair," I add despairingly. "This will all happen again. I'll relive tonight after I die."

He doesn't speak for several measures of music. Smooth

strings and gently insistent percussion drown my heartbeat in swooning sound. His next words are little more than a breath. "What do we do next?"

Finally, a productive question. I exhale sharply. "Figure out how this is happening, ideally. Maybe keep everyone in the Alcázar from getting killed, if we have time."

"Nonsense," he shoots back, quite decisive for someone who has never been murdered before. "If the king and queen are the primary targets of this attack, our immediate priority needs to be getting them to safety. Once they're safe, we can figure out what to do next."

Over on the dais, his parents are preening, so blithe in the fact of their power that it makes me want to throw up. Gaspard might approve of that kind of reaction, but I doubt the prince would.

We belatedly stumble to an end of the dance just as applause rings out. Looking toward the bewigged maestro instead of at me, Leo murmurs, "Follow my lead." I barely have a chance to retort before he swivels and drops to one knee.

I should have punched him in the face again.

"*Anaïs Aubanel!*" He trumpets my name in a mockery of intimacy. "My dearest, *darling* Anaïs, we have hidden our love for too long."

An hour ago, he didn't remember that I existed.

"*Vuestra. Alteza. Real,*" I push out through gritted teeth, "*please* get up, *please* don't do this—"

"Oh no, mi amor. You've left me no other choice." He bestows upon me his most beatific smile. Soft sighs from across

136

the ballroom flutter like ribbons down the careful quiet. "Doña Anaïs of Massilie, make me the happiest man in Ivarea tonight. Will you grant me the honor of your hand in marriage?"

The Alcázar erupts in a different explosion than the one I've seen time and time again. Leo's eyes burn with determination, not love, but judging from the indignant shouts and yelps echoing all across the ballroom, no one can tell the difference. If I look anywhere but into those eyes, I'll catch sight of the roiling chaos of the court, or the storm surely rumbling around the royal dais. I would absolutely freeze in terror if Rey Rodrigo and Reina Isabel marched down to—

Oh. This is how he's going to attract his parents' attention. To get them to safety without making anyone wonder why they're disappearing.

Only a Cardona would think a public marriage proposal could save his kingdom.

Idiot.

I clasp my hands together and summon the tears I didn't already shed tonight. "Oh, mi infante, I thought you'd never ask." The court froths and seethes in silence, waiting for me to complete the scandalous tableau. Eyelids fluttering, hands shaking, I do so with relish. "Yes! Yes, my Leo, light of my life, I will marry you!"

The wave of shouts that break out as Infante Leopoldo leaps up and pulls me into his arms could ignite the fuses of more bombs than are embedded somewhere in the veins of this palace. It could destroy kingdoms itself.

But if I'm honest with myself, so could his kiss.

If Leo is trying to punish me, or if he's merely taking advantage of the blank check I've given him for bad taste, I don't know. All I know is that his hands are soft on either side of my face, and his lips are ruthless. This is no chaste gesture for court, to convince chaperones that their charges are doing only what they're supposed to and nothing more. This is something that the chandeliers of this room are not supposed to see. A kiss better suited for shadowed alcoves or hidden balconies, gardens limned with moonlight and heady with tropical fragrances. His tongue parts my lips so deftly I don't realize how far this has gone until it's too late, and my arms are wrapped around his neck as if he really could save me.

He breaks off the kiss as easily as he initiated it. He presses another to my temple and whispers, "Just until we're out of here." Then he calls out, like an actor performing for the cheap seats at the back of a rapt theater, "Let us share the good news with Vuestras Majestades."

Whispers follow us to the dais like shadows. Leo seems to feed off them, turning his head to allow the crowd to behold the glittering triumph writ across his brow. I can't imagine what Gaspard would think to see my skin this flushed, my lips so swollen because of a Cardona. And my parents . . .

Rey Rodrigo and Reina Isabel are both standing by the time we arrive at the foot of the dais. Leo whirls me in front of him. I've already been presented to the king and queen tonight, but they stare at me from on high as if they've never seen me before.

"Papá, allow me to present my fiancée."

The king's dark eyes slide to examine me. "Present her? My boy, I find myself shocked that you *know* her."

Reina Isabel's reedy voice carries the richness of her scorn for all the court to hear. "Let us speak in private." She is half-way across the dais before I can even look up, guards and ladies-in-waiting scrambling to help her down the steps. The king leaps down alongside her, sending a breathtakingly dirty glare in my direction now that my shenanigans have reduced him to my level.

Leo glances over his shoulder at me. "Shall we, darling?"

My tongue trips over the memory of his. "You don't have to enjoy this so much."

He chuckles. "Neither do you."

With that, we set out to follow his parents under Arco de León and out of the ballroom. The crowds fall silent. All I hear are the grunts of people being shoved and elbowed out of the way by what I suspect is a middle-aged Proensan woman try-ing to find her daughter before she's swallowed up by the grim machinery and genteel terror of the Ivarean royal family.

The doors of the ballroom slam shut behind me before Maman can fight her way to my side. Leo lets go of my hand so he can catch up with his parents. I draw up the rear, a hand at my hip, at the stolen blessed dagger I have concealed there. I don't think I'll need it with the king, but I also didn't think I'd end up temporarily betrothed to his youngest son, so who knows what dangers I have yet to live through.

The guards herd me into a salon smothered with en-chanted porcelain fixtures—porcelain vines climbing the walls, porcelain flowers blooming and closing and blooming again underfoot, porcelain bees flitting between rustling porcelain petals, framing frescoes of dancing nymphs and keen-eyed fauns in a porcelain forest on the walls. Littering the room are porcelain chairs backed with velvet cushions and marble end tables lined with porcelain animal paperweights that preen and bray. I stand as still as possible so I don't accidentally break anything.

Rey Rodrigo is not nearly so careful. As his younger son relays the true story of our false engagement and the impending attack, Rodrigo stares as if Leo is trying to convince him that the ocean is red.

"We owe it to our subjects to at least *investigate* this allegation."

"An allegation," repeats the king in a low, thunderous voice, "raised by your *fake fiancée*!"

"It got your attention, didn't it? Come now, Papá, you can't think I'm stupid enough to just propose like that." He stops and glances up at me. "No offense, Doña Anaïs."

Maybe if I die in this room, I'll wake up as a porcelain insect. That sounds vastly preferable to the inevitable alternative. But Leo reminded his parents that I exist, so I bunch my wide skirts in my hands and take a cautious step toward them. They're both sweating, which almost makes me feel a little better. I've known exactly how *mortal* they are for a while now, but it is something else entirely to see them as human.

"Vuestras Majestades, forgive us for the charade. But the Alcázar is under attack as we speak. We *must* get you to safety."

The king sweeps his fur-trimmed crimson mantle behind his broad shoulders but makes no move toward me. The cool expression on his craggy face makes it very clear that any goodwill he might have felt for the sweet little daughter of the count of Massilie has long since melted—in fact, it probably never existed. "Your concern for the safety of your king is admirable, my child. But there is no threat that could shake this palace."

"There are bombs planted somewhere in these walls. They go off at midnight. The ballroom will crash down on your subjects. Imagine the destruction that would cause. The chaos that would stretch past the hills if the king . . ." I swallow rising bile. "I understand your skepticism, but we *will* all die if we don't get out of here now."

Reina Isabel's smile is the kind that keeps the beholder at a careful distance. Unlike the son she vaguely resembles, her expression makes no promises of warmth. "I do not know what game you have devised for my son, Doña Anaïs—"

"This is not a game, señora. The prince just—*believes* me. I would suggest you do the same."

Outraged, Isabel is stalking toward me, foaming pearl crests and mirrored waves crashing into the open ocean of her silk gown, when the door to the porcelain salon opens. With a huff, the heir to the throne pokes his head inside.

Príncipe Felipe is taller and leaner than his brother, a thin reed of a man swathed in more rich fabrics than anyone in their right minds would choose in Marenca this time of year. His dark auburn curls seem plastered to his forehead with sweat.

"What is going on here? Everyone's losing their *minds* after that little stunt. Especially the Castarans."

How unsurprising. Even in a situation as farcical as this, Castarans are liable to riot at the prospect of a lowly Proensan girl becoming a princess instead of one of their own.

Rey Rodrigo scowls at his firstborn for the interruption. "Tell them this is all a misunderstanding. A diversion of your brother's."

Felipe nods solemnly, not sparing a glance for Leo. I can't imagine what he's thinking, but it cannot be good. The younger prince simmers with energy that he inexplicably refuses to expend by sticking up for himself. Or for me.

Before the Cardonas can toss more orders at each other, the bells marking half past eleven interrupt, urgent and unfeeling. I seize my chance in their wake. "Señores, the longer you stand here and do nothing, the closer you are to being murdered and throwing Ivarea into untold turmoil. Do what you will with me if I'm wrong, throw me in a cell in the Torres, but *please,* we have to leave *now!*"

They stare at me like I've sprouted porcelain beetle wings from my back after all.

But they don't move.

I can't believe it. The royal family of Ivarea, the custodians of our kingdom for the past four hundred years, would rather go dancing to their dooms than think for a second that the world they built could come crashing down around them.

Felipe furrows his brows. "Who the fuck are you again?"

"You are Aliénor and Eduard Aubanel's only daughter,

aren't you?" Reina Isabel's voice curls cordially enough around my parents' names. She resumes her march toward me, a tide slowly rolling toward the shore to pull in unsuspecting beach-goers. "I do not know if this is your silly mother's influence or my good-for-nothing son's, but you should really know better than to get roped into such unseemly schemes. Whatever they have promised you—riches, or status, or power—it is not worth this humiliation. And it will not come to pass anyway. We will make sure of it."

Felipe smirks after his mother's tirade before backing out of the salon. Once his elder child is gone, the king doesn't so much as spare a glance at me. Instead, he turns his attention to his youngest. "You see? Your very existence destabilizes everything I have worked for my *entire life*. I could never hand this kingdom over to a selfish child like you."

Somehow, I think that's not at all what Rey Rodrigo means. "You mean you'd never hand the kingdom over to a *magician* like Leo. Don't you, señor?"

The king's head snaps so quickly toward me he might break his neck. "*You told her?*"

"He didn't have to! I know the same way I know that you and everyone in that ballroom is going to be dead in less than half an hour."

Remarkably, it's not me that Rey Rodrigo focuses on after that admittedly gloomy pronouncement: it's his immobile son. "Are you trying to stage a *coup*, Leo?" he roars with more fury than I've ever seen. "Unseat me and remove your brother? Is that your game, boy?"

This is Leo's father? This is our king?

It's not exactly a surprise to me that the monarchs are not the best parents, but it is now abundantly clear that this is no ordinary parental neglect. The way Leo's pointedly impassive stare bores into the spot between his father's eyes tells me just how much I've missed.

"Wouldn't dream of it," he says in a monotone.

It's impossible to tell whether the king believes this answer. But he sighs heavily and presses a hand to his shining temple. "Whatever you do, son, you will *never* have a right to this kingdom except what *I* deign to give you. Remember that."

The prince bows his head. Righteous ire whistles through his voice. "I will, Papá."

I would rather walk over broken glass than break into this conversation again, but lucky for me, I *have* walked over broken glass. A ballroom full of it. And corpses. And blood. "*Vuestra Majestad,* I beg you, take Leopoldo and Felipe and Cla—"

"Utter my children's names again and you will find yourself relieved of your prophesying tongue, Doña Anaïs." The queen turns to her husband with the defiantly triumphant air of having squashed a persistent mosquito. "We'll say it was a drunken prank. Everyone will believe that. We shall handle the Castarans in the morning."

Rodrigo nods. "The Proensans will not be happy to have their prize taken away from them."

Isabel waves her hand dismissively. "It was never theirs to begin with."

Without a glance backward at their son and his nominal

betrothed, the king and queen of Ivarea sweep out of the salon. The guards and maids that were waiting in the hall troop back to the ballroom with their monarchs. The prince and I are as alone as we've ever been.

As alone, and as helpless.

I sag against the nearest wall. Painted porcelain leaves cut into my bare back. Across the salon, Leo stares at the path his parents took.

"I'm . . ." I swallow uncertainly. "I'm so sorry . . ."

"Don't. I am a prince, Doña Anaïs. No one to be pitied." He leans against an end table, the sheath of his sword clanging against the edge like a little bell. I've never seen him so utterly drained. And it's all my fault.

But this feeling, the guilt and shame and anger and frustration, won't last. Not for me, and absolutely not for him. The next time I see the prince, he will have no memory of this whole episode. Neither will his parents. The suspicion Rodrigo has for his son, though, that he might be capable of a coup . . . that is an old wound, some constant paranoia. *That* did not raise its head tonight just because of what I said.

"Papá is right, anyway," Leo remarks tonelessly. "My existence *is* a threat to his reign. And to Felipe's, one day."

"That's why they keep your magic a secret." Because he is a Cardona magician who has come of age at a time when Cardona magicians have not been in power for decades. Rodrigo and Felipe must be deathly terrified of him. Of what he could do, if he ever decided to make such a move. "But . . . Clara's a magician, too, and everyone knows about her."

"That's because a magician-prince is more difficult for an ordinary king to control. My father, to his credit, seems to have learned the trick of it." He snorts at his own fate. "But a magician-princess who poses no threat to the line of succession? Now, that can be very usefully deployed. As an ornamental political bargaining chip, among other things. For Saints' sake, he managed to get her a crown of her own."

After the events of this night, I didn't think anything could surprise me, but: "Paloma Nelleda was *right*? Clara *is* betrothed?"

Leo chuckles, the sound as dry as bone. "Papá's supposed to announce the news tonight. His precious, talented daughter and the crown prince of Rasenna. Sounds like he never makes it that far."

No, no he doesn't. But that doesn't make Clara's betrothal any less real.

There have been mutters for some time now about the Cardonas turning their eyes to neighboring Rasenna, farther east up the Palancan Sea. If Leo is right, Clara's marriage to its future king would mean greater resources, increased military support, and of course, a whole lot more reales pouring into Ivarea. It might not be conquest in the way of the illustrious Cardonas of the past, but it would still be an expansion of Ivarean power, with Rey Rodrigo at the helm.

All that glory, and all it takes is the happy sacrifice of a young woman.

If I have complained about my parents' pressures, it is surely nothing compared to what Clara has been through. I carry my family name on my shoulders. She carries the magic and life-blood of a kingdom that she would soon be cut off from. And all she will ever have to show for it is that lovely painted fan, the symbol of her husband-to-be's favor—a poor gift.

But we are girls, Infanta Clara and me. We are meant to sacrifice ourselves for glory.

"Papá won't let his magician children challenge *his* Ivarea anymore just by *existing* in his general vicinity." Leo seems rather lost in his own story of sacrifice. "Once Clara's married off, he'll get rid of me somehow, too. Hell, maybe he'll banish me to Massilie."

After this, I no longer wonder why the Leo who would volunteer his deepest, most embarrassing secrets to a stranger can so easily become Leopoldo the Lush, the stumbling pleasure-seeker that the court enjoys watching but has little other hope for.

Pressure that has been building up in my chest ever since the prince got down on one knee bursts out in the form of half-hysterical giggles. I can't smother my laughter even as he stares at me like I've lost my mind. "At least we don't—live long enough—for that!"

"Are you *sure* you're not a witch?"

That shuts me up.

"Because if you are, I have no choice but to commend you. In getting rid of me so effectively, you've accomplished in one night what my family has been trying to do to me all my life."

Startled, I can only bleat, "Oh, I'm . . . no one."

"Somehow, I doubt that very much." He pushes off from

147

the table and eyes the door balefully. Bracing himself before battle, he straightens out his shoulders and readjusts the hilt of his sword. "Nearly midnight. The fun's about to start."

I heave myself off the wall. "Let's not describe the mass murder of hundreds of people as *fun*."

We are built to sacrifice ourselves. But I'm the only one who *has* to. And judging by how he cocks his head to the side, by the terrible smirk playing on the lips that crushed mine just a little while ago, Leo is absolutely not contemplating anything as noble as sacrifice anymore.

"You're a Proensan in the Ivarean royal court. Surrounded by people who hate you, and your people, and your magic. Don't tell me there aren't people in there you're not *glad* to see die."

A voice is screaming at me to say something. *Anything.*

"Am I wrong, Anaïs?"

All I can do is shake my head no.

He smiles again, more grimly this time. Poor little prince. Distrusted by his cruel parents, who would cut him off from the world he holds so dear.

From the *crown* he holds so dear.

"Come on, then," he says to me, soft as the whisper of a blade. "Let's watch them burn."

VIII

CHAPTER ONE

AS I STARE INTO MY BEDROOM MIRROR, EVERYTHING SEEMS to be the way it should. I look the same as before. *Whole.* It's not a lie, but I know none of it is true.

Blink, and I see myself as I have been specifically made up to be: powder-smoothed complexion, rosy lips, beguiling brown eyes. Blink, and I see fragments of myself shattered by things that have not happened yet: an unnatural ghostly pallor, a mouth stained with blood and ash, eyes frozen and unseeing.

I can't begin to reconcile what I see with what I know. Not even my face is mine anymore.

I wish I had *something* to rely on. Something that I will continue to recognize as *me* and *mine* when I am, inevitably, even further removed from my past self.

As Béatrice slides the last few pins through my hair, my thoughts circle the abyss that Leo's voice cracked open in me when he said *Let's watch them burn.* I don't know what to believe about him, either. Or about the royal family. And I haven't the faintest idea where to uncover the truth.

"Does Rey Rodrigo seem like a good king to you?"

We are close, Béatrice and I, but not share-politically-charged-gossip-about-the-royal-family close. Nonetheless, she doesn't completely balk at the question. I delude myself into thinking she can recognize the desperation behind it. "The kings of legend," she says slowly, "were always fair, and just, and brave."

It's all I can do to stifle my scoff. "What if there were a magician on the throne? Do you think we'd be better off with some legendary magician-kings again?"

"Not all legends are worth bringing to life, Mademoiselle." Béatrice touches her left thumb to the tip of each finger. This is an old gesture among our people, recalling the cuts those with the blessing must make to use our magic. "Let us hope that the next person who sits on the throne cannot wield that kind of power."

For some reason, I have a feeling that there's more she isn't saying. Such as, *cannot wield that kind of power against us.*

Which would be a fair concern. A thought that should put to rest any other questions about the throne of Ivarea.

But for several deaths now, I have not been able to think about anything else.

I've spent all this time trying to warn the Cardonas about what's to come at midnight. But disturbing as his comments were by the end, maybe Leo had a point. Why *should* I keep trying to save the royal family when they clearly don't care to listen to me? Why should I keep killing myself for them if they can't save themselves, let alone their subjects?

There *are* players in this night other than the Cardonas, after all. Like the actual people behind this attack. I can't do anything more if I don't find out who they are, who their connection inside the Alcázar is, and how exactly they manage to pull this off.

If nothing else, at least I have a feeling that I know what they want.

"What if there was no throne at all?"

Béatrice blinks. Her eyes are a clear, sweet brown, and freckles dust her nose as they do mine. We aren't so different, the two of us.

"Now, *that*," she says carefully, "is a story I have not heard before."

I meet her eyes in the mirror as she stabs one final pin through my hair. "Would you like to?"

Tonight, I have to do what I've been unable to since I last found myself at the firing end of a rifle: find the palace intruders and figure out who they are. Until then, I have to avoid Leo and everyone else at the ball at all costs. It's not as if anyone in the ballroom actually knows anything that will be of any use to me. I know that all too well.

Or do I?

Sure, the grandes and noble guests are useless, but they're

not the only people in the palace. The *really* important people are everywhere, made invisible by the fact of their positions: bringing wine to drunken provincial counts, standing at attention behind feast tables to clear still-full plates. Servants make places like the Alcázar work. They know everything.

And if they don't know, they can find out.

That's what I have to do. Become a maid, and I'll be able to leave the ballroom and investigate the attackers in peace.

It's very possible that running around the Alcázar as a royal servant wouldn't keep me alive any longer than running around as the daughter of a count would, but it's worth a shot. Frankly, I'm just pleased to have come up with a scheme that actually makes use of a cloth-magic-imbued blessed dagger. If I could tell Papa about it, I think he'd be thrilled, too.

Left to my own devices, I have to time my escape from the ballroom carefully. The dancing is off to a fabulous start; lords storm the floor with bejeweled ladies hanging on their arms, and the music is as vibrant and infectious as ever. The blessed dagger hums in its sheath, as if it knows it's about to be called upon for its extraordinary gift. I have nearly made it past the lions guarding the western archway when I hear someone calling my name.

Gloved hands behind her back, a small smile on her berry-painted lips, Jacinthe Vieillard sidles up to me—for the first time that I've seen, without a troop of hangers-on. "The dancing is over *there,* you know."

Maybe I should have roped Gaspard into helping me again.

To serve as a human shield against people like Jacinthe. "Yes, I know. I just, uh, need some air. If you'll—"

"Oh! Well, that's not a bad idea." The pearl dust slathered on the tops of her cheekbones glimmers in the chandelier light as she nods. "Won't you join me for a little walk, Anaïs? I heard there's a garden somewhere in the palace with every single variety of bluebell on the peninsula."

Oh *no*. It's as I told Gaspard: once you've seen one garden in the Alcázar, you've seen them all. And I very much doubt exploring a fastidiously designed Marenca garden with *Jacinthe Vieillard* is going to help me.

Which begs the question: If Jacinthe Vieillard has the upper echelons of the court practically eating out of her hands, why would she be willing to waste any more than a cutting remark on me?

"That sounds lovely, and I would just *love* your company," I say, "but I'd like to—I need to be alone for a moment."

In truth, of course, I've *never* loved Jacinthe's company, nor she mine. But now that she's being rejected, she digs her heels in. "Why, is everything all right?"

Now that I've inadvertently intrigued her, she will hold me hostage right here, and I'll never be able to search for the intruders. Unless I give her something else to believe.

No one believes me when I tell the truth. Which means it's time to simply lie.

"Honestly . . . no." My eyes dart across the ballroom in barely restrained panic. "I've been keeping a secret."

"Aren't we all."

I grab her hand and drag her through the other side of the arch, deeper into the corridor. The music is just a hair quieter this far from the orchestra, but we are not too removed from the action as to draw attention from the middle-aged women who think the worst thing that can happen at the ball is their young charges disappearing with each other into the dark.

Full of faux humility, I sigh deeply. "I might have . . . spent a night with the prince. And now he won't leave me alone."

"The prince? You don't mean . . . *Infante Leopoldo?*"

Sadly, I'm too busy floating outside of my own body to enjoy the sight of Jacinthe Vieillard speechless. I scramble to think back to some other event from earlier this season, a scaffold on which to build out my lie. "Remember . . . remember that premiere we all went to, three . . . no, four weeks ago? *The Thief of Varillo?* I saw Infanta Clara powdering her nose in the salon. We started chatting and became fast friends. During intermission, she introduced me to her brother, and . . ." The memory of him leaning against the bar of the Marenca Opera House that night, a complicated-looking drink in his hand as he scanned the season's new arrivals, makes me lose my train of thought. But I realize my starry-eyed dreaminess might help sell the story, so I lean into it. "He was so handsome, and witty, and . . . charming, and he and I . . . we never made it back to our seats."

Her eyebrows shoot up into her forehead.

I sink against the wall. "It's *bad*, Jacinthe."

At length, she sighs and leans against the wall next to me. She manages to compose herself as if she'd been directed by a portrait artist, one of the masters from the early days of Cardona reign. A splash of color artfully draped against intricately wrought tile and stonework. I, on the other hand, feel like a bloodied slug, crumpled against the walls of a palace that wants nothing to do with me.

"He was your first?" She smirks as I splutter. There seems to be less malice than usual in the gesture. "Brava, Doña Anaïs, brava. I had no idea you were so strategically inclined."

I shake my head hard enough to send some of my hairpins flying across the open hall. "It was *nothing* like that."

"Would it be so terrible if it were?"

"It was a moment of weakness. That I *immediately* regretted." Like how I immediately regret this. "And now he won't leave me alone."

The corners of her mouth tug downward. "I've never even seen him speak with you."

"Yes, well, he can be very good at hiding his true self when he wants to."

Jacinthe looks away for the first time since she cornered me and sighs, which tells me I'm not wrong about the prince.

"If he catches me again, I don't know what will happen," I continue. "I need to get out of here."

She glances to her left, down the corridor that will eventually lead to Night's Pavilion, and farther beyond that, into the western wing where the abandoned tower stands like a thoroughly useless sentinel. I can still make it there before the intruders arrive, if I hurry.

"If this story gets out," says Jacinthe, "you'd be ruined."

For less than an hour, but: "Yes."

"I imagine even your Don Gaspard might not be too pleased."

I blush despite myself. "Gaspard isn't *mine*, and even if he were—it was a *mistake*. Haven't you ever made a mistake?"

Suddenly she narrows her eyes, as deep and flat a color as jet beads. "Do you think this is a place where you can afford to simply *make mistakes*?"

I know I made up this story just to get rid of Jacinthe, but I did not expect her to express any concern for me or my life choices. Astonished, I stammer, "I—I only mean—"

"How could you have let yourself get carried away by something as base as passion? They are the Cardonas, and you are a Proensan. You can't afford to fuck up like this. *I* can barely afford it, and my father is the richest man in Ivarea."

Jacinthe's ancestors were merchants who crossed the Palancan Sea from Jazar, a country on the southern coast, to settle in what is now Galvain Province. Rey Rodrigo's father finally made Jacinthe's grandfather a baron in recognition of the riches that the powerful merchant and his family had amassed since they, too, were absorbed into Ivarea. I always figured the Vieillards' truly staggering wealth made up for their lower courtly rank—but perhaps that's exactly the sort of thing Jacinthe and her family would want people like me to assume. It's *hard* to ingratiate yourself into the highest echelons of Ivarean society, especially in the capital, if your place there is not already seen as a given. Because of where your family hails from, or your rank, or your magic.

No amount of money can buy true belonging. That's been very clear to me, especially since I came to Marenca. But I suspect Jacinthe knows it even more acutely.

"People like the Cardonas exist to prey upon your worst instincts, Anaïs. You can't give them ammunition. And if somehow you do, then you can't always expect to fix it by yourself. You may need someone else to pull you out of the range of fire."

Her expression softens from the censure of moments ago. I've not seen anything of her that even *approaches* tenderness before— except for that time, while Clara was bringing me to meet her brother, when Jacinthe and Marguerite embraced in the ballroom. That did not appear to be the weaponized gesture of warring favorites, or the expression of solidarity between mere friends.

Before I can dare ask whether she means Marguerite, Jacinthe exhales sharply. "But the world isn't going to end because you slept with a prince."

No, it's going to end whether I slept with one or not.

Which, again, I didn't. Wouldn't. Couldn't.

"Leo used you," she goes on, "and you wanted him to. That's fine. It's just how it works sometimes. The important thing now is that you don't let that night of passion, your mistake, whatever it was, be the end of the story. If you're smart, you'll figure out how to use him, too. For whatever it is that you really want."

I bite the inside of my cheek, considering. "I . . . I thought you were close with the royal family."

"Precisely why I'm telling you this."

Silence falls on us like a blanket, stifling in the heat. I swallow, but my mouth is dry. I wonder what terrible things she's seen or experienced at the palace, at the right hand of royalty, that would make her say something like this to me. How she really feels to be so closely tied to the most powerful people in the world and still be apart from them in some seemingly unimpeachable fashion. To not be the favorite. To still be different.

Mysterious warnings aside, this is still the same Jacinthe I've known for ages. The same Jacinthe who's taken every opportunity to poke fun at me. I can't help but ask, "Are you . . . will you tell anyone about Leo and me?" and find myself caring about her answer.

She only grimaces. "You're hardly the first person to succumb to one of them."

Just as I peel myself from the wall, Jacinthe raises her head. "One day, I will ask you for more details. And you're going to give them to me."

I would be more bothered by the almost threat if *one day* ever came. "So you can use me, too?"

She shrugs and averts her gaze. Perhaps to hide her wan little smirk. "Darling Anaïs, what else are friends for?" She spins away and heads back into the ballroom. She is not about to let anyone forget that she belongs there. Especially, I realize now, the Cardonas.

At last I flee down the corridor, following its twists and turns with no real sense of where I'm going, eventually slipping into another unused salon. I sink onto a slightly dusty but very comfortable sofa along the edge of the room and place the sharp edge of the emerald dagger on my lap. With a hand balanced on the hilt, I picture the maids and servants that have floated about the ballroom, their basquiña skirts sashaying unobtrusively along the tiled floors.

It takes no small power to manage a transfiguration like this, but, blessed with magic and watered in my family's blood, the dagger is not nearly as limited in its energy stores as I am. By the time I've finally turned my scarlet gown into a proper maid's uniform—olive overdress, cream apron, and a matching yarn hairnet—I'm no more tired than before.

So the blessing isn't completely *useless all the time,* I muse, winding my way through the western wing of the Alcázar complex. *Just* mostly *useless.*

I've nearly rounded the next corner when I notice a pair of shabbily dressed men tiptoeing along the corridor bisecting this one. I flatten myself against the inside of a decorative arch before they can spot my shadow. As they continue in silence, I stalk behind them, following the flickering flames of their candles. It's criminally easy to skulk when I'm not dragging fifteen pounds of gown along for the ride.

We approach a courtyard with a bronze fountain at its center depicting a winged horse. Water spurts from its mouth as its enchanted wings beat at the still summer air. I stare at it a moment too long from the shadows, transfixed by the effortless, abundant magic in Ivarea, which makes no demands of the people who would call on it, until suddenly the feathered wings become indistinct masses in my vision: the men I was following extinguished their candles. I see why a beat too late.

There are four others already here.

It's begun.

"The guards?" one of them calls to the new arrivals. His hand rests casually on the strap of the rifle slung over his back.

One of the men I was following responds, "Taken care of."

Just as the bells marking thirty minutes to midnight begin to chime, the first man steps out from the fountain's shadow. I can't see his features all that clearly, but he looks much like the others, dressed unobtrusively in a worn brown coat that dwarfs his tall, lanky frame. "Half an hour to go, my fellow citizens. Half an hour until our glory is realized."

His hoarse voice slithers against the columns of the courtyard, spreading like vines around their heads. Each pair of eyes burns as they gaze upon him, heedless of the marvelous enchantment at work behind and around them. This must be their leader.

He addresses the group members individually without referring to their names, calling each one "my friend" or "fellow citizen," as he quickly runs through their duties over the next few hours. Once the bombs have gone off, some will seal the ballroom doors to allow their fellows to finish off the guests that survived. Still others will secure the main entrances into the Alcázar.

I'm no military strategist, but I know you can't hold a fortress like the Alcázar Real with six men. Even if you manage to wipe out most of the people inside with a bomb blast. And if this group is comfortable flaunting their impossible presence and their already-murderous actions practically in the open, who knows what else lurks in the rest of this place.

Maybe one day—one more iteration of this night—I *will* know what else is out there.

Until then, I will count myself lucky to have heard the voice of their ringleader. Its coarse texture belies wicked intent, genteel cruelty. He switches between Ivarea's two official languages, Castaran and Galvaise, more smoothly than I can, and with no obvious accent. Does that mean he's one of the educated rabble-rousers Paloma talked about? Or is there some other possibility I'm not seeing yet?

To my right, another pair of men appear from the shadows of the palace corridors. At the sound of new footsteps, I hurl myself against the wall again, out of the reach of moonlight—

It's not enough.

I barely have time to cry out before one of them wrenches my arm and drags me out into the courtyard. The rest fall abruptly silent.

The main conspirator peers down at me, his blond hair shining in the dark. "What do we have here?" he sneers in Castaran.

I am still dressed as a maid in the Alcázar Real de Marenca, so I keep staring at his feet and say nothing, until someone kicks me and I collapse flat on the ground at the base of the fountain.

"Please, señores, I mean—I didn't mean . . ."

I break off my frantic half-formed pleading when the leader offers me his hand.

"Ignore them," he says. "There's nothing to fear, my Pro-ensan friend."

I wouldn't trust that voice if it told me the sky is blue. But I have nothing to lose. I look up into his face for the first time.

Wait.

This is not the first time.

I've seen this man. I've spoken to him. He and his friends stalked Gaspard and me from the tower through the corridors. He cornered us and asked me if I had found what I was looking for.

Then he shot me. Without doubt. Without remorse.

There are some people who could look exactly like a hundred others and somehow still stand out. He seemed like one of them, even when he was one of three strangers in that empty room, a gun slung over his shoulder. I thought his eyes were green then, but I can't make out their shade in the moonlight.

He pockets his hand in his coat when he realizes that I won't take it. "What could you be doing so far from home?"

The only thing to do is spin a lie that goes with the uniform as well as the accent I can't disguise. "I—I work here. I heard a noise, and . . ." I let fear well in my eyes, set my voice trembling, chin wobbling. Nothing is as terrifying to men as a young woman in panic. "I didn't hear anything, señores, I swear on my life."

"Señor? I am just a citizen of this great country. No more and no less." He crouches down, suddenly at my eye level. "Just like you."

This close, there's no mistaking the murky green color of his eyes, the broken line of his nose. There even appears to be bruising somewhere along his cleft jaw. He may not do much manual labor, but he has not had an easy time of it.

"What is your name, fellow citizen?"

"B-Béatrice." I think of the real Béatrice, of what she and Petronilla and the rest of the servants would be doing half an hour before midnight while the family they serve is about to fight for its future in a royal ballroom. I could have asked her this afternoon. She wouldn't have been able to answer me.

"I understand how much of a shock this will seem, but everything you heard tonight is for *your* sake."

Like hell is any of this for my sake. I can't swallow down my fury anymore. "You mean blowing up the Alcázar."

His men let out low hoots and hollers, too assured of their impending triumph to be afraid of a little Proensan maid at the feet of their leader.

He already killed me once for talking back to him. Since I don't have to hope to make it out of this alive, I might as well bait him into giving up some information, some motivation for all this, maybe even his identity. I push myself up to my knees and stare into his face, memorizing his features before I can lose them again. "I don't see how killing all those grandes would help anyone but you."

He cocks his head, the enchanted horse's wings half

shadowing his face. His eyes glitter with amusement, shiny and hard as beetle wings. "Tell me, Citoyen Béatrice. What has the royal family ever done for you?"

"Th-they did give me a job. . . ."

His hand snakes forward, as if to pull me up to my feet, but he grabs for my throat instead, and suddenly I can't breathe at all. In the middle of my violent coughing frenzy, I realize that it's not his grip that's choking me—it's his hold on my necklace. He squeezes the chain right above the opal locket, cutting off my air supply as casually as he would have smiled, and clasps its bloody depths in his palm like a gaping wound.

"What do we have here, my fellow citoyens?"

I should have remembered to lose the valuable jewelry.

The leader smiles, his blond ponytail preternaturally still at his shoulder. "A gift from your lover?" With his free hand, he flicks open the locket, digging into the casing as easily as he could my skin. "One smart enough not to leave a trace of his identity, it seems."

My eyes swim with tears. Then the pressure at my throat disappears and I'm shoved back to the ground. I cough and splutter at the boots of the men crowding around me. One of them crouches to leer at me from under his cocked hat. "He must not be able to keep his hands off you," he coos.

"Nothing like—no, please—"

The leader clicks his tongue at his compatriot. "Believe me, I am the last man to judge a woman for her dealings with high-born men. It is a dangerous game you have no choice but to play. Is that not so, Citoyen Béatrice?"

Last man to judge a woman. I wish I had the breath to laugh.

"Now, why do you feel you must indulge the attentions of the rich and powerful you serve? Why is it incumbent on us to give our bodies, our minds, our lives, our magics, to a kingdom that has done nothing to earn them? To a kingdom that lines its coffers with our earnings and fleshes out its armies with our brothers, without a care for us, the citoyens who make possible its very kingship? *Why must we submit?*"

My hand flies to massage my neck free of the marks of the chain. "Y-you're going to kill hundreds of people. Grandes and nobles and royals, yes, but also guards and serving boys and maids like—" I cannot dare say *like me.* "Innocents who are only trying to provide for their families. To *survive.* Like you."

The men around us stamp their feet, seemingly more riled with anticipation than concerned at all about what I said. Then the leader steps forward. The hard glimmer of his green eyes melts, burning with a fire only he can feel.

"The price of revolution is dear, Citoyen Béatrice. It must be, or it would not be revolution. But I promise, it will all be worth it in the end. For all of us."

He flips his rifle around and trains the long barrel on me.

"Even for you."

If only he knew that there is no end.

If only he knew there never will be.

IX

CHAPTER ONE

IT WOULD BE EASY TO SINK INTO DESPAIR. TO WANDER LIST-lessly through the world. To let it wash over me and do nothing to stop it from sliding toward that foretold end, over and over again.

God, it would be easy.

All it takes is one glance at the Alcázar, proud and ancient and lazy on the hills above the river, to snap me out of it.

This isn't about me. Not when so many people depend on dawn breaking over a kingdom that's still *whole,* if nothing else. Whatever the revolutionaries want, whatever that leader of theirs aspires to, I'm pretty sure that inaugurating a new era in the blood of a thousand innocents is not a good way to achieve it.

Still, I need to know: Who was he? Who helped him and his followers get into the Alcázar?

There can't be too many people in Ivarea that have followings like his. He personally killed me twice, for God's sake—once in the courtyard, and before, when I was hiding out with . . .

Gaspard.

Technically, yes, he already failed to recognize the man who chased us down from the abandoned west wing tower. But he is the only person I know who understands Ivarean politics that would also answer my questions without needing to be cajoled or flirted with first. Leo or Clara might eventually let slip some ideas, but looking at the Cardonas even now stirs acute anguish in my chest.

In the aftermath of the interminable feast, I sidestep into Gaspard's path as he stalks away from his anxious-looking parents. "Everything okay out there, Plamondon?"

"You have met my father, haven't you?"

In sympathy, I offer Gaspard my hand and we make our way out of the ballroom. He's too put out by whatever grievances he has with his parents to complain about me dragging him into yet another courtyard, this one bordered with scarlet bougainvillea arches that curl like script and stretch to the night sky. It's as if he, too, wants to put as much distance between himself and the ballroom as possible.

I can hardly blame him for that.

Inside, this courtyard contains lawn furniture made wholly of flowers. Gingerly I perch myself on a bench of pomegranate blossoms that sigh and bend with my weight. Gaspard doesn't seem as eager to test its magic. I clear my throat before he can drift away. "What was it your father said?"

"Let me think . . ." He starts to pace. "Ah yes. Something

along the lines of, *Draw the name of your future bride out of a hat by morning if you must, but if you have not chosen correctly, you will never earn my respect as a man and my heir.*"

In his way, Marquise Fabian Plamondon is as demanding a parent as my mother, albeit less prone to public histrionics. After his marriage to an elegant Landaulan noblewoman forged an unexpected alliance between two marginalized provinces, it seems Gaspard's father now expects his son to do him one better.

"Who does he have in mind for you?"

Light from enchanted poppy torches throws flickering shadows over Gaspard's face as he paces. "I believe the name *Paloma Nelleda* came up once or twice."

"What? Paloma Nelleda is *awful*. You have no idea how awful." How was it she so blithely described Gaspard all those deaths ago? *Half-Landaulan, unfortunately.*

"Her grandfather," he adds with fake cheer, "is the duke of Cadeira."

"So?"

"*So?* My father thinks I could do a lot worse than that for a bride."

"If you're chasing beauty or fortune or status, yes, but—"

"What else is there?" he retorts bitterly.

"I very much hope that you would not debase yourself for that arrogant Castaran *bitch*."

Only now does he halt his anxious marching up and down the courtyard. "I've never heard you talk like that."

The truth of it strikes me like a scythe across the middle.

"It's just that these people, they're so . . . They treat *me* like the dust on their shoes to my face, and they treat *you* like shit when your back is turned, and behind closed doors they just attack each other—and the idea that *this* is the place we're sacrificing our homes and names for, *these* are the kind of people we have to become, it just—it's *eating* at me. Why do we have to contort ourselves to fit into a terrible, broken world that doesn't even want us here? Why do we have to sub—?"

Oh. Oh my God.

I clap a hand to my mouth. Warmth floods my cheeks. The rush of blood drowns out the clamor and hiss of the words I barely stopped myself from repeating.

How could I let a man who happily killed me twice—who would have killed Gaspard if I wasn't murdered first—who has engineered the mass murder of innocents time and time again—worm his way into my head with just one speech?

Gaspard takes me by the shoulders. "Anaïs, are you . . . What happened?"

There's a hint of a breeze in the air that should help calm my nerves, but this whole night, the journey of my deaths and resurrections, feels as thin and flammable as paper. My tongue is tied in knots I cannot begin to tease out. The thread of linear time has folded and woven and tangled with itself far more than anyone should ever be able to see.

But for some incomprehensible reason, it's *all* I ever see.

"By any chance, do you know of a revolutionary with a passionate following determined to murder the royal family?"

"What in the f—."

I heave a shuddering sigh. "Can I tell you a story?"

He looks as though he wants to protest. Or possibly be sick. Instead, he takes a place on the bench, and I begin.

Again.

Gaspard's expression droops more and more as I speak. By the time I'm finished, he seems to be drooping, too.

"I know—Gaspard, believe me, I *know* how this all sounds, but whatever's happening to me is not the important thing."

He makes a faint, strangled sound. "You mean, the most important thing is something *other* than how in the hell you're reliving the same night over and over again?"

I flinch. The trauma of this nightmare is like black powder under my skin, liable to explode at the slightest, most horrific trigger; it needles at my brain, drives my heart faster and louder than it should be capable of beating. I shut my eyes against it, yet still it comes for me in that abject darkness.

But I can't succumb to that fear right now. There's no use dwelling on things I can't change.

"It's not." I take a deep breath and finally open my eyes. "The man I saw. Figuring out who's behind this attack and how they do it. *That's* what matters. It's all going to happen tonight, and keep happening, so if we're ever going to stop it—"

"*We?*"

I sigh. "This is not the first time I've asked for your help."

His shoulders roll inward until he's almost doubled over.

The sight of him brought so low would break my heart if I had not already died for him. I grab his limp arm and give it an urgent shake. "You go to the University of Lutesse. Which infamously has a not-insignificant amount of radical activity." Of course, I only know this because of Marguerite's story about the arrested students and their scandalous pamphlets, but Gaspard doesn't need to know my source. "If their leader is some urban intellectual type, you *must* have some inkling of who it could be."

"I . . . Anaïs, I appreciate your trust with all this, but I—frankly, I don't know the first place to begin." His expression goes strangely opaque, as if he's shutting himself down in front of me. As if to keep something of himself from slipping out. As if to keep me from recognizing it, whatever it is.

What is it?

All the things he's ever said to me across our lives and deaths start to bleed together, turning into a fractured whine in my head. I remember his simmering frustration with the Cardona dynasty. I remember the fervor in his eyes when he spoke of the discontent he's seen in Lutesse. I remember now, with the sharpness of a freshly ground lens trained on a once-distant object, the way he addressed the revolutionary leader when he cornered us after the tower. I thought he just didn't know what to say to a man who was definitely not going to let us leave that room alive.

But what if it was more than that? The whole fatal exchange, it felt so terribly genteel . . . as though Gaspard was speaking to a peer here at the ball. To someone he knew. And didn't Gaspard say he'd try to get that man what he wanted? How would he have known what that might be?

"Don't you?"

He startles, sitting straight up on the pomegranate blossom bench. "What's that mean?"

The words refuse to come together even on my tongue. My question comes out slow and disjointed as a result. "I mean, are you quite sure you don't know more than you're letting on?"

"About what?"

"We aren't children anymore, you know. I'm not some sheltered little girl." I swallow a sour breath, and hope it will embitter my heart as well, so I can get through this. So I can get to the truth. "I understand you have principles. I understand that Rey Rodrigo will run us all into the ground one day. I understand that things right now are horrible, but—*you* have to understand *me*, too. Just . . . tell me what you know."

He leaps up, ruddy-faced and indignant. "You really think *I* know anything about your attack? What, you think I'm part of it somehow?"

It's even more ridiculous coming from his mouth than it is in my head. But there's nothing I can do to dislodge it. I wonder if the idea was planted in me so many deaths ago that I can't even trace the moment. Now it's sprouted, and its unfolding is driving me mad.

"You've heard those radicals in Lutesse, haven't you? You certainly seem to agree with them. You've been grousing about this place and everything it represents since the day you arrived. The last time you and I ran into that man, it was like you recognized him. You understood what he wanted and were willing to give it to him." Behind my lips, my teeth seem to chatter. Never have they felt so much like exposed bone. "I don't know what you know or what you might have told him, but please, Gaspard . . . If you've ever thought kindly of our friendship, please tell me what's going on. Just put me out of my misery."

He gapes at me like a fish. "I'm not a conspirator, or a spy, or— *Fuck!* I couldn't." He begins to pace in agitation again, hands twisted in the blossom-perfumed air. "I have certain beliefs, which apparently doesn't come as a surprise to you, but premeditated mass murder? You? My parents? I . . . *no*, Anaïs."

God. Oh God. Not again.

First I accused Leo of masterminding the attack on a whim. Now I'm interrogating Gaspard.

I'm a fool.

A desperate, useless fool.

I slip off the bench, and my knees land on the stone of the courtyard floor with a dull thud. I heave low, throat-scraping sobs right there, the tears hot and angry down my ever-painted cheeks. Gaspard lowers himself to the floor with me, though he settles in an uncomfortable crouch, whereas now I'm half sprawled out on the ground, giant gown and all.

"I'm sorry," he whispers. "I don't know what I said or did to make you think this way, but I have *nothing* to do with whatever happens here. I'm . . . You tell me. I'm going to be killed at midnight, too, aren't I?"

Oh no. Oh God.

Gaspard shifts from his crouch to sit with me, leaning back and propping himself up with his arms. "The truth is, I have no idea who could pull off an attack like this. I don't know who the radicals in the capital are. What they want, how they're organized, nothing." He sighs, eyes raking over the floral furniture, the way each rose lounge chair and wrought-vine table seems to bloom and reshape itself with every press of wind, without really seeing it. "I mean, back in Lutesse, there was . . . I knew of one man who had a little following of *citizens,* but I don't know if there's anyone else like that here, or—"

My memory snags against his words. I push myself upright. "Did he call them *citoyens?*"

"What?"

"That man you just mentioned. In Lutesse. Did he call his followers *citoyens?*"

Gaspard's brows furrow. "Why would you ask me that?"

"Because the man who just murdered me in the courtyard kept calling me that."

Gaspard leans forward, but for the first time since I accused him of conspiracy, he can't look me quite in the eye. "It can't be," he mutters to himself. "It's impossible."

Oh my God. So I was *right.* "You *do* know who he is! You did recognize him that time!"

He buries his head in his hands. "Fine," he mutters through the lattice of his fingers, exasperated. "If I saw him head-on in some previous time, I would have recognized him. I can only assume I was too busy keeping him from killing us both to introduce you properly. But it couldn't really be him."

"Why not?"

He takes a deep breath and lets his hands fall away. "Because that's Mathieu Faucher."

My head spins, and it seems like a small mercy that my body doesn't sway with it. I *do* know that name. Though I can't say where I know it from. Papa must have mentioned it. Or maybe I read it in the papers. Wherever it was that I learned Mathieu Faucher's name, though, I know why.

He's been in a cell in the Torres de Paz for a year. And all of Ivarea knows that once you're sent to the Torres, odds are you're never getting out again.

Every Ivarean child grows up with the threat of the towers if they don't go to bed on time or if they misbehave in front of their elders. I've seen it once or twice since I've come to the capital: a fortress dating back to the Landaulan era, defending the eastern gate into the city. The Cardonas rebuilt the exterior to resemble an illustrated storybook castle more than a prison, complete with a renowned garden on the grounds. I very much doubt the irony is lost on anyone, since it's infamously the closest-guarded and most heavily warded prison in the kingdom.

"You're sure?"

Gaspard nods. "I . . . I saw him a few times, once he moved to Lutesse and tried to establish himself as a barrister. He frequented a coffeehouse I'd go to when I needed a break from those snot-nosed Galvaise students. He seemed like just another unemployed struggling hothead to me at first. But over a few weeks, I noticed more and more people gravitating toward him, listening to him talk. Soon the place became his territory. You couldn't even hear yourself think when his citoyen crowds showed up."

"And . . ." The words burn on my tongue. "And what would he talk about?"

"Certainly not how to establish a legal practice." He hums tunelessly. "More like, why is it that we give the royal family and their grandes power when they've made sure we can never rise above our station, how might we build a more equitable system, do we need a system at all. Seizing power from grandes who can't see past their estates, and kings who can't even save themselves, and giving it to the *people*. I've heard whispers along those lines from others before, but when he said it, it sounded righteous, not just aggrieved. That was . . . attractive, I admit. *He* was attractive." A staccato sigh. "The more I heard him, the more I wanted to get closer to him. I wanted to understand. I wanted to—hell, I wanted to help him, if I could. But once he found out that Safiya and Fabian Plamondon's son was hanging around like a sad, rebellious puppy, he made it very clear that I'd never be welcomed among his citoyens. So I stopped seeking him out. Rededicated myself to my studies. Moved on. I hadn't heard of him or his people since the police sent him to the towers last year. Some trumped-up treason or sedition charge, I think. And *just to be clear,*" he adds, pinching the bridge of his nose, "Faucher never said we should *kill* anyone. Not even the king. Or me, for that matter."

Perhaps not. Yet I can only imagine, when Faucher cornered us in the palace, that Gaspard's decision centered on not reminding Faucher of their acquaintance in Lutesse. Perhaps he realized then that there was no way Faucher would leave us alive.

But I can't ask Gaspard now what he was thinking then. I couldn't bring that Gaspard back, even if I tried. I can only look at the one I have now.

The one I'm about to lose.

"You fancied the man who murdered you."

I can sense that he wants to huff in indignation, but recognizing the precarity of this moment, he only exhales again, slower, more mournful. "I fancied a man who had ideals who was later sent to prison. We don't know any more than that."

He's right, technically. "Well, if it is Faucher who shows up here before midnight, then he must have escaped the Torres."

"Which is impossible."

"Say he managed it anyway. If Rey Rodrigo cares so much about political prisoners, wouldn't he have ordered a manhunt?"

"Sure. If he knew about it."

"Then . . . then Faucher must have only just escaped. Maybe even today." I stop in my tracks. "And the palace doesn't know."

Gaspard nods minutely, as if a movement more violent than that will make him well and truly sick. "Rodrigo really doesn't expect anything to happen tonight, does he?"

"Not even when I tell him."

"Then . . ." He pauses. Averts his eyes. Blinks rapidly at the leafy feet of an overstuffed chaise made of fiery carnations. "Then maybe he deserves what's coming."

For a moment, I can't even make a sound.

By the time Gaspard dares meet my suddenly watery gaze, I've almost successfully smothered my memory of Leo in the porcelain salon, asking me if I was glad to see Ivareans burn. The despair in his voice. The challenge. I see echoes of it now in Gaspard, too. But unlike the prince, Gaspard is not defeated by the idea. With his dark irises slitted with pinprick focus, he seems almost energized by it. "I'm not saying I support it, Anaïs. I'm just saying . . . if it *was* Faucher you heard that time, then you see the point of what he's doing. On some level, it must appeal to you too."

What if there was no throne at all?

I blink away the image of Béatrice's face when I asked her that, just hours before I was killed bearing her stolen name. It felt . . . not easy, exactly, imagining an Ivarea without a king, but . . . possible, in the way that only generations of misrule and repeated time-related trauma might make it seem. But now that the man who might be trying to make that happen— Faucher—has murdered me point-blank *twice,* most recently when he thought I was a maid being taken advantage of by her royal employers, I see right through to the rotten core of that story. I know a man like Faucher cannot be trusted to tell it.

Gaspard might not have known there would be an attack at the ball, but now that he does, the idea that he could still readily throw himself into Faucher's story, even after Faucher cut him out of it himself . . . I hoped Gaspard would be able to see through it, too. But what he's saying now seems more than a little naive. Dare I say, even selfish.

"Faucher might talk about returning power to the people," I snap, scrambling to my feet with no small difficulty, "but that's not what he actually *does*. How can you not see that?"

Still on the ground, Gaspard stares up at me. The tight lines of his mouth relax but that only sets me on edge in turn. "You don't understand, Anaïs. He's from Massilie, too. Mathieu Faucher is Proensan."

A stone drops down the dry well of my chest. *He's—he's one of us?*

For most of my conscious life, I've been trained to appeal to the peninsular Ivareans that dominate this kingdom. Leaving everything and everyone I love, becoming a stranger to myself—that was what I had to do to carve a prosperous future for myself and my family. I saw no use in pushing against what I couldn't control, what I couldn't change for myself. So I succumbed.

Whatever else he is, this Faucher person clearly hasn't given up on what he believes in and given in to the rules, unspoken and otherwise, of Ivarean society. Apparently, even imprisonment hasn't stopped him. We are countrymen, we even have the same hometown, but he's fighting a world that has never bent for us, and I . . .

I am here.

Trapped in time.

The sight of Gaspard standing brings me back to myself. He doesn't try to approach me, but he does raise his voice so it carries through the open air. "Don't you owe it to your people to see what he really plans?"

Faucher might be a Proensan revolutionary, but that only represents one side of the coin. "I *have* seen what he really plans. I've been murdered because of it. So have you."

Gaspard presses doggedly on. "And after that? You don't know what *else* he's planned."

"I can promise you, it's nothing good."

"Nothing good for *whom*?"

I know what I'm supposed to say. I know what is right, at its most basic level. But . . . I said it already, didn't I? So did Mathieu Faucher himself.

Why must we submit?

"You have to find out the truth, Anaïs." Gaspard's jaw clicks in place. "Or after all this time running around with royalty, did you *completely* lose yourself?"

I thought Gaspard was being selfish. But I once was, too.

"Fine."

It's his turn to blink at me. "What?"

"You want to sit up there and do nothing as your parents and friends get blown apart? Great. Let's go."

Then maybe he will understand, even if it's just until his next death, what I go through. What the stakes really are.

He gestures beyond the bougainvillea. "Lead the way, Mademoiselle."

"A *broom cupboard*?"

"You need to be far enough to survive the blast and close

enough to see what happens in the ballroom after. I'm open to suggestions."

Gaspard shuts his mouth, lifts up a stolen candle, and shuffles inside after me. While he settles down on an upturned bucket and props up the candle on a shelf, I contemplate the door. I'm in no mood to risk Faucher and his cronies shooting blindly into random rooms. Not again.

Just as I did when investigating the abandoned tower, I peel off my gloves and plunge my blessed dagger into my finger. I trace the cupboard door and its frame with the open wound. Memories flashing through my mind—the Alcázar collapsing, the burst of rifles, hundreds of years of history reduced to a heavy haze over all of Marenca—help me narrow my focus so I can set the protective spell.

Do not let the same thing happen again. Keep me safe from harm.

"Are you—?"

"Trying to keep you from dying an *immediate* grisly death?" My skirts threaten to topple a case of feather dusters as I turn around. Gaspard gasps as he sees the emerald dagger. "You're welcome."

I don't bother telling him that keeping this place from collapsing is not going to be as easy as sprinkling blood on the threshold. It feels as though the very stone of the Alcázar is eating away at the blessing, wriggling past my spell like a weed at the edge of my consciousness—the opposite of what the palace did when I eventually unsealed the upper landings of that tower. Even if the blessing is generally well-suited for protective magic, I wouldn't be able to sustain this spell for more than ten minutes in a magically warded space any larger than this broom cupboard. It would surely cost every drop of an entire blessed army's blood to keep the Alcázar standing in the face of the bombs.

Nearly spent, I collapse on my backside and unceremoniously kick off my shoes. While I still have time, I draw protective patterns on the floor in blood, pouring all my will and all my fear into surviving just a few minutes longer.

Gaspard mumbles, "Why don't you cast this spell every time you . . . every time you come back here? To protect yourself?"

"There's no point. I have to keep dying to have a hope of stopping this someday."

His expression grows grief-stricken. "God, Anaïs . . . I . . ."

"I know."

The minutes tick by in agonizing silence. I stay on the floor, facing the threshold and bleeding lightly from each of the fingers on my left hand, as well as from a new gash on my palm. The spell will only hold firm as long as I do, and probably not even then.

Between the sixth and seventh chimes of midnight, the ground begins to shake. The cries of the court carry across the palace like thunder, the shock from the explosion like lightning. Every scream and crash from the ballroom feels like it's being refracted upon my body. Every burst of gunfire and avalanche of stone pummels the small part of my brain not painfully tracking every droplet of blessed blood I've spilled. My spell can't stop the cleaning supplies from tumbling down from their high shelves onto our heads, can't keep the walls from rocking and wailing and shuddering from the violence of the explosions, can't clean the air of dust and grime and gunpowder and the metallic scent of fresh blood.

But through it all, the blessing holds. The debris doesn't leave a mark on either of us.

When I'm certain that the bombs have been spent and that the intruders' new battle is underway in the ballroom, I finally let my eyes fall shut. The darkness I find there feels thin and precarious, as if the flames of the past are slowly eating at the skin of my eyelids and will leave me unable to look away.

Unsettled by the thought, I force myself to turn and check on Gaspard. He's huddled in a corner, making strangled noises, gagging on the smell. But he's not dead.

He raises his head. "Do you hear that?"

All at once, I do. A sharp, high-pitched hum. Like a lightning rod held aloft in a storm, sizzling with electricity not yet discharged.

The walls of the cupboard start to quake.

That's new.

It's coming from outside. Behind that strange buzzing lies a cacophony of human sounds. Men laughing. Boots stomping. Guns going off.

This sound isn't coming from the ballroom. It's right here.

Gaspard and I scramble to our feet at the same time and huddle against the smoking door, trying to listen beneath the humming.

Then a chunk of stone the size of a well-fed rooster lands

with a *thud* on my shoulder. Gaspard seizes me by my bloody palm and barrels us through the door. Fifteen seconds later, the wall collapses completely.

I don't have time to thank him. Now that we're in the open, the humming is louder. It sounds like an alarm of some kind, but what's left to alert anyone about? The corridor we emerged into is littered with broken torches and crumbling arches and more smoke than I've inhaled in several deaths. We scarcely turn the next corner when I spy a knot of people ahead of us. I crouch behind a section of crumbled wall and pull Gaspard down beside me.

He pokes his head up to get a better look. "That's . . . that's Faucher."

I can hardly hear his awed whisper over the insistent, impossible humming, but I peek around the stone and—yes, yes, I think I see him. Faucher, wearing the same brown coat as before, pacing the abraded corridor. Not out of agitation, of course. Why would he be agitated when his plan is working out again?

"And what on *earth* do you plan on doing next?"

Another voice. One I know.

"You may think yourself very clever indeed, sneaking into this palace under my father's nose, murdering every innocent person—"

"My dear girl, I thought you were the smart one in your family. In what way do you suppose those people were *innocent*?"

I strain my eyes and clap my bloody hands over my ears to risk another look down the hall. Mathieu Faucher's cronies have Infanta Clara on her knees. I can see a sliver of her face covered in ash and blood, her hair wild and singed, her hand wrapped so tight around the base of her fan that it seems like an extension of her own body. She spits at the former barrister's feet.

He stops and crouches down in front of her the way he did before me. "Be glad, Citoyen Clara. You alone are the most fortunate of your late family. You will see dawn break over a new Ivarea before you die."

Still huddled behind the rubble, Gaspard nudges me in my very sore arm, horror rising in his voice as he watches his old idol bully a princess. "What should we do? Do we help her?"

"How?"

Down the hall, Faucher presses the barrel of the rifle he used to murder me against the princess's forehead. "First, you will tell me how to stop this abominable sound."

Clara once said that there were more magical defenses in the Alcázar than she knew about, or knew how to disable. She must have been right, since I've never heard this impossible alarm before. I think my ears are bleeding. The revolutionaries tug at Clara's gown and kick at her knees, and Faucher keeps the gun trained on her head. The sound doesn't stop.

Then the princess—no, I realize with a jolt, the *queen*—gasps, and the walls tremble.

Her voice, worn down and threadbare, barely carries past the humming. "I think I'll enjoy this."

Faucher shoots. The bullet slams through her skirts and blows out her knee. But the clap of gunpowder is hardly audible as the humming crescendos violently. Gaspard and I fall back against our barrier and gaze in terror at the corridor as it vibrates and shudders more than it ever did during the bombings. Those were localized attacks that began and ended in linear fashion, a chemical reaction that catalyzed and combusted. This—this is *growing*. From the palace itself.

No.

No, it's coming from Clara.

The men are shouting now, panicking rather than celebrating. Something emerges from the darkness down the way Gaspard and I just came, whipping down the walls to the floor and up the walls again. As it bursts through the walls like a river no longer bound by a dam, it seems to know where it's going.

"Is that a *dragon*?" shrieks Gaspard.

The closer it gets, however, the clearer it is that he's wrong. This is not an animal. It's the stone of the Alcázar abrading itself. Clara has unleashed the magic lurking in the walls and turned it into a deadly current of energy sweeping with hunger toward her enemy.

And the rest of us.

"I didn't know—" Gaspard starts.

Neither did I. I didn't know *anyone* could do this.

The last thing I hear before our queen buries us alive is Mathieu Faucher screaming.

It does not feel as sweet as it should.

X

CHAPTER ONE

IN THE LIGHT OF DAY AND WITH THE MOCKING OF MEMORY, Clara's last stand is all the more haunting. She became queen of a burning battlefield, was taken hostage by her family's murderers, got *shot*, and *still* brought the Alcázar to its knees. She accomplished more than I ever have by killing Mathieu Faucher, the chief architect of her family's and kingdom's doom.

I could bleed myself dry every night, and I would still never be enough. I could give everything I have to this hellish, unending night, and I would still fail.

Maybe I shouldn't be so surprised. Clara is the princess of Ivarea. The world lies at her feet, waiting for her to crack it open and use it however she likes, even to destroy the Alcázar itself. I am Proensan, and as my mother believes, my own world has nothing to offer me. *I'm* the one who knows exactly what's coming, and the best I could do was keep a cupboard upright. I couldn't even stay alive.

Maybe if Clara's revenge succeeded, she could have risen to the occasion as Ivarea's queen. She could have taken her father's throne and led Ivarea to a new dawn—bloody and bruised, but still together. There might still have *been* an Ivarea when morning came.

But there was no dawn. There is no morning-after reckoning for this kingdom. No hope.

Because of me. Because of my curse.

I don't understand how I started repeating this night or why it came to be, but even if I did, there would be no getting around it, would there? I can't make myself leave the Alcázar to its doom, so no matter where I am or what I'm trying to do, when midnight strikes, I'm going to die. And whatever was happening before that moment—whatever would have happened next—becomes immaterial. As far as the world is concerned, it never even happened.

Nothing will ever matter. No one will ever escape.

It's all my fault.

It always will be.

The feast at the Anniversary Ball has gone to ashes on my tongue for what feels like the thousandth time when I retreat into the shadows of the walls that Infanta Clara unmade. And promptly get run over by Infante Leopoldo.

I have not spoken with him since the night he proposed to me. All I remember when I look at him now is what happened after that. Fire and debris and screaming, and his voice, reverent, bitter: *Let's watch them burn.*

He bites back a perfunctory apology almost as soon as he's offered it and hands me his wine instead. "You look like you could use this more than me. Which is truly saying something."

Not really. Still, I take the glass and drain it to the dregs. He stares at my wine-dark lips through the empty glass, a single brow arched, either concerned or intrigued.

"You're welcome, Doña . . ."

Intrigued it is. "Anaïs."

Without another word, he draws closer, careful of the skirts that tripped him up a moment ago, and leans against the wall next to me. I always thought his ability to melt so seamlessly into the world of the palace came from knowing it better than I ever will. Now I wonder if it's something more—if he magically manipulates the walls of the Alcázar to cloak himself in shadow. If Clara can tear the palace apart to save herself and her kingdom, why can't Leo contort it to suit his wishes?

"Poor Doña Anaïs." His half-lidded gaze feels like a knife at my throat. "Don't tell me the royal court isn't everything you've ever dreamed it would be."

"I've *never* dreamed of the court."

"Then what?"

I shut my mouth before I confess something absolutely useless, like *I haven't been able to dream for a long time.*

Then again, what do I have left to lose by telling him the truth?

"If I told you that Mathieu Faucher is going to kill you and your family and everyone else here at midnight, and I'm reliving it again, and again, *and again,* what would you say?"

He drops his gaze to the wineglass dangling from my fingers.

I chuckle flatly. "Right. Of course. Thank you, Alteza. I'll remember this for next time."

I leave him at the edge of the ballroom, pass the bears of the western archway, and find a wide staircase yawning at the end of the corridor. I dash upstairs, my gown dragging against the stone steps, and reach a mezzanine level that looks over the broad painting- and tapestry-festooned galleries that surround the ballroom. The chandelier light here feels brighter and more diffuse than it does on the ground floor, twining more fluidly with the moonlight streaming in from the windows.

I've barely made it beyond the steps when someone seizes my gloved wrist from below. My wineglass shatters on the stairs.

Leo steps over the broken shards and twists me around to face him. "Did you say *Mathieu Faucher* is about to kill us?"

My breath stops in my chest. Taken aback by his interest, I dredge up the presence of mind to tell him all about it one last time.

We wander the length of the mezzanine, walking more closely together than we would in full view of the palace. Something about this elevated level of the Alcázar makes me feel like it could keep us from death itself, let alone the ravenous court below. A ridiculous idea, I know. An open mezzanine would be the first place to crumble from the explosions.

All I can look forward to up here is a new view of our coming doom.

By the end of my story, the prince's face has grown paler than it was when I first ran into him. "I see," he says, running a hand over his face. "So . . . so, it looks like we'll never be able to stop Faucher if we keep waiting until the last minute to act. We need more time."

We. He said *we.*

The rush of dizzy relief I initially feel quickly slams into the brick wall of my reality. The last time Leo actively tried to help, he proposed to me and then sent his family off to their deaths. I can't begin to fathom what he might come up with next. And there's nothing he could promise now that would make a difference. I can't keep staking our survival on the mere possibility of his help. For better or worse, all I have—all I'll ever have—is myself.

But he's not wrong: I do need more time to hope to accomplish anything. Which means—"Next time, I'll have to break into the Alcázar before the ball starts."

Leo blinks, almost more taken aback by this than the repeated–mass murder story. "You can't break in. There's no way."

"I think Faucher and friends would beg to differ."

"Just . . . tell the Guardia Real that you're my personal guest. The guards would believe anything of me. It'd be easier on you that way, too." He pauses to give me a slow once-over. "Spare you from committing a crime just for an audience with the infante."

Oh no. He thinks he's important. "You could be a kitchen boy, for all I care. You just have to help me."

His stare glances off mine. I wish I understood what he sees when he looks at me, and why he doesn't always head right back to a floating tray of drinks when I'm stupid enough to open my mouth.

"Perhaps a kitchen boy would be more useful," he muses.

"Perhaps. But I can't count on him having sworn to give his life and death to Ivarea. Even if it was only pretend."

Leo curls his hand around the mezzanine banister behind him, discomfited at the revelation that I know of his past secret. "Ahh. So you would bind me to a ten-year-old promise."

It can't be easy talking to a stranger who drops impossible futures and lifelong secrets into the conversation every other minute. But I don't know how to stop, so I join him at the banister, letting one gloved hand hover over the edge, as if tempting death to drag me down ahead of schedule. "I will ask you now. Can I count on you to help me, or can't I?"

When he raises his eyes to mine, his gaze seems more fluid than before. An ocean of feeling I can't begin to navigate threatens to cascade across the space between us, spill over into the gleaming galleries below. He has no right to look at me like that. If anyone should be drowning in panic, it should be me. It *is* me.

"I suppose I've said this before, or I wouldn't have told you about my . . . *incredibly* childish exploits. But . . . yes. Saints, come to me. Please. Count on me. I'll be here, waiting for you." He pauses, averts his eyes again. "I hope."

192

A rasping giggle escapes my throat. "You *hope*."

Leo raises his head. I've slaked myself on the sight of him in the dark more than once, and still my breath hitches every time I catch him like that. Still, I forget myself.

Do not forget yourself, Anaïs Aubanel.

We both go quiet. Music from the ballroom creeps in toward us on balmy winds, kicking up my skirts, teasing the locket at my clavicle. Now that we are as far removed from the prying eyes of the court as we have ever been and have exhausted the desperate practicality of our usual topics of conversation, I can think of no words that could fill the space remaining between the two of us. Nothing worth saying out loud. Nothing that would matter.

"We have till midnight."

It takes all the shards of my splintered dignity to not crumple where I stand. I can see phantom wounds on that face, ghostly blood pooling at the corner of his lips. The way it did the last time he said those last two words to me.

"I want to ask you something, if I may." He takes my silence as a signal to go on. "What would you do if you got out of this?"

"Home." I'm unable to resist its invocation. "I would go home."

"And?"

"And . . . and I—I don't know," I stammer, thrown by his interest in Massilie, of all places. "Go back to the way things were. Drawing lessons in the solarium. Tea parties in the gardens. My father debating obscure points of Proensan history

193

over dinner. My mother hunting for a husband on the peninsula for me. The way it should be."

"Of course. But what I really want to know is, what do you *want* to do?"

A faint, uncanny feeling clambers through my heart. Is he asking what I actually want with my life? Because that is not a question I'm equipped to answer. I can barely conceive of my own life for myself, especially not in this unending nightmare. But Leo asked, and . . . and no one else ever has.

"I don't know what I want. I never have. Even when you asked about my dreams before, I didn't—I don't dream. I can't." My hand curls around my locket. "Family responsibilities do that to you, I suppose."

Leo clenches his jaw. "Yes. They do."

I know how Leo's parents view him: the constantly looming threat underfoot, the black sheep who must be restrained at all times. How lonely an existence that must be. Perhaps that's why Clara shoved us together that time, why she wanted her brother to open up to me: because Leo and I are both magic users in a world that has no use for us.

Even though he has endured a lifetime of neglect and suspicion from his family, however, there's no doubt that Leo has dreams. And he's not exactly been shy about them.

"Do you really believe you'd be a better king than Felipe?"

"If I were king," he repeats with a dark chuckle, "I would believe you when you came to me and said my palace is about to be attacked."

"That's what you think now." I let go of the locket and

twist so I'm leaning back against the mezzanine banister. "Do you have *any* idea how difficult it's been trying to get through your drunken selfishness every single night?"

He pushes off the railing so we're no longer right next to each other. Without its support, he holds himself gingerly as he paces back and forth, as though my words could fell him as easily as a well-aimed gunshot. "Then why do you bother trying to save us?"

"Would you rather I not?"

"You're Proensan, aren't you? You should have every reason to want the Cardonas to go up in flames."

A new chill unfurls along my spine, despite the suffuse heat up here. Even though he *did* once want his own family to go up in flames, too—for himself, his pride, his pain, his anger— there is something terribly thrilling about a prince consigning himself to death for wronging your people.

For you.

For a brief moment, I wonder what Mathieu Faucher would do if he heard Infante Leopoldo say this. I respond in a way I can only imagine he never would. "Just because I'm Proensan doesn't mean I want to see innocent people die." Here, Faucher would push back on *innocent*, and perhaps he would be right; the grandes are, as a rule, not great people, which I know as well from the conduct of their children as I do from accounts of their governance. But for me, the point remains: "No idea is worth people's lives."

Leo grimaces. The expression tugs at the knot in my stomach. "I ask you again, Anaïs. Why are you killing yourself to save us?" He abandons his pacing to stare down into the galleries below, at a dynasty's ransom in art and power. Eventually, he turns his back on the glories of the past. His voice drops, almost uncertain. "Saints know we don't deserve it."

I close my eyes, unable to follow his gaze. "Maybe not." I will never be able to disentangle the feelings this night has bred in me, and this prince more than anyone else. But even if I don't know *how* I'm doing this, I do know why. "I just can't be the one to doom you to death."

"Then you're a better friend than any I've ever had."

"We are not friends."

He chuckles, a soft, rumbling sound like distant thunder come to break the hold of a cruel summer. I open my eyes to see a slow smile spread across his face. "*If* you save us, then. Would we be friends when this is over?"

"I don't see how. I'll go home to Massilie, remember? And you'll be here."

"I would say that's what letters are for, but I'm told my handwriting leaves something to be desired."

"Then you'll have to come visit Massilie," I volunteer, as cheery as I don't feel. "You could stay at our château. The goats would just *love* you."

"And if you're married to your peninsular husband by then?"

I'm half tempted to ask him *who* he imagines I would marry, but everyone else in this court, this palace, they all seem so very far away right now. "Then you could visit me here. You'd just have to say the word." Rolling my eyes in a way that might at certain angles appear like I'm fluttering my lashes, I add, "How could I possibly deny Leopoldo the Lush?"

I could track the amount of time it takes for him to speak again by counting discrete heartbeats. By the time he inhales, I have no idea how much of my life I've surrendered to him, or how much more I will give up.

"You have all the power in the world, you know."

I did not know.

"The only thing you really need to do is not die tonight, and you'll decide the fate of the kingdom by morning. You can change the future. And the past, I suppose." His voice gathers a new and fragile conviction. "If you've sacrificed yourself all these times for all of us, I think you owe it to yourself to figure out what you truly want next."

All of this feels wrong in a way I can't describe. It threatens to unravel me. "I just said I don't want you all to die," I bleat.

He shakes his head again. The expression on his face is more melancholy than I've ever seen. A sadness that resides deep in his bones. "But what are you sacrificing yourself for?"

"For you all to not d—"

"Anaïs."

We are barely a hand's breadth apart now, and he towers over me, his shadow almost blocking that of the gently swaying chandeliers above us.

"It's okay to not know what you want, for now. But one day, in a real future, a real tomorrow, you won't be able to wipe away your mistakes and regrets every night. You'll have to live with all of your failures, and go on living them. You'll have to remember them."

I haven't given myself permission to think beyond the madness of time. To truly consider the ramifications of my actions for my sake, and the Cardonas', and the country's. To ensure that if I ever make it to a new dawn, I will be able to face the world I shaped. Permanently.

Which means there are two questions I really should be asking myself. Two questions that have been buried at the heart of this nightmare from the beginning. The first is what Leo asked me once in Night's Pavilion and once now, when I explained our tragic story: *How is this possible?*

The other is what he asked me before I understood the truth of what was happening to me, before I even knew I was trapped: *So what are you going to do about it?*

The longer I avoid those questions, the longer the blood of all the people who die here at midnight will stain my hands. And . . . loath as I still am to acknowledge it, especially to myself, I have to figure out how I ended up at the center of this curse and how to end it. If I can't do that soon, if I don't even try, nothing else I do tonight will matter. Neither Ivarea nor I will ever have a future of our own.

To Leo, I can only say, "*Maybe* you have a point."

He nods sagely, which elicits a laugh that bubbles up like champagne from my chest. I feel like I could tumble over the banister or fly up and crash into a chandelier. I don't know. There's so much I don't know—about tonight and how it came to be. About myself.

"Have we ever kissed before?"

Great. Fall over the banister it is.

"Forgive me if that seems forward. It just . . . I feel like it's something that might have happened before."

"As a matter of fact," I admit wryly, "you have kissed me once or twice."

He accepts this with nary a blink of an eye; he can clearly imagine just how his past selves would have acted. "But you've never kissed me?"

"Did I give you the impression that I have time to waste when I have a kingdom to save?"

"Did you want to?"

I have nothing left to lose. I tell him the truth so I can torture myself forevermore. "Yes, I suppose. Before."

"Well, you can now. If you still want to."

We must be minutes, moments, away from midnight, so I'm the only one who will live with the consequences of this.

As it happens, I am exceedingly good at living with consequences.

Everything I didn't know I learned from our last kisses comes flooding back when our lips meet. I know that if I pull him farther down, he will bend and not break. So I do, my hands greedy on the sides of his face, and deepen the kiss before he can. He grins into me, giddy wonder and delight gilding the warmth of his embrace, and matches my lead, slipping his tongue between my teeth.

The last time we kissed, I didn't know what was happening, and was desperate to stop it when I realized the truth. For better or worse, I don't care anymore. We will never have this again, and from the way he pulls me in even closer, until it feels like my absurd skirts are little more than tissue paper sparking from the scorching of his hands, he knows it, too. He breaks off the kiss to spin me around, deftly lifting me off my feet, and pushes me against the mezzanine wall.

Pressed between the doomed palace and the doomed prince, I sense dangers that I've never even conceived of before.

Before this.

Before him.

He has only just taken me back in his arms when the bells begin.

True fear breaks across his face like a growing tide, threatening to drown everything that was blooming before. He glances back down at me with another unspeakable question in his eyes.

I answer him as a twisted kind of mercy. "There are worse ways to die."

Counting down the chimes, at last, the prince nods. "You would know," he whispers, and lowers his mouth to mine for the last time.

XI

CHAPTER ONE

IN THE END, I DON'T KNOW IF I WAS RIGHT. BUT I KNOW THAT Leo never let go, even when the palace began breaking above us. And when I wake again, it is with his name on my tongue, and the ghost of his touch on my swollen lips.

That kiss was my fault. That much is clear in the cruel, ever-dimming daylight. Leo offered himself up to me because he knew that we were already doomed, and I let him do it. I wanted him. I chose him. Without hope for anything more than that moment, I kissed him. And from there . . .

No. Nothing could have happened between us after that. Our fate was sealed the first moment I woke back up, in this exact spot, at this exact time. That's the only truth I have had to cling to since I started dying. And now I must do the impossible: find out why this time curse started and how I can hope to stop it.

It's just that *deciding* to figure out how to stop my repeating night doesn't mean I have any idea how to actually *do* so.

No one I know has heard of anything like this. I don't know if there was a reason for it, if someone actively cursed me—though why they'd pick me rather than literally anyone else in that ballroom, I have no idea—or if it simply *happened* to me, the way great cosmic events do to unsuspecting humans. I don't know which of those possibilities is most terrifying. I don't know which is most likely.

Maybe I'll never be able to end it.

I'm already stuffed into the scarlet gown by the time I remember what *else* Leo and I discussed on the mezzanine: a play for more time at the Alcázar to stop the attack. How I could reach him next.

The guards would believe anything of me.

As much as I once would have shuddered to spend more time than absolutely necessary at the palace, I might as well continue with our plan while trying to figure out the origins of this nightmare. If any other avenue to investigate my curse presents itself, I'll take it, but now I suppose I need to get back to the scene of our doom long before it actually happens. I need to get back to Leo's side.

And once you're there?

I don't know how to answer this question, either.

But I can't stop imagining the possibilities.

The rank-and-file guards stationed at the main doors of the Alcázar Real might believe that Leopoldo the Lush would indulge in terrible, bratty shenanigans when it comes to eligible young ladies, but that doesn't mean they believe *me*. Even my forged letter featuring Leo's signature, lifted from the dance card he signed for me lifetimes ago at the Tarrazas ball, only seems to complicate my case. But as much as they snicker at the shameless, wide-eyed girl desperate enough to show up for a *private salon* with the infamous infante—the lie I garbled to Maman to make sure I could come here like this at all—the guards do not dare keep the prince from what he may want.

The one escorting me slows before a pair of shining walnut double doors in the palace's residential wing. A captain I assume is assigned to Leo's service glances suspiciously out from the shadows. He has a face like a hunting hound—the same keen eyes, prominent nostrils, and even wide, almost floppy ears. If he's Leo's guard, I wonder why I've never seen him in the ballroom before, shadowing his prince.

"Capitán Noguera, I have Doña Anaïs of Massilie for Vuestra Alteza Real."

The captain steps aside and peers at me with what I suspect is no small amount of disdain, but he does not betray any feelings he may have about his prince or the stupid girl who's managed to worm her way here. Before my escort can elbow me across the threshold, I follow Noguera inside.

The prince's chambers are dominated by ornately carved wooden bookshelves stamped all over with what must be Leo's crest, the king's gilded dragon in flight against a diamond of night sky. Some of their many tomes bear spines etched with letters I can't make out, or in languages I can't read altogether, while others practically hum with energy—imbued with magic from the world that made them. None of it seems like Leo's taste, but it's not as if I know what that actually is. It's not as if I truly know him at all.

The captain stops before what I desperately hope is the last door in the suite. As it swings open, I brace for inquisitive looks from another guard.

I am not prepared for the haughty censure on Infanta Clara's face.

"How lovely to see you, Doña Anaïs."

"Doña—Vuestra Al—"

She rolls her eyes and physically pulls me across the threshold of what is clearly *her* dressing room, not Leo's, and in so doing, jolts me out of the most pitiful attempt at a curtsy of my life. "Thank you, Capitán Noguera. That will be all."

Once he's closed the door behind him, she strides toward the elaborate vanity, leaving me at the mouth of her bedchamber. Jewelry and fans that should be locked up with the rest of the Ivarean treasury are sprawled before a mirror backed by a gilded sun that glimmers with its own radiance. Its reflection shows the horror on my face plain as day.

The princess flops down on a generously upholstered chair. She's still getting ready for the ball: pins jut out from her dark brown hair, and she's only wearing a shift underneath her periwinkle silk robe.

"You're not in trouble," she says without preamble. "I simply wanted to meet the girl that managed to capture my brother's attention but not a written invitation."

Blood rushes to my cheeks. "Vuestra Alteza Real, where exactly is the infante?"

"With the king."

After Leo and Rodrigo's confrontation in the porcelain salon, I can imagine only too well how such a talk might be going.

Clara adds magnanimously, "You're welcome to attend me until the ball begins. No sense in you going all the way back home when you're already dressed."

As much as I might want to go right back home and lie in the dark of my bedroom, I would be a fool to pass up uninterrupted time with Infanta Clara, especially if she hasn't even invited her new favorite, Marguerite Lorieux, to attend her at the ball. Clara has clearly studied magic long and hard—if I can keep on her good side, she might be willing to help me untangle my repeating night. So I hasten with her preparations and wait for the right moment. Though none of the maids seem especially glad to have a pair of useless noble hands around, neither they nor their mistress say anything.

After one last dusting of pearly powder on the princess's cheekbones, the maids depart. The only thing they did not do is select a fan to complete the ensemble. Seven of them lie at haphazard angles on the vanity, unfolded to reveal the miniature masterpieces painted on their silk and vellum leaves. I grab the carved whalebone handle of the fan I know she always carries at the Anniversary Ball. As well she should, if Paloma Nelleda's rumor from all those nights ago was right about it being a favor from Clara's fiancé.

"How exquisite," I remark idly. "Where did you get this piece, señora?"

Seated once more at her vanity, Clara glances at me in the mirror and holds out her hand. "Thank you, Doña Anaïs. That will be all."

I drop the fan as if it burns. I don't want to annoy her into dismissing me.

How fortunate that I have all kinds of impossible magical phenomena to pull her back in.

"Have you ever heard of magic that can turn back time?"

"Don't tell me you wish you could take back your decision to come here tonight."

I feel the color draining from my cheeks. "Not at all. I just wanted to ask you about a magical phenomenon that I—"

"You want to talk magic, do you? Then why ignore the obvious?" She turns around in her chair to face me. "That amulet on your neck."

"I—I beg your pardon?"

She leans forward, the folded fan digging into her palm like a blunt knife. "I don't know much about your people's *blessing,* but I am very curious indeed as to what made you think it was a good idea to waltz into the Alcázar Real for what you intended to be a private meeting with my incredibly eligible brother displaying what I can only guess is a formidable magical object in your décolletage." She scoffs. "I didn't take you for a bold thing, Doña Anaïs. I see I was mistaken."

Part of me would like to snap, *Yes, you were,* but in this case, it wouldn't be deserved. I'm not as bold as Clara thinks

I am. I'm just a colossal fool. This is nowhere *near* the magical phenomenon I wanted to ask her about. In fact, it isn't even magical. My hand crawls up to the gold chain at my throat, but I don't clasp the opal locket. "With all due respect, that's . . . simply impossible. I carry the blessing. I would know if I'd been wearing a blessed object for half my life."

"Perhaps you have become desensitized to its magical energy."

"That would imply that at one point I felt its magical energy."

She cocks her head, less than impressed. "You're that sure?"

"This heirloom belongs to my mother's family. They lost their blessing generations ago." Maman's line was not the first Proensan family to experience the loss, and it will not be the last, whether I get out of this night or not. "Even if the necklace *had* been blessed centuries ago, its powers wouldn't have survived without someone else of its bloodline renewing the magic."

But, whispers the voice in my head, *you* have *bled a lot while wearing it.* And the copious blood of a blessed descendant *would* be the closest connection a blessed locket might have had in decades with the bloodline that forged it.

Still. I've worn it all my life, and it's never recognized me the way the Aubanel daggers do. It's never displayed any magical energy or helped me cast a spell. This is just an object, touched by no higher power, meant to serve no higher purpose.

"If that is the case," the princess murmurs eventually, half to herself, "then it seems that perhaps dead blessings can be resurrected. By the right person."

The locket suddenly feels very cold and almost clammy around my neck, as if caught in the grip of a corpse. "I *really* don't think so, señora."

"Oh, you can try to deny it if you will. But ultimately, there's no denying truth. Or power." She stands abruptly and proceeds to drift through the chamber as if guided by a path that only she can see. "I admire your audacity today, Doña Anaïs, I really do. You knew what you wanted and you did what was necessary to make it happen. But let me tell you, cariño: You *do* have power of your own. More than you know, and more than what people like my brother could offer you. You must learn how to use it before someone else takes it from you."

I know I've said *That's not how the blessing works* a lot, but *honestly.* "Who could want my power?"

"Haven't you heard the story of Clemencia of Lereda?"

First she beats me over the head with an accusation of magic; now she wants to lecture me on history. The Cardona siblings and their morbid stories are just too much. I shake my head.

Clara sighs, leaning against the closest bookshelf and folding and unfolding that lovely little fan. It's a nothing gesture, a reflex while lost in a reverie, but she makes it seem like magic, too—that thrilling self-possession, even in the middle of a story.

"Clemencia was a magician of some renown in the western Tarracuña countryside. Her connection to the land meant she could coax greater yields out of her and her husband's farm and use the proceeds on charity work. Building a hospital, schools, angelic endeavors like that.

"One day, her husband went blind. No one knows why. Out of his mind with terror, he begged and pleaded and *demanded* that Clemencia save him with her magical ability. But as much as she tried, she could not heal something like this on her own. So, three nights after her husband went blind, Clemencia knelt at her altar to Santa Lídia and swore that she'd give anything to restore her husband's sight. And, lo and behold, the next morning, the husband awoke and saw the sun shining again. But Clemencia didn't. She was the one who was blind."

A prickle of unease ripples down my back. "She—what?"

Clara crosses her arms across that crisp green bodice. "That's how the story goes. She put herself at the saints' mercy, *begged* them for help, and they plucked out her sight so her husband could have it instead." She chuckles to herself. "What a metaphor."

That same unease unfurls and sends goose bumps down my arms.

"Clemencia became a folk hero. Her husband did his best to enshrine her legacy. But over time, her *sacrifice,* as they call it, has largely been forgotten. A *sacrifice,*" she adds, "made for a *man.* So yes, Anaïs, there is always something they can take from you. Your body. Your magic. Your *amulet.* Your name. Before that day comes, you must learn how to protect yourself." The princess rubs her left hand.

Where, as Paloma knew and Leo admitted, Clara will soon bear a wedding ring.

I never thought that I would *pity* a girl destined to become a queen, especially a Cardona. But Clara is still a girl. Her predicament proves what I've seen at home and in Marenca for all my life. It doesn't matter who we are or to whom we were born. Our lot in life will never be without sacrifice. Of our dreams, of our homes, our love, our power.

Sometimes, the world will even demand we sacrifice ourselves.

I only have a few more minutes before she goes back to being Infanta Clara, royal magician and puppet master of the Ivarean court, collector of amusing things and even more amusing people. It's a minor miracle that I've made it this far. I may not have gotten the magical help I wanted from Clara, but it's not too late to tackle the *other*, more immediate problem. After all, it's one she faces, too.

"Señora, I do know where your fan came from."

Of all the things I have said, this takes her aback the most. "Do you?"

"From your fiancé. The crown prince of Rasenna."

Folding the fan again, she exhales very carefully. "Did Leo tell you that?"

"He didn't have to." I would have found out somehow, someday. For now, however, I can feel her patience wearing thin. I have no choice but to cut to the chase. "I know a lot of other things, too. And you're in great danger."

Unlike her younger brother, Clara doesn't call me mad. Since it seems for now that she can't help me untangle my time curse, I simply tell her that I'm plagued with visions of the future and have seen the calamity that awaits us all at midnight. Maybe that explanation, absurd as it must sound, is why she doesn't kick me out immediately.

"Do you know who's behind this attack?"

"A failed barrister turned revolutionary from Proensa. Mathieu Faucher."

The princess, who has retreated to her vanity for support, buries her luminous face in her hands. "*Mathieu Faucher. You're sure?*"

"I've seen him here multiple times. I've heard him talk about his plans."

"But you haven't seen anything after the bomb blasts?"

I've seen everyone I've ever known die with their limbs mangled, their mouths caught in frozen screams. I've seen innocents smashed by the debris of everything you and your family have built and stolen and remade in your name. I've seen your brother become king and die in my arms, and I've seen you become queen and demolish everything in your wake.

"Not much."

She peels her fingers from her face. Her skin is flushed with—panic, hysteria? "Mathieu Faucher," she repeats like a curse. As quickly as the wave of hysteria struck, it dissipates and leaves behind a steely-eyed magician-princess. "Right. Good. We can handle this."

"Can we?"

Clara isn't listening to me anymore. She grimaces like she's daring the world to try to stop her, grabs her fan again, and strides decisively toward the door. I suppose even when her life is at stake, she can't afford to be anything less than perfect outside of these apartments.

Right before she rams through the door, she whips around to set me with a stony glare. "I'm going to take Noguera and the Guardia Real to make sure Papá flushes out these cockroaches. In the meantime, *you* have to find the bombs for us."

Oh. A plan! How exciting. "Wh-where would I even start?"

"Well, if *I* were trying to hide something dangerous and magical, I'd go to the catacombs."

"The *what*?"

She smiles. "Don't worry, Anaïs. I won't send you down there alone." She turns and opens the door to utter a command to the waiting Capitán Noguera on the other side. "Bring me Infante Leopoldo at once."

CHAPTER TWO

*THIS IS WHY YOU CAME HERE, ANAÏS. TO MEET HIM AGAIN.
This is what you wanted.*

Yes, but that was before I had to look Leo in the eye and pretend I didn't remember the desperate crush of his lips on mine, my name a death knell on his tongue.

Imagine if he remembered it, too.

Once we are introduced and I recount the whole sordid tale, Leo fights his sister on the specifics of her plan. But as she told him, "If there's the slightest chance that Anaïs's visions are right, then the future of Ivarea depends on what we do right now. And we can guarantee our future. *If* you do as I say."

So here we are now. Doing as she says.

He only speaks to me when we've escaped the gravitational pull of the ballroom, and then it's only to say, "You know what it was about your little forged letter that nearly gave the game away? The lack of a seal."

A glint on his pinkie finger catches my attention—his signet ring. The flat bezel is fitted with an engraved carnelian bearing his actual crest, not the one I saw stamped around Clara's quarters: the Cardona dragon silhouetted underneath a crescent moon. According to her crest, Clara has the whole of the night sky in her grasp. And while a crescent moon is the symbol of a second son, I can't tell whether Leo's moon is waxing or waning. What kind of omen it's meant to be for his future.

I look back up and return a terse smile. "I'll remember that for next time."

He doesn't ask how many more times I plan to do this. I don't think either of us can fathom an answer.

We begin to descend endless flights of narrow stone staircases. The medieval fortress undergirding the royal palace yawns ever wider before us, and we march into its mouth, the teeth of history closing in behind us. Slowly the windows disappear, leaving enchanted torches to illuminate our way through the barren stone. The humidity here is worse than it is in the palace proper. Leo turns down a corridor and stops at an innocuous stretch of wall, holding himself hesitantly. He closes his eyes and presses his palm to the stone.

The seconds bleed between us until, all at once, the temperature in the corridor plummets. Goose bumps erupt down my still-sticky arms, and my nose twitches in the unnaturally crystalline air. Leo lets out a frosted breath and drops his hand. I stare at the mark of his palm on the wall—because there *is* a mark there, visible in the near dark. A singed handprint that melts into the stone before I can convince myself that I didn't see it. Then the wall dissipates.

I stumble backward, my heel catching on my skirts. A double door of black alder materializes where the wall used to be, with basalt knockers in the shape of more dragons. Without warning, Leo grabs me by the arm, shoves open the doors, and tugs me through. The threshold pummels me with an even deeper veil of cold, and then . . . then, we're inside the royal catacombs. The torches along the walls seem to burn more dimly than the ones outside; the shadows they cast muddle the impossible angles of this place.

"Surprised?" His voice sounds unnaturally loud in what appears to be a vestibule of some kind.

"No," I lie, just a little haughty. "I already knew you're a magician."

He deflates a little. "You take all the fun out of chasing our doom."

"You mean *stopping* our doom."

"Is that not what I said?"

My shallow breaths cloud before me. This cold is nowhere near our mild Massilie winters; it's more like the prelude to a bitter night on a barren mountainside than the caress of a chill against rosy cheeks. "Fine. I didn't know you could do *that*."

The guttering dark seems to bend around him as he smiles, more bittersweet than triumphant. "When the walls know you, it's easy to make the door manifest. One of the few perks left of being a magician in this family. No keeper's key necessary." He raises a hand again, and the torchlight perks up. The fires are set in the open mouths of more basalt dragons, their eyes as bright as if there are jewels embedded in their sockets.

I cast my eyes around the vestibule, everywhere finding a new elongated shadow or a too-smooth curve of wall to marvel at, and rub my arms to fight off the unease. I already had incontrovertible proof that the Alcázar obeys Clara; evidently, it knows Leo, too.

Discomfited, I wander through the vestibule, which stretches into several equidistant paths of greater darkness, like spokes of a wheel. Leo follows behind me, sweeping his arm to brighten the rest of the torches as we go.

"Why did Clara send us here, anyway?"

"Because the diabolical people who want all of us dead may well know that this is the best place in the whole of the Alcázar to hide illicit magical objects you don't want anyone to find," he says. "They'd need a keeper's key, but once they were in, they and their bombs would be safe from discovery. The catacomb wards have to guard much worse than bombs on a normal day."

I raise an eyebrow at the knowing cold. "What's *that* supposed to mean?"

He sighs, as if the question has struck a nerve. "You know the charm peddlers you see everywhere on the peninsula claiming they can sell you shards of San Arturo's right shin or Santa Lídia's knuckle or something? They can't, obviously. But can you imagine if they had charms made of, say, Rey Carlos's pinkie finger?"

"I thought you people value saintly charms the most."

He sucks in a breath at *you people*. "The saints and their remains wouldn't have any effect on Ivareans' ability to manipulate earthly magic. I don't know why people believe otherwise. But using the bones and reliquaries of powerful people who were actually historically renowned for their magical ability? Now, *that* would make a difference. Which is why we are very careful to guard our remains and those of other powerful magicians in Ivarea's service." He pauses. "Nothing safer than a magical fortress that has survived war and conquest and magic and my sister."

Nothing about this place screams *safety* to me, but I suppose Clara was right: it's as good a place as any to search. In silence, we separate to investigate either side of one of the catacombs' many paths of bones. They're picked so clean that they seem unreal compared to the burning stumps and gored flesh I've seen in the ballroom. Here, I can almost understand how a young Leo, first neglected by his family as the youngest child and then ostracized from them as a magician, might have thought playing with a saintly relic and swearing his life and death to Ivarea, to the service of the saints, was a normal thing to do. Death doesn't simply lurk in the Alcázar: it's painted across the walls in broad, unforgiving strokes, woven bright as thread-of-gold through the tapestries, through the foundation of this palace and this family and this country. Of course a nine-year-old would have imbibed a narrative of service to the kingdom after death in this place, even if it was pretend. It was the only way he knew how to assert his connection to his own family. Through stories. Through death.

How awfully bleak.

"You're Proensan, aren't you?"

I startle and almost upset one of the bone shelves. "Y-yes?"

"So you really believe in little winged creatures flitting about the countryside?"

After the despairing tenderness of our *last* night together, his words sting. I can't tell if he's being facetious or an asshole, or both, but I am not interested in indulging him either way. "First of all, the fairies supposedly disappeared centuries ago, so I can assure you that none of them are *flitting about* any-where. Secondly, my beliefs are none of your business, Alteza. And in all honesty, such a question seems rich for someone who did a blasphemous blood ritual with San Pedro's relic."

His footsteps stop. The silence across the catacombs now presses against my windpipe. "What did you—how did you know—"

"Your people's beliefs, saints and all, are *not* better than mine. Whatever they may be."

"Agreed," he ventures immediately, abandoning his earlier question. "What matters is our faith in the stories that belong to our people, and the duties we have to them."

"Duties to our people, or duties to the stories they tell themselves?"

"To the people, Doña Anaïs. Always to the people. No matter what they believe in—Ivarean saints, Proensan fairies, anything and everything in between. That's the price of duty." I hear his voice like an echo refracting through time off the walls. "Don't tell me you don't know what that's like."

I almost break out into a fresh wave of hysterical laughter

when the crack of what sounds suspiciously like a footstep re-sounds in the darkness.

"What was that?" Leo yelps.

"It wasn't you?" I try to peer out toward the main vestibule we entered from, but I can't make out any additional move-ment, strange flickers of the torches, anything. Maybe it's Clara coming to rescue us. She and the king found the bombs aboveground, arrested Faucher, seized his co-conspirators, and secured the palace. Ivarea is safe.

You did it, Anaïs. You can be at peace.

A hand at my shoulder dissolves the dream. The only rea-son I don't scream and leap into a sheaf of skeletons is that I recognize Leo's touch instantly. I draw backward against him, a bulwark in the insidious cold.

I turn my head just as he circles in front of me, a finger at his lips. The hilt of his sword is in his other hand, so I draw my blessed dagger from my sash. We shuffle forward in silence, side by side, pausing every few steps to listen for any action. As the third set of footsteps begins in earnest, Leo draws his sword. Now the footsteps mimic ours: searching, pausing, searching again.

There's only one reason anyone else would be down here when there's a ball going on overhead: one of Faucher's citoy-ens has a keeper's key for the catacombs.

They really are here to plant the bombs after all. Or they already hid them here and want to bring them to the ballroom before midnight. Whatever it is, I need to see what's happening before it kills me.

I break pace with Leo, taking the lead on our slow crawl to the vestibule. But right before I step out from the relative shelter of the catacomb wall, Leo pulls me back and shoves me into the wall of bones, pinning me in place with his chest.

"*What are you doing?*"

"Me?" His eyes practically leap out of his head. "What are *you* doing?"

I'm about to snap, *What the hell do you mean, and also, please stop staring at my breasts,* but I realize a beat too late what Leo means.

My locket is glowing.

No—the *amulet* is glowing.

My breathing grows shallow, my legs faint. Light is emanating from the locket like burning coal in a furnace. There's no denying it. Leo doesn't seem like he knows whether to hold me or keep his distance.

The fingers of my free hand dance down the length of the chain, but I don't dare touch the locket itself: it burns like a tiny star affixed to the hollow of my throat. Leo's face is bathed in its light.

Clara was right. She literally *just* told me this stupid heirloom is magical, and I didn't believe her.

"*Make it stop,*" Leo mutters tersely.

Suddenly, the amulet begins to burn an oval-shaped hole in my chest, and I scream.

I can just hear our guest leaping through the vestibule, but I can't see past Leo. He wraps his free hand around the amulet's chain, trying to break it. Then the burning at my chest stops as quickly as it began. The amulet flares like the fireworks that were supposed to go off at midnight, drowning the catacombs in amber light. The three of us all cry out, now blind and help-less.

I have to take advantage of the intruder's brief incapacity. I try to push Leo away with the flat of my dagger, but he doesn't get the hint.

Which leaves me no choice but to turn the sharp edge of the blade into his arm.

Before a dark spurt of his blood soaks into my skin, I slip out of his grip and make a run for the vestibule. Leo yells my name, but I don't pay him any mind. Ahead stands the intruder, a bearded man clenching his teeth in concentration, the barrel of his rifle swinging toward me. But behind the man and his rifle, the black alder doors to the catacombs have turned incandescent from the amulet's light—and they're thrown wide open.

From the hallway outside, a pitch-black shadow stretches across the threshold.

Then, a whispered command: *"Now."*

The bullet goes through my brain like it's made of paper, and all at once, darkness is all there is to know.

XII

CHAPTER ONE

THE LAST MOMENT OF MY LIFE BREAKS APART IN MY MEMORY like it, too, suffered a mortal wound. It splinters my latest murderer until he is just shards of bone, no different from those of the kings who saw me through death.

The person who gave the command must have been Faucher himself. I didn't expect he would be down there so early in the night, but maybe his task was important enough that he didn't trust his followers with it. Maybe he was taking the smuggled bombs into the open, beyond the catacombs' heightened magical protections. But who fired the shot? Someone in the palace already? A courtier? A servant? One of Faucher's men in disguise?

I abandon that train of thought as quickly as it comes to me. That is not the most pressing mystery I now have on my hands.

Or rather, around my neck.

Perched before the silver-backed mirror in my room, I undo the chain and set the locket down on the vanity. I don't know if I'm imagining it after my last death in the catacombs, but I can almost sense its dormant power. Like a pinprick of a chill in the depths of summer—unlike the Aubanel daggers, which only flare to life when called upon.

Never in my wildest dreams would I have guessed that the little opal locket I've worn since I was a child bore any kind of power, but Clara identified it after only an hour or two in my company. Now there's no use in me wasting time on a scheme to get into her good graces again just to ask her about the locket.

Not when I can ask the person who gave it to me.

"Does Papa know you're hiding a blessed object from him?"

Maman barely glances sideways from the selection of gloves that Béatrice is setting out on my bed for her inspection. "My family lost all of our blessed objects in the conquest, you know that."

The chain rattles in my hand as I give it a good shake in her direction. "Then what the hell is *this*?"

"Such dramatics, Anaïs. This behavior is really not becoming for a young lady."

"Tell me, or I'm not going to the ball. *What is this?*"

She turns my way at last, hands on her hips, affront in the straight line of her brows. "What kind of question is that? You've had the locket for years and never once—"

Because I was a fool. "I'm asking now." For some reason, the image of Leo throwing himself against me in a futile attempt to save us both hovers behind my eyes. "Tell me what I need to know."

She shifts where she stands, either frustrated or uneasy. "I really don't—"

"*Please,* Maman. The truth."

For the first time all afternoon, perhaps the first time in years, she actually looks at me. Past her vision of who she wants me to be. Straight through to the desperate girl shaking like a leaf in a summer breeze, begging for something real.

At last, she dismisses Béatrice with a murmur, and when she closes the door behind her, she huffs and settles down on the bed. "You asked for the truth, Anaïs. And perhaps it *is* time you knew."

Taken aback, I only nod.

"Hundreds of years ago, I had an ancestor named Mireille Laborde. She was the eldest daughter of a Proensan duke that owned one of the most celebrated vineyards in—"

"The short version, Maman." I don't have all night to go into every twist and turn of my family's history. I don't even have now.

"Oh, very well. Mireille had an encounter with a fairy."

In no world, at no time, could I have anticipated the *fairies* coming up when I asked my own mother about her empty locket. I only just manage to keep my jaw from unhinging. "Your ancestor *met* a fairy? A real fairy? *How?*"

She crosses her arms. "How many times have I told you the fairies were real?"

More than I can count. More than I can remember.

In truth, I've always imagined that the fairies were just one more of my mother's fancies; I couldn't quite bring myself to believe in them, let alone worship them, but I could never wholly close the door on the possibility of their existence. Not when the story was so meaningful to Maman and other Proensans like her.

But if they're *not* just a myth . . . if they *were* real . . .

It feels cruel to use a phrase I've been dismissed with time and time again on my own mother, but I can't help it. "This is *insane*. What do you mean, an encounter?"

She doesn't respond at all for a moment; she only bites her lip and watches me, as if I'm going to erupt. When I don't, she raises her head and adds, "It was, I should say, an *intimate* encounter."

It takes me several extra moments to process her word choice. "And by *intimate* . . . you're saying she . . ."

"They were lovers."

So now not only were fairies real, they could lie with humans? Sure. Why not. Makes sense. I've come this far down the path of madness with her, why not throw myself into it, too?

But why would my mother feel the need to recount Mireille Laborde's alleged dalliances with an apparently not-so-mythological being to me? What does that have to do with the origins of the locket? Just as I open my mouth, I notice the drawn expression on her face. Something breaks open within me, and I understand. "Your ancestor had *children* with a *fairy*?"

Maman makes a soft noise of assent.

The locket lands with a metallic clang on the lacquered surface of the vanity.

So . . . so my family is descended from fairies. Centuries back. The fairies my people remember and worship as gods. Those fairies. Does it mean anything for us now? Are we not just as human as we should—

I tear my gaze away from the cursed thing on the vanity. This cannot possibly be true. Fairies didn't exist. They cannot be our ancestors. We are not . . . I could not . . .

No. No, this is just a story. A legend that's been passed down from generation to generation. Kind of like—

"The blessing itself is a sign of descent from the fairies. Their blood is the source of your magic."

"That *cannot* be right."

"It's not just you and me, darling. Any Proensan that carries the blessing has fairy blood somewhere in their family tree. But not everyone with fairy blood also carries a strong blessing. Magic cannot be passed through bloodlines down the generations indefinitely. That's why the blessing weakens with every birth, every generation." Her hands twitch in her lap. I've never seen her so agitated. "I know what it must sound like, but it *is* the truth."

Her quiet conviction now scares me more than her bombastic declarations about my great destiny ever did.

"You see, the Proensans who survived the Ivareans' invasion saw the power and cruelty of their new king. They feared for their survival should the Cardonas find out that they were the children of fairies. What if they conscripted them into their armies? Tortured them for the crime of existing? Killed them outright? Used them to try to bring the fairies back? So they—"

I'm going to faint. "Bring the fairies *back*? Where did they *go*?"

Maman exhales through her nose. "You really think anyone knows?"

"Ten minutes ago, I wasn't even sure the fairies *existed*!"

She glowers down her nose at me for a few moments before recovering herself. "I mean to say, there was no telling what the Ivareans would do if they knew fairies had been real and that their descendants still walked the earth. So our ancestors wrote the fairies out of the explanations they gave the Ivareans about the source of their power. Our ancestors did what they had to do to protect us all. Sometimes I worry they did it too well. Just look at your father's family." She sniffs, almost mournful. "The Aubanels had a fairy ancestor somewhere down the line. They simply don't remember it anymore."

Then how is it that my mother, of all people, knows this many secrets about blood magic? How could she have hidden these monumental stories for all this time? Where could she have heard them? Maman has always had a wild imagination, but this is . . . If any of this is true, her hiding it for so long would be a deception so much bigger, so much more complex, than I would ever have thought she was capable of. "Why should I just *believe* you?"

She touches her thumb to each fingertip, over and over again, as if to ward away misfortune. "Ask your locket to reveal itself."

I should check her for fever. Tuck her into my bed. Nurse her back from madness here, in this burning house, in this doomed city, until we've forgotten everything we've ever heard about the locket, the fairies, the blessing, the ball.

But I can't bring myself to touch her. I can't even try.

With my back to her, I withdraw the Aubanel dagger I stole when I first woke up this afternoon, my knuckles white against the emerald of the pommel, and prick my ring finger. As my blood beads at the fingertip, I shove the dagger back into its sheath before Maman can see it and flick the locket's mechanism. It splits open with all the grace of a melon falling off a table. In this case, no overripe flesh spills out from the break; no seeds and no possibilities slip into my fingers. There's just the dull gold backing of each half of the locket, staring up at me like pupil-less eyes.

I dab them each with a drop of blood. My eyes flutter shut.

Reveal yourself. To the girl you were maybe trying to help in the catacombs. Tell me what I need to know. Reveal yourself and tell me what I am. I don't care what happens to me next— just tell me what I need to know now.

I feel my palms prickle as numbness hastens through my veins. I open my eyes just in time to see portraits emerge from the interior of the locket, as if the gold of the casing were as immaterial as mist rolling off the sea.

At first glance, the little portraits appear to be silhouettes. But they are too intricately wrought to be ordinary cameos— the paint so vibrant and fresh it could have been mixed this morning, the tiny gemstones too brilliant to have been locked away for centuries. The first portrait depicts the oval-shaped face of a pale brunette woman with a circlet of tiny seed pearls about her brow. Behind her glimmers a peerless blue sky studded with painted treetops. The second portrait is . . .

Is . . .

It's a fairy.

I know it is. Not because it looks anything like Leo's *little woodland creatures,* or the gods some Proensans cling to; at first glance it actually seems human, and handsome enough that it deserves to be immortalized, even if only in enamel. No, it's mostly because there's something uncanny about the curve of its cheekbones, jutting against the blazing sky. A suggestion of fey strangeness in the way its raw diamond eyes slide toward the woman's portrait.

Toward Mireille Laborde.

My gaze darts between the two portraits, of my ancestor and my . . . other . . . ancestor. They *are* looking at each other, warmly, across the hinge. It's beyond belief. But there they are, and for all the impossibility of their precious, hidden portraits, it's like they exist, still. Like if I just flicked my wrist one way or another, their painted eyes would break from each other and meet mine. Like they could see me, and know who and what I am. It seems that their locket does.

Why now? Why did it light up in the catacombs when it's done nothing every other time I've been killed?

I bring the locket back up to my eye level for a closer look. The evening light dancing about the surfaces of my room makes the portraits glow against their painted sunset-drenched skies.

Wait.

A second ago, the portraits depicted Mireille and her fairy lover during the day.

Yes, I can see it now: the skies in the portraits are changing. Day bleeding into night and back, sunlight streaking through storms and storms dissipating at the touch of the sun, trees blooming and wilting and blooming again, all subtle enough that it's practically invisible from this close up. The figures themselves remain the same through the cycling of the days, frozen in the constant churn of time.

A dark thought steals my breath.

Frozen.

It can't be.

But there they are. The lady and the fairy. Caught in a single moment as time circles them, never pausing, never breaking, a coil from which the portraits can't escape.

It's just magic, right? A cunning trick hidden in an old heirloom. That's all it is. There's no meaning there. No other possibility. A necklace couldn't trap people in time. No. No, that's not possible. I know I've said that about everything Maman has claimed so far, but . . . but this isn't the same. Can't be. I refuse to believe it.

But if I'm wrong now, too . . .

As Maman watches, I press another bead of my blood into the newly revealed portrait of the fairy. Once again, I ask it, *command* it, to reveal the truth. For what feels like a long time—nothing.

Suddenly, I see a shadow cross between the portraits. The suggestion of a silhouette watching Mireille and her lover. Following them. But it's not another enamel figure.

It's not *in* the locket at all, is it?

Obeying some strange magical instinct, I lower my eyelids. A vision takes shape behind them.

A tower room. A young man, with hair the brown of late autumn leaves, cheekbones too sharp to be merely inviting, and eyes like a clouded diamond—an uncanny combination of the key features immortalized in the miniatures. The locket is in the vision, too: the young man, clearly the result of Mireille's *intimate* fairy encounter, pores carefully over his parents' portraits. They are the brightest things in the vision, but their backgrounds aren't moving. The young man raises a hand and begins to draw circles in midair.

Slowly something takes shape out of nothing: a hilt of cloud wrought with rain, ice cut like a diamond in the pommel, a blade of scarlet lightning that sparks and fizzles and burns the air. He grabs at the cloud hilt and raises the impossible sword above his head. I can't hear what he's saying, can't guess at what's happening, but then he swings the sword against the sparkling innards of the locket and the scythe-sharp edge of the blade slashes across both portraits at once. A crash of thunder rings out in the tower, followed by the scent, even in the vision, of burning.

The man sheaths his sword of lightning. With a breath, he summons a wind so fierce it smothers the sparks wreathing the room. He bends to examine the mangled remains. But— nothing. The locket is still there. Whole.

He roars. I still can't hear anything, but the expression on his face, the anguish and horror, still manages to send a shiver down my spine. He shuts the locket for a final time and stalks away. The vision dissolves.

I have to blink several times before I can focus on anything in my bedroom, Maman included. All this time, Papa told me that the blessing can't offer visions of the future—but this was a vision of the past, wasn't it? Like . . . a memory. The amulet's memory. Of its own attempted destruction. By Mireille Laborde's half-fairy child. The ancestor whose birth meant that future generations would have blood magic.

He was trying to destroy the locket. And failed.

But . . . *why?* And what did the attempt do to the amulet?

"What—the hell—is this?"

Maman blinks impassively. "You see the portraits, no? They're supposed to be lovely."

"Supposed to—" I brandish the open locket in her direction. "Look at them! They showed me a *vi*—"

"It's no use, Anaïs. The locket doesn't reveal itself to me. It looks to me now as it has all my life."

Because she carries her family's fairy blood, but its magic didn't survive long enough to reach her.

I swallow my tear-prickling melancholy, but I can't make myself look back down at the open amulet. "Maman. Please. What *is* this thing?"

This pulls a shaky smile from her pursed lips. "My own maman, your grand-mère, she told me the locket had been a gift to Mireille made by her fairy lover himself. That it was forged with the stuff of gods." Meeting her pure, moonlit gaze is like looking back in time. At Maman as a young girl at her own mother's knee, learning about all these fantastical things that were in her blood, even if magic was not.

Did her heart break then, to not have the blessing? To not be able to see the amulet forged by her mythological ancestor? From her tone as she continues with her story, I think I can divine the answer.

"In its day, the locket was said to have a host of powers. Like freezing time so Mireille would not age and could stay with her fairy lover forever, if that was what she wished. I don't know for sure, though, darling. No one does."

My stomach drops.

I don't have to beg to see that vision again to understand what happened next.

If that amulet was forged by a fairy to stave off death, the way a portrait captures a likeness so that it may never grow old, never decay, never change—then that fairy's half-human son stabbing it with a magical sword, as if to *force* his mother back to the mortal world he dwelled in, must have warped the amulet's magic. Instead of just freezing time, now . . . now the locket loops time around itself.

It's all I can do to not break into sobs. Or laughter. Or launch myself out of my bedroom window because it'd be quicker than stabbing myself with my dagger.

This . . . this is it. The answer I thought I'd never find. The question I have killed myself and my family and my countrymen over and over again to avoid asking.

It was hanging around my neck the whole fucking time.

This fairy amulet, which has hung like a noose above my

heart for years, this thing that, apparently, has a mind and a corrupted ancient magic of its own—was it always going to reach out into my life and drench it in amber, preserve a single moment, a single horrific night, and trap me within it?

I think back to my first death on the ballroom floor, with Leo dying a king in my arms. I vaguely remember an amber light bursting from above my chest. I thought it was a shot or an explosion but . . . but what if that light was actually from the amulet activating for the first time? What if being drowned anew in my blood awakened it, pulling me into the embrace of a time that never ends?

Leo's words echo in my head: *So what are you going to do about it?*

Right. Well. If my curse comes from the locket, then destroying it would seem like a plan. But if my half-fairy ancestor's lightning sword couldn't destroy the amulet, then there's no way in hell that I can.

Which means there's no way to escape this night. Right?

Wrong again, sneers the voice in my head. *Just lose the locket.*

My intuition feels feeble, even to myself, but the more I consider it, the more I'm afraid that it's right: if I die without wearing the locket, maybe I won't come back.

It would be over.

Forever.

It would be so easy.

I wouldn't have to bear the weight of the whole kingdom anymore. A kingdom that, as has been made horrifically clear to me time and time again, does not care whether I live or die, let alone whether it lives or dies. I wouldn't be forced to haunt the scenes of my failures over and over again. I wouldn't keep ruining everything for anyone who might make it out of tonight alive.

I wouldn't have to build a future.

It's not as if I know how.

Even so . . . I cannot possibly risk being right. No, death, real death, a death that does nothing for anyone but me, a death I can't undo—no. I can't afford that. My family, at the very least, do not deserve that. Not even after this.

Fury compresses into resignation in the pit of my stomach. Wordlessly, I flip the locket shut.

Maman gives a tiny sigh. "House Laborde was able to protect it after the conquest because it's been dormant for so long," she says. "We kept the story of its provenance alive, but in secret. Now, more than two long centuries later, all we have are fragments. Memories. But the past is a heavy burden, even when it's so distant, and I didn't—I couldn't bring myself to tell you, Anaïs. It was too much."

"*Too much?*" I repeat. "Too much for whom?"

"For you," she answers peaceably. "I thought—I *hoped*—sparing you of its weight would make things easier."

I snap back to myself, suddenly less woozy than I was before. "Make *what* easier?"

"Your future." She seems bloodless and practical again, no longer wistful or nostalgic or, God forbid, mournful. My countess mother once more. "It would do you no good to settle down in Marenca if you cling to stories about fairy blood running in your veins."

235

"How could you keep this from me?"

Maman draws up behind me in the mirror. Iron-willed. Impossible. "I thought I was protecting you."

She knew. She always knew. Maybe not the amulet-time-loop-magic part, specifically, but she always knew there was something different about me, about us, something important—and she never told me what it was. She lied to me.

No, worse. She never thought to tell me.

I thought, if nothing else, that I had an anchor in myself. I thought I knew who I was. Who I'm supposed to be. Where and what I came from. As long as I knew that, I could keep going. I could keep fighting to return to myself, to the life that I thought was mine.

But it wasn't.

It was never mine at all.

Teardrops as dark as acid rain roll down my cheeks, mixing with the kohl on my lashes. My crying is quieter than the last time I broke down here, overwhelmed without any other recourse.

I very well can't blame my mother for getting me trapped in time. It would be like blaming her for the sunset. Hell, if she was the one who'd been wearing it for that first Anniversary Ball, maybe the amulet would have roared to life for her instead, and she'd be the one stuck like this.

I grab a spare handkerchief from a drawer and wipe my face completely dry. Maman has not moved the entire time I've been crying. She stares at the powder and rouge smeared on the kerchief and just barely manages to suppress a comment about all the work I just undid. I hold myself preternaturally still as she reaches out to tuck a loose strand of my hair behind my ear. In the early-evening sunlight, the gold of the ringlet looks akin to the chain in my palm.

"Like this locket," she ventures quietly, "our people are very good at surviving."

A fresh sob breaks off midway up my throat. "Are we?"

The weight of years gathers in the lines of Maman's eyes. "I'm sorry, Anaïs. I'm sorry for keeping all this from you. But I love you. No matter what happens." She plucks the amulet from my prone hands and loops it back around my neck. Her fingers are cool as she tries to grip the clasp of the chain, but her gaze in the vanity mirror is warm. "Now, promise me that you'll do your best tonight. Be a credit to your ancestors' legacy. Make your people proud."

It feels like centuries have passed since Leo made his confession: *sometimes I think we've been doomed for a long time.* Even though I didn't understand why he would say something like that then, now I rather think we were all doomed, long before the first strike of the midnight bells at the Anniversary Ball. I certainly was.

Whatever is happening to me now, however it began, whatever it makes of me, whatever it means, *I'm* still the one that comes back. I'm the one who remembers our suffering.

I can't let that mean nothing.

I have to keep going. I don't have another choice.

"I . . . I promise."

But I don't meet my mother's eyes again.

CHAPTER TWO

FOR PERHAPS THE FIRST TIME SINCE I WAS INITIALLY KILLED, I am genuinely glad to be at the Alcázar. Solely because it means I cannot be tethered to my mother's presence anymore.

She's around, of course. Watching me weave through the crowds from afar, nudging me toward notable grandes' single relatives, urging me to smile or flirt or dance, with facial expressions better suited for a stage actor than a countess. But I ignore her unsubtle little hints. I have to, or I'm going to fall apart all over again.

I can still feel the amulet, cold at the base of my throat. I sure as hell don't understand what the full extent of its powers are or why it gave off light in the catacombs, but after Maman's story, after the locket's own vision, those now seem like incidental mysteries. I feel all at once like my life was just stolen from me—by a necklace, of all things—and also like it's just begun, and it's too much. Still, I keep the amulet exactly where it's always been around my neck. It feels tight enough to strangle me.

I take a page out of Leo the Lush's book and drown my angst in drink. Just as I snatch up a fourth flute of fizzy summer wine, a hand at my elbow makes me whip around.

"Slow down, it's just me." Gaspard Plamondon holds up his hands in mock surrender. "Everything all right?"

I down my wine in one gulp and replace the empty glass on its tray. "Um."

"That bad, is it?" He gives me a curious once-over. "I feel like I haven't seen you sit still for more than three minutes. How am I supposed to badger you about the horrors I've been subjected to tonight if you don't slow down?"

"Your father wants you to marry Paloma Nelleda, yes, I know, how absolutely tragic."

"No, my father wants me to court Palo—wait, you knew about that?"

Not because you previously complained to me about this very situation on this same night. Definitely not that. "Oh, sure. The both of you are landed and wealthy and attractive. Sounds about right to me."

"Yes, well, I don't think Paloma's ever going to give a *Landaulan* the time of day." A glower pushes through his studied resignation, but he forces it back down like acid. I know the feeling. "Pity dance?"

I nod, because what the hell else am I supposed to do, and we take our places. The music starts anew, a moderate-tempo Lutessian waltz. My limbs seem to have lost all memory of how to comport themselves. I can't even follow Gaspard's lead without stumbling over my feet. He has the good grace not to draw attention to it; he only tightens his grip, making himself an anchor for my churning seas.

"How about you?" he asks, companionably enough. "Don't tell me your dauntless maman hasn't cooked up some brilliant scheme for the rest of your life, too."

The question throws me back into my earlier, more sober despair. I have to force my eyes to focus on Gaspard's face— the curls plastering on his forehead, the tension melting from his features despite himself as he sways with the music. Gaspard, who can't disentangle himself from his family any more than I can. Gaspard, who has even more complicated feelings about Ivarea than I do. If there's anyone I can confess to about what's eating at me, surely it's him.

Even if it will only mean something right now.

"My mother told me our family is descended from fairies."

"My mother likes to say that our family is descended from warriors and philosophers. I suppose the former line skipped me."

"Gaspard, I'm serious. She said the fairies were real and that we're *descended* from them, and that's where blood magic actually comes from, so anyone with the blessing is also just *like* this, I suppose. Also, my locket—this one, right here—was made by a fairy and it has *horrible* secret powers that, miracle of miracles, are only now manifesting themselves and have in fact *actively* ruined my life."

He raises his eyebrows so high that they disappear behind his disheveled curls. "Is . . . that all?"

I try to think back to this afternoon in my bedroom, but after all that wine, my brain skips over the memory like a stone along a lake. Maman thought it would be easier for me to not know. She thought I wouldn't be able to handle it. She doesn't know about what the amulet did to me, but that doesn't matter.

She was right.

"Also, my half-fairy ancestor summoned a sword made of lightning clean out of the goddamned sky."

I can practically see Gaspard's tongue tying itself in knots. "Well. Um, don't go around telling any Ivareans that last bit. They'd just try to claim them as one of their saints, and he'd never just be your ancestor again."

"Please be serious for a minute. Have you *ever* heard of this before? You know, fairies being real . . . and l-lying with people . . . and . . ." I blink back a fresh fall of tears. "You don't think it could really, actually be true?"

He sucks in his cheeks, making him look like a gaunt fish flopping on a beach. In another life, another time, I might have laughed. "It's folklore, Anaïs. There are so many stories about the fairies—what they were like, what happened to them—it's hard to know what's possible. But even if those of you with the blessing are, you know, *part fairy*, you've always seemed human enough to me."

"Human *enough*?"

"Well, do you feel at all non-human?"

"What does that even *mean*?"

"I don't know. Anything strange happen to you lately?"

I choke on my chortle. To distract myself, I stare behind Gaspard's shoulder at the southeastern doors of the ballroom, which are carved with great dueling bulls. The clash of their enchanted horns sends sparks down their wooden expanse. I think of the tension between Maman and me today, and the tension between Proensa and the peninsula, and the nights I've lived and died, and I, too, feel like the bull on the carving, throwing myself at an implacable enemy, sacrificing myself, forever, for nothing.

After a moment, my gaze slides away from the bull carvings. And lands on something else.

Some*one* else.

Gaspard tightens his grip on my hand. "Anaïs?"

I blink, jolted by the pressure squeezing my palm. The world comes back into focus.

I blink again.

"Back there."

Gaspard tries to follow my gaze. "Back where?"

At the southeastern doors. The guard there. He looks . . . well, not familiar, exactly . . . but a faint, whining alarm goes off in my brain, forces me to keep looking. I try to drag myself out of my despair. Why does it matter that I've seen that particular guard before? I've seen everyone here before. More than I ever wanted to. And in any case, it's not a crime to have patchy facial hair.

Maybe it's not just the face that matters. Maybe it's where I saw it.

That's when it hits me.

The catacombs. The man who killed me. On his leader's orders.

It's him.

And eventually, he will go to the catacombs again.

Clara must have been right, that evening in her chambers: Faucher *is* hiding the bombs somewhere in that underground graveyard, and this man knows it. Maybe he's the one who retrieves them for his citoyen leader. Or maybe they're powerful enough to overcome whatever special wards that place has, and he's the one who sets them off.

He may not be Faucher, but if this man is the reason the bombs go off at midnight, then *he's* the reason I'm stuck like this. Not Maman, not Mireille Laborde, not her fairy lover, not their horrifically powerful child, not the time-looping magical amulet he corrupted. *He's* the sole reason we're all doomed. And if the sole reason for our doom is right in front of me . . .

There are still those bombs, of course, and still the mob, and still Faucher himself. But bombs can be dismantled if you know where they are. Mobs can be controlled eventually. And men . . . men can be killed.

That's the price of duty. Don't tell me you don't know what that's like.

I don't have a choice.

Do I?

The minuscule amount of space in my brain left for dancing dissolves in the stagnant ballroom air. The only real thing in this room is that man at the doors.

The only thing in my pounding head is the overwhelming need to see him gone.

To end it.

All of it.

"Anaïs?"

Applause for the orchestra swells out of the ballroom. The dance is over. Well and truly over.

I slide my hand out of Gaspard's. "Oh. Sorry. Just— thinking. Sorry for dumping all of this familial nonsense on you."

A wry little smirk blooms on his face. "You know me. I love familial nonsense."

Couples part and reform to get ready for the next dance, and the next one, and all the ones that will never come. I back away.

If I'm lucky, I will never dance here again.

His name is Quirós. Or at least that's the surname emblazoned on a badge on his uniform. Up close, his face is in no way remarkable. Patchy facial hair, sweat gathering down his chin.

Giggling into a fresh glass of wine, gloves abandoned in a distant corner, I stagger toward the doors with the bull carvings. In the instant their enchanted duel falters, mine begins.

I trip and dash myself against the doors, shattering crystal below the bulls' hooves, flooding their wooden battlefield with wine. While knocking myself to the ground, I discreetly prick my arms with the blessed dagger.

With an uncertain glance at the rest of the courtiers, all of them too wrapped up in their own glories to notice a drunk girl caterwauling on the ground, Quirós sighs and reaches out a hand to help me up.

I was already drunk before I decided on this suicide mission, so it doesn't take much to push my voice into an even higher, more unstable pitch. "Oh . . . thank . . ,"

Quirós pulls me to my feet and belatedly notices the fresh blood on my arm. "You have been injured, señora."

"I *what?*" The wine flute crunches under my feet as I flail and examine my arms. "Why, that's—you're right, that's—my bl*ugh*—" I don't bother suppressing a dramatic, wolflike howl into his shoulder. My skin crawls to even touch him, and I long desperately to drive my dagger into his jugular right here, right now, but . . . no. No, that isn't the plan.

I think.

"The inf—the hosp—I have to go—to the *infirm*—"

Quirós doesn't say no outright; there's more time until midnight than he knows what to do with. I whine and whimper the whole way out of the ballroom. I don't even have time to look for my parents one last time before he and I disappear past Lion Arch.

I wait until the corridors have emptied of intrepid explorers and amorous couples and servants whiling away the time. He takes me toward a stairwell at the end of the corridor. Marble lion statues with gilded manes and tails that whip in nonexistent winds flank either side of the banister. It's easy enough to stumble on the closest enchanted tail. It's even easier to draw the dagger from my sash while my body is still folded in on itself.

And slashing the blade upward across Quirós's throat? That's easiest of all. Like taking a perfectly good blank canvas and flinging paint across the middle. Impulsive, but nothing that cannot be painted over with a surer hand.

Nothing that can't be covered up.

His body falls to the ground, the pistol at his side clanging down the stairs. I hear it echo forever and ever, clattering around in my suddenly and furiously empty mind, and don't feel the blood splatter on me for a very long time. I can only see the blood-slicked blade I have not yet relinquished. It feels like the first time I died, pitching myself across the bodies on that horrible battlefield.

And now . . .

Well, what's one more death when the blood of an entire palace has already been etched into my skin a hundredfold? Why should this matter?

The ghost of Leo's voice rings in my ears. *What are you sacrificing yourself for?*

This, I answer.

Them.

You.

I root around in Quirós's uniform, looking for something

that ties him to the bombs or to Faucher. The closest I can find is a tiny wrought-iron key buried in his trouser pocket. Did Leo once say there were physical keys to the catacombs, or is that a delusion like the hazy and blood-splattered one I'm seeing now? I slip it into the now-empty sheath at my waist. With my head still down, I drag the body behind the banister, shielded by one of the marble lions.

I press my fingers to the wound on my arm. The pressure splits my skin further, as if shards from the crystal flute really did get embedded there, and I have to force my arm back to my side before I cleave myself in two. I crouch down and smear my blood, the blood of fairies, on the floor.

Hide all trace of what happened here. Just for now. Just until we are safe. Then I will answer for my crimes. I will pay for what I did.

Just like in the broom cupboard with Gaspard, I have to fight to press my will into the palace, to make it do what I want. My feet ache, my knees quake, my arm burns. This place will never yield to me, and maybe it never should. Not to a murderer.

Soon, the bloodstains disappear into the floor. The spell even wipes the blood off the banisters and the lions. With Quirós dead, I've bought us precious time, but it's not over yet. I have to clean my gown and return to the ballroom to raise the alarm. I'll *force* the king to act. To get his people out before the revolutionaries storm the palace, and stop Faucher *now*.

After that . . . I don't care what happens to me. I'll toss the fairy amulet into the river and hope that will end my repeating night forever. And if Rey Rodrigo sentences me to death for Quirós's murder . . . fine. After all the times I've already died and come back here, after the terrible things I've done to save these people from their doom, I'd deserve such a sentence. I'd accept it gladly. As long as Ivarea is safe. As long as I'm not sent back.

But for now . . . there it is. Quirós's body. Incontrovertible proof that I *can* do something. That what I do *will* matter.

And it will all be worth it.

After midnight, anyway.

I wipe down my blade with a glove and press it anew to my skirt. With an intake of sharp, iron-tanged air, I close my eyes, and—

"Anaïs? Is that you?"

My eyes fly open. For a second all I see are lions prowling around the landing, pupils narrowed, muzzles pink and dripping. Then my sight focuses.

Oh no no no no—

Maman cries out again. "What happened to you?"

I'm dressed in blood. Made up with it. My face, my gown, my hands. And there's not a drop anywhere else.

Despite everything from this afternoon—the truth, the lies, the magic, the tragedy—the sight of her tugs at my paralyzed, benumbed heart. My voice cracks and splinters, my heart dropping with it to icy depths unknown. "M-Maman, I . . ."

She was frozen in the corridor where she spotted me, but she rushes forward at the sound of my voice. She skids to a stop just inches from the hem of my ruined gown. "What happened to you?" It doesn't even feel like a question. It feels like a prophecy about to be fulfilled, the promise of inevitability. "I heard that you'd fallen, and I thought . . . Why do you have one of your father's daggers?"

I can hardly remember the last time I made a real effort to tell her the truth. But I'm supposed to live past midnight. This is all supposed to mean something. It's supposed to be the end of the attack before it happens. It's supposed to be the end of death.

I'm not going back.

I can't.

"The palace is under attack."

I could be speaking in another language entirely, for all the comprehension on her face.

"There are explosives. In the catacombs. Under the Alcázar. If we don't find them now, they're going to go off at midnight and kill us all. They're going to . . . We have to find them first. We have to find them all first before they kill us."

"Before *who* kills us?" She takes another careful step forward, eyeing the dagger still in my hand. "Anaïs, tell me . . . What did you do?"

I was always going to be found out. I wasn't going to *hide* what I did to Quirós. That was the price of fulfilling my duty to these people, this place, this goddamn country. But I was not supposed to be discovered by my *mother*. Anyone but her. Anything to spare me the look on her face, the crashing certainty that something bad happened to her daughter just around the corner, just behind the ban—

Behind the banister.

Faster than should be possible in that massive satin gown, Maman darts around me. I cry out just as she rounds the base of the banister and finds a heap of human flesh below.

Her eyes flash up and search mine.

I throw myself to my knees, even though they scream in protest. "That's the man who was going to set off the bombs. I've *seen* him do it. The fairies—this amulet"—I drop the dagger on the floor and grab the locket tight enough to choke me, the gold stark against my hands—"the fairy amulet, the one with the portraits, you know? It has powers. It has so much more power than you know. I *felt* it today, I saw a vision of— Maman, this thing is keeping me trapped in time."

"Y-you've lost your mind." Her voice comes out warped with stress and sorrow. "This is my fault. Oh, this is all my fault. I shouldn't have told you. It's driven you mad. I drove you mad."

"*Shut up.*" Scorn shoots up from the pit of my stomach. "You have no idea how many times I've died because of that man. And you, too! You have no idea—*you*, and Papa, and all of us, we've all burned alive and been crushed to death and all kinds of horrific things, and when I saw him, I couldn't let him do it again. I *had* to buy us time. To buy *you* time."

She stays behind the marble lion, in the company of death. "You killed him."

"He killed us first! He killed *you!*"

Her skin has gone paler than I've ever seen. "What were you *thinking*? The king will never let you see the light of day again. You'll never come *home* again."

"I don't care. I had to do it, Maman, don't you see? I had no choice! I have to—I did this to save you. *All* of you. But it will only work if we can evacuate the ballroom and capture Faucher before—"

"Anaïs, you are a *murderer*. You have only doomed yourself."

"No. No, it will work. It has to." The dam of my demented panic finally breaks and sends me sobbing to the floor. "We just have to act now, or it'll all—all have been . . . for . . ."

A pulse like an earthquake. Cracks dart down the floor like a boulder down a frozen lake.

The Alcázar erupts again a few heartbeats later, the sound like a lightning strike that sizzles with growing proximity. Maman's head swivels so fast toward the epicenter that she could give herself whiplash, but all at once, the ceiling begins to crumble and the staircases disintegrate. Giant chunks of marble chase us down, and Maman runs once again, this time toward me, swinging her skirts over my prone body like a satin shield, her screaming like nothing I've ever heard before, nothing I want to hear again.

The last thing I see is the marble lion roaring as it goes up in flames. As if its anger means something.

As if what it does matters.

XIII

CHAPTER ONE

NOTHING I'VE EVER FACED IS HARDER THAN WAKING UP THE afternoon after Maman died trying to save her murderer daughter. She barks at me to get up the way she always does: as if she never has before, as if she has nothing else worth saying to me.

You have only doomed yourself.

I wish that were true.

But I need all this to stop. As soon as possible. In any way possible. And I don't know what else I can do. What else could possibly make a difference.

So when I go back to the Alcázar at night, I do it all over again.

This time, I wait to kill Quirós until we're on the other side of the palace, where there's no one to interrupt my plan. When it's done, I race back to the ballroom and raise the alarm. Quite literally—I storm the king and queen's dais and scream at the top of my lungs for the guards to search the catacombs for bombs. The ensuing stampede of grandes out of the ballroom is almost more chaotic than the explosions. Which, to my great shock, go off anyway.

The night after that, bewildered but sure that digging into the situation with more subtlety will be more successful, I bleat everything to Clara and enlist her to help interrogate Quirós. He *is* a legitimate guard, and *also* a true believer in Faucher's revolution, and he *did* smuggle the bombs into the catacombs, and he is *glad* to be the one tasked with pulling the trigger from there and watching the edifice of the Ivarean state go up in flames. When Quirós decides to stop talking, Clara shoots him with his own gun. It's quick and clean when she does it, as easy as butchering a chicken. She's just headed off to the catacombs to find the bombs herself when the explosions strike the ballroom anyway.

The night after *that,* I don't waste time on thinking through other options or avenues, on my own shenanigans or orchestrating plans with allies. I skip past the royal dais and plunge a dagger into Quirós's heart. The same guards who arrested me the first time, back when I was only a prince puncher, somehow believe me when I tell them of the danger facing the kingdom. Oleastro and Mendoza even find the bombs nestled in a shelf in the catacombs. I know because the guards they left to watch me are called down to help disable them.

They aren't fast enough.

They never are.

Anaïs, tell me . . . What did you do?

I told Maman that I was trying to save her—to save all of us. As much as I could use death and time to tell myself the story I want to hear, I know the truth. I can't make myself forget it.

I killed a man. I killed him over and over again, as viciously, as definitively, as I could. I was so desperate to believe that killing one person would save the palace from the bombs and the people from a doomed revolution and myself from death that I kept doing it. Even when killing him failed to have an effect, even when it made no rational sense, I was so sure that if I could just do it the right way, at the right time, then I would finally break free of this night.

And yet every time I killed him, the Alcázar was still destroyed. Every time, I was still killed and sent back.

No matter what little scheme I hatch, though, no matter how far back I trace the mechanics of this conspiracy, someone will always be there to set off the bombs, storm the palace, assassinate the royal family, shoot the survivors in the ballroom. It will never be as easy as only slashing a blade or firing a gun, smashing a portrait frame on someone's head, or getting pummeled by a current of magic. There is no one person I can kill that would actually save us from every compounded doom facing this kingdom. For there is a rot in the soul of Ivarea, and *that* would survive even if I killed Faucher and all his cronies, or if I let them kill every grande in the palace. And running away from it . . . fleeing blind into the hills of the Marenca countryside rather than facing it . . . that's not an option.

Not for me.

Not ever.

So where does that leave me now? How am I supposed to get everything right in a single night without getting killed first, and then be able to break myself out of this nightmare?

Well, understanding what's brought Ivarean society to the brink of a violent revolution would be a start. If I can figure out what either Rey Rodrigo is really after with his repressive policies or what the Mathieu Fauchers of this kingdom want most out of their new world, I might be able to begin untangling my curse, even end it. *If* the time is right.

What the world would look like then, what makes a single moment in time the right one, I don't quite know yet. I can hardly bring myself to imagine it. But this much I do know: if this country is to survive, we have to make it better than the one we woke up in this morning.

And instead of consigning myself to permanent death, my parents to misery, my world to the flames, I want to see that morning. I want to be worthy of it.

The problem I face now, however, is figuring out what's really going on at court and in Ivarea at large while I'm stuck at the ball. With Leo too unreliable on this front, Gaspard too sanctimonious, and Clara too slippery to pin down, I only have one decent option.

Decent being very much a relative term.

"Oh, I'm so glad I found you!"

Jacinthe Vieillard gives me an unimpressed once-over. The powder on my face must have melted, giving me the ruddy-cheeked, sweat-gleaming expression of everyone else in Marenca, except, of course, for the cool-tempered Jacinthe herself. "Enjoying yourself, are you, Anaïs?"

"*No.*" My lip wobbles dangerously. "I have *no one* to turn to in this vipers' nest but you."

True to form, she can hardly hold back her glee at my misery. "Oh, how absolutely awful! In ordinary circumstances, of course I would lend you a shoulder. But I'm supposed to dance with Don Godofredo next."

Godofredo Saraiva *is* one of the great catches of the night— mostly because of his family's grand castle in Caladur, on the edge of the Great Ocean, not because he is in any way a memorable figure. But Jacinthe is the only person here whose opinions about Ivarean politics I haven't heard before or can't entirely guess; close as she has been to the royal family, she still warned me against them on the night I first found Faucher in that Alcázar courtyard.

Maybe that was only petty jealousy about Clara picking Marguerite as her new favorite at court. But I don't think so. I think there's more under her polished surface than she's likely to admit. And if I don't start somewhere with her, I'll never get anywhere.

"Just my luck. *You* get to dance with a gentleman like Don Godofredo, and here I am, stuck to that *godawful* lush."

My wording doesn't escape her notice. "I'm sure I have no idea what you mean."

I sniffle pointedly.

Her brows arch halfway up her forehead. "Really? You and . . . *How?*"

"Oh, it's a long, sad tale, I'm afraid, so . . . don't let me keep you from your night." With another pathetic little sniff, I grab two glasses of summer wine from a floating tray. "Unless you'd like to join me for a drink first?"

A stolen bottle or three later, cross-legged on the floor of the porcelain salon, Jacinthe squeals, "FUCK Godofredo! You just made my *night*!"

I've only been drinking to be polite, which Jacinthe ceased to notice once she got caught up in the twists and turns of the story of mine and Leo's secret, sordid, season-long affair, but apparently, I've had enough to make giggles bubble up my throat. *"How?"*

Mesmerized by the enchanted wildlife in this room, she manages to peel a shiny porcelain beetle off the wall and cackles as it weaves around her fingers. I've seen her tipsy before, but never like this. "You're going to ruin Leo's life!"

I know better than to be actively offended by anything she says. But it's hard to remember that with the haze of wine clouding my thoughts.

"Infante Leo, with a pathetic nothing Proensan girl? He'll never hear the end of it! His *parents* will never hear the end of it! No one will trust them ever ever ever again!"

That's not what she said the last time I lied about Leo and me. We both knew that *I'd* be the one who would be ruined if such a thing were true. If it were even possible.

But Jacinthe doesn't know what she said in past deaths, and right now, I don't, either. She just chuckles again and raises a finger to the ceiling. The beetle climbs up her hand, its blue-and-white wings fluttering. "A toast to you, Anaïs!" Her glass lies empty, tipped over on the ground. "To the beginning of the end!"

"The end of what?"

She lowers her hand to the floor and gently shepherds the beetle toward the glass, sighing with satisfaction as the intrepid porcelain explorer climbs inside.

"You mean the end of the Cardonas?" That doesn't seem specific enough. So maybe . . . "You mean a *revolution?*"

She raises her head, blinking ponderously. "That," she whispers, "is *treason.*"

After explosions and sacrifice and revolution and murder, I'm well past treason. And I kind of think Jacinthe is, too.

I've never known her to be anything but proud of her place in this court, but . . . what was it she told me? *People like the Cardonas exist to prey upon your worst instincts.* I can't imagine Jacinthe as someone who would actually get her hands dirty, but perhaps that's not the standard by which to judge the richest noblewoman in Ivarea.

"You hate the Cardonas, don't you?" I ask.

"And? You're having an affair with one of them and you *still* hate them. Deep deep *deep* down." She glances down at the little beetle, who's been stopped short by a sticky puddle of half-dried wine. "You still have hope?"

"Are you asking me or the beetle?"

She gives the enchanted insect a look, as if to say *See what I have to deal with?* "You, for fuck's sake! Do you still have hope? Or are you just *full* of despair all the time?"

I choke on my own tongue. "About *what?*"

"You know." She gestures vaguely at the rest of the salon. "Our *situation.* Our *society.* Our . . . our fate." She curses under her breath at the break in her alliteration. "Just, it—it truly doesn't matter who you are. *Or* what you have. *Or!* What you care about. In this! Fucking! PLACE!"

Oh, dear. I knew she was drunk, just not *this* drunk.

Still. I would never have guessed that Jacinthe Vieillard, of all people, has felt as alone as I have, even before I started dying. I thought she was made for the court, or that the court was made for her. But it seems that this night has unlocked something strange and unhinged in Jacinthe, and I don't quite know what to make of it.

"I don't know if I despair *all* the time"—*mostly because I don't really experience time in the same way you do anymore*—"but you're right. You are! We're all caught in this, this same *cycle* of—of courting and courtship and . . . there's no escaping it." *Unless you keep dying.*

Jacinthe's lips crack into a shard of a smile. "Think so?"

"Course. Just look at Infanta Clara, right? If she can't get out of that, none of us have a prayer of it either."

"That?" she repeats quizzically.

"You didn't know? She's betrothed. To the crown prince of Rasenna. They're supposed to announce it tonight."

"Hmph. I'm sure she *loooves* that."

She's right to be sardonic. Clara's story about Clemencia of Lereda's legacy sticks in my mind: *Her* sacrifice, *as they call it, has largely been forgotten. A* sacrifice *made for a* man.

We both fall quiet.

I try to consider what else could be behind what she's saying about hope, or her lack thereof. Maybe Jacinthe is more an abstract, elite-salon sympathizer than a real revolutionary devotee. Or maybe she's simply taking out her personal frustration with Clara deciding to favor Marguerite by daydreaming about the destruction of her family. I suppose anyone who has known a Cardona for as long as she has would do the same.

"VULTURES!"

I duck so fast that I accidentally smack myself in the face before remembering there are no porcelain vultures in the salon. They wouldn't match the enchanted-forest theme.

"This whole COURT! Are VULTURES!" Jacinthe slaps the ground at the end of every exclamation, sending the beetle scurrying back to the wall where it belongs. "Circling the—the CARCASS of the past! Carcass? Carcasses?"

"Carcass," I answer faintly.

"Honestly, why's everyone *so* obsessed with the past when they could think for two seconds longer and make this kingdom, I don't know, *just*? Wouldn't *that* be fucking revolutionary!" She hiccups. "JUSTICE!"

"So you do hate the Cardonas! You think Felipe and Leo and Clara—"

"CLARA! Oh, she's the worst. I *know*, Anaïs." She pauses significantly, hand poised to come down hard on the floor again. *"Things."*

Oh my God. I kick away the empty bottles and glasses and slide forward just as she raises her hand even higher—and holds it there for at least ten seconds.

"Jacinthe, darling," I prompt her, "what do you know about Clara?"

"That BITCH!"

"Use your words."

Nothing. She has her head bowed down, not even returning my glare, and her hand slumps to the floor. I peer closer.

She's asleep.

She *fell asleep* right in front of me.

I bury my head in my wine-stained hands. We're going to explode before I get anywhere with her. This must be my punishment for murder and also for choosing to embroil myself in Cardona drama over and over again.

I have no choice but to slap her in the face.

Jacinthe's hand flies to her face immediately, which now bears high color. "Oh, *fuck* you." She rubs her cheek. "What was I saying?"

"Something about Clara."

"Oh, that awful little—"

"*Why*, Jacinthe? Because Marguerite's her favorite at court now instead of you?"

"I—I mean, *yes,* but—*ugh!*"

I give her a pointed look that says *I have all night.* That we really don't is neither here nor there.

Finally she sighs and takes several deep breaths, trying at least a little bit to steady herself. When she looks back up at me, she seems to have a bit more presence of mind. "Look. Clara and me, we were close. All our lives. Sisters." As she settles into her story, the words start to flow more easily. "Then . . . the king realized Clara was, I don't know, some crazy magic prodigy. Now she was *valuable.* And she fucking *loved* it. All of it." She makes an exaggerated vomiting face. "Papá doting on her. Showing off in meetings. Telling grandes what she thought. Wasn't even just the trappings of power. I would've understood *that.* It was the—the actual power part."

I'm not entirely sure what the distinction is. "What are you really trying to say?"

"I just said! She's fucking horrible now! Obsessed with power! An evil reactionary!"

"So what?" I scrunch my brows. "She's a Cardona—of course they all would hate the commoners agitating against their throne. So what if Clara hates them specifically?"

Jacinthe shakes her head so hard that her braids start to wilt down the crown of her head. "No no no no no. *They* don't hate them. Not even Rodrigo! He just thinks they're annoying little gnats." She flaps her hands at imaginary insects, though not the porcelain ones scurrying through the gently swaying undergrowth. "Unimaginative old bastard. It's all Clara."

"Wh-what's all Clara?"

"I! Just! Said!" She almost topples over the skirt of her magenta gown in her sudden fury. "The way everyone criticizing the monarchy turns up in *jail*? The torture in the Torres? All those laws banning public assemblies and slander and all the . . . She thinks she's saving the throne! Saints, she'd have that Le Nas de Sanglier place burned to a crisp if she knew what really went on there!"

That last reference escapes me, but taken together, none of it sounds all that great. The gears of my mind start to turn and grind against one another. "But she's still just a princess."

"*Just a princess*," Jacinthe sneers with a truly withering scoff. "You've met the two of them, haven't you? Clara and her *charming* Papá? Which one do you think has the VISION, and INTEREST and—and VISION to pull off something like this?"

I don't answer. I can't answer. Rodrigo never struck me as someone with *vision;* he simply wants to secure his reign and profit off his forefathers' legacy. It's one of the reasons Leo secretly wishes he were the next king. And if his sister has been given the strings of actual political power for all this time, unbeknownst to the rest of the kingdom, even if it may not have been exactly what her father intended when he discovered he had a once-in-a-century magical talent on his hands . . . then Clara may well be unwilling to give it up to be an ornamental queen consort in Rasenna.

What am I saying? This is too absurd to be true. Even for me.

Or is it so absurd that it *has* to be true?

But if she's behind the attack, *why?* Why not go straight for the jugular and take the throne herself? It would be much less of a logistical headache than contracting a very much imprisoned revolutionary to break in and blow up the machinery of her father's rule.

Of course, if she *was* involved . . . well, that would explain how Faucher and his citoyens enter the Alcázar complex undetected; there couldn't possibly be a better inside man than the magician-princess of Ivarea. And why the explosions keep happening each time, even when I killed Quirós, Faucher's man in the catacombs. Even how Leo and I were discovered in the catacombs that time in the first place: Clara was the one who sent us there. She may even have been the voice that told Quirós to kill me. But why would Clara ultimately kill Faucher, her chief co-conspirator?

I don't notice exactly when Jacinthe's attention snaps back to me, but at some point, I feel the weight of her stare. Her gaze seems almost lucid.

"Wait, wait. What does any of this have to do with Marguerite being Clara's favorite? You're not jealous of her, are you?"

For a very long moment, I think I've lost her. Then she blinks. "Saints, no. I'm fucking terrified for her."

Their smiles over talk of treason. Their embrace in the ballroom. Jacinthe saying that she needed someone to pick up the pieces.

Finally, something I knew before it was revealed to me. Sort of.

"Once that mean, evil vulture girl finally realized what I

thought of her, she banished me from the winter court. Sent me back to Lutesse in ingom—igon—"

"Ignomin—"

"Inmoginy," she pronounces smugly. "Marguerite's the only one who never asked why I came back. Even my parents didn't spare me."

She wipes away a stray tear. I pretend I didn't see, just in case she would feel worse if Anaïs Aubanel, of all people, caught her crying. But something tells me she might not feel so bad about it now. That she wanted to talk to someone tonight. To someone who was not completely hopeless all the time.

She could have picked anyone else. But she picked me.

"I never had a friend like that, you know? Who's there for me just 'cause I needed her." The fallen tears leave a bit of a glow on Jacinthe's face, and a surprising measure of peace steals over her. "Then we stopped being just friends. So maybe I still don't."

"You're lucky to have each other." I try to ignore the pang in my chest for someone similar, who would be there for me just because I needed them. Without me having to beg and blackmail them into doing so. Without having to prove that I deserve them. Need them. Want them. "At least you're not alone."

She hums contentedly in agreement. "Course, we still have to do the season. Marry grandes, make alliances, gain titles, stability, power. All that shit." She lists the reasons on her wine-stained, ring-laden fingers. "As long as I have Marguerite, I don't care if I have to marry a man. I just need to beat the rest of these goddamn vultures at their own game."

Vultures like Clara.

Jacinthe continues. "See, I know Clara's being nice to Marguerite to get to me, but Marguerite doesn't. She thinks it's real, this favorite thing. But Clara is only loyal to herself. Not her friends. Or her family. Or her people." She glances back up at me, eyes full and clear. "She'll have my head if any of this comes out."

I can feel myself swaying, as though poised over a cliffside. At least now I can almost make out what awaits me at the bottom. "I won't tell anyone, Jacinthe. Not about Marguerite and absolutely not Clara. I swear on pain of death."

I'm not sure what use a promise is when it's built to be broken, but Jacinthe doesn't know that's what I'm doing. Wouldn't understand.

The real issue is this: How can I possibly find out if I'm right?

In the end, there's only one possibility. I find it lurking in the shadows of the ballroom, as if determined to melt into them.

"*There* you are, Vuestra Alteza Real!"

Leo cocks his head to the side in a way most would read as *flirty* and I read as *confused*. "Can I help you with something, my lady?"

After spending most of the night plying Jacinthe with alcohol, I only have a few moments left until midnight. I have to do what I can now to make certain that next time I'll be able to investigate Clara. For that, I'll need easy, unquestioned access to the Alcázar. And if Leo was right the last time I tried to sneak in . . .

"There's going to be a coup at midnight, and your sister might be behind it. I need your signet ring."

Leo stares at the space above my head. It's as if he's hoping a sign will materialize that reads *You heard the girl correctly.* He steps back toward a gilded mosaic, but his hands don't unclench at his sides. "That's not funny."

"It's not supposed to be." I advance, the sweep of my skirts wide enough to swallow the prince whole. "We can't stop what's going to happen unless you give me your signet ring. Trust me."

"If your friends back home ever doubt you once danced with Infante Leopoldo, let them. You and I will remember the truth."

I'm going to kill him.

I hurl myself into his arms, and before either of us can process what's happening, my hand is aloft and sailing right into his cheek.

To me, the slap resounds like the crash of a cymbal in the hall, but the actual cymbals are still going strong, and for once, the court is more intent on pursuing its own midnight pleasures than in tracing the silhouette of the drunk girl falling over Leo the Lush.

For now, he stares at me as he rubs his cheek, his expression suddenly too blank to hold any danger. After a terrible, weighty moment, I reach for the hand still holding his face and wrestle his signet ring off as quickly as I can.

"Are you *insane*?" he asks in a hushed voice. "What do you think you're doing?"

A great question. To which I have no answers.

To the prince, I say, "I'm sorry."

To Mireille and her fairy beloved, I whisper: *Please.*

For the first time since that terrible afternoon, I flick open the opal locket. The portraits of the lady and the fairy inside are still visible to me. Still staring at each other like nothing has changed, even as time forever circles their enamel selves.

I have no idea what this thing really is or what it can really do. But not knowing hasn't stopped me before. And since it already suspended me between life and death and time, it owes me a favor or two.

I wedge Leo's ring into the locket.

For several long seconds, nothing happens—it's just a gold ring, and too big for the locket to close around it. Then, without warning, the ring disappears into one of the portraits. I can't even see which one, for the locket snaps shut. I stagger forward, my neck now weighed down by something new.

Leo exhales deeply through his nose and stares at my throat, at the locket. In his eyes, I see a reflected light too furiously red to come from the chandeliers—the opal amulet.

"What the *fuck* was that?"

I don't bother trying to explain it, with what little time we have left. I want to tell him to trust me again, but . . . looking at him, his drunken indolence cracked open with confusion and awe, his eyes bright but focused, his cheeks flushed and lips parted . . . my words don't come out the way I want them to. Something else, some other feeling, starts to unfurl in my chest. It reaches up and weaves around my thoughts, twines with my suddenly shallow breath.

I don't know what's happening to me. Where it came from. Why it's happening now, of all times. But I know it will ruin me. That much I can feel, down in my quivering bones. So I strangle the feeling even as it flutters in my chest. Because I have to. Because this is one curse I cannot bear. Not now.

Dear God, not now.

The bells begin right then, as if to put me out of this particular misery. The cheers of the royal court shake me to my bones, and still he keeps staring at me, and all I can trust myself to say is, "I'm sorry."

"What did you say about Clara? What do you need my ring for?"

Tears fill my eyes by the fourth chime. "I'm *sorry*."

"*Why? Why* are you sorry? What's going on? Who are you?"

I choose selfishness in these last moments and lift my hand to his reddening skin. He shudders under my touch but does not move, transfixed, as I am, by the thunderous tableau behind us.

"I'm sorry . . . but Leo, I . . ."

The words die out in the back of my throat. Different ones leap up to take their place, impossible ones, but I choke them down before I can say them, before they are immortalized on my tongue, before I doom myself to live with their new and raw and terrible truth. He opens his mouth, but ash coats his lips, and long before we manage to die, we are torn asunder.

XIV

CHAPTER ONE

I SPARE MYSELF ONLY A MOMENT TO MAKE SURE THAT I DIDN'T leave an eye or spleen or bone behind on the dance floor before shooting up in bed and yanking the amulet from my neck. It doesn't seem as heavy as when it first swallowed up Leo's ring in the ballroom. The vagaries of time, maybe. Or my silly, dramatic gambit failed.

I know I don't technically need Leo's seal ring to get into the palace and investigate whether Clara is truly involved in this attack, but I would much rather have it than risk getting dragged directly to Clara's chambers like last time. That would just be a waste of time. Especially if she just sent me off to be murdered again.

So, back to the locket it is. The opal seems like an open wound in my hand, the gold setting nearly translucent in the sunlight. I don't even remember when Maman first showed it to me, or let me wear it, or what she first told me about it. I don't know how much of my life it has seen me through. How much death it has suffered with me. How much of my and Ivarea's blood it's drowned in.

I don't own a palace that changes shape to please me. I don't have a whole world that bows to my will. Now that everything I thought I knew about myself turned out to be a lie—my heritage, my blood, my magic—I don't even really have my own memories. But I have this amulet, and after all this time, after all this bloodshed, it *knows* me.

And it knows what I want.

For several long seconds, my fingers scrabble at the little clasp. Then finally, almost reluctantly, the locket swings open.

Something hard and shiny falls into my lap.

Ironically enough, the Guardia Real is more wary of me now that I have a royal signet ring to return to its owner than they were when I forged a letter inviting myself to the palace. But they cannot argue with the golden Cardona dragon glaring up at them from my palm, so they usher me into the residential wing of the Alcázar, and after some dithering before his door, through to Leo's apartments. It's only once they've left me alone with the prince that I realize this is my first time here.

Now, to me, Leo has always seemed too much of a piece with the ballroom—a statue hewn of the same stone as the Alcázar come to life. But these rooms are his domain, not his father's, and the story Leo tells himself here, the one he falls asleep to and wakes from, is quite distinct from Rey Rodrigo's grandiose vision of the Cardonas' power.

Trinkets and other curiosities crown towers of books that teeter on the polished floor and line the armoires and tables: animal-shaped paperweights and incongruously gleaming letter openers and empty inkwells and cheap pins and jeweled goblets and more, so much more. I can only assume they are charms, but I wouldn't know how to use them, or why one might have so many. The walls here are smothered in painstakingly assembled mosaics and gleaming oil paintings and enchanted tapestries of different styles—some expensive heirlooms, many clearly market-day finds that were never meant to hang in the Alcázar Real. They whisper with the magic of hammers and glass, of brush and ink, of thread and needle, the fairy tales and local legends of all the provinces of this kingdom, of the myriad Ivareas. There's even a framed sea-glass mosaic of the port of Massilie on the southeast wall. The sight of it fills me with bitter despair; I have to turn away before it takes over the whole of my heart.

I look at Leo instead, who regards me with a nonplussed stance and a gaze lit with flickers of daylight, and find myself even more confused.

I've never seen him at ease before.

As much as I might trick myself into believing otherwise, I've never known him at all. Not really.

It's only been a few seconds since the doors shut, but it feels like a whole life and death later when he finally clears his throat, staring at the glint of gold in my half-outstretched hand. "My lady, I could not guess where you got that ring, but I assure you, it's not mine."

I swallow. My mouth is dry. "Yes, it is. You gave it to me yourself, Vuestra Alteza Real."

"Somehow I think I would remember that. And if you *were* right, I wouldn't still have it myself, would I?" He raises his hand, and indeed, there it is, complete with a dull red gem winking on his pinkie finger.

"Yes, well, it happened in a past life. We each have the same ring, from two different times." My signet ring seems like it's burning a hole in my palm. "We also both know about your heretical fake blood oath."

His lips part and close a second later. For a perilous moment, I think it's all over for me, even though the end is many hours away.

"Is there anything *else* we both know that I should know about?"

"Well, Alteza, there's a not-insignificant chance that your sister is planning to kill you."

Without another word, he sinks onto an overstuffed armchair in a graceless heap and waves his hand.

When the story is over once more, Leo cranes his neck against the headrest and stares at the ceiling. My gaze catches on the bob of his exposed throat as he swallows, head tilted back.

I've kissed him there, haven't I? I've felt his pulse racing in his jaw, gasped as his breath tickled my ear. The memory of it seems clearer than it should, as if overlaid on what I'm seeing now.

I would be okay if I never felt any of that again. I would be okay if I never touched him again.

The response in my head comes out of nowhere, somehow both earnest and sly. *But what if you do?*

Seeing Leo again—alone, in his own space, as his real self—has distracted me. But . . . but no more. No longer. I can't give any more attention to the sneaking, ruinous feeling that's warping all my thoughts, all my plans . . . all my desires. I absolutely cannot give it any voice.

Not even to myself.

Across from me, Leo is wholly unaware of the contortions my heart is putting my mind through. "Before we can begin to convince any *sane* person of any of this, we need to know if Clara is truly behind these attacks. Without a shadow of a doubt. And as far as I can tell, there's one simple way to find out."

I inhale sharply. "Which is?"

He raises his head again, and with no particular feeling, his eyes lock onto mine. Again, I don't know if he's noticed my staring, the flush in my cheeks. I don't know if he reads anything else, any other secrets, in my countenance. But I know that I couldn't bear it if he did.

"We wait to die."

❦

At the ball, the prince is in great form as Leopoldo the Lush. When I'm on his arm, the night does not so much unfurl before me as it seems to spiral down to a central point I still cannot quite see. He brazenly drags me out beyond Arco de León before the feast is even over. Too flabbergasted to object, I let him steer me up a flight of stairs.

"Clara's guard captain has been missing all night."

I nearly trip over the last step. I remember meeting the captain when I was taken to her chambers. I remember his disdainful gaze at me from across the princess's threshold. "You mean that Noguera fellow?"

He doesn't ask me how I know the captain's name. "If he's working with Clara . . . what could he be up to right now?"

"Breaking Faucher out of prison. Smuggling more of his men inside the palace. Keeping the rest of the Guardia Real from finding out. Who knows?"

Instead of weighing these options, the prince pulls me along the landing and into a room dominated by a great ceiling fresco of scenes from the life of a saint I can't identify in the dark. Along its far side is a pair of finely wrought glass-paneled doors overlooking some courtyard below. Leo lets me go at the threshold to wander toward the center of the room, craning his head back to take in the fresco.

I clear my throat as gently as possible. "What are we doing here?"

He tears his gaze away from the saint and doesn't answer. "You really think this is all her doing."

It seems like a silly question, considering that he's the one who just raised suspicions about Noguera, but I understand. Of course I understand. "Truthfully? I don't know." With no small hesitation, I finally step inside. The saint in the fresco above is not mine, and I feel it judging me all the more for it. "But the longer I spend not knowing, the more often we all die for no reason, and I don't want that to happen again. And again."

He cards a hand through his dark, wavy hair. "You've suffered for a long time trying to find out."

Suffered rather puts it lightly.

"If you don't mind me asking," he continues with careful deliberation, "why do you keep doing this?"

My heart flutters with uncertainty. "You've asked me something like this before."

He starts working his jaw. As if it's easier for him to rearrange the world than to say what he means. "*I'm* asking you now, not that past person. To me, it seems like you could save yourself from all this at any time. Run home to Proensa and be safe enough. For a while."

Perhaps, as he says, for a while. But what's happening in the capital tonight *will* reach Proensa sooner rather than later. And even the possibility of safety, however small, however temporally bound, is not enough to force me out of the orbit of the Alcázar Real.

At least, not anymore.

"I . . . I did run away, once."

I've never let myself remember that night. I don't think I could have if I wanted to—and I absolutely did not want to. I couldn't bear the weight, the shame, the failure of that memory. For all these deaths now, I've glossed over in my own mind the time I never made it to the Alcázar, only able to think around it in glancing asides, not head-on.

Now that lost night, from those deaths right after Leo first told me about his childhood play oath, wavers in the back of my mind. My memories of that night have become so pressurized by guilt and time that they seem like visions of someone else's past, like the one the amulet showed me. Something beheld from a distance. Not something I lived through and blocked out of my own mind for so long after. Not something I died for.

I only tell Leo the story now because if I don't, I will lose it, and I've already lost so much to this nightmare. I can't let everything keep slipping away. Even when it hurts.

Especially when it hurts.

"I'd tried to tell my parents what was going to happen before. They usually didn't understand, or would say I'd lost my mind. But that time, I got them to run. We bundled everyone into carriages, servants and all, and drove east out of the capital before the sun had set. Not an easy feat, as you'll know if you've ever met my mother."

He hasn't, not in all our deaths, but that doesn't matter. I fear I barely know her anymore. I lose more of her every time I wake up.

"We were fully in the countryside by the time midnight struck. And even though we were miles away and safe from the violence, I just—I felt so *empty*. I didn't know what would happen if I stayed away from the Alcázar and let it all unfold the way I knew it would. So I . . . I decided I couldn't risk it."

Leo's gaze pierces through the distress in mine.

"You got yourself killed."

I shake my head, less as a response than a reflex. There is terror and despair lodged so deep inside that I can't begin to rattle it free, no matter what I do. No matter what I say. "Leapt out of the carriage." My voice comes out a strangled whisper, struggling across time and death to be heard. "Dashed myself against the side of the road. But I survived the fall. So when my father came to get me, I stole the pistol off his belt."

His eyes grow bright with—pity, or awe, or something else I don't have a word for. His fists clench at his sides like he's holding himself back from rushing toward me. "Why would you do that?"

Leo once asked me that before, too—what I'm sacrificing myself for. What do I actually want out of my life. I didn't have an answer then, and I still don't. The only thing I know now is what I've always known. "I can't let everyone die."

He has no words for this, at first. I don't either. Not anymore. At last, he mutters, "I don't think anyone else in this whole goddamn kingdom would be able to do that."

"Oh, dying is easy. What you do when you come back is not."

Leo cracks a morbid grin. "All right, I couldn't do it."

"That's a shame. I seem to recall you swore an oath that you would."

He recoils in no small horror. Then he catches himself,

shakes his head at what he didn't say, what he didn't ask. "I was just playing. I didn't know what something like that meant. What it would do. Your case is extremely different from mine."

My chuckle is too dark for the starlight to reach it. "If you find someone whose case *is* like mine, please send them my way. I'd like to compare notes."

Leo sighs. "You must be tired, though. All those horrible things. All that dying. Do you ever . . ." He glances up at me. "Can you ever just *rest*?"

His question makes me want to curl up then and there, under that oppressive fresco, to sleep through my trauma, his doom, the end of a thousand lives and that of a kingdom that has been led by centuries of kings and tyrants.

Even if I did—even if I fell asleep for years on end, a cursed village girl whose slumber holds a world hostage, prey only to what she perceives in her dreams—I fear that when I woke, I would still not be okay.

"Well," he murmurs in the face of my silence, "I hope you can. One day."

I nod, my mouth dry, my heart heavy. "One day."

The silence between us is vast. The terrifying ambiguity of it sparks a wave of panic that I haven't felt in a long time. I begin to withdraw, my steps echoing in the cavernous space.

"Wait! Wait, no, don't leave. Please." His words grow softer, rounding out into melancholy. "Clara's waiting down there. All of the bullshit that was already there is still there. I can't take it anymore. I—honestly, Anaïs, you seem like the only real thing left in this whole damned city."

Goose bumps erupt on my bare arms. "What would that make you?"

"Oh, I'm *definitely* not real. Not even to myself." He chuckles again. "I'm . . . Believe me, I'm no one."

"Don't say that."

"Why not? It's true. In nineteen years, what have I ever done that's been worthwhile? Even now, I can't . . . There's nothing I . . ."

I swallow down the bitterness. "You don't have to worry about it, señor. You don't have to do anything. Go back to the ball. Dance and drink and forget all this." Glaring at the floor, I try to soften my voice. "You'll be fine again soon. You won't even remember."

"I don't want to dance."

"For God's sake, then, or your saints'," I snap, "what do you want?"

He averts his gaze from mine. His breathing is slow and heavy, weighed down by something stronger than gravity that threatens to suck me into its maw, too. "Some other . . . impossible thing."

"What's that supposed to mean?"

He doesn't answer. And I realize, belatedly, bleakly, that the reason he isn't saying anything is because he *can't*. Speaking his desire out loud, confessing to a feeling, would make it real. Undeniable. And he can't risk that. Not here. Not now.

I know the feeling. I know it all too well.

The instinct to hurtle myself toward certain doom makes me whisper across the room. "Why is it so impossible?"

He smiles again. "Because I am no one," he says, "and she is our savior."

My stomach flutters, either with butterflies or because I'm about to be sick. "Don't say that," I repeat, voice bright with terror.

"Why not, Anaïs?"

I feel light-headed even as my heart pounds in my ears. Whatever I thought would come of this night, it was never this. Whoever or whatever I am, I never thought I could be this person.

Until suddenly I tell him, "Because you could just kiss me instead."

Just like that, he closes the distance separating us and takes my face in his hands with as much devotion and wonder and respect as he would a weapon—one he knows how to use, or be used by—and obeys.

We drink in each other's fevered breaths and burn in the heat of each other's skin. My arms loop around his neck as I stretch up on the tips of my toes and open my mouth to his just as his hands drop to my hips. I toss my gloves behind him and drag my bare hands through his hair. He breaks off the kiss to scoop me up by the waist. I hitch up my skirts and wrap my legs around the column of his body like this is something we've done countless times before.

Time skips and stutters before us like our doomed heartbeats. He pushes me against the glass doors and presses fresh bruising kisses to the tender underside of my jaw, the fluttering hollow of my throat. I fumble at his scarlet cloak so it pools at our feet, then tug blindly at his jacket and vest until only his shirt stands between me and his bare skin. He makes a wordless, disbelieving sound as I rip the cloth and the staid air hits a sliver of his chest. With a wicked grin, he starts toying with the laces of my bodice. The glass door behind me is the only reason I'm not spilling out of my dress and into his arms, and we both know it.

One step forward, and everything between us could change forever.

No. Not forever.

Just until you die.

I plant myself firmly on the ground. My voice comes out ragged, my lips swollen, kiss-bitten. "We can't."

His face falls, but he shifts his grip so he's only holding me by the waist. As if I will be able to concentrate when he's still touching me.

"It's not—fair," I offer haltingly. "To you. You won't know. . . . It'd never have happened."

Leo cocks his head. "I want you, Anaïs." He adds, "I think . . . I think I always want you, even if I don't say it. Even if I don't know it."

I find myself snarling, "You *never* know it," even as my brain kicks and screams at me.

"I don't care what those past Leos knew or didn't know. I just know that I want you *now*. Me. The person standing here now. Don't I exist to you? Are we not supposed to have feelings if we're saving the world? Or act on those feelings?"

And what exactly does he think he feels now? There's lust,

clearly—I felt that in his gaze, in his hands, in his kiss. But if it's not just that . . . If he thinks he *feels* something for me . . .

No. No, he doesn't. He can't. Where would he get the idea that he could—what gives him the right to believe—

Overcome, I shove him away. The swelling of my lips and the flush on my skin seem like the only signs he was ever here, that he was—is—real. But the expression on his face is rapturous, like the paintings of his precious saints as they behold the divine, or true magic, or both, and I can't pretend that I don't know why the sight of him coming undone terrifies me so, why it cracks my heart wide open. I can't pretend I don't see him all the time, even when he's not there, even when I'm caught up in a cycle of death and life and death that I can't, won't, break.

Even when I close my eyes.

Especially when I close my eyes.

Shaking more than I ever have before midnight, I murmur, "You don't understand."

He looks like he wants to grab me by the shoulders until an answer rattles from my mouth, but he doesn't. He pleads, "Saints, just tell me what's wrong."

Oh, you are a fool, Anaïs Aubanel.

The moment I realized I was falling for him, after I slapped him across the face and he stared at me as though the strike had jolted him awake from centuries of slumber, I knew it would ruin me. I didn't realize just how much it would hurt.

I should not be brave enough to confess this at last. But I can't deny it anymore. "You don't understand. I'm in love with you."

Leo flinches. I don't think he meant to, but he does, and I know it.

"See?" I say bitterly. *"Feelings."* I withdraw into myself, resting my hand against the sash that has gone askew. The blessed dagger still hangs there, having survived the roaming of the prince's hands. I'm seriously considering drawing it and remaking the laces of my bodice, but the spell of our suspended despair breaks with his voice again.

"Anaïs . . ."

My name seems unrecognizable when he speaks it, with his capital-bred accent, with the crashing waves of his confusion. His lust. His longing.

"I don't know . . . anything. But right now, we want the same thing, don't we? We want each other. We want to not be alone. We want to—in what time we have left—"

"Oh, *fuck* you, Leopoldo."

His jaw goes slack. I can't remember the last time I cursed at him. I can't remember a time before I loved him.

"Don't tell me you love me, too. You *don't,* and we *don't* want the same thing. Because I love you, and every moment I spend with you breaks my heart. Every time you *look* at me, or *speak* to me, or God forbid try to *help* me . . . You don't understand, you'll *never* understand—"

"Fine! Then stop trying to make me understand! I didn't *ask* to be dragged into any of this!"

"Actually, you did. Several times. Lifetimes ago."

He recoils in horror. "That's not fair."

Oh, now that I throw his own past words back at him, it's

not fair. But when I put a stop to our kiss, when I denied my-self everything I didn't know I wanted, to protect *him* and *his* future selves, it doesn't matter. Of course Leo the Lush doesn't care that I care for him. How could I have thought him to be anything but selfish? "You . . . You're the most manipulative bastard I've ever met."

"Then let me *die*, for Saints' sake! I know I didn't *ask* you to turn yourself into a martyr. Just let us burn! All of Ivarea! It's what we deserve, isn't it?" The look in his eyes, the furor and terror and the earth-shaking fear, makes me want to hide, want to cry, want to fight. *"Isn't it, Anaïs?"*

"You *idiot!*" I howl through my hands. "I can't let you die, *I'm in love with you!*"

"You have a funny way of showing it!"

A beat of silence. Grim and terrible and, yes, impossible. Wonder and dread, love and death, magic and more magic, swirl in the space between us. I look up and find him slouched over, the force of his anguish leveling him like a punch to the gut.

Oh, Leo.

Just one step unravels all the fury of moments past and present and future, and also the bodice of my scarlet gown. He rises to catch me before I become completely undone. I press my forehead to his chest. We stand there a moment before he takes a finger and tilts my chin up. His eyes are still clouded, but now they water at the corners. The harshness of his words dissolves in his inexplicable, unshed tears, as the cruelty of mine gets drowned out by the drum of my heartbeat.

When we kiss this time, it's not because we have no other choice.

It's because once, just this once, we don't want to choose anything else.

It's not love, at least not in the way that threatens to carve the stupid heart out of my exceedingly breakable rib cage, but it's the only thing we have, and if it kills us, then the fact remains:

I love him.

It will never matter.

CHAPTER TWO

SIX CHIMES. SIX CHIMES IS ALL IT TAKES TO STEAL THE LAST words from his tongue, the sound from my ears, the ground beneath our feet.

By the time the blasts are over, the walls of the cupboard that Leo and I hid in before midnight—the very one I once marked with my blood in an attempt to prolong Gaspard's life—are still upright, and the door only partially caved in. Still the minutes wear on before the marching begins in earnest. Faucher is on his way. I can feel it in the air, as sure as a storm rolling past the hills at home.

"Let's go."

Without another word, he draws his sword and accedes.

Outside, the Alcázar is in disarray. People bearing bloody wounds and congealing burns stagger down what's left of the corridor, its stone innards barely holding together. Leo and I push against the crowd, heading forward whence they're fleeing. The sounds of fighting, the thumps of bodies crashing to the floor, hit me like so many blows to the head.

We skid around the next corner and find a cell of revolutionaries clinging to the pillars of Arco de León. They fire gunshots wherever it strikes their fancy—into the smoking ballroom behind them, at anyone fleeing. They're so busy with their game that only one of the men notices Leo gesturing toward a boulder the size of the enchanted lion's head and . . . and levitating it into the arch.

They don't have time to scream.

Neither do I.

For a wild moment, I wonder if his power really could stand a chance against Clara's. If tonight is all her doing, could he just kill her and save us all?

A new spate of gunfire erupts in the ballroom. Above it, a single garbled note rings out, higher-pitched than my delicate eardrums can handle anymore. And then—

Laughter.

It rolls and twists and decimates the demolished ballroom. It reaches into my exposed heart and tugs at the tissues that connect it to the rest of my body. I lurch forward, transfixed, and pick through the wreckage to grab a lost pistol. I know whose laughter it is.

Mathieu Faucher loves an audience, and we are the last and greatest he will ever have.

"Men of Ivarea." He raises the trace of amusement in his voice so all can hear and tremble. "MEN OF IVAREA."

They wave their gun barrels and bayonets in the air, whooping for their leader. His face is bloodstained, his coat singed at the edges from the feral fires. But he is still Mathieu Faucher, his green eyes uncannily bright across what used to be the ballroom.

I sink to my backside and crawl toward a collapsed pillar, behind which Leo and I take shelter. Bodies stiffening with rigor mortis fortify the ground. Broken glassware and dented headpieces are the weapons they left behind.

"For four hundred years, the Cardonas have demanded you sacrifice your blood, your gold, your children, your *dignity*—for *their* kingdom. *Tonight,* men of Ivarea, you are reborn! From the dregs of the Cardonas' corruption of this land, to-night, you become *true men!* Citizens! *Brothers!*"

Behind me, Leo tenses, but does not say a word. Then Faucher leans down and reaches for the nearest body.

Shit.

I whip around on bleeding knees and grab Leo by the shoul-ders. "Don't look. Don't look. Look at me, okay? Just look at me, not—"

"Men of Ivarea, Citoyen Rodrigo Cardona stands before you now. What do you have to say to your fellow citizen?"

The look on Leo's face as he takes in the sight of his blood-ied father with the barrel of a rifle at his temple sets my vision alight. I hold so tight to him that I could leave bruises on his skin, but he doesn't move, doesn't wince, not so long as his fa-ther is there, looking upon all that was granted to him by birth coming apart in fire and blood.

"What does Ivarea's justice demand we do with Citoyen Rodrigo?"

I bury Leo's head against the curve of my neck, the chain of my locket stamping across his forehead. But the answering cry of the revolutionaries, in all the languages of Ivarea, sparks in him an instinct for self-destruction, and he struggles anew and—

And then the shot.

Leo roars and leaps to his feet. The sound is lost in the bellows of triumph that ring out with the death of the king. Still slumped against the broken pillar, I dry-heave into my lap before daring to peek back up. But Leo hasn't left my side, hasn't charged Faucher, hasn't even magically attacked the regicide as he could.

All at once, I don't know how to touch him. How to look at him.

Then he glances down at me, a wild, desperate look in his eyes.

"You swear tonight won't end like this?" he asks in a hail of celebratory gunshots.

I swallow ash. "I won't let it."

With one last look at his father's dead body, Leo crouches back down with me. Tears and soot coat his cheeks, tarnishing all that was left of his golden aura.

With the king dead, Faucher quickly rounds on his men to seek out the rest of the Cardonas, and dispatches a few others to report on the goings-on in the rest of the Alcázar. Both searches signal a new license for the victors to shoot and maim and murder. Faucher's men take to their new tasks with aplomb. But they do not look too far into the rubble of the ballroom.

Leo licks his cracking lips. "Where's Clara?"

I shrug. Every tiny movement I make is heralded with a barrage of gunfire, or the last screams of the dying. It all stops, though, when the erstwhile princess emerges into the ballroom, alone and unarmed.

I can't quite see the expression on her face from this far away, but as she looks upon the burning ballroom, it's like I can feel the tension coiling in her body. I've seen Clara at Faucher's mercy before, when he shot her in the aftermath of the bomb blasts, but I didn't know then the kind of revenge she could exact. I didn't know then what else she might want.

I still don't know exactly. That's what I'm here to find out. That's why I kept Leo from avenging his father's murder and putting a premature end to the story I most want to hear. But looking at her now, I can't imagine Clara would ever give up what she wants. Especially if it requires giving someone else any kind of power over her.

To a girl who can uproot a palace to suit her wishes, any other power must not feel like power at all.

While the remaining guests in the ballroom take in the sight of the latest Cardona surrounded by a band of commoners, Faucher's cronies push her to her knees. She barely manages to throw her arms out in time. I hear the crunch of bone clean across the way, but I can't tell if it's hers or that of her fan, hanging on a thin ribbon around her right wrist.

"Citoyen Clara," says Faucher over the jeering and cruel, lascivious whispers of his crowd. "So kind of you to join us for this momentous occasion."

She raises her head. Even from the ground, even possibly hurt, her gaze seems to calcify the churn of the ballroom. "I'm glad you got to see it before you died."

He curls his lip, breathing fire out of his gnarled nose. "Justice, men."

All at once, they fire.

And all at once, the bullets bury themselves in Mathieu Faucher's flesh.

No one realizes at first that Clara manipulated each bullet, that such a thing could even be possible, until Faucher collapses on top of the king's body. Then the closest of the revolutionaries rush her, only for her to spin out of their grip as if they are clumsily trained dancers. She slashes her left hand through the air. A pulse of energy jolts the ballroom like a blade slicing it across the middle. One by one, the revolutionaries slide to their knees and crash, breaking their skulls on the floor slicked with the grandes' blood.

Survivors of the blasts start to stir, murmuring fearfully about what exactly is going on, until Marguerite's grandfather, the viscount of Tuvronne, a spry old man whose arm is now a stump, gets to his feet and shouts, "Long live Reina Clara!"

As more bodies fall, the cry ripples through the ballroom. Clara takes it in silently. Maybe Leo and I are the only ones alive who recognize that there is more than grief and duty coursing through her veins.

She *loves* this.

She's *reveling* in it.

"There is much still to do, my friends," the young queen

calls in a quavering but clear voice. "First, we must take back our palace."

Echoes of approval hum against the walls. Wobbly-legged nobles and shell-shocked commoners alike stagger around to liberate the rest of the Alcázar. The wounded start keening more loudly, broadcasting their need for help.

"And," Clara continues, "we must take Ivarea back from the traitors in our midst."

A pulse of magic shoots through the floor. The Alcázar preparing to unmake itself at her command.

"Traitors who let our kingdom rot from within these long years. *Traitors*," she shouts now, pacing as Faucher once did, "who sold Ivarea to the men who just murdered my father."

The elderly survivor hobbles closer to her. I can't see Marguerite anywhere. Or Jacinthe, for that matter. "Vuestra Majestad Real, take it from an old man. Our priority must be to rescue—"

Clara holds up her hand, clutching the remnants of her fan. "Incompetent. Venal. *Sympathizers*. Mathieu Faucher, that rabble-rousing *pig*, killed your king in front of your eyes, and you did *nothing*." Her breathing is harried, as if she's been chasing something a long time and is only now beginning to catch sight of it. "How is Ivarea to survive your *wisdom*?"

New cries of alarm start to ring out in the ballroom, but it's too late for the viscount; Clara releases a brutal slash of energy, and Marguerite's grandfather falls to the pockmarked floor in two uneven pieces. Wherever she is, whatever happened to her at midnight, I'm glad Marguerite isn't here to see this, and that Jacinthe isn't here to see her heart break. Because this time,

Clara isn't using her inelegant unraveling magical force against the palace. She doesn't want to destroy the Alcázar now that she rules it: she only wants to purge it of the people who would challenge her hold. Not just stray Faucher supporters, either. The grandes with the wealthiest and most resource-rich holdings are the ones she's targeting with the same brutal force she just turned on Faucher's men—the ones who contribute the most in taxes to the Ivarean treasury and conscriptions to the Ivarean armed forces. No matter who they are, or how close she may have been to their children and grandchildren.

Because they are the last people who can exert leverage over the crown. *Clara's* crown. Because they are the last people who can stop her.

The new queen stalks through the ballroom, sending rubble flying with even less effort than Leo had needed at the arch, checking for survivors and deeming, seemingly on the spur of the moment, whether they are worthy of joining her. She just made a big show of freeing Ivarea from the corrupt traitors in its midst, but to me, it looks more like she's terrorizing it, training her new subjects to love her for her *mercy*. The people Clara spares leap up sobbing to kiss her feet, her bloody emerald hem dragging behind her. She pays them no mind.

She's looking for her brothers.

And if she finds Leo alive . . . Leo, the magician . . . Leo, whose claim to the throne is above hers . . .

"Kill me. Kill me now," I say. Leo doesn't seem to hear me, so I shove the orphaned pistol I stole earlier into his clenched hands. "You have to kill me now, or she'll kill you, too."

"I . . . You don't have to . . ."

"Leo, for God's sake."

He stares at the gun for longer than he should while his sister twirls around in the ever-widening whirlpool of her triumph. His eyes flick back up at me, and he remembers, again, what has happened tonight, what will happen again, what he will lose, what he will never be able to mourn.

Then, as if it was never a question—because it never was—he takes up the pistol. I pretend I don't see it. I track the way he leans toward me instead, the kiss that tastes more of salt and iron than anything else, blood and tears and gunpowder on our tongues. He tells me something, but it gets lost when he takes the shot, and instantly, so do I.

XV

CHAPTER ONE

THE DEATHS ARE ENDLESS.

There is the time when a guard holds out a hand to help me down from the royal dais, Rey Rodrigo's smile cool at my back, and I spot Clara chatting with a flushed Capitán Noguera. I steal the pistol holstered at the guard's side and fire a shot in the princess's direction. I live just long enough to see it strike true before she staggers toward me, the bullet wedged impossibly in her chest where she has stopped it from penetrating her heart, before she sends the nearest mosaic column crashing on my head with a peaceable smile.

Another time, right before my parents present me to hers, I manage to push my dagger deep into Clara's side. It cuts through the layers of satin and lining and human bones like a dream. She stares at the jeweled hilt jutting out above her hip and laughs as she sends me to my knees with a delicate flick of her wrist. My father's screaming as she plucks the dagger from her gut and turns it on him is the last thing I hear.

I break into her apartments, into Capitán Noguera's room, into the suites of her ladies-in-waiting, searching for letters, charms, keys, magic, *anything*. But Clara and her attendants are fastidiously tidy. I can find no physical proof of her plot.

I waste more lives than any one person could ever want forcing Clara's friends to tell me about her desires, her motivations, her facade. I even spend an entire night flirting with Príncipe Felipe under his wife's nose, just to get him to reveal something about his sister. All of these unsettlingly high-ranking nobles marvel at the freedom the king and queen gave the talented princess and are aware that she used it to explore the realm of magic, but they don't know what exactly that looked like. And they don't care. *Some girls at court practice embroidery or paint landscapes. The princess practices magic. So what?*

Some nights, she is willing to share general secrets about how to become undeniable with another much-derided girl magician in Ivarea. Some nights, in the chaos and crumbling glory of this place, I have a feeling she would like to find someone like her. Some nights, she fools me into thinking that if she knew how much I know of her plans, she wouldn't murder me where I stood. Some nights, I don't think she is trying to fool me—not consciously, anyway. She sees something in me the way I once did in her.

Clara, the princess I thought could be queen. Clara, the only one in this terrible place to understand what it feels like to be burdened with the future of a people, let alone your own. Clara, who I wanted to befriend. Clara, who I wanted to be.

But I *am* a fool. And rarely more so than when I let myself fall into Leo's orbit again.

And again.

And again.

We never have a night quite like the one that ended with him killing me. We fight. We scheme. We kiss. We die.

I don't know how to stop loving him.

I don't know how to not kill him.

I thought I'd learned after Quirós that just killing one person cannot be the key to freeing myself from this night. But what I forgot in the midst of my delirium was that he was just part of the plan. A single gear in the machine. Killing him made no difference, saved no one.

Because *Clara* is the one at the center of this scheme. She is at the apex of Ivarean society and has a crown that's been promised to her, and despite that, she still would rather manipulate a whole kingdom for her own ends. She despises her people so much that she would take advantage of their grievances just to cover up the blood on her own hands. She is a singular presence of singular evil, and after all I've seen, I have to believe that getting Clara out of the equation would change *something* about this night in a way that killing Quirós didn't.

Maybe I'm wrong. But if Clara is the heart of our destruction, then I have no choice but to try to stop her.

However, that would require her to actually die.

I have fully buried blades and bullets into her body, and she still manages to survive. If I can't get to her, then I can't save anyone else. If I can't save anyone, then I can never save myself. And if—

No. No, I won't succumb to that darkness again. I don't understand *why* simply murdering the princess won't work, but it doesn't. So . . . where do I go next? What else can I do?

Although the responsibility for the attack ultimately rests on Clara's shoulders, her coup still relies on triggering a revolution first. And I very much doubt that someone like Mathieu Faucher would ever partner with Clara Cardona if he knew what she had in store for him.

At the beginning of my deaths, I could not have imagined wanting to appeal to or even ally with the architect of the attack that killed us all. But so much has changed in my thinking since then that I know I need to connect to my countryman somehow. If I can make Faucher understand that his revolution is doomed, if I can persuade him that there is a bigger threat to him and his movement than Rodrigo Cardona's continued reign, we could form a united front against the immensely powerful Clara.

Back in the porcelain salon, a drunken Jacinthe mentioned one specific place Clara hasn't managed to burn down: Le Nas de Sanglier. According to Béatrice, the Boar's Snout is a

Proensan-run tavern down by the riverfront. She doesn't *say* it's a hotbed for radical activity, but Jacinthe implied it, which makes it seem as good a place as any to gather information on Mathieu Faucher and his followers.

So once again, I tell Maman that I have a secret but mostly proper rendezvous with Infante Leopoldo. Instead of heading to the crest of the hills, however, I direct the driver down toward the valleys of Marenca proper, and eventually, into the warren of convoluted byways and pockmarked streets of the riverbank district.

Walking into Le Nas de Sanglier, having transformed my ballgown into plainer traveling fare on the drive, I can instantly tell why people like Clara or even Jacinthe would never venture here themselves. The tavern resembles a country home in old Proensa—all whitewashed walls and stucco molding, aged furniture that appears to be made of driftwood, and scuffed, untreated wooden floors. It must seem hilariously unsophisticated in the cosmopolitan capital. Underneath the humidity, though, hangs a scent in the air—of rich wine and mild herbs and somehow, miraculously, even a tang of salt water—that jolts me right back home. It seems like all the Proensans in the capital feel the same. But they're celebrating a kingdom that soon will die.

I sit down at one of the last unoccupied tables, opposite a shadowed staircase next to the bar. If this place offers rooms upstairs, and if it is actually a hub for revolutionaries, this would be the perfect place for Faucher to lie low between his prison break and his appearance in the abandoned tower in the Alcázar complex before midnight.

A sallow-faced, snub-nosed barmaid that I suspect is only a few years older than me stomps over and asks my order. She barely manages to stifle a snicker as she looks me up and down. "New in town, are you?" she asks in Proensan.

"Visiting. From Massilie."

The girl tugs her worn white cap back into place before it slides off her chestnut hair. "How're you finding it?"

I can still taste the Alcázar's terribly perfumed air at the back of my throat, so heavy and cloying that I don't know how I've survived with it pressing down on my windpipe for all this time. "It's . . . so . . . *humid.*"

"Oh, I know. You could live here the rest of your life and never get used to it." Her gaze lingers on the fine silk taffeta ribbon of my conjured traveling cloak. "A girl like you shouldn't be out alone on a night like this."

There may well be worse things in this place than a perceptive barmaid, but it won't do to waste this chance. At least this time, I didn't make the mistake of leaving my locket visible. "What's your name?"

"Vitòri."

I push the hood of my cloak all the way down and lower my voice, forcing her to lean closer to hear me. "Vitòri, I have traveled very long and very far to be here tonight, so I would appreciate an honest answer to my next question."

I should have stopped at the Plamondons' manor and bullied Gaspard into telling me more about Faucher's teachings and supporters before coming here. Too late for anything else now. With nothing but my life to lose, I repeat the question

Mathieu Faucher asked me when he thought I was just a Pro-ensan maid in the Alcázar Real. The one I have not been able to shake entirely since I first heard him say it.

"Why must we submit?"

Vitòri sets her sharp jaw. "I think you're in the wrong place."

"Do you doubt your fellow citoyen?"

"There's a difference between citizens like you and citoyens like me."

"There shouldn't be."

She rolls her hazel eyes and begins to back away, her path complicated by the closeness of the tables and haphazardly sorted chairs of the patrons. I leap up before she can disappear.

"Mathieu Faucher broke out of the Torres de Paz. At midnight tonight, he will attack the Anniversary Ball and murder the Cardonas and everyone else celebrating. Tell me I'm wrong, Vitòri. Tell me he's not about to change the face of Ivarea as we know it. Tell me he's not hiding out in a room upstairs as we speak."

She shuts her gaping mouth and blinks moodily at the rushes on the floor. "What *are* you?"

My arm snakes out and firmly clasps hers. I feel quite unlike myself and yet unable to remember what the difference is between me before this and me now. "Let me talk to him. Let me help you."

Hails for her service have begun to break out across the tavern, but Vitòri ignores them with a practiced air. I know I haven't seen her at the Alcázar before, but if women like her are so close to Faucher, it's a wonder that he only addressed the men of Ivarea at the moment of his triumph.

Well, he's still a man. Not a wonder at all.

Vitòri pushes me back down onto a chair. "What did you say your name was?"

The great fugitive is huddled by himself over a worn oak table in an airy little room when Vitòri finally leads me upstairs and pushes me inside. Faucher barely startles from the map of the Alcázar complex laid before him. Judging by the faint scent of lemony soap in the air and the curling of his damp sandy hair about his ears, he's taking full advantage of his freedom.

"Of all the people I expected to meet here today, the daughter of Conte Eduard Aubanel was not one of them." His street-worn Castaran and Galvaise accents seem like flimsy things to me now that I hear him speaking in Proensan, his—*our*—mother tongue.

I swallow down my nerves, willing my hands from knotting themselves in my skirts. "Please . . . please just call me Citoyen Anaïs."

His laugh is a coarse bark. "And how exactly did you come by that title?"

I have no idea how well he knows House Aubanel, but I'm more concerned with making him understand that I actually want to help him. In my way. "We are not blind to the suffering of our people, Citoyen Mathieu. And after all this time at court, I've seen how this country functions up close, and . . . and it makes me *sick*. I can't bear to see Ivarea sleepwalk into the future while the king and his grandes go on as if nothing but their pleasure matters."

Faucher seems unperturbed by my zeal, but he stands, his hair darkening in the dying sunlight, and gestures me forward. "Citoyen Vitòri says you have some notion of what I'm doing. And at this hour, on this night, when all of Ivarea waits to be liberated, I find myself here wondering how Anaïs Aubanel could know exactly where and when to find me."

I may not have known Faucher would actually be here, but everything else should more than make up for that. "A captain in the Guardia Real broke you out of the towers, didn't he? Daniel Noguera." Faucher doesn't react, which I hope to God means that my guess was correct. "Are you aware of who he works for?"

Behind me, Vitòri shifts on her feet, uneasy.

"You've hidden the bombs in the royal catacombs in the Alcázar. Which are accessible only to those with the Cardonas' magic—unless you have a keeper's key, as Alberto Quirós does. Where did *you* get that key?"

Still, Faucher doesn't answer.

"Who removed the wards from the empty tower in the west wing so you and your fellow citoyens could sneak into the palace undetected?" I take a daring step closer. I let my cloak part so he can see the hilt strapped to my side before he reacts. "How do you think you survived this long?"

Faucher's brows, wild after years of imprisonment, dive into a deep V. "*This long?* Citoyen Anaïs, I've barely begun."

How obtuse can the man be? Does he really think the captain of a reactionary princess's guard converted to his cause? Or does he think that his followers are just so powerful and numerous that they could manage a plot like this on their own?

"You're not a revolutionary, Mathieu. You're a straw man," I say. Vitòri pushes forward, cleaving the air with a pistol. Its metallic clicking is as loud as the Alcázar clock tower bells. I go on: "Infanta Clara is the one pulling your strings."

Faucher has not moved all this time, hands uncurled and relaxed at his sides. A vein pulses in his temple, but his countenance is otherwise still. "Let it not be said that Proensan women are retiring types."

"She wants the crown for herself. But she can't just *take* it, no. She needs someone else to do it for her. And if that person is someone *she herself* threw in prison when her father would have let him go free? Can't you imagine what kind of regime she would build in the wake of your aborted revolution?"

Vitòri steams with rage just behind me. "This devil girl is only trying to distract you."

Compared to *barbarian* and *witch, devil girl* at least affords me a modicum of respect. "If anyone else at the Alcázar knew what I did, you'd have been dead before Noguera knocked on your cell door. I'm trying to *help* you. *Don't play into Clara's hands.*"

At last, Faucher rounds the table and draws up in front of me, his once-broken nose just inches from mine. I wonder if that happened to him in prison or before, at some point in the journey that brought him to this day, which trapped him as thoroughly as it did me. "I admit, there are pieces of what you've said that no one but my closest brothers and I know. Not even faithful Vitòri here knows where the palace bombs are hidden." The barmaid makes a muffled, indignant noise, but her leader does not waste his breath on her confusion. "How exactly did you come by this information?"

I could say that I had visions, or turned Quirós, or make up any number of other lies. But Mathieu Faucher is like me in one crucial respect: we're both Proensan. I wonder if he believes in that connection as I do.

"I have the blessing. Turns out that means I'm descended from the fairies themselves. They gave me the power to see everything that happens tonight." The last time I said anything about fairy descent aloud was to Gaspard in the ballroom. It feels a thousand times more ridiculous to say as much to Faucher in a tavern chamber. "And I'm telling you now, Mathieu, going down this route by yourself is not enough to change Ivarea for the better. It will never be enough."

For a second, it looks as though Faucher is more thrown by my last words than the first. Which, frankly, I wouldn't mind. Then his smile drops, leaving behind a strangely compelling emptiness, one that invites you to search it for something, anything, to pin your hopes on—a search that will always be in vain. "This is what I find so remarkable about people like you. You sincerely believe successful husband hunting in the capital would mean something to your people. But you arrive and are promptly rejected by the very Ivarean grandes you came here to ensnare. You cry over the *injustice* of it all, curse the rigged game that lured you out to the capital in search of more, and then . . . then you go home. To your grand châteaus, to your sumptuous downtown mansions, and to living as you and your kind always have. A noblewoman. An Aubanel. *Blessed* with blood magic. *And,* as you now claim, a descendant of the fairies themselves. This is injustice? It sounds to me like a *fairy tale.*"

Without looking, he pulls out another map—of all Ivarea. His hand drifts to the curling edge of the northeast to hover over our hometown, marked with an anchor for the port and fruit orchards in the countryside.

"Your people cannot live off storybooks, Citoyen Anaïs. They cannot slake their thirst with arcane blood magic. They want the power to change their own lives and society. *Real* power. And they, unlike you, are willing to fight and die to take it. So as your magic continues to wither away within you, and your people demand justice from you, who failed them for all these years, perhaps you will come to see yourself as I do." He looks up from the map and smiles. "As a *dying breed.*"

I swallow. The taste of lemon and oil fills up my mouth as if he actually shoved a bar of soap into it.

I know how the story that Faucher tells himself and his followers will end. I know what his vision of Ivarea's justice is, what his mercy looks like. The blood it requires. The cruelty and selfishness at its core.

I may be much better at dying than anything else I've ever

done in my life, but if I am still here, I have to hope for more. For all our sakes.

"We still have time, Mathieu. If you don't stop now and stand against Clara, you're going to lose everything. You'll consign Ivarea to nothing but fire and vengeance and blood."

"Fire and vengeance and blood is all Ivarea has ever known." He claws at the edge of the table. "We are simply balancing the scales in the people's favor."

Something sharp and cold presses into my side. Vitòri's calloused fingers tangle in my hair, smashing my scalp against the table. Struggling against the grip on my head, I catch the corner of Faucher's smile again, only now it's accompanied by a rifle in his hands, withdrawn from beneath the table in one sure movement. There's no excising all the terror laced deep in the workings of my heart, the traceries of my veins. There's no freedom from it, either. Not even in death.

A bullet bursts from the gullet of his gun. I collapse on top of the table and drown Ivarea in my blood.

XVI

CHAPTER ONE

AGAIN AND AGAIN, I SNEAK OUT OF THE TOWNHOUSE AND head for the Boar's Snout. I storm into Mathieu Faucher's rooms, with Vitòri and other citizens hot on my heels, blades bared and barrels aimed. Again and again, I tell Faucher that his coup was engineered to fail and that none of us will survive if we can't stand together; once, I even plead my case at his bath-side, staring determinedly at the wall above his curling blond hair and nowhere else.

Most nights, he has me killed. A few times he does it himself. Once, Vitòri gags me with Le Nas de Sanglier's famous herbed soap and ties me to the bedpost, leaving me there when Faucher departs for the Alcázar. I have to fall forward onto the blade of the blessed dagger to die.

There are a few times when he seems to believe me, or at least seems like he could be convinced that there's some truth to my story. But instead of helping me outmaneuver Clara, he only vows to make an example of the conceited princess who dared try to harness the movement of an awakening Ivarea for her own gain. I can only imagine how well that will go. If he ever lives long enough to do it.

Unable to figure out how to persuade Faucher into compromising by myself, and without any allies at Le Nas de Sanglier, I have no choice but to admit defeat for now. I have to focus on the *other* intractable problem that's keeping me from taking off my locket and possibly, maybe, one day breaking the cycle of my own deaths: Clara's seeming inability to die. If I can figure out why that is, if I can find a way around it, that would be a huge step toward saving this country from doom and saving myself from constantly repeating it.

After all my recent failures, however, I know I can't hope to get to that point alone. So it's a good thing that I have other allies waiting for me at the palace.

Even if they don't know it.

It takes strategic flirting, unsubtle whining, and outright threats in the form of a blessed dagger to lure Gaspard and Leo in one place together.

Leo is already inside my favorite broom closet, basking in the light of a stolen candelabra as only he could. He looks up from beneath his lashes as I bustle inside—and jumps back when he notices the gangly young man shutting the door behind us.

Unable to help himself, Gaspard guffaws. "If this was what you had in mind, Anaïs, you should have just said so."

Leo waves his hand, unruffled. "You should be so lucky."

One of the many past Anaïses I've been would rather have melted into the walls than let this conversation go any further. But I would like to not have to die for once in my lives.

"Infanta Clara is planning to murder the entire court and steal the throne."

The broom closet stills. Even the cleaning supplies we disturbed seem to be suspended in midair. For a long moment, no one breathes.

"*What?*" Gaspard squeaks for them both.

At least this way, I don't have to explain it twice.

When I'm finished, the pair of them are speechless. Leo seethes on an upturned bucket, head in his hands, knees knocking together in agitation. Gaspard stares at me from a stand of feather dusters as if he's never met another human person before. I don't feel bad for beating them over the head with merciless, excruciating detail of what is to come. Tonight, I need them both for one reason:

"You have to tell me why Clara isn't dying."

Gaspard curses under his breath. Leo remains deadly silent.

"I've stabbed her in the side. I've shot her in the chest. I've convinced Jacinthe to pour poison down her throat. I've watched the whole goddamn Alcázar fall down around her. And every time I manage not to die long enough, she just bounces back like nothing happened." I take a deep breath.

"Alteza, you're her brother, and Gaspard, you're supposed to be smart. Between the two of you . . . why can't she be killed?"

Gaspard seems to be knocking his head against a support beam, or maybe the handles of the feather dusters, as if to get his brain working again. "Um . . . a powerful charm?"

And here I thought he'd finally hit on something useful. "There's no way a throwaway market-day trinket is saving Clara from getting blown up."

"You just said Clara seems impervious to bodily harm. How else could that be possible?" Even with the pressure of our lives and the kingdom's survival hanging on what we say now, Gaspard seems almost invigorated by academic debate. "An Ivarean magician would try to manipulate the physical world as a defense—you know, reinforce the walls around them, destroy debris. But Clara's not doing that. That's not possible unless she's using a charm to alter or amplify her own powers somehow. Hell, even the great Cardonas couldn't have survived a direct attack like that on their own."

"Of course not, Plamondon. The great Cardonas were never on their own." Balancing on the knife's edge of a bucket, Leo chuckles darkly under his breath. "They used the bones of their dead ancestors to make talismans of power."

Oh fuck. Oh *fuck*. Why does this sound horrifically familiar?

Can you imagine if they had charms made of, say, Rey Carlos's pinkie finger?

Because Leo told me all about it in the catacombs.

For the first time in a while, I find it briefly, keenly impossible to even look at him. I bury my head in my hands instead. "And you all think Proensan blood magic is barbaric."

Leo sucks in a breath, stricken. Through the lattice of my fingers, I notice him drumming his fingers against his knee in anxiety. "I . . . I know. But that's the heart of the Cardonas' type of power for you." He drops his hands and straightens his back, as if belatedly trying to own up to his family's secret, dark magical legacy. "The Cardona magicians used the bones of their dead magician ancestors to amplify their abilities for ages, even once they'd taken over the peninsula. But about two centuries ago, after they crossed the sea, their command of magic began growing more tenuous. They decided it was no longer safe to carry on using powerful talismans they could not control. So they destroyed the surviving ones and re-interred their ancestors in the catacombs here in Marenca, where they would be protected. They couldn't afford other, more power-ful magicians figuring out their secret and raising that same power against them." He snorts. "Little did they realize they should've worried more about the people *within* the Alcázar than the people without."

Gaspard clears his throat with a flourish. "I'm sorry," he says, not sounding sorry at all, "but how does this . . . enlight-ening but extremely disturbing fun fact help us with this Clara situation?"

Leo grimaces. "I think she's made a talisman out of our ancestors' bones to survive the attack."

All of Gaspard's indignant confusion compresses into a single strangled noise.

"Actually," the prince continues, gaining a strange, almost macabre momentum, "if Clara is already using a talisman for herself, planting the bombs in the catacombs might make sense. She might have figured out how to use the magical potential of the catacomb bones to amplify the explosive power of the bombs to overcome the wards. Which means that not only can she decapitate the palace, she's also destroying a massive cache of potential talismans that could have been used against her." He exhales through his nose, as if overwhelmed by his own realization. "Two birds."

Two birds indeed. Except I somehow feel like the stone that Clara's using to kill them. What was it she said before she sent me and her younger brother to be murdered? *You must learn how to use that power before someone else tries to take it from you.*

I wish I could say I don't understand how Clara could extrapolate that lesson to this terrible plot . . . but the truth is, I do. Perhaps it was only a matter of time before she decided to resurrect her ancestors' legacy. The Cardonas' luck with magical talent is not what it once was, after all, and Clara became the most powerful magician in her family in nearly a century. Leo has similar ambitions, but he tried to fulfill them by promising to *serve* his kingdom, even in a childish game. Clara went for deceit, mass murder, and tyranny.

The moment I raise my head from my hands, my gaze slides to Leo's. "What exactly *is* a bone talisman, anyway? What would it look like?"

Gaspard rakes a shaky hand through his already-loosened

curls. "Couldn't be too different from typical Ivarean charms, right? Little paperweights, bits of jewelry, pottery shards, accessories—"

My stomach has already dropped to the floor out of some base instinct I can't immediately unravel. My mind catches up a beat later.

"Her fan. It's made of bone."

Whalebone. I thought it was whalebone. Assumed it was whalebone. Who could have ever assumed otherwise?

You, Anaïs. You could have assumed something else.

Yes. Yes, I should have. She had that fan in her hands even after Mathieu Faucher shot her; she must have used it to bring the Alcázar down on our heads. She clung to it like it was an extension of her own body when she felled Faucher's men in the ballroom. She didn't even let me lay a hand on it back in her chambers.

It was right in front of me. It's always been right in front of me.

And I always missed it.

Leo and Gaspard are each as lost in furiously churning thought as I am. Our combined concentration seems to be raising the temperature in the broom cupboard; new beads of sweat roll down Gaspard's face, and Leo loosens the clasp of his cloak, letting the whole thing fall to the floor.

"Parading an incredibly powerful ancient magic talisman in public in the hours before you use it to usurp your father's throne seems . . ." Gaspard casts about for the right word. "Risky? Foolish? Audacious?"

"I expect that's the point." Leo glances back at me. "So. What do we do now, Anaïs?"

Neither he nor Gaspard seems dumbfounded by what I say any longer. They're honestly, truly seeking my guidance. They're looking to *me* for leadership.

Gods and fairies and saints save us all.

Somewhere, Contesse Aliénor Laborde Aubanel is begging her fairy ancestors to knock some sense into her intransigent daughter for ignoring all the eligible young nobles making eyes at her in favor of her childhood friend, but I choose not to see her. Gaspard and I have been dancing for ages now, lying in wait. At least our plan is a simple one:

Ram into Clara. Steal her fan. Die.

If it were up to me, I would have charged at her long ago. But to stall for time before our immediate deaths, Leo wants to make a decoy fan to switch with hers. While he's off searching for pig bones left over from the feast, Gaspard and I stay in the ballroom, clinging to each other in a way that probably lends credence to the assumptions about us at court.

Which is fine. We have a lead *and* a plan, and it's not yet midnight. I can afford this. To do nothing but dance. For now.

Can't I?

The sound of Gaspard chuckling to himself jolts me out of my reverie. "What're *you* laughing at?"

"I just can't believe you're the same girl who once begged

me, on bended knee, to not tell her mother about her traipsing around the undergrowth outside your family's château."

"I had to! Maman would have throttled me if she knew I'd snuck out of that important garden party or whatever it was to run around in a muddy forest and ruin my dress. You were the only witness. I *had* to beg you to keep my secret. It was an act of self-preservation."

"Was it?" His expression sinks with the weight of melancholy. "Anaïs, do you ever think about what this is like for the rest of us?"

My breath suddenly shrinks into itself, until it's so soft that it couldn't disturb a soap bubble. "I'm sorry. I really am. I know it's unfair, it's just that I don't . . . I can't do this alone. I've tried, and I just . . . I can't."

"That's just it," he responds earnestly. "Listen, I understand feeling powerless. Forget this disaster of a season. My father banished me to school without even once asking whether thirteen-year-old me wanted to spend years in a chilly northern dormitory, far away from everything and everyone I knew. But after the first year or two, I realized, for all that Lutesse was hell on earth, I could still make something of this experience. I could try and find something that was *mine* to live for. I don't know that I've found it quite yet, as my time on the fringes of Faucher's movement proves, but I've been trying.

"You, though . . . I don't know, Anaïs. All these years I've known you, and you were always just resigned to what your parents wanted for you. You were always so passive, I never knew what you were really like."

I move only because Gaspard is technically still holding me. Passive, indeed.

"Now I wonder if I was blind all that time. Or if I just can't remember." He lowers his head, and his eyes almost seem to shimmer with uncertainty under his furrowed brows. "I'm starting to think that even before this happened, deep down, you were always this Anaïs. The one I'm talking to now. The one who's determined. Assertive. Compassionate. *Brave*."

That can't be right. It has to be wistful nostalgia talking, a side effect of imminent death. Because after all this time, all these deaths, I feel so far gone from the Anaïs he remembers, the Anaïs that was supposed to be, that she sounds almost like a stranger. I'm not sure I could bear meeting her in the flesh.

But if he thinks it's possible, if he thinks it's true, then I can let him go on believing it. "You're just being nice to me because you know we're closer to midnight than not."

"Don't worry about that. I just want to say . . . I believe in you. I think you can do this."

"You remember the part where I die every night?"

There's increasing despair in the crinkle of his eyes, and in a balance I can't comprehend, greater warmth in the curve of his lips. "You come back every morning."

"Afternoon."

"Same thing."

For a moment, out of a self-destructive impulse, I debate telling Gaspard that I once accused him of being part of the attack. That I truly, if briefly, believed he was helping orchestrate the deaths of hundreds of people. But I can't make myself admit this past shame. Not now. So, breaking with form, I rest my head on his shoulder. Even now he smells faintly of cedar and dried orange blossoms. Like winters in Massilie spent huddled beside roaring fireplaces, the crash of the sea a suggestion in temperamental winds.

The music dies down, and I raise my head again before anyone can comment on the intimacy of the gesture. Gaspard's mouth is slightly parted, as if torn between saying something and not, but then he releases his grip on my hand.

I understand why when I feel the tickle of Leo's murmur against my ear. "May I have this dance?"

Gaspard inclines his head to the prince and steps away with a woeful half grin for me. "Good luck, Anaïs."

The last time he said that, I ended up with a bullet through my heart.

As I take Leo's hand and Gaspard melts into the crowd, I throw the prince a glance of impatience for good measure. "What took you so long?"

His fingers uncurl and slip through mine, so my hand gets caught in his jacket sleeve. Just inside his cuff, I feel something smooth and cold strapped to his shirtsleeves.

The decoy talisman.

Judging by the feverish heat behind Leo's eyes, making the fan has already cost him energy and magic. I withdraw it and press it between our hands, a joint supplication that what he's already sacrificed for this, what we're about to do, will be worth it.

A minute or two later, Leo tightens his grip on my waist. "Ready?"

I look up and finally glimpse Clara and her current partner, Tristán de la Cueva. Her fan dangles from an emerald ribbon around her wrist. Her head is back, her cheeks flushed with giddiness. She's enjoying this last hurrah as a mere princess. Counting down the minutes until midnight and all that happens after.

So am I.

With a flush of euphoric brass and searing percussion, the song barrels toward its high point. The ballroom bursts into motion—sweeping spins, limbs flying, skirts whirling, the high color of passion sweating the powder off women's faces and elderly men's wigs alike. I can feel the crest of the crescendo growing in my head and in my heart. Leo and I ride its wave of energy together—

Right into his sister.

Infanta Clara's scream is brutal. Louder still is the *crack* of our arms on the floor as we collide and fall, she with her hands outstretched to protect her face, me strategically flailing. By the time I push myself onto my protesting elbows to see the aftermath, Clara's fan has whirled off her wrist to a stop a few steps away, its emerald ribbon already streaked with dirt from the dance floor.

With the press of concerned courtiers around the fallen princess as my cover, I stretch my left arm until I feel the carved bone handle of Clara's fan. Quick as a snake, I snap it back to my side and stuff it into my sash, just before—

"Why, Doña Anaïs. How *lovely* to see you."

I extricate my right hand from below my skirt and try to

push myself up. "Vuestra Alteza Real . . . mi infanta . . ." The decoy fan clatters on the floor, as if it has been trapped beneath me this whole time. "I cannot *begin* to express how sor—"

"Save it, you stupid Proensan *pig*."

My arms give out. The gleeful viciousness of her tone catapults me back in time far more efficiently than a mysterious fairy amulet could. Collapsed on the floor before her, I'm the pathetic little country bumpkin I used to be again. The one Gaspard pitied all our lives. The one whose greatest pain came from cruelty, not death.

I shouldn't be surprised. I know Clara is a lunatic regicide murderer. But even when executing Faucher and his followers, I've never seen her so briefly and violently overcome with rage.

"Saints, Clara, where are your manners?" Leo strides forward, his slightly dirtied crimson cloak practically floating above the floor even as he crouches down to help me. "I'm so sorry, Doña Anaïs. Got a bit carried away. You're all right?"

Ignoring the new titters, I lean into the prince's body and try desperately not to look at his sister, the floor, or the fake fan at my feet.

Leo curls his arm around me so his hand rests on top of my sash as if in a familiar caress. Or as if making sure something else is safe there. "Come, let's find you a place to rest. The farther from these vultures, the better."

Clara's smile burns, but she says nothing. With this crowd on her side, she doesn't have to.

I wonder what they would do if they knew how thoughtlessly she'll turn on them soon.

Something tightens at my waist. Panic briefly flares in my chest before I remember that Leo is still holding me. Trying to protect me. From his sister. From the world.

At least I'm not the only fool.

Oblivious to the pain she's caused, Clara crouches down where I just lay. Expression neutral, she picks up a fan by an emerald ribbon.

The decoy.

Before Clara can do or say anything, Leo finally leads me away and out of the ballroom. I barely breathe, let alone spare a glance backward, until we've hurtled into the broom cupboard and slammed the door shut behind us.

Leo wipes his brow with the back of his hands. "*Shit.* You were brilliant. I didn't even *see* you make the switch. Are you okay?"

Banishing the glow of Leo's praise before it clouds my mind, I extricate Clara's real fan. Now that I have more than a millisecond to examine it, I can feel that the bone of the handle is unnervingly smooth to the touch and carved with vines that twist and transfigure into flames. At its base is another carving of a gilded dragon against a diamond of night sky—Clara's personal crest. It's truly a piece worthy of a princess.

But it doesn't exactly feel *magical* to me.

I frown up at Leo. "Is there any chance we're wrong and we did all this for nothing?"

All excitement gone, he plucks the fan from my palm.

His expression as his fingers close around the handle stops my breath cold. Leo's eyes are glazed over and unseeing, mouth slack, hand clenched around the fan. Without touching him, I can feel a fever beginning to churn below his skin. It spreads to the very walls of the cupboard, imbuing the worn stone with an impossible energy that threatens to shake loose whatever binding agents sealed them in this formation all those centuries ago.

Not good. Whatever this is, it's not good at all.

I grab his free hand and dig my nails deep into his palm. It's only when I nearly draw blood that he finally flinches and I can wrench back the stolen fan. He slumps against the door with a thunderous clatter, as if I've knocked his knees out from under him. He pants heavily, which means that he might not have been able to breathe before.

Extremely not good.

"L-Leo?" I watch his breathing slow in the dark. "What happened?"

He doesn't respond, only blinks. He presses his empty hand against the wall beside him as if to right his relentlessly tilting world. "*Fuck.*"

I feel rather the same.

Seemingly much later, he stammers, "How . . . can she . . ." He stares at the fan, ominously inert in my hands. "You don't feel it, too?"

As I have not unwittingly reduced the cupboard to rubble in the last few seconds, I shake my head. "You're the Cardona. Maybe its magic only recognizes you."

The drawn expression on his face tells me I am right. Leo may not be able to control his sister's talisman, but the very foundation of this city would still probably split itself open at his command. *If the talisman is carved of the bones of Cardona magicians past, why should it respond to me?*

Clara said it herself. *I'm just a Proensan pig.*

How terribly unfair it is that I'm the one left to save this kingdom from her.

I begin to lift the folded fan up toward my locket to bring it back with me for next time, but Leo grabs my wrist, aghast. "What are you doing? Anaïs, that thing is *not* safe for—"

"The only other person in this cupboard who could use it?"

Wounded, Leo lets me go. "Just because you don't feel anything now doesn't mean that talisman won't affect you over time. Or when you go back."

I have no idea if that's true or not, but the longer we fight about this, the likelier it is that Clara discovers the fake and exacts her vengeance on us. Without taking the locket off, I wrench it open and jab the guard of the fan into its center like a dagger. Then all at once, and faster than last time, the fan disappears and the locket slams shut. The opal glows like a bloody winter sun at my throat. I stagger forward and crash headfirst into Leo's chest, knocking him fully against the wall. My head begins to whine.

Groaning as we both struggle upright, he brushes off the gilded hairpins that got caught in his vest buttons. "What in the fuck was that?"

Trying to steady my breath against the new weight on my chest, I offer up a wan version of a smirk that I must have picked up from him. "Can't you tell? It's *secret magic*."

I can just make out the whites of his eyes as they roll in the semidarkness. "I suppose I deserve that."

The melancholy twist of his voice makes me erase my smirk. "In all honesty, if it weren't for you, Leo, we would never have made it this far. You've given so much of yourself to help me when I asked, even if you didn't really believe me, and I . . . I can't express how grateful I am."

His breathing pauses. Then he mutters, "Yes, well. Anything to serve Ivarea."

Ah yes. His embarrassing little oath. Luckily, I already blackmailed him with that secret to make him meet me here earlier tonight, so for once, I can ask *him* magic questions. "*Why* did you use your blood for a fake ritual?"

"I don't know. I suppose it just felt right at the time." He coughs. "Tell me, how exactly did I explain that night to you?"

It's been so long since he first told me that story that pulling out the specifics is harder than it should be. I hadn't needed details before, after all. The very mention of his earnest little gesture of devotion was often all I needed. "Something about you being a sad, lonely little boy desperate to connect himself to his family through a hero."

He blinks rapidly at the ground. "That was all?"

"I don't know. You put a drop of blood on San Pedro's sword relic and swore to serve Ivarea. Honestly, it was almost endearing."

"I didn't tell you what came after?"

For some reason, my lungs contract and my breathing goes slightly shallow. "There was an after?"

He doesn't answer me directly. "You haven't heard the story of Clemencia of Lereda, have you?"

I choke on my own spit. Because I *do* actually know this story. Clara told it to me in her chambers before she sent me and Leo off to the catacombs to be murdered: the Tarracán magician who asked the saints to restore her husband's sight and lost her own. But I fail to see what that has to do with Leo's childhood heresy.

At my silence, he buries his face in his hands. "It seems that I . . . I misled you, all those deaths ago. A lie of omission, maybe. I don't know what I was thinking, but if Clara has been relying on dark, esoteric magic all this time, then who knows, you might need to know this, too."

Somehow, I'm not sure I really want to. "What do you . . ."

"That silly ritual I did with the espasa òssia? Swearing my life and death to Ivarea, sealing it with my blood? It wasn't a game, Anaïs. It was binding."

My brows furrow, and my confusion only makes my head ache more. "Have you lost your mind?"

"Everything I told you before is true. I *was* a pathetic boy starved for heroism. My father made it very clear that I would not have a real place in my family and that I would have nothing much to hope for out of my own life, so I imagined myself in San Pedro's place. I thought I was playing a game. But after I said my piece, I offered the saints my blood, and then . . . I can't explain it, but it was like the whole world had *shifted* around me. I just *felt* what had happened.

"The saints had accepted my oath and bound me to them.

From then on, my life and death would forevermore be in service to Ivarea. It was . . . magic. Like I never knew existed."

My eyes cross and uncross as I try to follow his logic, trace the roots of this latest impossible story of magic, but trying to understand only threatens to split my skull open, laying bare all the gristle of my bewildered brain. "I have never heard anything even *beginning* to approach this."

"Of course you haven't. My illustrious ancestors made sure of that." He grimaces. "Blood oaths are older than Ivarea itself. But the medieval Cardonas thought ordinary people binding themselves to the saints or forcing them into mortal business was heretical. Dangerous, even. So when they came to power, the Cardona kings said that blood oaths were blasphemy against the saints, and successfully turned Ivarea's attention to the magic to be mined and manipulated from the earth. In their own image."

His eyelids keep fluttering, as if he's communing with some ancient power to tell his story. With his saints, perhaps. Or whoever else might be listening. "Now the practice of blood oaths has been forgotten. *I* definitely didn't know what it was until I accidentally invoked it. Afterward, I chased down explanations anywhere I could. Like in that Clemencia folktale. The magic there is real: you ask for the saints' intercession, for someone else or for yourself, agree to pay the price, bind your promise with blood." He scoffs again. "Turns out Tarracuña and Proensa aren't that different after all. We both trafficked in blood magic."

Impossible.

This is all impossible.

But . . . if Leo *is* right, and a form of blood magic *was* once practiced on the peninsula, why is it that *Proensans* are now the barbarians? It feels wrong in a way I can barely conceive of, and trying to just increases the pressure building up behind my eyelids. My headache spreads through my body, causing my hands to shake. I shove them behind my back, where my knuckles scrape themselves raw against the stone of the cupboard wall. I breathe in deeply, trying to calm myself, but whatever is happening to me is as befuddling as Leo's story.

A little boy playing pretend promised to serve his kingdom and sealed it with blood—only to invoke some ancient magic. And . . . and that act was *binding*? What does it mean, to be bound to a saint?

"Leo, I—"

Before I can finish my question, the bells begin to strike.

Only now do I realize we never left the broom cupboard; ensconced within the Alcázar walls, the bells feel louder and more resonant to me than ever before, as if they're not in the palace at all, but embedded behind my eardrums, pounding at my heart. Head in my shaking hands, I sink to the floor and cry out.

"Anaïs?" Leo's voice is as distant as the lapping of a wave along a shifting shore. "Anaïs, can you hear me? Are you okay?"

For the first time in all my lives, I don't feel the bombs explode all around me.

I don't feel anything.

XVII

CHAPTER ONE

HUDDLED BESIDE MY BED FRAME TO HIDE THE PROFUSION of amber light pooling in my hands, I stare as Clara Cardona's talisman tumbles out from my amulet. The locket seems as eager to get rid of it as I am to have it in my hands. As if this token of Mireille and her lover recognizes the horrors that the bone talisman helped perpetrate—and, I suspect, the weakness it caused in me before midnight.

If that feeling was indeed the effect of Clara's talisman, then it's just more proof of what I've known to be true ever since I arrived on the peninsula: Ivarean magic is averse to fairy blood. I don't know how, I don't know why, but sure as the Alcázar itself undoes spells I cast upon it with the blessing, I know that this bone fan and I are not going to get along.

The last time my opal amulet glowed like it is now, I was in the catacombs, surrounded by the bones of Ivarea's most powerful magicians. It glowed again when I stowed Clara's bone fan inside. So maybe, after it awoke at the moment of my first death, the amulet is now trying to warn me about talismans in its vicinity. Why it would do that, I'm not entirely sure, but there's no use in me wasting time by spiraling about the amulet's impossible magical mysteries when I could simply spiral over Leo's equally impossible blood-oath story instead.

I can't get over it: I, a Proensan, carry the magical blood of fairies in my veins; and Leo, an Ivarean, unknowingly, unintentionally, bound himself to a saint with a blood oath.

Perhaps he was right. Perhaps we aren't that different after all.

Now that I know the truth behind this secret, I can almost understand why Leo told it to me as ammunition against his very self. He may not have told me that his pretend oath was in fact not pretend, but he said it that night, too: he knew how seriously he would take a stranger who knew the first thing about it. For all I know, maybe he thought his oath to serve Ivarea *forced* him to offer me his help. I don't know what's more unsettling: the idea of his wanting to help me, or the idea of his being magically bound to do so.

Haunted as I am by those possibilities, I cannot bear to chase him down again and force him to unearth the secrets of his past. Especially if he can no more tell me what he was thinking when he first told me about his childhood oath than I can. No, all I can do is honor what those past Leos did for me. All I can do is move forward. Figure out what comes next.

But he is all I can think of.

We are at an impasse, my heart and I. I've had lives and deaths to make peace with my feelings and with their futility, and while I've failed to actually do so, it's not as if I'm holding out hope that one day, Leo will take one look at my face and fall desperately in love with me. That's not how the world works. That will never change.

So I love him without hope. That is the bargain I have struck with myself. Knowing him, having the privilege of loving him from afar, from yesterday and tomorrow and now, always now, is more than I could ask for. My love is a fact that no one knows to be true and that, in the grand scheme of this endless day, will change nothing.

But if I can save him—if I can save all of them—it will be enough.

I wanted proof of Clara's involvement in the attacks, and here it is, the fan plain and inimical as day. And until the stroke of midnight, there's still only one real power in all of Ivarea who can do anything with it.

I haven't been able to make him listen before, but this time, with proof of his daughter's magical plot hanging on my wrist, Rey Rodrigo might believe me. He has to. He's the only one who can turn the might of the Ivarean state on our shadowy magician-princess. Maybe he and the magicians of the Guardia Real can hold her long enough to save everyone trapped at the palace.

This is the king's last chance to stand up for the country he was born to rule. I'm hoping against hope that he'll take it.

Blinking hard against the growing ache in my head after I reach the palace, I am ushered through to a cavernous chamber, practically wallpapered in gold leaf, that's easily five times the size of the sitting room in my family's château. A pair of guards push me into a curtsy before a tall man in shirtsleeves that I don't fully recognize until he bids me rise.

Without royal regalia, Rey Rodrigo almost seems like he could be another middle-aged patron of Les Nas de Sanglier, albeit with a less pockmarked visage. He regards me as he would a well-trained horse. "My men tell me you've spun quite a story, Doña Anaïs of Massilie," he begins nonchalantly. "Something about a dissident mob in the Alcázar."

When I told the guards about Mathieu Faucher's prison break and coup, they rocked back in shock, their armor squeaking in protest. The king is not so easily taken aback. He may not take the threat of revolution seriously—and how could he, in a room as absurd and isolated as this?—but even he can't *always* wave away anything that makes him the slightest bit uncomfortable.

Unfortunately for him, Mathieu Faucher is not the most contentious part about this story.

I take a deep, unsteady breath. "Your daughter is helping them, Vuestra Majestad Real."

The king frowns deep enough to swallow all the palace in its crags. "Tread carefully now, child."

I *am* trying to be careful—I don't want the king to summarily dismiss me again, especially not if he thinks I'm simply hysterical—but if he thinks I'm too calm, he might not even entertain the possibility that he's in danger, and then who will mobilize the Guardia Real? Then what chance can we ever have?

With a ramrod-straight back, I look him in the eye and make myself seem as iron-willed as he is. "Infanta Clara is using Mathieu Faucher to do the dirty work of bombing the Alcázar and assassinating you. Then she'll swoop in to kill him, save the day, and take over Ivarea herself. Search out the royal catacombs and you'll find bombs hidden among your dead if you don't believe me. Send a contingent of troops to Le Nas de Sanglier in the river district and they'll find Mathieu Faucher and his supporters biding their time there before midnight. And as for Infanta Clara . . ."

I shake the ribbon off my wrist to unfold the bone fan. Its skeleton seems to soak in the evening light even from underneath the vellum leaf. "She broke every norm of Ivarean magic to create a talisman of power out of the bones of your ancestors. See? That's her crest on the handle." Clara's diamond dragon winks knowingly at her father in the last of the sunlight. "Your magician-guards can confirm what this is. They'll tell you what it means. They can tell you how powerful a talisman made from Cardona magician bones would make the magician who wields it. But you are not a foolish man, Majestad, of course you're not. You have to know what a Cardona magician armed with a weapon like *this* would do next. You have to know, on some level, what your own daughter wants most." I snort despite myself, but it only sounds like I'm choking. "And it's not the foreign crown of a consort."

Rodrigo drifts forward, as slowly as if a dream creature himself, and studies the object in my hand. "Quite a story indeed."

Stories, stories, everyone in this capital is obsessed with stories. About themselves, their kingdom, their peoples, their pasts. Rodrigo is no different than his children in that respect. But if this kingdom has any hope of surviving tonight, Ivarea has to look beyond the stories it tells itself.

Even, perhaps, the ones sealed with blood.

"It doesn't have to be this way, Majestad. Mobilize all the magicians at your disposal. Do it now and you might save yourself and your kingdom from untold destruction. You don't want to die at your daughter's hand, do you?" Frustration and desperation twine and rattle my bones, make my hands shake again, the way they did in the cupboard at midnight. *"Do you?"*

I don't know that I even have reason on my side now. But after all I've suffered, all I've done to others, it's clear that I *still* don't have any power here. None that will make a difference without the king's stamp of approval. He keeps looking at me like I'm some jester brought in for his entertainment—not that he is much enamored by my performance. His look tells me exactly what my words are worth. What my curse, its powers, amounts to, in his eyes.

Nothing.

He's going to fail us. Again.

And I can't do anything more about it.

My voice comes out as a snarl, though it sounds toothless

334

even to me. "I would have hoped you could care enough about your own kingdom to care whether it's in danger—"

"Who are *you* to question *my* devotion to this kingdom?" Rey Rodrigo erupts. "You have no idea what it takes to rule so many and for so long as I have, as my ancestors did before me. You Proensans never had any culture, never made a civilization of your own. *Ivarea* gave you all you have. You should be grateful for it. You should be grateful to *me*. Instead, here you are, slandering my daughter, questioning my governance, attacking my great dynasty's rule! The audacity!"

I don't know why I hoped, even for a second, that showing the king proof could get him to act. Not against Clara. Not if it ran up against his pride.

What a complete waste of time.

"Your daughter is going to kill you! Isn't that *audacious* enough for you?"

Rey Rodrigo passes a hand over his face, weathered despite having seen so little in the way of legitimate challenge. "Ivarea does not need saving. But you, my dear . . ."

He raises his head and a new set of guards diffuse into the room, as if they were waiting for his signal from behind secret panels in the wall. Maybe they were. Maybe his magicians were right here the whole time, and they didn't lift a finger when I told their king that he was in danger.

Maybe no one else ever will.

"The girl is deluded. Let her clear her head in the dungeons."

The moment the guards leap to action, a crushing wave of

dizziness from the talisman hammers my brain. As unmoved by his certain doom as he is by my dimming consciousness, Rey Rodrigo stands resolute in his own power as I crash to the ground.

⁊

I wake up on the floor of an eerie dungeon cell. I have no idea how long it's been or where exactly the Guardia Real took me. My head seems to weigh a thousand pounds, as if it's growing heavier the more pain and suffering it absorbs. Like my amulet.

Through the haze in my head, I lift a hand to my neck.

It's gone. The amulet is gone.

Panic dissipates the worst of the pain, allowing me the clarity to run through the possibilities. Between the legend of the amulet's original powers, the vision it showed me of its failed destruction, and a base instinct bought of my suffering, I don't see a way around it: If I die without the amulet, I think its spell on me will be broken. I don't think I'll wake up again this afternoon.

I won't wake up at all. Ever again.

Faucher's revolution will go on as he thinks he's planned it. Clara will co-opt it and plunge Ivarea into tyranny.

I don't want to know if I'm right. I just know that this is not my time to die. This is not how it's supposed to end.

I force myself to crawl toward the iron bars of the cell door, my hands and gown dragging on muck and gravel and the cold bone of the fan talisman, clearly tossed in after my prone body.

The corridor beyond resolves itself into a shadowy set of stairs, watched over by what appears to be an officer. I try to strain my neck to see more through the bars, but my hair starts to burn.

With a muttered curse, I smother the sparks with my grimy hands and scuttle back. The darkness wrapping around the bars seems to dance. More cautious now, I raise the back of a limp hand toward the cell door. And . . . there it is: a current of light glancing against my skin. Wound like lightning around the cell bars.

What is this? And where the fuck is my amulet?

New footsteps land like a crack in the hallway. The retreating of several pairs of boots up the stairs forces me back up against the cell wall. Before I can even begin to compose myself, Clara draws up before my cell.

She recognized my locket as an amulet before I even knew what it had done to me. If she knew I was unconscious here . . .

I'm going to throw up. For the first time in my lives, I send a prayer to Mireille Laborde's fairy beloved and beg him to make the amulet glow, dissolve the cell bars, *send me back in time,* before Clara can kill me. Forever.

"Wh-where is my—"

"Save it, Doña Anaïs." The princess edges closer to the bars. The shellacked gentility I've seen from her before has melted clean off her face. What's left is something raw. Something that, for the first time ever, might be true. "There is one thing I'm dying to know. *Where* did you get that fan?"

Oh . . . right. The magical talisman I brought back in time. That fan. "Where do you think?"

With the flick of a wrist, she unsheathes hers—the one belonging to this time, to this Clara—admiring the way it glimmers clean as greed in the speckled half-light. "There's only one of these in existence."

"Sure about that?" If she saw the fan I stole on my cell floor, she must know that's not true anymore. Clearly she was not worried about a Proensan being able to use her talisman if she took my amulet but left that here. "I understand, though. No one except you would dare resurrect forgotten magic to make a talisman out of the bones of dead Cardonas, would they?"

"What did you say to me, you little Proensan pig?"

Hearing this drivel from a person I once admired makes me want to crawl out of my own skin. But she's out there, I'm in a cell, and the only way I can hope to undo this is to keep her talking. "Raiding the royal catacombs for raw material is awfully tacky, Alteza. I don't know what you were thinking."

"Frankly, I was thinking that no one would understand what I was doing, and if by any chance they did, they still wouldn't be able to stop me. And I was right." I'm sure she understands that I'm baiting her, but she doesn't seem to care. She flicks her wrist again, and the fan snaps shut. "My ancestors mowed your people down with talismans like these. I didn't realize until now that it was because you *literally* couldn't stand up to them."

She begins to pace before the cell, the edges of her emerald gown sweeping up dust and cobwebs in the golden blossoms along its hem. "Tell me the truth and you just might survive. How do you know about my talisman?"

"Mathieu Faucher loves reminding the people what they're fighting for. But we both know he's rarely specific about how to wage that fight." She flinches at his name. "And now that your father is sending you off to a foreign kingdom to be married, there's a ticking clock over your head. Even if you'd get a crown as a consolation prize for your banishment, you couldn't just *leave*. Not when you could take Ivarea for yourself."

Her lips curl into a sneer so venomous it could knock me unconscious. Though right now, that would not be all that difficult. "After all I've done in service of this kingdom, taking my father's crown is really just a formality, I promise."

Not for the first time but perhaps for the last, I'm struck by just how much Clara differs from her younger brother. Despite being shut out of power in his kingdom, despite being turned into an outcast in his own family, Leo swore to serve Ivarea, and he *has*. Almost every time I've asked him to. No matter what it's taken from him, over and over and over again. Clara has had an outsized part in governance because of her father, but the only thing that experience instilled in her was lust for power. She serves nothing and no one but herself and expects the world to reward her for it with a crown in her own right.

She heaves an aggrieved sigh into the silence of the dungeon cell. "I'm not stupid. I know what an alliance with Rasenna could do for us. For this kingdom, I could have spent the rest of my life in that glorified-banker royal family. *If* my dearest, darling Papá had asked me first."

A terrible feeling unfurls in the pit of my stomach. "He—he

never told you?" How many times have I heard this sort of story before?

"Not until after he signed my betrothal agreement." She rolls her eyes so witheringly that I flinch. "Credit where credit's due: I haven't seen him try so hard to keep a secret since Leo."

But why would Rey Rodrigo have kept his plans from his favorite daughter? He'd already effectively ceded at least some of his governing responsibilities and power to her. Did he so fear that she would say no to his plan? Didn't he trust his treasured magician princess?

In the end, I suppose not. Despite all her gifts, despite all she'd done for her father's rule, Rodrigo thought she was still most useful as . . . how did Leo put it? Rodrigo turned his daughter into *an ornamental political bargaining chip, among other things.*

Her father treated her as the most important girl in Ivarea. He used her magical prowess to bolster his image and power at court, which in turn bolstered *Clara's* image and power at court. And when he found a better use for her, he changed course. He did what kings do. He did what the pursuit of power demanded of him. Clara's tragedy is that she believed the story her father always told her about being better than the noose of his ambition.

I feel briefly but keenly betrayed, as if it were my father who had sealed my fate without doing me the courtesy of telling me about it. So for better or worse, I sort of understand why that breach of trust set her on the path that led her to this moment. I don't know if I truly believe that Clara would have gone through with her father's plans if he had asked, but she deserved to know. To have a hand in her future. We all do, no matter where we come from, what we believe, who we are.

But I've been holding the future hostage.

The only reason she hasn't been able to keep her stolen crown is the fact that I'm incapable of surviving past midnight. So . . . maybe she deserves that crown for now. Maybe the best we can do in the face of inevitability—maybe all I can hope for—is a bloodless revolution. Let her take over Ivarea tonight and stave off the mass murder. Maybe a Reina Clara wouldn't be able to hold the throne against a real revolution. Who knows? The future is broad and full of possibility. We just have to get there.

If she would accept that compromise, then as long as I'm trapped here without being guaranteed another death and another chance, I might as well try.

"It's not too late, Clara. You could call off Faucher and the bombs. Force your father to abdicate. He would give way if his life depended on it. Which . . . you know." I swallow down the bitter taste in my mouth. "You could still have your revenge. You could still be queen. Just don't inaugurate your reign in blood."

She blinks down at me, still huddled on the cell floor. I wonder if she's ever considered a less sweeping plan for her coup, or if it was always going to be this way—the botched revolution, the palace choking on its own death knell. If she's ever thought Ivarea could change of its own volition, or if that change could only happen with a burst of black powder.

Finally she asks, conversationally enough, "And my brothers? What do you propose I do about them?"

A strange question for an alternative coup. "What could they do, duel you for the crown?" She flinches again, and the realization cracks across my brain like a whip. "Oh. Oh, of course. You're scared of Leo. Because he's like you."

"Like *me*? That pathetic little lush?" She chuckles, but it doesn't reach her eyes. "Oh, he's got his delusions of grandeur, too, but he is the *most* incapable of realizing them of all of us. Which is saying something, since Felipe is our brother."

"I didn't know *not orchestrating mass murder* was a character flaw."

"It is if you wish to rule." She steps up to the bars, close enough to make them crackle with warning. "Anaïs, for nearly a century, Ivarea has been ruled by a succession of venal, incompetent, cruel kings who have let our society decay. My selfish, inconsiderate father is just the latest iteration. Because of their narrow-mindedness, our whole system of government, our way of life, is in peril. Ivarea needs a monarch with *vision*. Someone who can resurrect this kingdom's legacy of *greatness*. If the choice is between letting utter fools let Ivarea slide into chaos and saving it the way I know only I can—it doesn't seem like much of a choice to me."

"You don't have to murder hundreds of people to save Ivarea. You know that. *It doesn't have to be this way.*"

She is absolutely unfazed. Just like her father was when I

begged him to act. "How are we supposed to grow a garden if we're not willing to uproot some pesky weeds now and again?"

I wince at the garden metaphor, but at least she's too distracted by her monologue to remember she wants to murder me. I knew getting her to modify her coup was a long shot, but her conviction now chills me to the bone. Clara should absolutely never be trusted with the fate of Ivarea. I wasted this time trying to persuade her to compromise. But I can't let her kill me. Not now. Not when my death wouldn't change the future.

I need my amulet.

"If you keep killing people to secure your power, you'll never be able to stop . . . pulling weeds. Faucher, for instance, is not the only revolutionary in Ivarea. You could imprison the rest, or kill them, but eventually, more and more people will agitate against the crown as they once did. You'll turn them into martyrs." I lick my lips. "The people are never going to stop believing in their cause, and you killing their leaders will just make everyone venerate them. Like new saints."

"Saints. Fairies. *Gods.*" Her voice drops to a growl by the end. "You know, cariño, I tire of stories that use fantastical beings to absolve us of responsibility for our actions. If you truly want something in this world, you must take it. That's what power is about." She pauses before me, on the other side of the cell bars. "But you know this, of course. Don't you?"

How did Gaspard put it, all those deaths ago? *What use is magic when you have power?* This whole night proves just how right he was. Clara and her father didn't need magic to throw me in the dungeon, though I suppose my talisman-induced fainting was helpful for them that way. She didn't need magic to steal my amulet. They are Cardonas. Ivareans. They were born into power. They will die because of it.

Now so will I.

Clara stops short before my cell door. "Now tell me where you got that fan."

"Give me my locket first and I'll tell you."

Out of the corner of my eye, I see her hand clutch at something in the folds of her emerald skirts. After several beats, Clara finally gives in to her curiosity and tosses the amulet through the cell bars. I flinch as the bars sizzle around its flight path, but if a locket forged by a fairy couldn't be destroyed by a conjured sword of lightning, I highly doubt a Cardona cell door is going to manage anything of note. I scramble forward, scrabbling in the muck until I feel the opal cool and welcoming under my bleeding fingers.

"I don't have all night, Anaïs," Clara adds, "and if you don't answer me, neither will you."

The amulet doesn't actually lend me any strength, which certainly seems like an oversight in its design, but *knowing* I have it, *feeling* its slight pinprick of energy as I clasp it around my neck, is enough to get me to stagger to my feet at last.

I shuffle toward the mad princess. "It happens the same way every night. The bells. The bombs. The mob." I trip on my gown and hit the floor with a cry. I use the commotion to grab for the abandoned fan talisman in the grime of the cell and stuff it into my locket before Clara realizes what I'm doing—yet another bait and switch. "So much death. I don't know what to do with it. I don't know how to stop it. *Clearly.* Why else would I be wasting my time with you?"

For once, Clara seems completely unsure of what to make of me. She sinks down to the ground, as if she perversely cares to stay level with me. "What," she says gently, "the fuck?"

Dredging up the last of my determination, I drag myself forward on hands and knees. "And *every night,* it all happens again."

"How traumatic." She clicks her tongue in a mockery of sympathy. "The truth, now, little Anaïs, or you're going to wish you had simply waited to die at midnight with everyone else."

"Oh, that is the truth. But why should that matter to you?"

Once upon a time, I told Leo that dying is easy.

I didn't know how to tell him how much it can hurt.

I lean my forehead against the cell bars. The magic woven around them sends sparks behind my eyes and fire through my arteries, and I could swear I hear Clara cry out, but she doesn't move to help me, and despite the urgent panic of my remaining survival instincts in these last moments, neither do I. I have to die. Before it's too late.

"You won't . . . even . . ."

I press my face harder against the bars. The taste of rust and iron and magic is salty on my tongue.

". . . remember it."

The last of my certainty shatters.

XVIII

CHAPTER ONE

CLARA WAS WRONG. I DON'T WANT TO BE A HERO.

If we survive tonight, I don't want the king to grant me new titles and lands and a royal husband. People to raise statues of me in their town squares. Bards to immortalize my name in song. But if that's what saving Ivarea would make me, then fine. Fine! I can be a hero. I just have to decide how far I'm willing to go to become one.

I know I've already done terrible things. Caused thousands of deaths. Let innocents die for me. Murdered people with my own hands. And there are probably a thousand more terrible cruelties I have yet to commit.

After the dungeons, though—after failing to even mediate Clara's plans, after staring her delusions in the face and seeing both more and less truth in them than I ever wanted to— I know I have to do whatever I can to stop her.

But . . . what?

The most obvious first thing to do, if the most difficult, is to figure out a way to use Clara's talisman against her. If I can harness the same power she does, then we'd be evenly matched, and I might have a chance to defeat her.

The problem is that the talisman is a leech, and it's killing me.

The light-headedness is always there, sometimes from the second I wake up with the amulet heavy around my neck. By the time I reach the Alcázar, my head usually feels like a driftwood raft on the open seas, whipped to a frenzy by merciless waves and furious winds. Once the dancing begins, I feel unmoored from my own body. By the end of the night, if I make it that far, I'm never quite sure I even *have* a body. All this vessel of flesh knows is that there is some foreign energy invading it, and fight as it may at first, it cannot hope to win.

I would bear the pain and suffering gladly if I could get the talisman to *do* something other than take out its maker's evil on me. One afternoon, I even slice open my palm in my bed, soak the naked skeleton of the fan in my dripping blood, and try to use it as I would a blessed object. Before I can think of what to ask of it, my mother finds me and faints at my threshold.

The next time I try to use the fan, I lock my bedroom door. And when it fails again, I press the dragon of Clara's seal into my wound and wait for it to kill me.

I don't remember how long it took. I just remember the

sounds of my parents screaming from the hallway. Begging me to let them inside.

❧

Once, I give Leo the talisman.

I try to brace him for its impact as best I can. I warn him of how he felt the first time he held it. I tell him that I'm here for him, always here for him. I promise I will save him.

He takes the talisman gingerly, with all the awful respect it deserves, and again, the light goes out of his eyes. Again, the fever builds beneath his skin, hot enough to scald me just for making the mistake of looking at him. Again, it spreads from his body into the floor, up the walls, and into the chandeliers swaying above him. But when they begin to fall this time, he doesn't let me claw the fan back.

Screams I never thought I'd hear because of him echo down rippling corridors. Crystal and glass explode around us. Leo staggers into a courtyard, utterly overcome, and the ground uproots itself at his calling. Crawling across the broken landscape, I sneak up to strangle him from behind.

The talisman has not left him completely senseless, though. He whips around, and the courtyard comes with him. I let him kill me, because this was my promise.

I'm going to save him.

❧

How can I save him?

How can I save any of them?

⤫

Breathless after yet another heist of Clara's talisman, which I lost when Leo last killed me, the prince takes me to another garden that somehow I have never seen, a maze of marine grass lifted from the Palancan Sea and populated with enchanted coral creatures, to once again await our death.

"So." He takes a brisk breath. "What now?"

"Excuse me?"

"We just spent all night stealing the talisman for you. You're going to bring it back in time. But what will you *do* with it then? If I can't be trusted with it—"

"You really cannot," I interject in a flat tone.

"—what else can we do? How are you going to make it work? And if you *can't* harness its power, what do we try next? How do we get to Clara?"

These are the same questions that have been rattling around my empty brain for ages now. And I have nothing to show for all my pondering. Just a re-stolen talisman in my locket that's going to kill me if midnight doesn't first. "If only I had your magic instead," I mutter, exasperated. "Then everything would be a hundred times easier."

"If only." He rolls his eyes. He steps back into the maze wall, the touch of swaying marine grass almost pulling his frustration into its depths. "How in the hell is any of this even possible?"

Now, here's a question I'm finally able to answer. Even though it's the third time he's asked. Even if it will sound fundamentally ridiculous.

"Because of the fairies."

"The *what?*"

I pause beside an outcropping in the maze, where a lobster carved of red coral snaps its claws against Clara's fan hanging off my wrist. I've never told Leo about my ancestry before; the only people other than my mother that I ever discussed it with were Gaspard, who asked me if I felt *non-human*, and Faucher, who murdered me again. How very long ago all that seems now. "The fairies. You know, the otherworldly-slash-godly figures of Proensan myth and legend." I smile to myself. *"Magical woodland creatures."*

He recoils. "I did not say that."

No, but you did. I tuck away the memory with no small amount of wistfulness. For those times, for those Leos; even, in a distant way, for those Anaïses. But, for the first time, I tell Leo every impossible thing I know or suspect about my curse: about Mireille Laborde and her fairy lover, his gift of an amulet, their child's failure to destroy it for reasons unknown. Holding this wholly impossible magical history in my head alongside the events yet to pass in this repeating night is like looking into the ancient past with one eye and staring into the immediate future with the other. Even if the bone talisman's magic wasn't pounding insistently in my head and making my extremities feel disconnected from my core, this conversation could easily unmoor me.

But Leo doesn't make me stop. He leans back against the maze wall opposite me, its marine grass bending around his sheathed sword, and stares at the amulet the way one might stare into the sun.

Once I'm done with my explanation, it takes him several moments to emerge out of his contemplative fog. "So you're telling me . . ." He pauses, collects himself all over again. "Not only did this—*fairy* ancestor of yours have the power to *freeze time*, but their child broke a magic necklace and made time *loop around itself*?"

"I . . . I think so."

He raises his head to stare back up at me. I still find myself wanting to squirm under the force of his gaze. I could almost run back through the maze to the palace, the way I did the first time he kissed me.

"This is . . . all of this . . ." Leo's breathing goes shallow. "It sounds impossible, doesn't it? Like a fucking miracle."

A miracle.

I remember Leo's story of San Pedro: he was the Tarracán blacksmith whose sword turned to bone with his death; Leo's ancestor, the founder of the Cardona dynasty, took up that relic and single-handedly defeated a Castaran siege. Then there was the story Clara first told me about Clemencia of Lereda, where the saints collected on her blood oath by robbing her of her sight. I've never seen or heard of such powerful magic—except perhaps during the age of the fairies. Except from Mireille Laborde's fairy beloved and her half-fairy son.

"I don't know about miracles, but all these stories . . . Your saints' powers and my fairy ancestor's magic kind of sound similar, don't they?" I think back to how he put it before, in that cramped broom cupboard, in the dark. "Maybe your people and mine aren't that different after all."

Leo stands up straighter, as if he, too, can hear the echo of his past words on my tongue. "You really think so?"

I don't know what I *think*. Still, surprised at myself, I nod.

"Maybe you're onto something here," he muses. "Let's say there was something, some belief or practice or story, that connected Proensans to the Ivarean peninsula. Something that we forgot over time, or that my ancestors erased from the throne."

I cock my head. "The way they wiped out the practice of blood oaths on the peninsula?"

He stares at me for a second, but the gears in his head are turning without him being conscious of it, and the words flow like time from his lips. "Exactly. And maybe that connection lies in blood magic. Your fairy blessing and my—*our*—blood oaths. It would make sense, wouldn't it? Magic passed down from fairies . . . magic as a bridge connecting people . . ." He breaks off, hesitant. "What if . . . your half-fairy ancestors were Ivarean saints?"

For the first time in a long time, I'm the one who can barely string words together. "What do you . . . what?"

"Anaïs, think about it. The saints were humans. Mortals.

But they wielded magic that's impossible to replicate with earth magic. Magic on the scale of *miracles*. What if their extraordinary powers came from being the children of fairies? You're the one who just said their powers seem similar. If it were possible . . . if it were even true . . ."

Could it be possible? Could it be true?

The first and only time I told Gaspard about my locket's provenance and not-destruction, he *told* me not to tell any Ivareans about the man with the lightning sword. *They'd just try to claim them as one of their saints, and he'd never just be your ancestor again.*

Now that Leo's said it, too . . . I don't know. I have never really cared about what Ivareans think is blasphemy, but this theory definitely would count as such. A link between Proensan fairies and Ivarean saints? A *blood relation* between them? And me as . . . what, their descendant?

And Leo once called *me* mad.

The way he looks at me, though . . . I've never seen anyone so broken open with wonder. So overcome by magic.

It's not just magic he's overcome by.

That's not possible. I'm more likely to be a true-blue Ivarean saint, one to be invoked and worshipped by the masses, than Leo is to have fallen in love with me now.

I feel a shift in the close, humid air as we stand there together, blocked from the sight of the world, as if we really were at the bottom of the sea. Something in the silence compels him to reach for my hand. "You have to know, I would do anything to save this country. I'd give anything I could."

I bite the inside of my lip, turning it white. "Saving Ivarea is never going to be as simple as some grand gesture or promise. Believe me, I know."

"Yes. Of course." The muscles in his hand tense. "However."

Bewildered, I break our grip.

"Have you ever heard of Clemencia of Lereda?"

A peal of foreboding snakes down my spine. If I never have to be lectured about this particular folk story again, it will be too soon. "Why . . . why do you ask?"

"Because." His throat bobs with uncertainty. "*I* could be your Clemencia. Except instead of offering you my sight, it'd be control of my magic."

"*What?*"

"You're fairy-blessed, aren't you? Your blood magic is weaker than your ancestors', but it has to mean *something*, right? So if I could bind my life and death to San Pedro when I was a kid, why couldn't I swear a blood oath now and share my magic with you? What if that is the secret for you using the talisman and defeating Clara?"

Somehow, I am very much regretting telling him the origins of my curse.

"Anaïs, our only chance of killing Clara is using her bone talisman against her. Which, at the moment, neither of us can do." He glances at my locket, where the fan lies in wait, with a sort of longing. He cuts off the air of whatever curiosity he found in himself, then raises his gaze back to meet mine. "But *you're* not like us, are you? If you could use this talisman alongside your fairy blessing, you'd be more powerful than Clara. She'd never see you coming."

"Of course she wouldn't. Because this doesn't make *any* sense."

"You said it yourself. If you had my magic instead, all of this would be so much easier."

"I—I didn't—" I splutter incoherently. "I didn't mean that *literally.*"

"But if I *could* open up a channel for you to access my magic, you could still use Clara's own talisman against her. And your fairy blood would keep you from being consumed by it."

This just sounds like a whole lot of desperate, wishful thinking, even to me, and I'm fully aware that I've been running on desperation and fanciful thinking since I got stuck here tonight. Besides, there is one massive hole at its center he hasn't addressed.

"Even if you could . . . what, make yourself my living conduit to Ivarean magic? . . . my blessing is too weak." Right on cue, I can feel the ache in my head from the talisman beginning yet again. "I think combining our magics would kill me."

He blinks, considering. "Even if that happens . . . what's the harm in trying?"

He's got me there, and he knows it. After all, if nothing I've ever done in one night stretches to the next, this absurd blood oath's effects likely wouldn't reach beyond my death.

And although I still don't understand how this plan could actually work, nothing else I've tried has borne any fruit, and Clara remains frustratingly impervious to harm . . . but . . .

"What would a magic-sharing blood oath do to you?"

Leo startles. "To *me*?"

"Clemencia went blind in her story, didn't she, when she gave up her sight for her husband?" I say. "So—would an oath like this mean you lose your magical ability? Your *life*?"

We're plotting to kill his sister, for God's sake. If we go through with this . . . if *I* choose to go through with this, and it still doesn't work, or if Leo gets hurt, or loses more of himself to an oath, to *me* . . .

Haven't I asked him for enough?

"My life and death already belong to the saints. You know that." He grimaces, immovable. "So what's one more sacrifice for Ivarea? Why shouldn't we at least try?"

No. No, that's—no. It can't be this way. I will not make him suffer because I was too weak, too stupid, to find a way to save us that didn't require him to sacrifice more than he does when I die every night at midnight. Whatever the terms of Leo's childhood blood oath, I will not make him sacrifice anything more for this kingdom. Especially not for me.

I can't let him do that. Not now. Maybe not ever.

But Leo doesn't need to know that. I just need to make it to midnight and he'll forget all about this mad theory of blood rituals and power sharing. So I only say, "Okay, it's a plan. I'll remember it for next time."

His hand hovers over the hilt of his sword, as if he is about to draw it right now and make his oath. "Next time? Why not now?"

"Because!" My brain whirs desperately to catch up to my body as I dig around for another explanation, one that will make sense to someone outside of a time loop curse. Something he couldn't possibly argue with me about. "Because— there's no time left to get everything right tonight. If you—if we think this blood-oath magic-channel theory could be the key to defeating Clara, we have to be able to deal with Mathieu Faucher, too. And the bombs. And your father. Otherwise there will still be a revolt, and we'll all still die, and I'll be sent back and have to start from the beginning, so . . . so there's just—we need to get everything right first."

His voice deflates, but not his delicate conviction. "Oh. I see. You're waiting for the perfect moment. Then you'll make your move."

I nod vehemently. "It may take time, but I have to wait for the right time. *That's* the only way to do this." *Not your far-fetched ancestry theories.* "Otherwise, honestly, what's the point of being cursed if I can't take advantage of it?"

Suddenly his attention is sharp as a harpoon. "And you're sure you'll be able to give up your time loop when that moment comes? You'll be able to let go?"

I remember the last time he expressed such a concern. *One day,* he said to me on the gallery mezzanine in the Alcázar, *in a real future, a real tomorrow, you won't be able to wipe away your mistakes and regrets every night. You'll have to live with all of your failures, and go on living them.*

He was right, more than I even knew then. Because my curse, horrible as it's been, as much as it's taken from me, is precious, too. It's given me the chance to pave the way to a new world, and I have to use it. If that means I have to keep dying until I can get to the moment that will shepherd Ivarea into the best possible future for all of us, if it means I continually defer a future for myself that I was never built for anyway . . . I'll do it. I have to do it. That's the price of duty.

He should know that, too.

"Of course. Of course I will."

Maybe he does recognize the cost of my duty. Maybe that's why he doesn't press me again. Instead he asks, "Do you believe in destiny?"

Ah. He's feeling morbid in the wake of calamity. In part out of love, but mostly pity, I indulge him. "I don't know. I mean—I don't think everything has already been decided, or I would have figured out everything about tonight by now. But . . . I believe in the inevitable. And I believe—I *have* to believe—that our choices here and now shape the people we need to be in order to face destiny. Inevitability. Whatever it is. *When*ever it is."

Leo stares up at the sky instead of meeting my gaze. I trace the line of his profile against the night, look to the stars that would fall to his feet at his command, to find themselves reflected true and whole in his eyes.

"So is this always how we're going to face our destiny?" he murmurs. "By hiding from it in a garden?"

"What? No!" My voice slips out of me before I can claw it

back. "Leo, I'm sorry, but we're going to get there, I promise. It won't always be like this."

He turns his head and looks askance at me. "Saints, I really hope not."

That's when it begins. The stars turn to gravel and dust at our feet.

He glances down at the detritus of the world in horror anew. "Don't let it end like this, Anaïs."

But it *does* end this way.

Because maybe, just maybe, there's a part of me that will make sure it always does.

XIX

CHAPTER ONE

THE AFTERNOON LIGHT FEELS HARSHER THAN USUAL WHEN next I rise to meet it. It carries none of the indolent oppressiveness of this particular Marenca day, as I've seen it over and over again. It's as if the world remembers how I reacted when Leo asked me if I would let go of the time loop and is watching what I do now. For his sake or my own, I don't know.

He was right to ask me that. I know he was. Maybe I *am* too far lost to my curse to be able to see beyond it.

Why couldn't I let him swear that oath? Because it really was a ridiculous idea that I didn't need to indulge? Because it would require me to open myself up to a magic that has always been inimical to me and mine? Because I couldn't stand for Leo swearing a blood oath to me? Because if it worked, he might end up hating me for it? Whatever the reason, I didn't even try. If these magical blood oaths are bargains, I couldn't allow myself to enter into one. Not when the sacrifice at its core would be Leo's.

There's no use regretting it now. Today is—not a new day, exactly, but it *is* a new chance. And if Leo really thought combining our magic would allow us to harness the talisman's power without getting destroyed by its hunger, maybe we can still do that. Just not by him swearing a wholly absurd blood oath to me. Instead . . . instead, couldn't I use the blessing to cast a protection spell on Leo? That might be enough to ground him as he battles Clara and her talisman. And be a simpler, more elegant solution to boot.

I could do this, couldn't I?

Yes. Yes . . . of course I could. And it would work. It has to.

Because after everything I've seen so far, the truth is that even without his esoteric magic-sharing theories, Leo's magical ability and habit of indulging me make him the best chance we have to defeat Clara. Saving us all is *his* destiny, I see that now—I just need to help him meet it. And if my protection spell doesn't work, if the talisman turns him into a monster or Clara still kills him, then Leo would have sacrificed nothing he wasn't going to anyway. *I'm* the one who will suffer for failing.

It's the least I can do. It's the only thing I can do.

Well, not exactly.

Destiny aside, there *are* still many other pieces at play in the hellish puzzle of this night. Most significantly, Mathieu Faucher and his revolution. I wasn't lying to Leo, after all: I *do* have to get everything right before I can even think about going into the future. I have to do everything I can to make sure Ivarea is better come morning than it is now.

But since I failed every time I tried to get Faucher to help stop Clara's bloody tyranny, I'll have to come up with something new.

Or at least call on those who can help me do that.

When Maman bursts into my bedroom that afternoon and asks me what on earth I'm up to, I stare like I've never seen her before, hair wild, eyes already burning. "What does it look like I'm doing?"

She glances at my impossibly unscarred hands, at fingers that have never slipped in the blood of innocents and not-so-innocents. "Writing?"

I wave my little pen like a flag of victory.

"About?"

My other hand drifts toward the opal locket at my neck, which still hides Clara's talisman inside. This amulet is the only thing that brings me back to life, that tethers me to this exact point in time. And horrific as it has been to bear that curse, I owe all my lives to her for giving it to me all those years ago.

And all my deaths.

"You'll see, Maman."

"The only thing I want to *see* is you looking like a proper lady. *Béatrice!*" she barks out the door without missing a beat. "Béatrice, we *must* do something about mademoiselle's hair. It's the most important night of her life!"

Early that evening, Le Nas de Sanglier is packed with the Proensans of Marenca eager to celebrate any occasion whose spoils will spill over into their cups. Vitòri bobs and weaves around the patrons, too busy to think twice about the blond girl with the blood-red locket in the corner. Who could blame her, when the hour of her glory is so close?

Ignoring that girl, however, becomes slightly harder to do when two more young people turn up at the pub's threshold, stare at each other with abject loathing, and tiptoe gracelessly in her direction.

Both of the new arrivals are taller than me, and far better dressed. I glance pointedly down at the bench opposite me so they sit down before anyone recognizes them. Conserving my ever-waning stores of energy, I offer them warm smiles. "You made it. Both of you."

Jacinthe Vieillard holds her nose high, as if the elevation affords her cleaner air not tainted with the smell of hops and sweat and humidity. Her rich blue traveling cloak sweeps obnoxiously over the edge of the well-worn bench. "You wrote that it was a matter of life or death." She leaves deliberately unsaid, *Perhaps I should have chosen death*. I wouldn't have blamed her if she did, frankly, but I'm grateful she came anyway.

Next to the richest young woman in Ivarea, Gaspard Plamondon twists a cap in his hands like a rag and glances plaintively at me. "I still don't understand. What do you mean by *time loop*?"

Although I wrote this all out to both of them *specifically* to avoid that very question, I run a finger down the gold chain at my neck and explain it all again—the fairy magic that has shaped my imprisonment in time, Clara's perversely powerful bone talisman, the fact that unless we solve both her and Faucher's coups, we all die.

"Which is why," I conclude, tilting my head down so my voice doesn't carry, "our only hope is to get Faucher to strike a deal with the throne *now*."

Gaspard shakes his head. "Are you kidding? I knew Faucher in Lutesse, and—"

"Oh, I know."

Though he deflates at the reminder of all I've learned and taken from him over our deaths, a hint of stubborn defiance shadows his brow. "He didn't even like me being in the same coffeehouse as him. So believe me when I say he'd rather let Clara kill him after all than collaborate with the throne."

"I suspect the king would feel the same," Jacinthe adds dryly.

Of that, I'm well aware. I remember his spitting anger before he threw me into the dungeons. Even though I've done everything in my power, everything I didn't know I could do and wish to God I couldn't, to save him and his people. He refused to see it then, to countenance the possibility that a Proensan girl could know something about his family, about his kingdom, that he didn't—but for better or worse, I did then, and I do now.

"Gaspard, I've done everything else in the book. *We've* tried everything else. I have a plan to deal with Clara tonight"— *I hope*—"but the hard truth is that none of us, no one in this whole country, will survive if we can't get them to make a deal. Right here. Right now."

Underneath her cloak, Jacinthe knots and unknots her

hands together, a nervous tic I've never seen before. "Suppose we start with Faucher, then. What exactly do you plan to say to get him on your side?"

"No idea." I smile brightly and tell myself the ache building in my head is just anticipation, and not the stolen fan making its presence known. "That's why you two are here."

For after all I've seen, after all I know that still awaits us, I don't see another way around it. Ivarea cannot go on the way it always has.

Which means we three—a Proensan, a mixed Proensan Landaulan, and a Galvaise of Jazarian descent—have to change it.

"Saints *above*, Anaïs," snaps Jacinthe, "the man's trying to overthrow the king, not *partner* with him."

It takes all my self-control not to wince at her invocation of the saints. "You both understand what he and his supporters are fighting for. You both see what's at stake tonight. You *must* be able to come up with something."

Jacinthe shudders. "This is treason. You're asking us to commit *treason*. Not to mention risk the lives and safety of everyone we know and love."

The tender, faraway look in her eye tells me she's thinking of Marguerite. I don't blame her for being scared. I am, too. Even now.

Perhaps especially now.

I can't let this opportunity pass me by, though. Not if it could save Marguerite and everyone else at the Alcázar. "Do you have better ideas?"

Gaspard turns to Jacinthe with a tight grimace. "I don't

know about you, but if we're probably going to die anyway, I'd rather die trying to change Ivarea for the better, not just to inaugurate a tyrant. We all deserve more than what we've been given." He offers me an only slightly warmer version of that grimace. "Besides, committing treason sounds like fun."

"*Fun.* Naturally." Jacinthe forces her hands apart for the last time and places them on the table. One of her fists curls inward, her knuckles going pale and sallow. "I . . . suppose if you have any chance of making this work, we would all need to pour our blood, sweat, and ink into it first."

I've asked both Gaspard and Jacinthe for their help plenty of times before, and they often, eventually, say yes, so I shouldn't be this surprised that they would agree now. It must be because I've never asked them for help with Faucher, because I myself have never tried a plan like this before.

Which means that, for the first time I can remember, I don't actually know what's going to happen next.

Mercifully, when we barge into his room, Mathieu Faucher is not bathing. Less mercifully, the former barrister is lounging on the little bed wearing only a linen shirt and breeches without stockings. I stare for several seconds as Faucher ponderously swings his bare calves over the bed, props his elbows on his knees, and contemplates the strangers at his door. He doesn't seem to recognize either Gaspard or Jacinthe from Lutesse. But then he takes a second look at me.

"Anaïs Aubanel. A pleasure." Faucher gestures at something behind me; I assume that the begrudging scuffling I hear is the still-armed Vitòri falling back. "Correct me if I'm wrong, but I suspect you and your friends are supposed to be somewhere else."

Though Faucher spoke in Proensan, Jacinthe clearly got the gist. She huffs, "And I, for one, would *love* to be there."

Oh, for God's sake. We need Faucher to *like* us, not think that we'd rather be drinking with the Cardonas during the Anniversary Ball. I swallow my groans. "*However,* there's something more important on the horizon, and we think it's our duty as Ivareans—as *citizens*—to come forward. We know all about your prison break, you see."

"Do you?" Faucher asks with a bit of a smirk.

Gaspard bristles at being dismissed. "And your men in the palace."

Jacinthe adds, "Also that ghastly business with the catacombs."

"You mean the *bombs* in the catacombs," interjects Gaspard.

She shoots him a scandalized look. "The ones Alberto Quirós planted there, yes, I *know,* Gaspard."

"*Most importantly,*" I cut in, "we know that Infanta Clara is the one who bankrolled your whole plot. The planning, your prison break, the catacombs, all of it. It's a *trap,* Mathieu."

Not for the first time, I've rendered the revolutionary speechless. But for once, I didn't have to do it alone.

Jacinthe's posture is so brittle as she stalks forward that it's noticeable even in the way her cloak hangs off her shoulders. Faucher seems unperturbed, as ever, and pushes off from the bed to meet her advance.

"After you do her dirty work, she's going to kill you and your fellow citizens here to seize the throne." Jacinthe swallows, as if there's a lump in her throat. "She'll make sure nothing like this ever happens in Ivarea again."

Gaspard slides a step closer to me without breaking his gaze from Faucher. *"Nothing will ever change."*

"Also," I point out, "you will still be dead."

Faucher scoffs, his nostrils flaring beneath the jagged bridge of his nose. "You expect me to believe this tall tale? Clara Cardona organizing an entire coup with a man she put in prison?"

To her credit, Jacinthe doesn't quail in the slightest. "You know what she's capable of. A coup is no great stretch. Especially if she can pin the first move on someone like you in order to retaliate against your supporters."

Faucher stops in his tracks. His linen shirt is undone at the chest, and from where I'm standing, he seems flushed.

Good. I could use a Faucher that's angry.

I think.

"That little princess is a fool if she thinks murdering me will change anything," he hisses. "She will never be able to kill an idea."

Any hope I had for him dissipates as that intense demagogue look rises up again in his arresting green eyes. I clear my throat to draw his attention. "She's the most powerful magician Ivarea's seen in centuries. You may not understand what that means, Mathieu, but we do. Your only chance—*Ivarea's* only chance—is to cut a deal with Rey Rodrigo and join forces against her."

Faucher begins to advance again, catlike, predatory. "Have you never poked your head out of your château to hear what your people *actually* want?" he sneers. "They tire of royalty denying them their rights. And they would never abide by the toothless compromise a venal man like Rey Rodrigo would—"

"We could make you prime minister."

All of a sudden, each pair of eyes in the room fixes on me. Racked by a new and acute wave of nausea from Clara's talisman, I clutch my amulet, wishing it could give me strength as well as the inability to die properly.

Maybe I should have talked through what exactly we could offer Faucher before we confronted him.

Too late to fix it now.

I break from Gaspard's shadow and Jacinthe's blank glowering to approach him directly. "Tell me, if we could make you the head of a new Ivarean government—a *representative* government, whatever it's called—would you do it?"

A beat too late, he snarls, "You think I would betray my fellow citizens? Our cause? What do you take me for?"

I consider the question. "A man who would rather see his cause realized in life than after he's gone." *In* this *life, at least.*

Faucher unfolds his arms, then folds them again. To my right, Jacinthe places her hands at her hips in an implacable pose. Gaspard keeps a safe distance from Faucher while using his gaze to bore a hole in the man's temple.

"I . . ." Faucher breaks off. "The king would never—"

"Oh yes he would."

"We'll make him," says Gaspard.

Jacinthe adds, crushingly sanguine, "It's not as if *he'd* have a real choice, either. His daughter's the one plotting to kill him."

The room falls silent. Clara's fan, lying in inimical wait in my locket, makes me feel as though a whole menagerie of animals is stampeding across the suddenly and violently empty fields of my brain. I feel my breathing grow shallow. "M-Mathieu?"

He licks his lips, very dry after his bath, and shoots a look up at the ceiling, at the heavens, the saints, the fairies, the gods. "There is much at stake tonight, my friends. You seem to know it as well as I do. So before I go to the trouble of killing you here . . . I will give you a chance. *One* chance. To outline your proposal."

Knowing only too well how serious he is about the murder, I screech, *"Thank you!"* without wasting a breath protesting, as Gaspard and Jacinthe seem to be preparing for. "Stay here for now, and *don't* let your people make any moves on the Alcázar. Gaspard and Jacinthe can help you draft a satisfactory power-sharing agreement."

Faucher's brows shoot into his damp sandy curls. "You're Jacinthe *Vieillard?*"

She curtsies mockingly. "A pleasure, Monsieur Minister."

Gaspard flushes angrily, indignant that the reveal of his identity didn't spark a similar shock after the lengths Faucher went to just to keep him from his citoyens in Lutesse. With more force than strictly necessary for an unarmed man, he steers Faucher to the table still strewn with the schematics and maps that have haunted me for more than one death. "Come on, we only have . . ." He glances up at me as Jacinthe steals Faucher's usual chair. "How long do we have again, Anaïs?"

"No time at all." I take a deep breath, trying to clear the acute pain in my head. Somehow I only manage to concentrate it into a single point, a harpoon rather than an ocean. "So . . . so I'm going to go. I'll get the king and meet you all near the Alcázar when you're done." Beyond Clara's watching eyes, I hope.

Faucher briefly looks as adrift as I feel. "You truly think you can pull this off," he remarks after a beat, a casual, cool observance.

"Not without you." I take as deep a breath as my unsteady body can handle. "All of you."

The truth is, I *don't* know if we can do this. Especially in just one night. But if this works, I'll have to give Leo the talisman again and hope that my blessing will offer him enough protection to fight Clara. And if by some miracle—over which I have *absolutely* no control—we *do* stop her . . . then I'd have to do as Leo said. I'd have to let go of the power that has tethered me here and now. I'd have to move on. And live with my mistakes. Forever.

And if it doesn't . . . well.

It wasn't an oath sealed with blood, but I can hold this promise as dearly as Leo did his:

You swear tonight won't end like this?
I won't let it.

CHAPTER TWO

BY THE TIME I MAKE IT TO THE ALCÁZAR, THE PAIN IN MY head has begun to flow down into my very fingernails. Luckily, flirting and cajoling and "Now, you see here"-ing my way into the Alcázar has become second nature for me, and before I know it, the guards posted at the palace doors are once again walking me down to Leo's chambers. With panic blooming in my chest, I try to rattle off the whole story for the ever-bewildered prince: the fairies, their amulet, and the curse it laid upon me; Mathieu's revolution and our possible deal out of it; Clara and her budding tyranny; the bone talisman and its blind hunger; and my plan—*my* plan and none other—to save him from it.

But what if this Leo doesn't believe me? What if he wouldn't surrender himself to a dangerous magical talisman to help a political prisoner remake his country's monarchy and kill his own sister just because a random Proensan girl asks him to?

"I don't want to hold you hostage with any of this, Leo. So if you can't help me right now, or you don't understand, please just—tell me now." I swallow a lump in my throat. "I promise it'll be okay."

He stares into his lap as he turns the story over in his head. *"Fuck."* His voice is dry and brittle as kindling. I could set it aflame with a well-placed glare. But I don't. I can't.

Eventually he looks up, his always-molten gaze hardened. "You're right. I don't understand. But if there's even a slight chance that you're right, it'd be my duty to help. No matter what it takes. Right?"

From me. He means, *No matter what it takes* from me.

Because he is Leopoldo Cardona, and I think—I *hope*—this is who he really is. Not just for tonight, but every night to come.

Silence rises around us, thick enough to be almost tangible. I feel like we're each suspended over a precipice, waiting for the other to pitch themself into the abyss first. Tension throws long shadows over Leo's chiseled but drawn face.

"So . . . you mentioned my sister's talisman."

"A fan. I brought it back with me." Much good it's done us so far.

"To use to fight her."

As if the evil thing knows it's being invoked, the amulet holding it twitches against my skin, and a new wave of other-worldly dread lashes at my heart. "For *you* to use to fight her. I'm just here to help."

He blinks slowly. "If you said it's so dangerous for me

specifically, why wouldn't you use it? You said you're a magician, didn't you?"

I flinch where I'm sitting on a hastily cleared chaise longue, the knee-jerk motion enough to rattle my skull. "I have blood magic, yes, but it only means I'm descended from fairies. Like your saints were." I crack a pitiful smile, remembering his past shock, the wonder I once saw in his eyes. Now I see only bewilderment. I just hope this doesn't make him think of anything he shouldn't. Forgotten pathways forged with blood. Oaths sworn and sealed. "I can't use the talisman. At all. But if I cast a spell of protection on you with my fairy blessing, *you* should be able to wield it without losing control or dying. Besides, it shouldn't . . . it shouldn't be me. You're her brother. If anyone deserves to be the hero here, it's you."

His lip curls; he's clearly not quite sold on the idea. What did he tell me when I first told him about the attack on the ballroom, all those deaths ago? *You would have to be pretty desperate to think I could save you.*

He was right.

For now, he only folds his arms across his chest. "Aside from this protection spell, what's the rest of your plan?"

Long before he asked me if I could let go, I remember him asking, *But what are you sacrificing yourself for?* The question evoked sheer panic in me then. I don't know that I've vanquished it completely, but all that's happened between that night and this one—discovering who and what I am, realizing I have more friends and allies here than I ever thought, coming to terms with the power and responsibility I alone have, even falling for Leo himself—all that horror and all that wonder wash across my vision now, showing me all the fullness and possibilities of life itself. If it's real, not bound within a single night. If I can embrace it as mine, not continually run away from it.

That's what I'm doing all this for, isn't it? For a chance. For me. For Ivarea. To give us all the best chance I can.

Which can only begin at the right moment.

But Leo is still waiting for me to walk him through a brilliant kingdom-saving plan. I pinch the inside of my arm to leverage myself, however briefly, back to the here and now. "We need to have a united front to be able to stand against Clara *and* get Ivarea out of this mess. That's why we need to get your father to agree to share political power."

"You're not serious. Have you met my father before?" The prince scoffs, as if he didn't hear me the first time I said as much. Though there was a lot of information to digest, so maybe I can't blame him for missing some of the details. "What terms could you offer him?"

That depends on Faucher not having killed Gaspard and Jacinthe the second I left Le Nas de Sanglier. And Gaspard and Jacinthe not having killed each other since then. "I don't know. Exactly. Yet."

Leo bites the underside of his lip. The suppressed violence of the gesture sends a flare of foreboding up my spine. "Listen. Anaïs. I'm sorry, but if I'm going to help you, you have to help me understand. What the hell is going on here? What is this all about?"

What did I just tell myself? It's about fighting for the future. For Ivarea. For me. It's about our society and governance, our magic and belief, what we owe each other above all.

But I don't say any of that.

"I—I fell in love with you."

He doesn't answer at first. Maybe he can't trace the illogic of my confession himself. Maybe he's waiting for me to do it for him.

Stupid, stupid girl. What a moment to tell him. What good is it going to do? Who does this help other than me?

"And I . . ."

I could lie to him. I could spin an entire elaborate love story out of air that was always too thin to fuel my wildest fantasies. But I can't lie. Not to him. Not now. "And you didn't. How could you?"

He blinks at me again, once, twice, three times. "Right. Right, it would be impossible."

I put a hand discreetly to my temple, which hopefully seems thoughtful and not like I'm trying to keep my brain from spilling out of my skull. "It *is* impossible."

Time itself seems to be whispering in my ear, *Hurry, Anaïs. Hurry hurry hurry hurry*—

With great effort, I push myself off the chaise. My shoes seem too tight and the ligaments of my ankles stretched too thin to support myself, but I'm standing now, and will do my best to stay that way. "We have to find your father. Now, before it's too late."

I just hope it's enough.

"I did not think I had to tell you to keep your whores out of my chambers. Perhaps I overestimated your ability to read between the lines."

For once, I am grateful to the talisman for leeching away so much of my energy. At least I am now past feeling embarrassed at the king's words.

Hackles raised, Leo throws a downright mutinous glare at his incredibly unimpressed father before turning to the guards stationed at the chamber doors. "Leave us. I have something of grave importance to discuss with my father."

Rey Rodrigo rolls his eyes at the ceiling but wryly echoes the dismissal. Leo waits several beats before pointedly clearing his throat and gesturing to me. "Papá, allow me to introduce Doña Anaïs Aubanel. Daughter of Conde Eduard of Massilie."

I curtsy briefly to the king, but do not beg his forgiveness for the intrusion. "I'm here to warn you of a great danger, Vuestra Majestad Real. To the whole kingdom."

I hold up Clara's fan to the light streaming in from the filigreed windows behind him. Interest piqued, Rodrigo shuffles closer and spies his daughter's crest at its base. "What is the meaning of this?"

The last time I told him the truth, the king flew into a horrible rage and expected me to thank him for it. *Ivarea gave you all you have,* he sneered at me. *You should be grateful for it. You should be grateful to me.*

It was a lie then, and it absolutely is now. Ivarea has never given me anything. That was almost by design.

But what if it could? What if we could make this kingdom worthy of our loyalty?

I let my hand fall, and tell the king all about the threats from his daughter and his people awaiting him later tonight, that his best chance of surviving another day is making a deal with one against the other. As I finish describing the political power-sharing concept I hope to God that Gaspard and Jacinthe have been able to figure out, I can feel a shift in the mood of the room. A power-hungry Cardona is not nearly as fantastic as a commoner leading a kingdom's governance, and I just *know* Rodrigo is going to say I'm some mad Proensan radical out to undercut the throne or something similar.

Finally, Leo cuts in. His voice is as cold as a blade countering his father's building affront. "Doña Anaïs is right. With an orator who has proven himself willing to *serve* you and the kingdom on one side and a magician who would destroy all of us for power on the other, we have only one choice. We need to go *now.*"

The king erupts. "So now I am to act on the word of my jealous son and a thieving Proensan against my daughter? You would have me betray my country and break up the institutions that have given Ivarea four hundred years of glory? Guardados! Arrest this gir—"

With a wordless cry, Leo spins into me to block his father's path to the doors. His hands fumble around mine, and for a second, I let myself open up to his touch. He meets my gaze with a terrible depth of feeling, but all at once lets me go—only to immediately double over, as if punched in the gut. The king stops moving when he notices his son whimpering on his knees. Cradled in Leo's hands, a glint of bone catches my eye.

Before Rodrigo can ask me what's going on, his guards spill into the room. Rodrigo flings out an arm in warning to keep them from trampling over his son's suddenly prone body.

Then the ground starts to shake. Followed by the furnishings in the chamber. Dust and gravel leap from the walls of the immaculately kept room like sparks of fire.

There is no question, even from our incompetent king, as to why this is happening.

He wasn't supposed to take this on himself. Not without my help.

As the Alcázar trembles in its prince's magical grasp, I scramble to my knees and take Leo's chin in my hands. His expression is nearly unrecognizable—eyes blotted out by dark irises, nostrils smoking like a dragon lies coiled in his gut, like he is the dragon himself now, or has always been, and this—the talisman—has only unlocked it. He's gone absolutely silent, and stares back at me, unseeing.

With great effort, I peel back his fingers and pluck the fan out of his grip, sliding it securely onto my wrist. Even though it's sapping my strength, too, I would rather succumb than let Leo do the same.

It takes several long seconds for his eyes to clear, his heartbeat to calm. The guards behind me let out a collective sigh of relief. The king paces back and forth, relieving his agitation by righting objects that fell askew on the walls. Seeing him attempt the job of his stewards brings a hoarse, sardonic chuckle to Leo's lips. The prince sways with exhaustion and burnt-up magic but keeps himself upright long enough to fix his father with an icy glare.

"You see?" He's panting heavily now. "With this power in her hands, she'll burn up the last four hundred years of Ivarea's glory as kindling for her own tyranny. Don't tell me that's what you want your legacy to be. Not when there might be another way out."

Rodrigo's grizzled face grows flush as he remembers what was beneath Leo's demonstration. "Your *way out*," he spits, irascible all over again, "is the beginning of the end of the dynasty. That's what *you* want?"

This is our king?

Leo exhales sharply through his nose. "Times are changing, Papá," he says, and it sounds like a warning. "If we are to survive, it's time to change with them."

Rodrigo says nothing. I realize that it's no small thing to ask a king to give up his absolute powers, and I'm sure it will not be as seamless a negotiation as it is in my head, but I can't bring myself to pity him now. We shouldn't have to hold a palace hostage to effect change in our governance. But that's where we are, and there's nothing any of us can do about that now. We can only make our choices based on what we know. And we only have tonight to do it.

My deaths alone cannot change Ivarea's future.

With one more fearful, reverent look at Clara's talisman

on my wrist, Rodrigo suddenly snaps to attention. For the first time, he actually manages to dispatch a company of the Guardia Real's magician unit to disable the bombs in the catacombs, a sight I thought I wouldn't see for a hundred more deaths at least, and briefly gives me hope that whatever happens next, we might at least be saved from being bombed to the midnight sky. The king is about to send off another to fetch the rest of the royal family when Leo shakes his head, a drawn, sickened expression on his face.

"She'll notice if we all disappear before the ball. You and I are her biggest threats." He doesn't cede ground, even as his father looks wildly around the chamber for anyone he can force to shut up his son. "If the guards disable the bombs in time, Mamá and Felipe and Helena won't be in danger. Right, Anaïs?"

I swallow uncomfortably. Clara has always seemed perfectly happy to watch her mother, older brother, and sister-in-law die, and there's every chance she might try to use them against us. But Rodrigo doesn't need to worry about that right now. "Majestad, if you can strike this deal with Faucher, you can save them. But we have to go *now*."

Rey Rodrigo throws Leo a mutinous glare even sharper than the one he bestowed on me. He may be king, but he will never enjoy ceding control to the random girl in the corner and also his fuck-up son. No matter that his life and reign are at stake.

"If any one of them dies, their blood will be on your hands, boy."

Leo pushes past his father and plants himself in front of a tapestried wall. "So be it."

That's where they're both wrong. Their blood is already on my hands. And their fates, *Ivarea's* fate, weigh on my head as heavy as any crown the Cardonas have ever borne. But we cannot waste time on this debate. We need to get Rodrigo away from the keen eyes of the Alcázar Real, where he and Faucher can meet on slightly more neutral ground and argue their way to a power-sharing agreement. If Gaspard and Jacinthe manage to get Faucher to our chosen rendezvous point along the Río del Dragón.

Luckily, and as he only told me before we dashed into the king's chambers, Leo has a shortcut out of the palace.

A current of magic rises up from the floor where the prince stands. The amulet at my neck twitches, but the fan talisman is silent, perhaps seething about the power it senses that its keeper cannot harness. Rodrigo goes pale as the wall splits open and reveals a hidden tunnel carved of preternaturally smooth stone. Leo raises his hand, and torches mounted evenly along the tunnel walls erupt with light. He ventures into the maw of the wall as his father remains motionless, quailing at the magic laid bare in his home, the secret in his very chambers.

I lay a gentle hand on his elbow to steer him toward the wall. He scoffs at my touch but allows himself to be guided. The chain around my neck seems tighter than usual as we approach the secret tunnel, but I ignore that and the feeling of creeping doom. As soon as we're both inside, the wall stitches itself back together, the royal chambers mere chambers once again.

Rodrigo and I follow Leo into what quickly reveals itself

to be a whole network of hidden tunnels. They all seem more or less as well-maintained as the one that rose from the king's chambers. My mouth falls open and I breathe in centuries of the Cardonas' dust and wonders. The torches along the walls live and die by the prince's tread. I hasten forward before I get caught in the darkness trailing him.

"Clara and I found these tunnels when we were children," Leo mutters. "We must get to Faucher and the others before she thinks to look for us here."

Slowly, the tunnel floor leads toward stairs that stretch deep underground. At some point, beyond the Alcázar complex, the precise incline of the meticulously hewn steps melts down into a dirt track. The tunnel narrows until we can only travel single file down its length: Leo in the front, the king in the middle, and me drawing up the rear. The torches that Leo was magically igniting become less frequent landmarks the farther we go. I draw my blessed dagger out of an abundance of caution.

The journey grounds down any instinct for debate or invective among the fleeing Cardonas, which is good, since I cannot make myself concentrate on anything but staying upright. I can't even make the pieces of my precarious plan fit together in my brain anymore.

"Where are we going?" Rodrigo calls in a halting, hoarse voice. Perhaps I'm not alone in feeling lost and dizzy.

"There's an abandoned outpost by the river," Leo grits out. "You and Faucher are to meet there and sign your agreement."

"And then?"

"Then," I interject, "we defeat Clara."

"And how exactly do you think to do that?"

I whip all the way around, my back to the king's, to face down the tunnel. At my throat, my amulet flares like a torch itself—another talisman is nearby.

I should have tested the blessing's protection on Leo after his stunt in his father's chambers.

I thought—hoped—we had more time.

I back up in a panic, pushing the flabbergasted king behind me. The torches that Leo had extinguished flare up once more. The new flames burn so hot that they melt away the mounted torches themselves. Rivulets of molten metal and embers rush down toward us, turning to ash at our feet.

"Goodness gracious, Papá, is that you?" Clara's voice floats over my head, serene as a hurricane, as she strolls down her roiling ashen path, with me directly in her way. "Don't tell me you *believe* whatever lies this little Proensan told you."

Rodrigo fights my gown to try to pass me and face his daughter. "Clara! Clara, mi amor, it's not too late—"

"*Don't.*"

Between one frenzied heartbeat and the next, the fire turns blindingly bright, like fireworks going off all at once. I duck away and turn, only to find Leo shouldering his way past his father and toward me, to take the first line of defense against Clara's advance. Frantically I draw a line in blood on my arm and smear the cut against the back of Leo's hand, screwing my eyes shut and piecing together my desperate intentions: *Save Leo, protect him from the talisman, don't let him succumb, save him from harm, please, please, save him, protect him, I don't have anyone else, please, let this work, please*—

"Now, Anaïs!"

No more time. Quicker than I can blink, Leo yanks the talisman from my wrist. I feel suddenly, horrifically light without it. His hands burn with magic as they scrape across my bodice.

A sound like the roar of the Río del Dragón floods the tunnel. Clara's laugh is high and clear above it. "You picked the wrong time to be brave, little brother."

"And you, dear sister, picked the wrong time."

An invisible wall of energy shoots out from underneath him. Clara cries out as it slams into her, and her horrible light winks out.

Swathed in oppressive darkness, I whirl around behind me, where Rey Rodrigo is still blustering at his bloodthirsty daughter. "Your children are going to kill each other," I tell him urgently. *"Get out."*

I can feel his stare, but I don't think he knows what exactly he's looking at before a shudder of the tunnel wall knocks us both down. My palm cuts to shreds on my dagger. Clara's laugh rolls down to us once more, past Leo's frighteningly flickering silhouette.

Before my mouth even closes around the word "NOW!", the king scrambles off. I should have offered him a blessing of protection, too, but there's no time. I turn around to face Leo's battle with his sister, but his back is to me. As I watch, he generates gales out of the stale tunnel air to try to keep Clara from chasing their father down the tunnel.

Which might be the most specific, focused magic that I've seen from a talisman-wielding Leo ever. So maybe my protection spell *is* working—keeping him from being immediately devoured by it, at least.

Still, Clara staggers forward. Her own talisman seems fused to her palm, as though her illustrious ancestors' bones have overtaken her own. "Where *did* you get that little trinket, Leo?"

Blinking falling gravel out of my eyes and quite possibly my skull, I grope my way toward their fight. The hill above us groans with the new, unnatural pressures burbling at its core. I feel like I did the first time I was killed, crawling toward a duel that Leo will not survive.

My locket lets out a burst of light like a combusting star in the void of space—its most urgent warning yet. I see what warrants it a second later. Clara is rising—and *rising*.

Not just rising. *Flying.*

Leo throws up spears of packed dirt and sharp, greedy rock to try to block her path, but it's not enough. All at once, she's zooming over his head, then mine, in pursuit of her father, still heading for the Marenca hills. I can't see or hear Rodrigo ahead of her, but he's out there somewhere, and—and she will find him, and kill him.

What a failure this whole plan was. What a waste of time.

I have no choice but to die now. I need to go back before anyone dies again.

"Speaking of trinkets." Clara flips around in midair to face us, all the while hurtling backward down the tunnel toward where I hope to God her father has found the exit. "You. Girl. What is *that* on your pretty little neck?"

"Come closer," I spit, "and find out."

Kill me now. Let me go back and try again.

She's amused by my goading, but her eyes slide back to Leo. He's the bigger threat, for good reason. "Don't mind if I do." Her advance is lightning fast, enough to bring thunder roaring into the tunnel.

Or is it?

Something scalds my skin, hot enough to raise blisters on my arm. I jolt and see Leo's blown-out pupils, just as horrifying as the time he destroyed the Alcázar himself. Sparks of electricity leap off his bare skin. I can't quite *feel* the blessing's protection break, but one look at him tells me all I need to know. I can't control the talisman's magic. And without my fairy blood grounding Leo, the talisman is going to prey on his power. Corrupt it. Hollow him out. Turn him into a monster.

A thunderous crackle resounds in the fast-disintegrating tunnel. Almost like a real storm.

No, not *almost* like a real storm.

A real storm.

Underground.

Clara seems to sense it, too. She halts her flight to launch herself at Leo. The impact sends him flying against me, and I go sprawling to the dirt with them, my still-glowing locket bouncing on my chest. They claw at each other with brutal, wordless efficiency, and I can't disentangle myself from their

387

fight. I don't know what to do with my wounds except smear my blood on Leo's tingling, feverish limbs all over again and pray to my fairies and his saints for our deliverance, his victory, *an end*. I feel Clara clawing at my neck in the second before—

CRACK!

Lightning strikes right above us. Leo frees his bloody hands and raises them to meet the storm he summoned here in the tunnel. With a blood-curdling shout, he pushes his sparking hands outward and blasts Clara down the tunnel in an arc of sizzling power. She slams against the wall, her impact buckling the ceiling. Before she can scramble back up, the tunnel ceiling fully collapses at last, splintering in two, and Leo and I are buried side by side under the weight of the impassive Ivarean hills.

I awake with a splutter, convinced that the dust and dirt from the collapsed tunnels will never, ever settle, and I'm going to pass out again. When I'm reasonably sure I won't slip back into unconsciousness, I try to sit back up. The tunnel is indeed extremely collapsed between where Leo and I are and where Clara was before the cave-in. But if I survived that—for now, at least—there's no way a Clara armed with a talisman didn't, either.

I turn to Leo, who's still motionless on the ground. His eyes are bizarrely wide open and glazed with power as they weren't in the king's chambers. I have to crawl on top of him and use the flat of my dagger to wrench the fan talisman from his hand. The bone is ice-cold now. I cradle the fan to my chest like a grenade and slap Leo across the cheeks, but he doesn't wake up.

If he's actually dead, if the all-consuming power of that horrible talisman killed him despite my efforts with the blessing, then . . . then what do I do? I don't want to keep going without him.

Of course, I can always undo his death with mine. It would break my heart to lose whatever progress I made with Mathieu and Rodrigo, but—but at least now I know that a deal is possible, and that I absolutely cannot save Leo from Clara's talisman. So I'll keep going until I find the right way to do it. I'll keep trying until Ivarea is remade, and Leo is alive to see it.

It still seems impossible that I might love someone with whom I can never have a chance—and more impossible still that I love him enough to undo what I've done, with and without him, in this single iteration of tonight. But I don't care what happens between us come morning. I don't care if he ignores me or forgets me or banishes me for some reason. As long as he's alive and well, I'll be able to live with whatever happens to me next. I'll survive.

And if I die now, we all will. Eventually.

Just as I raise my blessed dagger to my bare neck, a sob echoes throughout the hollow stone chamber. It takes me a moment to realize that it's not mine.

Stunned, I drop my dagger and rush to pump Leo's chest. The sound of his name tearing from my suffocated lungs is all

I have to keep time until, finally, he coughs more cleanly than before.

"Are you okay?"

Leo blinks several times. It doesn't seem like he's able to speak. I wouldn't mind, but the longer we sit here, the more I worry about the stability of the remaining tunnel system. My hand returns to my neck, seeking the amulet for comfort, but—

It's bare.

My fingers scrabble for purchase against my skin. For the cool kiss of a chain. For a heavy pendant swinging below the hollow of my throat.

Nothing.

I crawl about the remnants of the secret tunnel, scratching my hands and knees raw. I dig into the debris, the extinguished torches, the crumbling walls. I twist my arms and legs this way and that to churn up the dirt. But there's nowhere left to look.

It's *gone.*

It must have been taken from me during that last scramble before the tunnel collapsed. Before a power-mad Leo brought down thunder and lightning on his sister. Clara saw my amulet for what it is; she must have pulled it from my neck before Leo blasted her back into the tunnel.

Which would mean . . . it's not just gone. Clara stole it. And with it, all my plans. All my hopes.

It's over.

It's all over.

If I die now, I don't think I can come back to this day, to this city, to this place. I don't think I'll come back at all. I could still be wrong, but I cannot afford to test this theory, the only thing that has made any sense to me, as absurd as it is. I don't want to die, truly die, and plunge Ivarea into irrevocable loss. Into bloodshed and cruelty and tyranny. Into everything I have killed myself to save it from.

So . . . this is it. There is no way to undo my mistakes now. To save anyone. To start over.

I can't go back.

Out of my bleary peripheral vision, I notice that Leo's just managed to push himself upright. Desperate, I go to him on my hands and knees. "You have to find my amulet."

He blinks, barely comprehending.

"My locket. With the opal. The *cursed one*. You have to get it back for me." I swallow grime. "I think Clara took it."

After his ordeal, only one word registers for him. "Clara . . ." His eyes go out of focus again, and then suddenly he shakes his head, hard enough to dislodge his teeth from his chattering mouth. He can barely push the words off his tongue. "Not dead. She's . . . hurt. *Angry*. But I can't reach her."

I couldn't care less about how Clara Cardona is *feeling*. "The locket. Focus on the locket." I unscrew both of my earrings, not just the one I gave him the time I only pretended to lose my locket. Before I knew what it was. Before I knew what it had done to me. I shove the earrings into his bleeding hand, embedding tiny stars of gold with drops of garnet into his palms. "I'm—I'm begging you, *please*, just get it back."

Much to his credit, he closes his hand around my earrings and tries. Despite what he just went through, what he's absolutely not recovered from, he tries. He closes his eyes, and a whisper of a breeze tickles my feverish brain.

But his magic dies out so quickly that even he flinches. He wipes a trickle of blood from his temple, his other fist tight over the earrings. He cannot even dredge up the strength to look me in the eyes. "If she has it, I can't sense it, Anaïs. I'm sorry."

I sink down against the crumbling wall. More dirt falls in my eyes, my hair, my empty, bloody hands. My lungs scream for something more than grime, but I have nothing left to offer them. I have nothing at all.

"Leo, if we don't find it . . ." My mouth has gone violently dry. "If I die without it . . . I think that's it. I won't come back. It's over. No second chances."

Gasping against phantom pains, he opens his hand, traces the grooves cut into the garnets. I can't blame him for failing to find the locket. Whatever happened to it, whatever Clara will do to it, it's my fault, in the end. Everything is my fault.

"So don't die," he says.

I wish it were that easy.

But . . . he's right, in his way. The future is here, and there's nowhere I can run now to avoid it. There's nothing I can do to stop it from coming, make and unmake it.

This is my destiny.

I have no choice but to finally meet it.

CHAPTER THREE

WE PUSH THROUGH WHAT'S LEFT OF THE DISINTEGRATING walls in silence, praying we don't find Rodrigo's body, until we hit fresh air. The sun above us unwinds toward dusk, washing the sky with warm colors that leave me as cold as Leo's touch as he helps me out of the tunnel.

Hidden from the palace by a curve of the Río del Dragón, the meeting place looks more like a miraculously standing collection of rocks on the valley floor than the ruins of a medieval outpost, but I don't care; I am near collapse, weighed down by the fact that I only have one life to live and also by the energy of Clara's stupid talisman, which I've now lashed tight as a corset against my ribs so I don't lose that, too. Before I can pitch myself into the river in a desperate bid to make it all stop, forever, the sound of vehement arguing catches my attention. A second later, I spy a figure lounging in exhaustion as the river laps at his clothing.

"Gaspard!"

He lifts his head before I crash beside him. Leo seems like he wants to crumple into nothing, too, but manages to plant himself like a sentinel between the outpost and the river.

"Don't you look like hell," says Gaspard mildly, propping himself up on his elbows.

"Oh, I just got back."

He gestures behind his head at the outcropping, still fully flat at the water's edge. "Jacinthe's helping Rey Rodrigo and Citoyen Mathieu get acquainted. For *some* reason, she didn't think I would be as useful in that situation."

His tone tugs a wan smile out of my empty heart. "Too inflammatory?"

"You wound me, Anaïs. I'm never inflammatory." His eyes go wide as he processes my dirty, scratched-up face. He reaches out a hand that's stained with ink, not blood. I flinch anyway. "Wait, don't you have your locket?"

The lump in my throat feels like earth itself. I can't force my voice around it.

Gaspard swallows. He clearly remembers everything I said this afternoon at Le Nas de Sanglier. "If you die without it . . ."

Suddenly, all the fatalistic asides I've made and thought about my impending doom, every speech about how nothing we do matters but also how everything we do matters, seem very cavalier indeed. The last connection to my heritage, the last proof of my power, the faces of Mireille Laborde and her lover, the embodied memory of their son, the saint . . . lost to the world that destroyed and remade them in the first place.

Also, I'm going to die.

And when I do, I'll be taking an entire kingdom with me.

"Tonight's our only chance."

Slowly, he forces himself upright. His face is more pale and drawn than I've ever seen it before as the implications of what I said come to him in waves. He looks the way I feel. Adrift. Alone. Anguished.

Maybe my parents have been right, all along. Maybe all this is just a nightmare after all. Maybe I'll wake up this time and –

"*Fuck* them to hell and back!"

I twist around to see Jacinthe storming down from the outpost. Her outburst startles even Leo from his stoic contemplation as he ducks out of her way.

Blinking in the orange of the sunset, Gaspard squints up at the fuming Jacinthe. "Not as easy to handle as you thought?"

"Staring oblivion in the face, and they're *still* locked in a pissing contest!" She huffs and falls to the ground, intentionally staining her luxurious cloak in actual dirt for what I suspect is the first time in her life. "*Idiots.*"

"What, you thought Rodrigo Cardona would happily sign away any ounce of his authority to a failed barrister? Like it wasn't at all hard enough for you and I to propose a new system of government in *two hours*?" To me, Gaspard adds, "You would not *believe* how close Faucher came to killing us back at the pub."

Out of habit, I rub my neck, but my fingers meet only dirt and dried blood. No cool metal, no fairy-forged magical amulet. If Faucher *had* killed them, I wouldn't be able to undo it. I wouldn't have been able to bring Gaspard and Jacinthe back.

Their deaths—permanent, true deaths—would have been on my hands.

All of their deaths.

I lick my chapped lips, staring at the placid surface of the water. "What stopped him?"

"*Somehow,* he was no longer so eager to take the risk that we were wrong. Good thing he didn't. Since we're not wrong." Jacinthe picks up a rock and skips it across the river. The three of us watch it sink with nary a blink. "Are we, Anaïs?"

Before I can respond, a pair of boots draws up in front of me. I look up at Leo's dirt-streaked face and swallow the feeble words I could have offered Jacinthe. I don't know how to comfort her. I don't know how else to explain that tonight truly is all that matters. That I'll never, ever know what else could have happened tonight.

This isn't how it's supposed to be. It was supposed to end when I said it should—when I decided to break the cycle. It wasn't supposed to break for me.

There's no going back now.

"I need to talk to you," Leo says.

With no small reluctance, I rise. Nodding up at the outpost, I tell Jacinthe and Gaspard to keep an eye on Rodrigo and Mathieu. "Please don't let this all have been for nothing."

Gaspard swallows. Jacinthe scoffs as I turn my back. "We should ask you for the same thing."

But she is, they are, and they know it. They only came here because of me. They're only staying because, until two minutes ago, they thought it didn't matter whether they did or didn't.

I should tell them to run. I should tell them to follow the river down to the sea and go as far as it will take them. But I tell them nothing, because Leo has me by the elbow, and he takes me around the far end of the outpost so we're out of their sight. Assuming Clara isn't burrowing toward us from under the ground like an overgrown gopher, the only witness to what is to come is the browning hillside, gilded by sundown.

Leo drops my arm, only to take me by the hand instead. "You were wrong," he says shortly. "I can't use the talisman. I can't stop her. We need another plan. *Now,* before she comes after us again."

I bury my face in my hands to stifle my shuddering breath. I know I was wrong, but to hear Leo say I wasted my last night on some stupid wishful-thinking magical technicality makes me want to abandon the world to the future and take myself out of the equation, the way I was about to do in the tunnel. But I don't have the luxury of falling apart anymore. Of choosing to stop and undo myself, erase my mistakes. I don't have anything.

Except . . . except for another wishful-thinking magical technicality. The one that Leo once thought would work, and I refused to go through with. A channel of magic opened up with a blood oath.

I thought I couldn't demand any sacrifice from Leo that he wasn't already destined to make. But if I've really lost hold of my curse, and as Jacinthe said, we're *still* staring oblivion in the face . . . then maybe this is it. Maybe this is the destiny he's been heading for all this time, and I've been keeping him from it.

I suppose all that was in vain.

Could I make Leo my Clemencia? Could I ask Leo to swear his magic to me and consign him, permanently, to whatever such an oath would do to him? And if he did do it, if his oath did allow us to share his magical ability . . . would it matter? What if it doesn't work? Or what if it works and I can access Ivarean magic, but I'm still not strong enough to actually defeat Clara?

Then . . . then that failure would be my destiny, too. And it *really* won't matter what happens next.

First, we have to get there. While we still can. Before Clara recovers from whatever Leo was sensing in the collapsed tunnel and finds us.

"What if there was another way we might be able to use the talisman against Clara? What if . . ." I bite my tongue and hope the pain will take me through whatever happens next. "What if it were me?"

His eyes widen. "But you said it couldn't be you. You said you can't use the talisman at all."

I know too well what I said. "Once upon a time, you told me that you swore a blood oath to the saints that was magically binding."

He recoils. "You . . . you know . . . about . . ."

I smile sadly. "You told me all about how blood oaths can

bind people to saints. You thought that if my fairy blood means I'm descended from the saints, you could swear your magic to *me*. And that would open up a channel for me to access your magic and use the talisman to fight Clara."

His jaw goes slack. "I came up with all that?"

"With some help."

He stares through me at the bloody sunset. Awe for his past selves that is always as sharp as a knife spills from his gaze.

"You're not telling me that I've lost my mind." I swallow down my dread. "You think this could work."

Whatever he was contemplating, he expels it with an abrupt exhale. "Clara won't be down there forever. If a blood oath is the last thing we haven't tried and failed yet, and we don't have any other brilliant plans . . . then let's make this our last stand. What do we have to lose?"

I've never made it this far into the night—a skirmish with Clara where I didn't die, a deal with Faucher that didn't kill me. I don't know what's next, and now I'll never know what *else* could have been. What other ways I might have made it to the right moment—the one I've been waiting for. The one I've been dreading.

I can't wait anymore. I can't defer the future. Right now, there is just me, just Leo, and the ridiculous, arcane idea between us, between our magics. It's all we have. It's the only real shot our people have. The ones huddled beside the river, hammering out at least the skeleton of a new government. The ones who love and believe in and follow them. The rest of the city. The rest of the kingdom. So when Leo takes a sure step toward me, I don't question myself anymore. Abandoning myself to some base instinct, I fall into his arms.

"Are you sure?"

He sighs into the crown of my dirtied hair in answer. One of his hands lifts from my side, and I see he's already taken my blessed dagger. It shakes slightly in his grip, but he wards me off when I move to take it back. "Whatever happens next . . . you're an Ivarean, Anaïs. Fairy blood, saintly heritage, and all. My power is yours, too. Now all we need to make it real is a promise."

Suddenly it feels like all of it is happening too fast, and I don't know if it will work, if it's worth it, but I'm here, and I can't make it stop, don't want it to stop. With this blood oath, Leo would open a channel of connection and forge a contract that his people and mine have never had. A contract as strange and unthinkable and new as the one between Rodrigo and Faucher.

We owe each other this. We owe Ivarea a chance.

No matter what it takes. No matter what it takes *from us*.

Leo takes a deep breath and grabs my hand again. Half-unseeing, I stare into his face and seek out a hidden undercurrent of doubt clouding his eyes. But—nothing. Just absurd, spluttering faith, in himself, in his country, in his magic, in me.

"Leo, wait—"

"Any power of mine is yours to share, Anaïs Aubanel. In your name, I swear this power to you, and seal it with my blood."

My heart roars like the river in my ears, lightning hissing

in my veins. Then he lifts my dagger to the arm still curled around me and drags the blade across his skin.

His blood wells and spills down onto me. We're still entangled in one another, but I feel something shift. A tremor that goes all the way to the center of the earth. Like the planet has been knocked off its axis. The rhythm of my heartbeat is decimated in its wake.

All at once, I'm aware of so much more than my own body. Too much more. Any emotion, any vestiges of confusion, none of it sustains itself against this onslaught of sensation.

Magic.

"Anaïs . . ."

Summer-wine woozy. Can't feel anything else.

"Are you okay?"

The talisman throbs at what should be my hand. Dizziness knocks me to my back. I don't cry out. Don't feel any pain.

Not good. Must do . . . something. Maybe get up?

I try. Push myself onto my feet. Doesn't work. I swoon. The earth rises to meet me and breaks my fall.

That's new.

Hesitant, I reach out and bury a fist in the raised ground. The grass around me wilts.

Somewhere, I hear Leo inhale sharply.

He's still here. Not dead from the blood oath or the channel of magic. Good. I guess he can feel it when I call on his power. Mindlessly I sweep my hands across the grass, and the browning blades start to glow gold. Every wildflower past its peak stands taller, more vibrant at dusk than they should be.

Everything more sharply etched against the waning of the day. Etched as if with intention.

Intention. That sounds familiar.

"Leo . . . ?"

Before I can translate my confusion into words, the earth below me rumbles and roils. I sense—*sense,* without seeing—a new presence at the crest of the hill. Why do I know this if I can't see it? I force my eyelids open and rake the hill summits anyway. What if I'm dreaming, what if it's not what I—

But there she is. Clara, her silhouette fire-lit. Impossibly beatific and beyond furious.

I remember lightning striking her underground. Maybe that has something to do with it.

I don't know why I can't pull my eyes away from her, but then sunlight flares on its way out of the heavens, and I see it. Her right hand.

Gone.

Leo attacked her with lightning and caused the tunnel to collapse. He must have struck her hand.

And destroyed the bone talisman she'd been holding.

That's why she didn't come out of the tunnels before. She was trying to heal her hand and find her talisman. Maybe the world chose to keep it from her when she demanded it back. Maybe she was even trying to remake one out of her own bones.

We're still alive, so whatever it was she was trying down there, it didn't work. Clara is at last just a magician now. Just like Leo.

And therefore, I suppose, like me.

Leo glances down at me still collapsed in my bed of too-vibrant wildflowers, utterly incapable of waging a magical battle, and exhales unsteadily. "Are you okay? Can you—are you sure you can *do* this?"

Tears of frustration roll down my cheeks. "I don't know, but . . . I *swear*, I'll . . ."

"Right." He sets his jaw, determined, terrible. "Then I'll try to hold her off for you. Stay down till you're ready."

Fear erupts in my chest as he turns toward the hill. It's not supposed to be this way. I'm not supposed to fail before I even get started. "Wait, don't leave—"

"You. Little. Shit." Each of Clara's footsteps as she stalks down the hill resonate in my head like physical blows. "You cut off my FUCKING HAND!"

"I should have cut off your HEAD!" His shuddering footsteps echo in my ears, too—galvanizing, somehow, where his sister's movements actively hurt. But I'm the only one who feels it. "Now we go to the death!"

Even from this far away, I can see her frown. "Isn't that a little premature?"

Just as I feel a *tug* of power in my gut—Leo seizing back control of the magic I cannot understand—Clara swipes her hand in the air and knocks him off his feet. The impact of his body against the earth rebounds against me, as if I'm the one physically breaking his fall. She leaps over his body like a deer without sparing me and my ridiculous bed of preening wildflowers a second glance as she speeds down to the river.

Where her father is waiting.

At that moment, Matthieu Faucher crows, "A new Ivarea dawns!"—only to duck when he realizes what's coming for him.

I try to force myself upright, but Leo's blood oath threw me into unknown, stormy seas of power, and I feel myself drowning in them, the pull of magic tugging me in his direction like a rope pulled taut in my gut. It's tearing me apart, burning my hand. Did he feel this way, too, when I was playing with the grass?

A series of thunderous *smacks* briefly jolts me out of my magical haze: Clara is tearing apart the outpost.

One by one, she sends the stones flying, marking a new battlefield around the crumbling outpost. Jacinthe and Gaspard are still there, huddled behind Rey Rodrigo. Watching her pen them all in, I know that I have to do something. I have to save them. But I don't know what I'm doing, and Leo has to fight for me because I'm just as useless now that I have access to his magic as I was before.

This was our last hope, and it's all going wrong. Because I'm not good enough. I can't do anything.

But you still have the talisman.

Oh. Right. I wrap my fingers around its handle. Suddenly I feel horrifically combustible with its power in my hands. Already it's eating away at me, just the way it always did to Leo. Except in this in-between state, I can't use the talisman's magic; it's only wreaking havoc on me, compressing me from the inside out, a vise of intense power. It's all I can do not to faint right here.

From the river, I hear a sardonic inquiry: "Oh, Papá, what have you done?"

I feel the impact in my shaking hands when Rodrigo sinks to his knees as if in supplication before his rampaging daughter. "Mi amor, please . . . *please* stop this. Stop this fighting! You don't have to—"

"Yes, I do, Papá. I really, really do."

More rocks uproot themselves as Clara crosses into the middle of her little battlefield, clearly not worried that any of those inside could hurt her even at close proximity. I force my heavy eyelids open just in time to see Jacinthe knocked to the ground, her leg pinned beneath stone. Still, she manages to twist around and glare at the princess with impressively acidic disdain. "So you're going to rule by killing everyone who stands up to you?"

Clara strides forward past her uprooted sentinel stones and towers over Jacinthe's shaking form. "If you were as smart as you think you are, you would have simply stayed out of my way. You wouldn't have had to suffer."

"No, I'd just have to die. Like everyone else." Jacinthe spits at her feet. "Isn't that right?"

Clara's grin is as wide and lush as the valley in spring. Instead of answering the girl she once regarded as her sister, she backs away.

Suddenly the world sways around me, and my entire body seizes along with it. A new and overwhelming horror cleaves the very air. It feels like—

Explosions.

I scream.

But the screams come from everywhere—the king and Leo and Gaspard and Jacinthe. Even Faucher can't help but gasp. My nose burns with the smell of smoke from up in the hills.

The bombs. The bombs were still in the Alcázar.

Clara's laughter dies in her throat as she beholds the sight of her handiwork. Maybe it isn't as satisfying from a distance. Maybe the Guardia Real did manage to disable some bombs. Maybe it's not as bad as it could have been.

But we all know what she did. What she has always done. What she will always do.

Clara grimaces at her astonished father and his unlikely entourage, all of them staring at the smoking palace behind her with slack jaws and teary eyes. "You might consider bowing. While you still can."

Faucher, the most self-possessed in the wake of the destruction, sneers right back at her. "If you think Ivareans will bow to your tyranny, you don't know your people at all."

"A lecture on legitimacy from the pathetic little traitor who sold out his whole *movement* to the very king he was going to depose." She shakes her head, almost genuinely disappointed. "Saints, Papá. You'd really rather destroy our crown with *his* sort than give it to your own daughter." She crosses her arms over her chest, dried blood covering the stump of her burned-off hand. "Last chance."

"Clara, please—"

"Wrong answer."

Without taking another breath, she sends the detritus of centuries soaring from the ruins to smash into the king's head.

A different, more deliberate wave of magic keeps his body from collapsing beneath the force of the blow—Leo, still stuck on the slope of the hill, just barely rallying himself to cushion the impact and to save his father.

It's not enough. And it never, ever will be.

Rey Rodrigo crumbles to the ground, rendered into brittle stone and dust himself.

I stare at my burning hands and let Leo's screaming tear through my heart. I don't deserve my heart. I don't deserve the power Leo shared with me. Clara is still alive, the king is now dead, *actually* dead, *forever* dead, and even though a Clara without the power of the talisman is our best chance to kill her, all I know how to do with Leo's magic is kill grass.

If this whole magic-sharing plan is doomed because I still can't figure out how to use it, then I need my amulet again. If she did steal it from me—if she didn't leave it behind in the ruined tunnels—if it wasn't destroyed by Leo's lightning along with *her* bone talisman—then I could just put it on and go back.

Maybe I can still make this right.

I force myself up again. Try to focus my intention. Call my missing amulet the way Leo did back in the tunnel. But the magic splinters in my head, unable to connect me to the world.

Still at the riverbank, Gaspard tears Jacinthe from the trap of the outpost stone, hoists her onto his wiry shoulders, and flees with her and Faucher downstream, toward the city and safety. Clara watches them go, head thrown back in glee.

"You can run, if you like. But"—she spins on her heel in the river sediment to face the hillside again—"who will you run to if all your loved ones are dead?"

With an incomprehensible roar of grief, Leo charges down the hill, stumbling and bleeding as he fires at his sister. Clara may not have a talisman anymore, but she still has far greater magical talent; Leo may have his limbs, but he was already injured by his sister on the hill and weakened from his earlier brushes with the talisman. He's fighting as though a grace period will be enough for me to learn to control the power he swore to me. Every blow they exchange feels like a club to my head, a stab in my stomach. Like I'm both the weapon in their hands and the one swinging them.

He didn't tell me it'd feel like this. But how could he have known what sharing a channel of magic would do?

I can't help anyone until I figure out how to take it back. How to control it.

Intention.

Hissing against the whine in my head, tugging back on the current of magic twisting in my gut, I tap a single blade of grass and make a wish.

In the valley, I see Leo stumble at the same time that a minuscule bud pushes out from the end of the blade of grass. As if it has always been there struggling for release, and only now has been freed. The bud opens into a blood-orange blossom, sunset-drenched and achingly ephemeral, that grows and grows until it's practically the size of a full-grown rose. I brush its petals with a finger. The blossom seems to shudder with a pulse of its own that stretches into the blade of grass that has become its stem, the roots it has taken over, the hill below, the river beyond, the world waiting.

But what more can I do? What more do I have to give?

The brutal rhythm of the Cardona siblings' fight mirrors my and Leo's struggle over this, *our*, magic. Territory ceded and gained, deaths tempted but not met. Until somehow Clara catches Leo off guard and sends him sprawling to his knees again.

"What about you, Leopoldo?" She kicks him until he's prone on his side, forced to stare at their father's nearly unrecognizable remains. "Are you going to be as stupid as dear old Papá?"

Leo staggers to his feet. One of his arms hangs at an awkward angle, but he's not protecting it, not screaming anymore.

A wave of power floods my senses, the way it did the moment after Leo sealed the oath.

The channel to his magic is mine now.

Leo fought as hard as he could. Whether I'm ready or not, it's my turn.

I push myself up to my feet and feel around stupidly for the Aubanel dagger that Leo dropped after the oath. It's a last, hopeless beacon of light at this curve of the river at dusk. The late-evening sky is festooned in streaking jewel tones that are more fleeting than magic.

"HEY!"

With my blessed dagger aloft in one hand and the bone

talisman at my side, I stumble after them. Clara's focus snaps on me for the first time since our skirmish in the tunnels.

"Ah, welcome to the party! I was wondering if you would ever make it." With a wave of her handless arm, she sends a volley of dirt crows at me.

Love and fury and desperation boil in the pit of my stomach, and with the talisman in my hand, I make the crows shatter in midair. Their dirt falls like acid rain, but somehow it doesn't touch me.

Taking advantage of his sister's brief distraction, Leo breaks free of her orbit and tries to retreat toward me. Clara makes a frustrated sound and stomps her foot. The Río del Dragón lashes out from behind her like the tail of its namesake creature. First it steals Leo into its current, sucking him up as if it were a whirlpool; then it grabs for me. Half-blinded by the churning vortex of water around me, I reach out for Leo's ankle with one hand and twist the talisman toward the riverbank with the other, forcing the current to spit us back.

Clara is marching up to the Alcázar to take her crown when we emerge back onto the riverside, sopping wet, freezing cold, ready to strike. Leo glances at me, and when I nod and relinquish control, he kicks at the earth. Cracks zigzag through the ground beneath her feet, opening up a massive ravine in the hill below us. He pours river water inside to try to drown her as she keeps falling deeper and deeper within. Even at a magical remove, I can feel her struggle against the earth, against the water, feel her fury rising and cresting, and I dare to think maybe—maybe this is—

At that moment, she catapults herself out from the earth and lands on her feet, face ruddy, the stump of her arm bleeding anew.

She stalks over to where Leo and I are still standing beside that pit. She spits at our feet and dissipates the currents of magic Leo was throwing her way with a kick. "Well, *that* was a splendid party trick. I'm rather impressed." She grins. But not at me. "Unfortunately, it just wasn't good enough."

With a flick of her remaining wrist, Clara draws a new and brutal energy from the air itself and wraps it around Leo's neck. He falls to the ground, choking and spluttering against its implacable pressure. As his lips turn blue, I fall to my knees trying to dissipate the wind that's strangling him, but it just whips around his neck without mercy, Clara's and my commands of magic battling each—

Suddenly, a rush of magic flares in my bones, a gilded glory like I've never felt before. The violence of its descent sends me flat on my back.

And next to me, Leo's head lolls slack against the ground. His eyes are vacant and terrible.

Oh no. No no no no no . . .

I turn and stick a trembling hand above his face.

No movement. No breath.

He's—

No.

No. No, gods, no. Gods, fairies, saints, no. No no no no *no*.

He's dead.

Leo. My Leo.

Gone.

I want to explode. Want to kill. Want to *die*. But I'm frozen again, paralyzed in place, and all the magic that he was supposed to share with me now somehow lies futile in my body, as stunned as I am to not feel his presence anymore. To reach for him and find—nothing.

Above me, Clara is as unmoved by having murdered her brother as she was by having murdered her father. "Oh, don't be sad. It just had to happen this way."

No, it didn't. It wasn't supposed to be like this. This wasn't what I was fighting for. Leo wasn't supposed to die. Not like this. Not forever.

He swore an oath to me. He gave up control of his magic to share it with me. All this power he bound in my name, and what did I do with it? Killed grass. Summoned flowers. Broke up dirt.

And let him die.

Why did I believe I could do this?

Why did he?

"Saints above, don't tell me you're going to *cry* over this boy." Clara slashes her arm and whips a thin, sharp current of air against my stomach. I topple onto the ground and double over as she continues striking me. "You really need—to have—more—self—respect."

My ribs are near to caving in. I cough up blood at her feet.

I'm going to die. I *want* to die. If I had my amulet, I could just succumb and end this pain. I wouldn't be free of my curse, but at least I could undo all of this—all of these deaths. Leo's most dear of all. But.

I may not be able to go back, but I do have power. And I can't let him die without making sure Clara follows him.

"Now, tell me, cariño, can you guess what happens next?"

In my ears, Ivarea cries out for action and peace and blood and water, savage and restless and weary and unmoved all at once. I curl up within myself and, using the blessed dagger in my other hand, I draw a crimson line down my arm.

Stop her.

More and more of my blood flows out, mottling my skin and the ground alike. Along the riverbank, new saplings shoot up one by one. Surrounding Clara.

She swipes the train of her ruined gown over the wobbly little stems, but they don't bend. Her intelligent brow creases. She steps forward out of the circle of saplings, only to be tugged back by branches that grow farther and faster than their little trunks should be able to support.

Please, I ask the little trees, the bone talisman shaking with potential in my hand, *please, keep her from hurting us.* Just as I would pour intention into the blessing, I direct my entire life into this spell—born of a syncretic magic that at once feels terribly ancient and horrifically modern as it coalesces in my body.

Like a gliding hawk finding a mouse miles below, Clara catches sight of me through the branches. "This is *your* doing?" No one else—not her dead brother, not her lover, not her father, and not her scapegoat—elicited such a bright tone at the time of their defeats. "You? A *Proensan?*"

"A Proensan with a claim to Ivarean magic," I choke out, trying for bravado and failing. "Who could have guessed."

All my energy, every bit of power I've stolen from this earth and drained of myself, is feeding this new, unreal magical energy. One of the saplings at Clara's feet begins to burn with smoke as crimson as the banners hanging in tatters in the palace. She engulfs it with her own flames.

"And who the fuck are you," she hisses, "to claim this magic? Who are you to claim my kingdom?"

Smoke the color of blood winds in skeins around my heart. It doesn't drift as it should up through my nose into my lungs. I breathe through the pain. Something whispers inside me: *The flames belong to you, too. Everything here belongs to you.*

"Don't you remember me, Clara?"

Fire blinks up through the saplings. Clara gasps, looks out at me over the flames with unformed questions in her gaze. The burning saplings grow wider and taller, encasing her in a forest of flames.

"I'm Anaïs Aubanel. But you're going to die, so I guess it doesn't matter."

I can barely see her knocking her fists against the trunks, trying to force the fire to obey her, but I can *sense* her struggle. Her rage and desperation and passion have no hold on the burning trees, however; she cannot touch the magic that feeds this cage of flames. Cannot dam the life and death and time I pour into its burning.

Soon, the cage built with fairy blood and kept burning by earth magic collapses around her. It smothers all her screaming. In my bones, I feel the furious corrosive energy of her presence, her power—until I don't anymore.

I don't believe it. I stand there, staring at the great burning forest, waiting for her to crawl out. Flesh melting off her own bones. Power deeper than any I'd ever felt before still curled in her skeleton.

And yet . . . nothing.

Maybe I shouldn't doubt it. The world that made Clara recognizes and even mourns her death, just as it did Leo's.

They're both gone.

I fought for this moment for so long. I sacrificed everything for it. And now it's here, but still it's . . . it's nothing like it was supposed to be. There's too much screaming in the air.

Screaming?

The palace. The bombs.

I failed. I did all this, and I still failed.

Finally, I give in.

They say sleep is like a small death. If that's true, I would happily stay dead. I would gladly let the world spin into a new day without me.

But when I wake, the sun is low in the sky, if only just; the gray smoke from the Alcázar explosions and the ruddy smoke from the blessed forest's burning nearly block it out. Then it's only been a few minutes since . . . everything. And with Gaspard, Jacinthe, and Mathieu gone and the court trapped at the burning palace, I'm still here. Still alone.

I push myself up, fighting yet another swoon. The talisman is still curled in my hand. The vellum of the fan has burned clean off the bone. But it doesn't look like anything to me anymore. It looks like another hand wrapped around mine. A second skeleton. A frightful scar.

Sprawled on the ground, unable to distinguish whether I'm breathing dirt or ash or ember or air, I make one last request of the earth. A tendril of the blood-orange blossom, alive but only just, snakes out and wraps around Clara's talisman. It pries the fan out of my death grip and crushes the bone skeleton. I feel an ache in the back of my head as it is returned to the world it came from, but I don't care. Not as long as it's gone.

I don't know what to do now. So I crawl over to the only one who might have understood the totality of what happened here. If he had been alive to see it all.

His body looks uncanny now. Like the portraits of my ancestors in the lost locket. A pale, unchanging thing. The sight of it triggers a new wave of dizziness in my head. Unable to help myself, I caress his waxen cheek. The touch sends a lick of flame through my body. Deeply confused and at this point deeply delirious, I place my other hand on his, and somehow get burned again.

Oh, for God's sake, will this night *ever* end?

I try to reach out and connect to the magic I felt before— the rush of energy that I felt at the exact moment of Leo's and

Clara's deaths. But there's nothing left to sense anymore. He's just a memory.

So much for whatever this is. With a steadying breath, I whisper my goodbye and shut his eyelids for good.

At this third touch, time splits open.

It comes apart from everywhere and nowhere, breaking around me like a wave against the shore. It pulls me under and steals the breath from my lungs and pummels me into the shape of its whims. Its tides send me in a thousand different directions. It feels like a pistol at my temple, a blade at my heart, hot irons at my feet. My consciousness shatters and is reshaped both seconds afterward and centuries ago. All of it is true and none of it is. The only thing that convinces me I'm real is that I'm not the only one trapped in time. There's another voice here.

And it sounds . . . so . . . familiar . . .

A vision coalesces around me. A small stone room. Starlight halted at a high, narrow window, unwilling to cross the threshold. A fat beeswax candle burning brighter than it should.

. . . *with my life, my magic, anything. No matter what.*

A child on his knees.

I'll serve even after death . . .

Around him, a shroud of shadows.

. . . *if called upon to do so.*

A sword of bone before him.

This I swear, in the names of all the saints.

For the price of my life.

A disbelieving giggle as he presses his wound to the blade.

"LEO, NO!" I scream.

The vision cracks apart. Midnight unravels into dusk. The stone room in that Bayirid castle crumbles into the hills that encircle the Alcázar Real. Ten years later, here Leo is, dead on the ground. I am here with him now and there with him then. Only the grip of my hands on his frozen face grounds me in my own time.

That was another vision of the past, wasn't it? Leo's first blood oath. The one he told me about all those deaths ago.

I keep staring at his body. His eyes painted enamel, his lips blue even in the last gasps of sunset. But beneath his death . . . no, *within* his death . . . I sense something. Like an ember smoldering under his skin still. Begging to be lit again. Begging to burn.

Leo swore control of his magic to me today. But ten years ago, he swore to give up the one thing his existence promised him in order to serve his kingdom—*an end*. If his saints called upon him to do so.

Now that he's dead, truly dead . . . what if he were called upon?

What if, as a descendant of saints and fairies both, *I* can call him?

Maybe once it was impossible. Or maybe not. Maybe it's always been possible, and it took the whole world breaking before me, and me breaking with it, to see.

There's only now.

Now all we need to make it real is a promise.

"Leopoldo Cardona, you swore that you would always

serve Ivarea, even after your death, if you were called upon to do so. You sealed that oath with blood." I bite my lip. It splits, fills my mouth with the taste of iron. Some power hums and takes shape behind my closed eyes, expectant, sinuous, strong. "I call upon you now to fulfill it."

With a gentle, bloody kiss, I bind us together anew, fulfilling an oath ten years in the making—and—

A spluttering breath. The sound of coughing. The twitch of his hand against me. A flush of power caught in midair, on its way from me to . . . to . . .

"A-Anaïs . . ."

Magic or miracle or delusion, I don't know. Don't care.

"My king."

A dark flower with jagged edges blooms suddenly across my vision.

The world turns black.

CHAPTER FOUR

I DON'T BELIEVE IN AN AFTERLIFE ANYMORE. I DON'T BELIEVE in eternal rest or reward or retribution. Life lasts for the blink of a cosmic eye. No less and, depending on how you define it, only sometimes more.

Which is why, when I wake once more in Marenca and the same heavy gilt rays of sunshine fall on my face, I start sobbing.

What was the point of everything I just did, everything I just sacrificed, if I'm still sent back after all?

The grief and rage and wonder of my last death rings so loud in my ears that I don't even notice when my mother alights again at the threshold and collapses at the side of my bed, her own face drawn and tear-streaked.

I stare at her, out of my mind with confusion. The unreasonably heavy embroidery of my blanket bunches in my fists. When my father also pops into my room, I let go and surrender to the day. I've seen a lot of terrible things, including my parents dying over and over again, but this just might be the worst.

Papa crosses the room in several long strides and takes up a vigil at Maman's side. "How are you feeling, dear heart?"

I wipe my eyes with the back of my hand. "Fine, fine. Shouldn't we be getting ready?" I try to sound chipper. A girl looking forward to the biggest night of her life. "For the ball?"

They exchange a look I can't begin to decipher. Maman cradles my face in her hands. I flinch as she brushes a bruise on my cheek.

I have a bruise?

"Darling . . . it's over. The ball is over."

I freeze. "What are you talking about?"

The corners of Papa's eyes crinkle as he tries to smile, but something unspeakably melancholy remains in his features. "The ball never happened. Infanta Clara tried to stage a coup, and damn near succeeded." His eyes dart from side to side. "A bomb went off near the ballroom. The royal family was half decimated."

Maman sniffs. "But you stopped it from being worse. Didn't you, Anaïs?"

This can't be happening.

She hauls herself on top of the bed, which I now realize is too big to be the one I've been resurrected in over and over again. Also, Maman would never furnish our rooms with Castaran embroidery. Papa sits down, too, his feet dangling off the edge, as Maman hugs me to her chest, letting my head rest awkwardly on the slope of her shoulder. "You did it, darling," she whispers. "Don't you see where you are?"

To appease her, as I have most of my life, I peer around her shoulder to study the fixtures of the airy but not quite opulent chamber. The sight of it all, utterly new and utterly disorienting, only heightens the doubt and desperation growing in my stomach. Doubt that the story is true, and desperation that it is.

"The . . . Alcázar?"

"Yes, Anaïs, yes. You're in the Alcázar now. Under the king's protection." Her chest swells with equal parts pride and sadness. "My daughter, the hero."

I scoff into the shoulder of her simple linen shift, which I realize now is not the gown she wears to the ball. This is something she could have put on without help, if she'd been keeping vigil at her daughter's bedside for a day or—wait.

The *king's* protection?

"Y-you said the royal family was decimated."

"Yes. Rodrigo you know, and Clara you . . ." Papa clears his throat. "Felipe and his wife got caught in the bomb blasts. The queen survived, if only just. Now Infante Leopoldo wears the crown."

"You mean *Rey* Leopoldo." Even now, my mother can't resist correcting my father, but I don't mind. It means that everything I thought I saw on the hillside before I passed out was real. It happened.

Leo came back.

Because I called him.

Perhaps sensing the enormity of my shock, Maman soothes me as she would a baby, patting my back and brushing the hair from out of my eyes. "He told us everything. About Clara, and their father, and . . . and your . . ."

"Your time travel," Papa supplies.

I disentangle myself from my mother's arms. "I don't time travel."

Under normal circumstances, perhaps Maman would wave her hand and utter some well-meaning, flippant thing, like *Well, yes, darling, you knew what we meant.* But she doesn't do anything. Curled up on top of the bed, her hands in her lap now, she looks very small indeed. Her eyes are luminous with tears. "So it's true."

I don't know what Leo told them. Rey Leopoldo, I mean. *God.* I don't know how much he knew, or understood, or even remembered of what was going on before he was killed. Or what's happened since he . . . since I brought him back and reawakened the magical channel between us. He's never going to know or understand or remember completely. None of them will, not without my amulet as proof.

For now, I can only nod.

Their faces fall and chests sag at the confirmation. But they don't ask for details, what it really was, how it could have happened. They cautiously reach out their hands toward me and say in unison, "We're so proud of you."

This should be the signal that sinks into my stretched-out

mind. This should be the close of the nightmare. I crawl to them on still-scratched-up knees and let them suffocate me with hugs and kisses and more crying, and I hug and kiss and cry with them, too.

I survived. *We* survived.

But it's not the end. And maybe it never will be.

By order of the king, I'm kept in a room of my own in the Alcázar Real de Marenca, far from the infirmary, the ballroom, the many gardens, and every other place in the complex marred by violence. The ballroom was not as packed as it would have been at midnight when the bomb went off, and the Guardia Real's magicians did manage to find and disable the rest in the catacombs, so the damage to the palace and to the court is really not as bad as it should have been.

That's no comfort. Not at all.

They say Clara's grave continued to burn with scarlet smoke for nearly a day before it finally died down. The new king was the first one to cross through that ashen field, and he carried her charred body back up to the catacombs. Now she lies with the ancestors whose legacy she wanted to resurrect. I don't know if she would like the irony, but I imagine she would understand it.

I wanted to go down to the valley, too, and see what was left of the blessed forest. Look for my still-missing fairy amulet before some unsuspecting innocent finds it and somehow triggers its curse for themselves. But Maman wouldn't hear of me leaving the room, let alone go hunting for lost jewelry, until I'm fully recovered.

I don't have the heart to tell my parents that it was Maman's gift that trapped me in time. I absolutely cannot tell them that we're made of the same stock as the saints. Maybe one day I'll find the words, but—not now. Not when Maman still walks on tenterhooks around me all the time, with a bemused and even melancholic Papa taking her cue.

Gaspard, bless his heart, tries his best to be normal. Mostly uninjured from his flight out of the valley with Jacinthe and Faucher, he manages to sneak into my rooms to keep me company. One time, he shows me a copy of the agreement he and Jacinthe put together in Le Nas de Sanglier. I can't get my eyes to focus long enough to actually read the written oath. Only one of its original signatories still lives, and the legacy of the document will certainly be contested by angry grandes and underwhelmed radicals down the line, but Gaspard says that with the new king's stated support, the changes it outlines will come to pass someday soon, somehow.

"It feels like we wrote this a lifetime ago. I don't understand. Is this how you feel all the time?" Gaspard chuckles wanly. "Don't answer that. You don't have to answer that."

I do not answer that.

Another time, he passes on a note from Jacinthe, who is being kept under a close watch in her family's sprawling city mansion while her leg heals. With just Marguerite for company, she seems more than content to not be enmeshed within the palace.

Mademoiselle Anaïs—

*I have no idea how to thank you for my life and our country.
I hope one day to be able to repay you in deed, rather than word.*

I look up and repeat the line aloud. "I would also accept
several thousand reales."

Gaspard crooks his head. "Would you, though?"

My mouth goes dry, and I go back to the letter.

*I suppose I could take this opportunity to apologize for any
difficulty I may have given you, but that, too, I will have to save
for another day. When the dust settles, you must come visit Marguerite and me in Lutesse. I'll take you shopping for gowns fit
for our great and wonderful hero. And in return, you will tell me
all about how our young magician-king finds political power-
sharing, and how you find sharing him with the rest of the world.*

*I doubt it will be easy. But for you, Anaïs, I hope the en-
deavor is worth it.*

I do not repeat any of *that* aloud. Speaking of Leo—Rey
Leopoldo—in such a manner feels like sacrilege. I don't blame
him for not coming to see me. He is king now, and his father and siblings are dead, and his country's wounds barely
staunched. I know he hasn't forgotten that I exist, but it would
be too much for us to see each other now. Before we're ready.

Ready for what?

I don't answer that, either.

I trace time by my healing wounds. It's been so long since
I've had to live with the consequences of my actions—the physical ones most immediately—that the whole process seems as
magical as time. The deepening of my bruises into purples and

blues, the scabbing over of cuts on my arms and legs, the ache in my head that waxes and wanes with the moon at night—all are absolutely uncanny to me now. Almost more than the two oaths that tie Leo and me to each other: the one he swore that opened his magic to me; and now, the one I called upon to leverage him back to life.

The magic that Leo gave me command of seems less present now, less potent, than it was when I wore the talisman. I'm glad it's dormant. I hope Leo empties the catacombs of all the other magician-king bones to keep anyone else from getting ideas. Himself included. *Myself* included.

For sometimes, I find myself seeking a blade. Darkly, hypnotically eager to see what I could make of our power.

At those moments, I screw my eyes shut against the light, and wait until the urge passes. Until the song in my head goes silent.

Very late one night, nearly a week after the hillside battle, I feel that pull come over me again. I never know what catalyzes it, but I know I'm not ready to pursue it, not now. So I close my eyes once more against the predawn darkness and count sheep and goats and cows and all the creatures of a Proensa that I still won't see for weeks or months yet until I feel like what I tell myself is *me* again. When I open my eyes, there is a silhouette at the chamber door.

I swallow. "Come in."

A snap of fingers, and a little fire bursts in the cold grate. In the crackling of magic, he shuffles forward. My heart lurches with him as he stops at the foot of the bed. I tell myself I don't know why that is.

"Vuestra Majestad Real."

"Doña Anaïs."

Just like that, we are strangers. King and subject. He does not bear a crown now, but that doesn't change who and what he is.

"What are you doing awake?"

"I could ask the same of you." He pauses. "I've stopped by here before, but you were always asleep."

No one ever told me the king came to visit. Is that because he didn't want me to know, or because I didn't ask?

"I'm . . ." My voice breaks, as if hoarse from lack of use. "I'm *so* sorry. You have no idea how sorry I am. About everything."

He sinks onto the little bench next to the bed and doesn't respond to my apology. In profile, his long lashes flutter in the dim light. "My mother still doesn't believe Clara could have done this. She blames me for their deaths."

It's me that the queen should hate, not her surviving son. Dowager queen now, though, I suppose.

"I understand," he continues, as easily as telling a story. "She's in mourning. She doesn't understand how I . . . how I came back and they cannot. I don't either, really. All I can do is let her grieve in peace."

Though I can't contradict it, I bristle at the hoarse sympathy in his voice. "What about your grief?"

"What about it?" he responds insouciantly, like Leo the Lush tossing bon mots back and forth across a ballroom. But his bleeding heart comes through in the set of his jaw. "There's too much to do. Too much to rebuild. No time for grief. But I want to hear from you. How are you feeling?"

No time for grief. Empathy and pity twist in my stomach. If he doesn't want to talk about the enormity of his losses, I can't make him. It's not as if I know how to talk about it, either. "Better, I think. Or I'm getting there."

"Good. Good, I'm glad to hear it." He nods and doesn't press the point. He looks sideways, into the fire. "I've been thinking about the . . . the oaths."

That makes one of us. I can barely bring myself to contemplate the breadth of magic unlike anything I've known or wanted before, and all I've done is lie in bed for a week.

It's strange to want again.

I don't know if I like it.

"And?" I prompt him gently.

"And . . . I don't know." Every word is a weight on his shoulders, the release of which eases absolutely nothing. He stares at me with a grimace on his lips, his head cocked at a curious angle. "Should I be calling you *Santa Anaïs*?"

My gasp is sharp enough to seal a new oath. I shake my head minutely, terrified by its . . . not truth, exactly, but its resonance across time. I am still what I always was, even if I didn't know it. Nothing more, nothing less.

"Oh, all right." He sighs, as bemused as he was when he first suggested that I might be descended from the saints. "But I do wonder . . . what does it feel like?"

The molten glint of his eyes persuades me to tell him more than I should. "I don't know. I don't feel the channel most of the time. If you were trying to heal a wound, maybe . . ."

Leo flinches at the reminder of what I did, what control I

could still wield over him, and I curse myself. It wasn't out of mercy that I called him to fulfill his oath. It was selfishness. I brought him back to watch his family die and his country teeter over the edge of disaster. My choice doomed him to a life as a living bargain.

But then he sighs. "I serve Ivarea, but I'm bound to you," he says with matter-of-fact wonder. I feel something unwind in the pit of my stomach. "I can't believe this is all real."

Drawn up short by memory, I flinch in turn.

"Please don't mistake my meaning, it's just—"

"It's just that you've said this to me before."

"Oh." He screws his eyes shut, his gaze a shooting star that blinks out of the night sky. "I'm sorry, Anaïs." It's the first time he's said my name, and only my name, since the riverside. I didn't know a sound other than the bells of midnight could be so traumatic. "I'm sorry for all of this. I shouldn't have sworn that oath to you. This—magic, this place, none of this has to be your burden to bear. Not anymore."

Now that I'm out of the loop of time, I see that this now, living with all my choices, my failures, is the real burden. I have to remember everything I did wrong and keep on living. I wring my hands under the covers so he doesn't see how much it hurts. "No. No, don't be sorry. I don't regret . . . this. Only that I couldn't do more."

"More than defeating the power-mad, invincible magician-princess who was going to kill us and suppress our people?" he erupts. "More than saving the palace from being destroyed in magical explosions and being overrun by violent revolutionaries? What more could you have done?"

"I don't . . . I just . . . So many people still died—"

"If anyone should know just how much danger we were in, it should be you. You saw it happen night after night, and you—Saints, you kept coming back. You kept trying. *How,* Anaïs?" Stunned, and numb, and mourning, and yet struck by awe, the king of Ivarea asks, "Why did you bring me back?"

I sit up straighter as if it will banish the exhaustion from my bones. "I didn't do it *for* you. I did it for all of us." I gesture vaguely toward the windows of the chamber, which overlook the river as it hurtles down toward Marenca proper. The city is only beginning to wake, but the river has not stopped flowing. "Help us build a better, fairer, more equitable Ivarea. One we can all belong to. One we can all begin to be proud of. We're putting our trust in you to do it."

"We?"

I sigh reluctantly. "Me. *I'm* trusting you to be able to do this."

"What have I ever done to deserve your trust?"

Leo will be officially crowned soon, and that is due in large part to me. The compromise I forced Rey Rodrigo and Mathieu Faucher to broker, the one Leo has to try to implement, might not be enough in the end—years, decades, centuries down the line. I don't know.

Perhaps I'm a moony-eyed fool, lovesick and unable to see the truth before me, or a fool that Faucher or someone like him will one day laugh at with condescension. But I believe the best ideas in the world mean nothing when those who fight for them don't actually care about their people. And Ivarea deserves a real chance.

With a leader willing to give them that chance.

"You've done more than enough, Leo." I belatedly realize my mistake. "I mean, Majestad."

"*No*. No, call me Leo. Please."

The fire crackles in our ears, painting our worn-out complexions with a rosy glow even in the near dark. The syllables of his name sit on my tongue. My fairy blood and the channel of Ivarea's magic call on me to say his name, to invoke him for myself as if he's a spell I can cast, a power I can command.

"There *are* still some advantages to being king, you know."

I snort in a distinctly unladylike manner. "Oh, are there?"

"All of Ivarea owes a debt to you, whether they remember it or not. So whatever you want, I could grant you." He clears his throat. "Make your father a duke? Done. Stay in Marenca to help advocate for our glorious new constitution? Be my guest." His voice drops so it sounds of a piece with the crackling of the fire. "Anything you want, Anaïs. You only have to say it."

I suppose his suggestions are things that a version of me would want as a reward for services rendered to the crown. And they are certainly generous gifts—elevating my family as they have always wanted, giving a Proensan girl a hand in reshaping the system that dictated the Ivareans' lives for centuries. No other king would grant me these. And yet—

"Right now, all I want is to go home."

He didn't expect that, I can tell. I will pointedly not think too hard about what he did expect. What he might have hoped.

"What you want right now," he repeats quietly. "And . . . in the future?"

I smile. "That's for time to tell."

Out of his not-unpleasant grin blooms a question. "Have we ever . . ."

Have we ever kissed before? I feel my back arching as if to meet the crush of his lips, but that's a sense memory that my body is trying and failing to will into reality. Leo is not a figment of my imagination. He is here, and real, and whatever it is he feels now is not the end.

Time will tell, indeed.

"Never mind." After a moment, he shakes his head, buries his hand at his side. "Before I forget, I brought something for you."

Puzzled, I peer closer as he offers his hand out. And suck in a stunned breath when I glimpse a chain coiled in his palm. "Where—where did you find it?"

He runs a thumb over the opal of my locket, which shines brilliant in the ember light now, just as it did when it first caught me in its spell. "Near Clara's body. After interring her in the catacombs, I went back down to the valley, and there it was. I thought of giving it back to you sooner. But I . . . I remembered you saying that you'd be able to go back in time if you had it. And I didn't want to risk you trying." He raises his head to look back at me, a furrow in his brow. "Now I don't know. Everything seems so . . . Maybe this isn't the way it's supposed to be. Maybe there was another way we were supposed to get here, and we utterly fucked it up. If we did . . ." He leans forward and presses my amulet into my suddenly cold hands. "Well. It's your choice, Anaïs."

Once upon a time, not very long ago at all, I let kingdoms die over and over again, I let my loved ones sacrifice themselves, to avoid the weight of those last four words. I killed myself so I wouldn't have to live with a future I couldn't change.

And maybe there *is* a time when everything turns out right. When no one dies at the Alcázar, or down at the riverbank. When Clara is called to account for her crimes. When our destinies don't hang in the balance of power-sharing promises and hastily scribbled paperwork.

But . . . but the amulet feels inert in my hands, in a way it hasn't for a long time. If I open it, maybe I'll find the portraits of my ancestors frozen, its curse broken, time no longer contorting itself around them. Or maybe the portraits will be exactly as they always were, and all it would take to resurrect the locket's magic would be the spilling of more of the blood I inherited from Mireille and her beloved.

Perhaps I should know how to use the weapon that's returned to my hands. Perhaps I could still have the power to undo time.

But Leo also asked me, not too long ago, if I'd be able to let go of this very power. And no matter what magic or miracles lie in wait inside the amulet, no matter what happens tomorrow, or the day after that, or in the months and years to come, I can't keep going back. I can't keep doubling back on my own life. I have to live it.

The only question that matters is this: What do I do with it?

I don't know how to say any of this to him, so I don't. In silence, I nudge open the drawer of the bedside table and drop the amulet inside. After I shut the drawer, I could swear I catch a glimpse of his bittersweet grimace, but whatever the expression was, it disappears quickly. He whispers, "Thank you, Anaïs. For everything."

"Please . . . please don't." I swallow. "It's you I should thank. Leo."

He gets up without a word. For the first time in our lives, he bows to me. When he rises, a glaze of contemplation plays over his flushed face. He lifts one of my limp hands to his lips. The kiss is little more than a press of skin on skin, but that's all it's ever taken.

"I should let you rest now. You deserve it." He lowers my hand, more slowly than he really needs to, and begins to back out of the room. He only breaks his gaze on me once, to snuff out the fire in the grate. The chamber now seems draped in gauzy darkness.

"I suppose this is goodbye," says the king.

I close my eyes against his voice. New and strange powers hum inside me, even as something larger than myself stirs in the darkness. When my eyelids flutter open, thin rays of sunlight stripe the room. Faint sunbeams graze Leo's face, and mine too, painting us both in gilded colors that will become stronger with time. As Ivarea will. As we will.

At least, I hope so.

I smile into the dawn.

"No. It's good morning."

ACKNOWLEDGMENTS

So much has changed in the years since that feverish eighteen-hour period when I plotted out what would become *Midnight Strikes,* to the point that I still have a hard time believing it actually happened. But looking back, I know I would not change a single thing about this journey—not the many twists and turns it took to get here, and absolutely not the wonderful people I got to do it with.

Thanks first go to my extraordinary editor, Hannah Hill, whose passion for and understanding of this book never fail to blow me away. From the second I got off the phone with you for the first time, I knew I had to work with you, and every day since has proven that gut instinct correct. Thank you for your sharp insight and dedication throughout this process, your pointed and extremely necessary questions about the magic systems, and your absolutely spot-on dating-show-franchise references. Anaïs and I would be lost without you. Massive thanks also to everyone at Delacorte Press and Random House Children's Books for all their fantastic work and support, including Beverly Horowitz, Wendy Loggia, Barbara Marcus, Tamar Schwartz, Colleen Fellingham, Alison Kolani, Alison Impey, Cathy Bobak, Nathan Kinney, and so many more. Special thanks as well go to Luke Lucas, for the gorgeous cover art, and to Priscilla Spencer, for bringing Ivarea to life in a map. Thank you all for making my dream come true.

To my incredible agent, Claire Friedman, who is the best champion and advocate I could have asked for. You have never once doubted Anaïs and Leo's story, or me, and I can't thank you enough for taking a chance on me. I can't wait for all that's to come. Thanks also to my fabulous film agent, Katrina Escudero, for her passion and wisdom every step of the way.

To the writer friends who were there through my triumphs and spirals and everything in between. Gina, look at us—twelve years of friendship, our debuts and a blurb later, and we're just getting started. I don't know what kind of writer or person I would be without you, and I don't want to. Haley, neither I nor this book would be what we are without you, and I have the screenshots to prove it. You're the best, and I owe you so much more than your next coffee. Diya, growing with you over the years has been a tremendous thrill, not just because you always knew where the journey would take us. You're taking over the world, and I'm so happy to be along for the ride. Em, I am beyond grateful that I get to do the whole debut thing alongside you. You are so wise, passionate, and generous, and you're who I want to be when I grow up. June, you always know just what to say, and every time I think *She can't get any cooler,* you prove me wrong. I can't believe I get to be your friend. Hannah, I am constantly floored by the depth of your talent, your compassion, and your friendship. I am so glad to have you as a friend, and can't wait for all the things you'll do next. To the wonderful writing communities and people who have been wonderful friends and cheerleaders over the years, including Kaavya, Sarah, Annie, Farah, Karuna, Jaria, and so many more. I can't overstate how much your support has meant to me. To Allison and Tasha, who were gracious enough to blurb this book. I'm so, so floored by your enthusiasm and encouragement.

To my dearest friends, who were there for everything else. Elma, what is there to say that we haven't said before, except a millionth I love you and thank you. Sayyada, in all these years you've never once failed to put a smile on my face, and I'm so lucky to have you in my corner always. Ayesha, we've come a long way from those after-school dances in your basement, and I'm so thankful to have you in my life. To all the wonderful friends and colleagues who didn't raise an eyebrow when I told them, at times rather conspiratorially, that I wanted to be an author: no matter where we may have ended up, your enthusiasm has rivaled my own, and I'm so grateful to know you all and have you in my corner.

To my cousins, for being my favorite dance partners, day-trip companions, and sleepover buddies. I'm not letting you get the check again. To my aunts and uncles, for being the most wonderful and enthusiastic supporters I could have asked for. Your duaas mean the world to me. To my grandparents, for all your love and guidance. If I can one day be half the people you are, I'll be more blessed than I can say.

To my family: Samina, I can't imagine my life without you. Thanks for letting me bask in your shadow (because as we know, you're both cooler and taller than me). To my mother, Zainab, my greatest inspiration, and my father, Shahid, my greatest role model. You are the smartest and most loving people I know, and I would be nothing without you. I didn't know how to respond all the times you asked me, with no small horror, why I was still awake at two a.m., but here's the reason. I hope I've made you proud.

And to you, the readers, bloggers, and supporters who picked up this book and gave it a chance. I hope you'll look back on it with a smile.